# A NOTE
## FROM ...

Dear Reader,

With two long-running series, BROTHERHOOD OF WAR and THE CORPS, I have tried to accurately portray the inner workings of the military community. With BADGE OF HONOR, I created an all-new series based on one of my favorite subjects, the fascinating and complex world of law enforcement. Books One and Two were originally published under the pseudonym John Kevin Dugan, to avoid any conflict with my military novels.

However, the police force and the military share a number of unique traits: astonishing courage, loyalty, and camaraderie that unite its men and women like no other profession in the world. For this reason my publishers and I have now decided to release the BADGE OF HONOR novels under the W.E.B. Griffin name.

I hope that the readers of BROTHERHOOD OF WAR and THE CORPS will share my interest in the police community—from the cop on the street, to the detectives, to the chief of police. And I hope these books capture the spirit, the pressures, and the controversies that face these brave men and women every day of their lives.

Sincerely,

W.E.B. Griffin

*Turn the page for reviews of*
*W.E.B. Griffin's bestselling series . . .*

# PRAISE FOR THE TRIUMPHANT SERIES BY W.E.B. GRIFFIN . . .

## BADGE OF HONOR

"Gritty, fast-paced . . . authentic."
—Richard Herman, Jr., author of *The War Birds*

"Readers will feel as if they're part of the investigations, and the true-to-life characters will soon feel like old friends. Excellent reading!"
—Dale Brown, bestselling author of *Day of the Cheetah* and *Silver Tower*

"Damn effective!"
—Tom Clancy, bestselling author of *The Hunt for Red October* and *Clear and Present Danger*

## THE CORPS

"Packed with all the love, action and excitement Griffin fans have come to expect."
—*Baker & Taylor*

"This man has really done his homework . . . I confess to impatiently awaiting the appearance of succeeding books in the series."
—*Washington Post*

"Griffin is a natural storyteller with a special flair for how military men channel strong emotions."
—*Publishers Weekly*

# BROTHERHOOD OF WAR

"Griffin is a storyteller in the grand tradition, probably the best man around for describing the military community. *Brotherhood of War* . . . is an American epic!"
—bestselling author Tom Clancy

"Extremely well-done . . . First-rate!"
—*Washington Post*

"Absorbing . . . fascinating descriptions of weapons, tactics, army life and battle."
—*The New York Times*

"A major work . . . magnificent . . . powerful . . . If books about warriors and the women who love them were given medals for authenticity, insight and honesty, *Brotherhood of War* would be covered with them."
—William Bradford Huie, author of
*The Klansman* and
*The Execution of Private Slovik*

"A crackling good story. It gets into the hearts and minds of those who by choice or circumstance are called upon to fight our nation's wars."
—William R. Corson, Lt. Col. (Ret.) U.S.M.C.,
author of *The Betrayal*
and *The Armies of Ignorance*

"Griffin has captured the rhythms of army life and speech, its rewards and deprivations . . . Absorbing!"
—*Publishers Weekly*

*By W.E.B. Griffin from Jove*

*BADGE OF HONOR*

BOOK I: Men in Blue
BOOK II: Special Operations
BOOK III: The Victim

*BROTHERHOOD OF WAR*

BOOK I: The Lieutenants
BOOK II: The Captains
BOOK III: The Majors
BOOK IV: The Colonels
BOOK V: The Berets
BOOK VI: The Generals
BOOK VII: The New Breed
BOOK VIII: The Aviators

*THE CORPS*

BOOK I: Semper Fi
BOOK II: Call to Arms
BOOK III: Counterattack

# W.E.B. GRIFFIN
# SPECIAL OPERATIONS

**SECOND IN THE <u>BADGE OF HONOR</u> SERIES**

Originally published under the pseudonym John Kevin Dugan

JOVE BOOKS, NEW YORK

This Jove Book contains the complete
text of the original edition.
It has been completely reset in a typeface
designed for easy reading, and was printed
from new film.

BADGE OF HONOR: SPECIAL OPERATIONS

A Jove Book / published by arrangement with
the author

PRINTING HISTORY
First published October 1989
Jove edition / April 1991

ISBN: 0-515-10148-6

Jove Books are published by The Berkley Publishing Group,
200 Madison Avenue, New York, New York 10016.
The name ''JOVE'' and the ''J'' logo
are trademarks belonging to Jove Publications, Inc.

PRINTED IN THE UNITED STATES OF AMERICA

10  9  8  7  6  5  4  3  2  1

*For Sergeant Zebulon V. Casey*
*Internal Affairs Division*
*Retired*
*Police Department, the City of Philadelphia.*
*He knows why.*

# SPECIAL
# OPERATIONS

# ONE

Mary Elizabeth Flannery first came to the attention of the Police Department of the City of Philadelphia at 9:21 P.M., June 29, 1973, when an unidentified civilian called the Police Emergency number and reported that as she and her husband had been driving through Fairmount Park, going down Bell's Mill Road toward Chestnut Hill, they had seen a naked woman, just walking around, on the Chestnut Hill side of the bridge over Wissahickon Creek.

The call was taken in the Police Radio Room, which is on the second floor of the Police Building in downtown Philadelphia. The operator who took the call was a civilian, a temporary employee, a twenty-two-year-old, 227-pound, six-foot-three-inch black man named Foster H. Lewis, Jr.

Foster H. Lewis, Sr., was a sergeant in the Eighteenth District. That hadn't hurt any when Foster H. Lewis, Jr., had appeared three years before in the City Administration Building across from City Hall to apply for a part-time job to help him with his tuition at Temple University, where he was then a premedical sophomore.

Foster H. Lewis, Jr., who was perhaps predictably known as "Tiny," had been at first more than a little awed by the Radio Room, with its rows of operators sitting before control consoles, and made more than a little uncomfortable by the steady stream of calls for help, often from people on the edge of hysteria.

Alone of America's major city police forces, Philadelphia police respond to any call for help, not just to reports of crime. It is deeply imbedded in the subconscious minds of Philadelphia's 2.1 million citizens (there are more than five million people in the Philadelphia metropolitan area) that what you do when Uncle Charley breaks a leg or the kid falls off his bike and is bleeding pretty bad at the mouth or when you see a naked woman just walking around in Fairmount Park is "call the cops."

Tiny Lewis had worked in the Radio Room two, three nights a week, and weekends, and full time during the summers for three years now, and he was no longer awed by either the Radio Room or his responsibilities in dealing with a citizen who was calling for help.

For one thing, he was reasonably sure that this citizen's call was for real, and that the citizen herself was neither hysterical or drunk, or both.

"May I have your name, please, ma'am?" Tiny Lewis asked, politely.

"Never mind about that," the caller snapped. "Just help that poor woman."

"Ma'am, I have to have your name," Tiny Lewis said, reasonably. Sometimes that worked, and sometimes it didn't. It didn't now. The phone went dead.

"Joe!" Tiny Lewis called, just loud enough to catch the attention of the Police Dispatcher, a sworn police officer named Joe Bullock.

Joe Bullock had had sixteen years on the job when he pulled a drunk to the curb on the Baltimore Pike in West Philadelphia. He had him standing outside his car when another drunk had come along and rear-ended the stopped car. Neither civilian had been seriously injured, but Joe Bullock had spent seven months in University Hospital. The Department had wanted to put him out on a Thirty-Two, a Civil Service Disability Pension for Injuries Received in the Line of Duty, but Bullock had appealed to the Police Commissioner.

The Police Commissioner, then the Honorable Jerry Carlucci, had found time to see Officer Bullock, even though his time was pretty much taken up with his campaign to get himself elected mayor. Commissioner Carlucci only vaguely remembered Officer Bullock, when Bullock politely reminded him that he used to see him when the Commissioner had been a Highway Sergeant, but he shook his hand warmly, and assured him that as long as he was either Police Commissioner or mayor, the expletive-deleted paper pushers on the Civil Service Commission were not going to push out on a Thirty-Two any good cop who wanted to stay on the job and had a contribution to make.

Officer Bullock was assigned to the Radio Division as a Police Dispatcher.

"What have you got, Tiny?" Officer Bullock inquired of Tiny Lewis.

"A naked woman in the park at Bell's Mill and Wissahickon Creek, around the Forbidden Drive," Tiny said. "I think there's something to it."

"It could be some girl changed her mind at the last minute," Joe Bullock said.

Forbidden Drive, despite the ominous name, was an unpaved road running along Wissahickon Creek, used in the daylight hours by respectable citizens for horseback riding, hiking, and at night by young couples seeking a place to park a car in reasonable privacy.

"I don't think so," Tiny said, repeating, "I think there's something to this."

Joe Bullock nodded. He knew that Tiny Lewis had a feel for his job, and very rarely got excited. He knew too that the location was in Chestnut Hill. It was said that ninety-five percent of Philadelphia was owned by people who lived in Chestnut Hill, very often in very large houses on very large pieces of property; the sort of people who were accustomed to the very best of police protection and who could get through to the mayor immediately if they didn't think they were getting it.

Bullock went to his console, and checked the display for the Fourteenth Police District, which was charged with maintaining the peace in the area of Northwest Philadelphia including Chestnut Hill. He was not surprised to find that an indicator with "1423" on it was lit up. The "14" made reference to the district; "23" was the Radio Patrol Car (RPC) assigned to cover Chestnut Hill. He would have been surprised if 1423 was not lit up, signifying that it was on a job, and not available. Chestnut Hill was not a high-crime area, or even an area with a traffic problem.

"Fourteen Twenty-Three," Joe Bullock said into the microphone.

There was an immediate response: "Fourteen Twenty-Three."

"Fourteen Twenty-Three," Joe Bullock said to his microphone, "report of a naked female on Forbidden Drive, in the vicinity of Bell's Mill Road and the bridge. Civilian by phone."

"Fourteen Twenty-Three, okay," Police Officer William Dohner, who was cruising his district on Germantown Avenue, near Springfield Street, said into his microphone. He then put the microphone down, flipped on the siren and the flashing lights, and turned his 1972 Ford around and headed for Forbidden Drive.

As this was going on, Tiny Lewis was writing the pertinent information on a three-by-eight card. At this stage, the incident was officially an "Investigation, Person." He then put the card between electrical contacts on a shelf above his console. Doing so interrupted the current lighting the small bulb behind the "1423" block on the display console. The block went dark, signifying that Fourteen Twenty-Three had a job.

Joe Bullock's Police Radio call vis-à-vis the naked woman in Fairmount Park was received as well over the radios installed in other police vehicles. Almost immediately, a 1971 Ford van, EPW 1405, one of the two-man Emergency Patrol Wagons assigned to the Fourteenth District to transport the injured, prisoners, and otherwise assist in law enforcement, turned on its flashing lights and siren and headed for Forbidden Drive. So did Highway Nineteen, which happened to be in the area. So did D-209, an unmarked car assigned to the Northwest Detective District. And others.

It had been a relatively quiet night, and a naked female on Forbidden Drive certainly required all the assistance an otherwise unoccupied police officer could render.

Joe Bullock's call was also received over the police-bands shortwave radio installed in a battered, four-year-old Chevrolet Impala coupe registered to one Michael J. O'Hara of the 2100 block of South Shields Street in West Philadelphia.

Mr. O'Hara had spent Sunday evening having dinner with his widowed mother, who resided in the Cobbs Creek Nursing Center, in the Mr. and Mrs. J. K. McNair Memorial Dining Facility. Mickey was a dutiful son and loved his mother, and made a valiant effort to have dinner with her twice a week. It was always a depressing experience. Mrs. O'Hara's mind was failing, and she talked a good deal about people who were long dead, or whom he had never known. And about fellow residents in the Cobbs Creek Nursing Center, who, if she was to be believed, carried on sinful sexual relations that would have worn out twenty-year-olds when they were not engaged in stealing things from Mrs. O'Hara. The food was also lousy; it reminded Mickey of what they used to feed him in basic training in the army.

After pushing his mother's wheelchair down the polished, slippery corridors of the Cobbs Creek Nursing Center to her room, Mickey O'Hara usually went directly to Brannigan's

Bar & Grill, two blocks away at Seventieth and Kingessing, where he had a couple of quick belts of John Jamison's with a beer chaser.

Tonight, however, he had gone directly home, not because he didn't need a drink—quite the contrary—but because there was a recent development in his life that left him feeling more uneasy than he could ever remember having felt before. And Mickey knew himself well enough to know that the one thing he should not do in the circumstances was tie one on.

Home was the house in which he had grown up, the fourth row house on the right from the end of the 2100 block of South Shields Street. He had been living here alone now for two and a half years, since Father Delahanty of the Good Shepherd Roman Catholic Church had managed to convince Mrs. O'Hara that moving "temporarily" to the Cobbs Creek Nursing Center was the best thing for her to do until she got her health back.

She was never going to leave Cobbs Creek, and everybody but Mrs. O'Hara knew that, but she kept talking about when she'd be going home, and Mickey didn't feel it would be right to go and see her and lie about selling the goddamned house and taking an apartment somewhere.

He went into the house and put the photo album back on the shelf where it had been kept since he was in short pants. He had carried the damned thing back and forth to Cobbs Creek two dozen times. She would ask him to bring it, and he would take it to her, and a week later, she would tell him to take it home and put it on the shelf; Cobbs Creek was full of thieves who were always stealing anything that wasn't chained down, and she didn't want to lose it.

Then he went into the kitchen and decided that one lousy glass of beer wasn't going to get him in trouble, and filled a Pabst Blue Ribbon glass from a quart bottle of Ortleib's, which was a dime less a quart than Pabst, and so far as Mickey was concerned, a better beer to boot. He went into the living room, turned the TV on, and watched a rerun of *I Love Lucy* until it was time to go downtown.

Bull Bolinski, who was probably his oldest friend, said his plane would arrive at half-past eight, and that Mickey should give him an hour or so to get to his hotel, and make a couple of phone calls. Mickey had offered to meet Bull at the airport, but Bull said there was no sense doing that, he would catch a cab.

When it was time to go meet the Bull, Mickey turned the TV off, rinsed out the Pabst Blue Ribbon glass in the sink, then went out and got in the car. He turned on the police-band radio without thinking about it. The "*naked lady in Fairmount Park*" call from Police Radio came before he had pulled away from the curb.

He had two reactions to the call: First, that what he had heard was all there was to it, that some broad—drunk, stoned, or crazy—was running around Fairmount Park in her birthday suit. If she was a good-looking broad, there might be a funny piece in it for him, providing she was drunk or stoned or maybe mad at her husband or her boyfriend. Every cop in Northwest Philly would go in on a "naked lady" call; it would look like a meeting of the FOP, the Fraternal Order of Police.

But not if she was a looney. Mickey had his principles, among them that looney people aren't funny. Unless, of course, they thought they were the King of Pennsylvania or something. Mickey never wrote about looneys who were pitiful.

The second thought he had was more of a hunch than anything else. It *could* have something to do with a real looney, a dangerous one, a white male scumbag who had been running around lately raping women. Not just any women, but nice, young, middle-class white women, and not just raping them, either, but making them do all kinds of dirty things, weird things. Or doing the same to them. Jack Fisher, one of the Northwest detectives, had told Mickey that the looney had tied one girl down on her bed, taken off his own clothes, and then pissed all over her.

Then Mickey had a third thought: Whatever was going on

was not, at the moment, of professional interest to Michael J. O'Hara. There would probably be a story in the *Philadelphia Bulletin*, either a two-graph piece buried with the girdle ads in section C, or maybe even a bylined piece on the front page, but it would not be written by Michael J. O'Hara.

Michael J. O'Hara was *withholding his professional services* from the *Bulletin*, pending resolution of contractual differences between the parties. Bull Bolinski had told him, *"No, you're not on strike. Bus drivers strike, steelworkers strike. You're a fucking* professional. *Get that through your thick head."*

Mickey O'Hara had been *withholding his professional services* for three weeks now. He had never been out of work that long in his life, and he was getting more than a little worried. If the *Bulletin* didn't give in, he thought it entirely possible that he was through. Not only with the *Bulletin*, but with the other newspapers in Philadelphia, too. The bastards in management all knew each other, they all had lunch at the Union League together, and there was no question in Mickey's mind that if the *Bulletin* management decided to tell him or the Bull to go fuck himself, they wouldn't stop there, they would spread the word around that Mickey O'Hara, always a troublemaker, had really gone off the deep end this time.

And it was already past the point where he could tuck his tail between his legs and just show up in the City Room and go back to work. The only thing he could do was put his faith in the Bull. And sweat blood.

Mickey reached over and turned off the police-bands shortwave radio, then headed downtown, via the Roosevelt Boulevard Extension to North Broad Street, then down Broad toward City Hall.

Bill Dohner, a wiry, graying, forty-two-year-old cop who had been on the job for exactly half his life, turned off his lights and siren when he was four blocks away from Forbidden Drive, although he didn't slow down. Sometimes, flashing lights and a howling siren were the wrong way to handle a job.

He reached over on the front seat and found his flashlight, and had it in his hand as he braked sharply at the entrance to Forbidden Drive. The unpaved road looked deserted to him, so he continued down Bell's Mill Road and crossed the bridge over Wissahickon Creek. He didn't see anything there, either, so he turned around, quickly, but without squealing his tires, and returned to Forbidden Drive and turned right into it.

His headlights illuminated the road for a hundred yards or so, and there was nothing on it. Dohner drove very slowly down it, looking from side to side, down into Wissahickon Creek on his right, and into the woods on his left.

And then Dohner saw Mary Elizabeth Flannery. She was on her feet, just at the end of the area illuminated by his headlights, on the edge of the road. She had her head down and her hands behind her, as if they were tied, and she was naked.

Dohner accelerated quickly, reaching for his microphone.

"Fourteen Twenty-Three. I got a naked woman on Forbidden Drive. Can you send me backup?"

He braked sharply when he reached Mary Elizabeth Flannery, then reached onto the passenger side floorboard, coming up with a folded blanket. Then he jumped out of the car.

Dohner saw the blank look in Mary Elizabeth Flannery's eyes when she saw him, and saw that his guess had been right; her hands were tied behind her.

"It's going to be all right, miss," Bill Dohner said, gently, as he draped the blanket around her shoulders. "Can you tell me what happened?"

At that moment, every radio in every police car in the city of Philadelphia went *beep beep beep*, and then they heard Joe Bullock's voice. "Assist Officer, Forbidden Drive at Bell's Mill Road. Police by radio. Assist Officer. Forbidden Drive at Bell's Mill Road. Police by radio."

Flashing lights and sirens on all the cars that had previously been headed toward Bell's Mill Road went on, and feet

pressed more heavily on accelerator pedals: flashing lights
and sirens went on in cars driven by Bill Dohner's Sergeant
(14A); Bill Dohner's Lieutenant (14DC); two of Dohner's
peers, patrolling elsewhere in the Fourteenth District (1421 and
1415); on Highway Twenty-Six, D-Dan 209, and others.

Bill Dohner took a well-worn but very sharp penknife from
his pocket and cut the white lamp cord binding Mary Elizabeth Flannery's hands behind her. He did not attempt to untie
the lamp cord. Sometimes a knot could be used as evidence;
the critters who did things like this sometimes used unusual
knots. He dropped the cord in his trousers pocket, and gently
led Mary Elizabeth Flannery to his car.

"Can you tell me what he looked like?" Bill Dohner asked.
"The man who did this to you?"

"He came in the apartment, and I didn't hear him, and he
had a knife."

"Was he a white man?" Dohner opened the rear door of
the car.

"I don't know. . . . Yes, he was white. He had a mask."

"What kind of a mask?"

"A kid's mask, like the Lone Ranger."

"And was he a big man, a little man, or what?" Dohner
felt Mary Elizabeth Flannery's back stiffen under his hand.
"What's the matter?" he asked, very gently.

"I don't want to get in the back," she said.

"Well, then, I'll put you in the front," he said. "Miss,
what did this man do to you?"

"Oh, Jesus, Mary and Joseph," Mary Elizabeth Flannery
said, sucking in her breath, and then sobbing.

"Did he do anything to you?"

"Oh, Jesus!" she wailed.

"I have to ask, miss, what did he do to you?"

"He made me—he *urinated* on me!"

"Is that all?" Dohner asked softly.

"Oh, Jesus," Mary Elizabeth Flannery wailed. "He made
me . . . he put his thing in my mouth. He had a knife—"

"What kind of a knife?"

"A *knife*," she said. "A butcher knife."

"What's your name, miss? Can you tell me that, please?"

He installed her in the front seat of the car, then ran around and got in beside her. She did not look at him as he did.

"What's your name, miss?" Dohner asked again.

"Flannery," she said. "Mary Flannery."

"If we're going to catch this man, you're going to have to tell me what he looks like," Bill Dohner said. "What kind of clothes was he wearing? Can you tell me that?"

"He was *naked*."

"He brought you here from your apartment, right?" Dohner asked, and she nodded.

"How did he bring you here?"

"In a van."

"Was he naked then?"

"Oh, Jesus!"

"Do you remember what kind of a van? Was it dark or light?"

She shook her head from side to side.

"Was it new or old?"

She kept shaking her head.

"Was it like a station wagon, with windows, or was it closed in the back?"

"Closed."

"And was he a small man?" There was no response. "A large man? Did you see the color of his hair? Did he have a beard, or scars or anything like that?"

"He was big," Mary Elizabeth Flannery said. "And he was *hairy*."

"You mean he had long hair, or there was a lot of hair on his body?"

"On his body," she said. "What's going to happen to me?"

"We're going to take care of you," Dohner said. "Everything's going to be all right now. But I need you to tell me what this man looked like, what he was wearing, so we can lock him up. Can you tell what he wore when he brought you over here?"

"Overalls," she said. "*Coveralls*. You know?"

"Do you remember what color they were?"

"Black," she said. "They were black. I saw him put them on. . . ."

"And what color was the van?"

"I didn't see. Maybe gray."

"And when he left you here, which way did he go? Did he go back out to Bell's Mill Road, or the other way?"

"Bell's Mill Road."

"And which way did he turn when he got there?"

"Right," she said, with certainty.

Dohner reached for the microphone.

"Fourteen Twenty-Three," he said.

"Fourteen Twenty-Three," Police Radio replied.

"Fourteen Twenty-Three," Dohner said. "Resume the Assist."

"Resume the Assist" was pure police cant, verbal shorthand for "Those police officers who are rushing to this location with their sirens screaming and their warning lights flashing to assist me in dealing with the naked lady may now resume their normal duties. I have things in hand here, am in no danger, and expect my supervisor, a wagon, and probably a District detective to appear here momentarily."

As police cars slowed, and sirens and flashing lights died all over the Northwest, Dohner went on: "We have a sexual assault, kidnapping, assault with a deadly weapon. Be on the lookout for a white male in a gray van, make unknown. He's wearing black coveralls and may be in possession of a black mask and a butcher knife. Last seen heading east on Bell's Mill Road toward Germantown."

As he put the microphone down, a police car turned onto Forbidden Drive, lights flashing, siren screaming. It skidded to a stop beside Bill Dohner's car, and two Highway Patrolmen jumped out of it.

Joe Bullock's voice came over the radio: "Flash information on a kidnapping, assault with a deadly weapon and rape on Forbidden Drive. Be on the lookout for a white male in black coveralls driving a gray van. Suspect fled east on Bell's Mill Road toward Germantown. May be in possession of a large knife. May have a black mask.''

"Mary," Bill Dohner said, kindly. "I'm going to speak to these officers for a moment and tell them what's happened, and then I'm going to take you to the hospital."

As Dohner opened the door, two more police cars, one of them another Fourteenth District RPC and the other an unmarked Northwest Detectives car, came onto Forbidden Drive, one from Bell's Mill Road, and the other from Northwestern Avenue, which is the boundary between Philadelphia and Montgomery counties.

When Bill Dohner got back into the car beside Mary Elizabeth Flannery, she was shaking under the blanket, despite the heat.

He picked up the microphone: "Fourteen Twenty-Three, I'm en route with the victim to Chestnut Hill Hospital."

As he started to drive off, Bill Dohner looked at Mary Elizabeth Flannery again and said, "Shit," under his breath. She was probably going into shock. Shock can be fatal.

"You all right, Mary?"

"Why did he do that to me?" Mary Elizabeth Flannery asked, wonderingly, plaintively.

# TWO

Mickey O'Hara drove the battered Chevrolet around City Hall, then down South Broad Street, past the dignified Union League Club. When he came to the equally dignified Bellevue-Stratford Hotel, Mickey pulled to the curb at the corner, directly beside a sign reading NO PARKING AT ANY TIME TOW AWAY ZONE.

He slid across the seat and got out the passenger side door. Then he walked the fifty feet or so to the revolving door of the Bellevue-Stratford and went inside.

He walked across the lobby to the marble reception desk. There was a line, two very well dressed middle-aged men Mickey pegged to be salesmen, and a middle-aged, white-haired couple Mickey decided were a wife and a husband who, if he had had a choice, would have left her home.

All the salesmen did was ask the clerk for their messages. The wife had apparently badgered her husband into complaining about their room, which didn't offer what she considered a satisfactory view, and then when he started complaining, took over from him. She obviously, and correctly, considered herself to be a first-class bitcher.

The desk clerk apparently had the patience of a saint, Mickey thought; and then—by now having gotten a good look at her—he decided she looked like one, too. An angel, if not a saint. Tall, nicely constructed, with rich brown hair, a healthy complexion, and very nice eyes. And she was wearing, Mickey noticed, no rings, either engagement or wedding, on the third finger on her left hand.

She gave the big-league bitcher and her consort another room, apologizing for any inconvenience the original room assignment might have caused. Mickey thought the big-league bitcher was a little disappointed, like a bantamweight who sent his opponent to the canvas for the count with a lucky punch in the first round. All keyed up, and nobody around to fight with.

"Good evening, sir," the desk clerk said. "How may I help you?"

Her voice was low and soft, her smile dazzling; and her hazel eyes were fascinating.

"What room is Bull Bolinski in?" Mickey asked.

"Mr. Bolinski isn't here, sir," she replied immediately.

"He isn't?"

"Are you Mr. O'Hara, sir? Mr. Michael J. O'Hara?"

"Guilty."

She smiled. Warmly, Mickey thought. Genuinely amused.

"I thought I recognized you from your pictures," she said. "I'm one of your . . . what . . . avid readers . . . Mr. O'Hara."

"Oh, yeah?"

She nodded confirmation. "Mr. Bolinski called, Mr. O'Hara," she said. "Just a few moments ago. He's been delayed."

"Oh?"

"He said you would be here, and he asked me to tell you that he will be getting into Philadelphia very late, and that

he hopes you'll be free to have breakfast with him, somewhere around ten o'clock.''

"Oh."

"Is there anything I can do for you, Mr. O'Hara?"

"No. No, thanks."

She smiled at him again, with her mouth and her eyes.

By the time he got to the revolving door, Mickey realized
that opportunity had knocked, and he had as usual, blown it
again.

*Well, what the hell was I supposed to say, "Hey, honey,
what time do you get off? Let's you and me go hoist a couple?''*

Mickey got back in the Chevy and drove home, nobly re-
sisting the temptation to stop in at six different taverns en
route for just one John Jamison's. He went into the kitchen,
finished the quart bottle of Ortlieb's, and then two more bottles as he considered what he would do if he couldn't be a
police reporter anymore. And, now that the opportunity was
gone, thinking of all the clever, charming and witty things
he should have said to the desk clerk with the soft and inti-
mate voice and intelligent, hazel eyes.

George Amay, the Northwest Detectives Division detective, who, using the designator D-Dan 209, had gone in on
the naked woman call, stayed at the crime scene just long
enough to get a rough idea of what was going down. Then
he got back in his car and drove to an outside pay phone in
a tavern parking lot on Northwestern Avenue and called it in
to the Northwest Detectives desk man, one Mortimer Shapiro.

Detective Shapiro's place of duty was a desk just inside the
Northwest Detectives squad room, on the second floor of the
Thirty-fifth Police District Building at North Broad and
Champlost Streets.

"Northwest Detectives, Shapiro," Mort said, answering
the telephone.

"George Amay, Mort," Amay said. "I went in on a Thirty-fifth District call for a naked lady on Forbidden Drive. It's at least Criminal Attempt Rape, Kidnapping, et cetera et cetera.''

"Where are you?''

"In a phone booth on Northwestern. The victim's been taken to Chestnut Hill Hospital. The Thirty-fifth Lieutenant and Sergeant are at the scene. And Highway. And a lot of other people.''

"Go back to the scene, and see if you can keep Highway from destroying all the evidence," Shapiro said. "I'll send somebody over.''

Detective Shapiro then consulted the wheel, which was actually a sheet of paper on which he had written the last names of all the detectives present for duty that night in the Northwest Detectives Division.

Assignment of detectives to conduct investigations, called jobs, was on a rotational basis. As jobs came in, they were assigned to the names next on the list. Once assigned a job, a detective would not be assigned another one until all the other detectives on the wheel had been assigned a job, and his name came up again.

The next name on the wheel was that of a detective Mort Shapiro privately thought of as Harry the Farter. Harry, aside from his astonishing flatulence, was a nice enough guy, but he was not too bright.

What Amay had just called in was not the sort of job that should be assigned to detectives like Harry the Farter, if there was to be any real hope to catch the doer. The name below Harry the Farter's on the wheel was that of Richard B. "Dick" Hemmings, who was, in Mort Shapiro's judgment, a damned good cop.

Shapiro opened the shallow drawer in the center of his desk, and took from it a report of a recovered stolen motor vehicle, which had come in several hours before, and which Detective Shapiro had "forgotten" to assign to a detective.

When a stolen motor vehicle is recovered, or in this case, found deserted, a detective is assigned to go to the scene of the recovery to look for evidence that will assist in the prosecution of the thief, presuming he or she is ultimately apprehended. Since very few auto thefts are ever solved, investigation of a recovered stolen motor vehicle is one of those time-consuming futile exercises that drain limited manpower resources. It was, in other words, just the sort of job for Harry the Farter.

"Harry!" Mort Shapiro called, and Harry the Farter, a rather stout young man in his early thirties, his shirt showing dark patches of sweat, walked across the squad room to his desk.

"Jesus," Harry the Farter said when he saw his job. "Another one?"

Shapiro smiled sympathetically.

"Shit!" Harry the Farter said, broke wind, and walked back across the squad room to his desk. When, in Shapiro's judgment, Harry the Farter was sufficiently distracted, Shapiro got up and walked to the desk occupied by Detective Hemmings, who was typing out a report on an ancient manual typewriter. He laid a hand on his shoulder and motioned with his head for Hemmings to join him at the coffee machine.

"Amay just called in," Shapiro said after Hemmings had followed him to the small alcove holding the coffee machine. "We've got another rape, it looks like, on Forbidden Drive by the Bell's Mill bridge over the Wissahickon."

Hemmings, a trim man of thirty-five, just starting to bald, pursed his lips and raised his eyebrows.

"Amay said that he could use some help protecting the crime scene," Shapiro said. "I just gave Harry a recovered stolen vehicle."

Hemmings nodded his understanding, then walked across the room to a row of file cabinets near Shapiro's desk. He pulled one drawer open, reached inside, and came out with his revolver and ankle holster. He knelt and strapped the holster to his right ankle. Then he went to Shapiro's desk, opened the center drawer, and took out a key to one of the Northwest Detectives unmarked cars, then left the squad room.

Shapiro, first noting with annoyance but not surprise that Harry the Farter was still fucking around with things on his desk and had not yet left, entered the Lieutenant's office, now occupied by the tour commander, Lieutenant Teddy Spanner.

"Amay called in an attempted criminal rape, kidnapping, et cetera," Shapiro said. "It looks as if our scumbag is at it again. I gave it to Hemmings."

"Where?" Spanner asked.

"Forbidden Drive, by the bridge over the Wissahickon."

"Who's next up on the Wheel?" Spanner said.

"Edgar and Amay," Shapiro said.

"What's Harry Peel doing?" Lieutenant Spanner asked.

"I just sent him on a recovered stolen vehicle," Shapiro said.

Spanner met Shapiro's eyes for a moment.

"Well, send Edgar if he's next up on the Wheel, over to help, and tell him to tell Amay to stay with it. Or, I will. I better go over there myself."

"Yes, sir," Mort Shapiro said, and walked back across the squad room to his desk, where he sat down and waited for the next job to come in.

Officer Bill Dohner used neither his siren nor his flashing lights on the trip to the Chestnut Hill Hospital Emergency Room. For one thing, it wasn't far, and there wasn't much traffic. More importantly, he thought that the girl was upset enough as it was without adding the scream of a siren and flashing lights to her trauma.

"You just stay where you are, miss," Dohner said. "I'll get somebody to help us."

He got out of the car and walked quickly through the doors to the Emergency Room.

There was a middle-aged, comfortable-looking nurse standing by the nurse's station.

"I've got an assaulted woman outside," he said. "All she has on is a blanket."

The nurse didn't even respond to him, but she immediately put down the clipboard she had been holding in her hands and walked quickly to a curtained cubicle, pushing the curtains aside and then pulling out a gurney. She started pushing it toward the doors. By the time she got there, she had a licensed practical nurse, an enormous red-haired woman, and a slight, almost delicate black man in a white physician's jacket at her heels.

"Any injuries that you saw?" the doctor asked Dohner, who shook his head. "No."

The LPN, moving with surprising speed for her bulk, was at the RPC before anyone else. She pulled the door open.

"Can you get out of there without any help, honey?" she asked.

Mary Elizabeth Flannery looked at her as if the woman had been speaking Turkish.

The LPN leaned into the car and half pulled Mary Elizabeth Flannery from it, and then gently put her on the gurney. She spread a white sheet over her, and then, with a little difficulty, pulled Dohner's blanket from under the sheet.

"You're going to be all right, now, dear," the LPN said.

Dohner took the blanket. The doctor leaned over Mary Elizabeth Flannery as the LPN started pushing the gurney into the Emergency Room. Dohner folded the blanket and put it on the front passenger-side floorboard. Then he picked up the microphone.

"Fourteen Twenty-Three. I'm at Chestnut Hill Hospital with the victim."

"Fourteen Twenty-Three, a detective will meet you there."

"Fourteen Twenty-Three, okay," Dohner said, and then walked into the Emergency Room.

None of the people who had taken Mary Elizabeth Flannery from his car were in sight, but he heard sounds and detected movement inside the white curtained cubicle from which the nurse had taken the gurney. Dohner sat down in a chrome and plastic chair to wait for the detective, or for the hospital people to finish with the victim.

The LPN came out first, rummaged quickly through a medical equipment cabinet, muttered under her breath when she couldn't find what she was looking for, then went back into the cubicle. The nurse then came out, went to the same cabinet, swore, and then reached for a telephone.

Then she spotted a ward boy.

"Go to supply and get a Johnson Rape Kit," she ordered. "Get a half dozen of them, if you can."

She looked over at Dohner.

"She hasn't been injured," she said. "Cut, or anything like that."

"I'd like to get her name and address," Dohner said.

"That'll have to wait," the nurse said.

A minute or two later, the ward boy came running down the waxed corridor with an armful of small packages. He went to the curtained cubicle, handed one of the packages to someone inside, then put the rest in the medical equipment cabinet.

Officer Dohner knew what the Johnson Rape Kit contained, and how it was used, and he felt a wave of mixed rage and compassion for Mary Elizabeth Flannery, who seemed to him to be a nice young woman, and was about to undergo an experience that would be almost as shocking and distasteful for her as what the scumbag had already done to her.

The Johnson Rape Kit contained a number of sterile vials and swabs. Blood would be drawn from Mary Elizabeth Flannery into several of the vials. Tests for venereal disease and pregnancy would be made. The swabs would be used to take cultures from her throat, vagina, and anus, to determine the presence of semen and alien saliva, urine or blood.

It would be uncomfortable for her, and humiliating, but it was necessary to successfully prosecute the sonofabitch who did this to her, presuming they could catch him.

The "chain of evidence" would be carefully maintained. The assistant district attorney who prosecuted the case, presuming again that the police could catch the rapist, would have to be prepared to prove in court that the results of the probing of Mary Elizabeth Flannery's bodily orfices had been in police custody from the moment the doctor handed them to Dohner (or a detective, if one had shown up by the time the doctor was finished with his tests) until he offered them as evidence in a courtroom.

Detective Dick Hemmings arrived at the Chestnut Hill Hospital Emergency Room twenty minutes after Officer Bill Dohner had taken her there. He found Dohner sitting in a chair, filling out a Form 75-48, which is the initial Report of Investigation. It is a short form, providing only the bare bones of what has happened.

Dohner nodded at Hemmings, who sat down beside him and waited until he had finished. Dohner handed the 75-48 to him. In a neat hand, he had written: *"Compl. states a W/M broke into her apt, forced her to perform Involuntary Deviate Sex. Intercourse, urinated on her, tied her up, forced her into a van, & left her off at Bell's Mill Road & Forbidden Dr."*

"Jesus," Hemmings said. "Where is she?"

"In there with the doctor," Dohner said, nodding toward the white curtained cubicle.

"Hurt?"

"No."

Dohner reached in his pocket and took out the cord he had cut from Mary Elizabeth Flannery's wrists. "This is what he tied her up with."

Hemmings saw that Bill Dohner had not untied the knot in the cord.

"Good job," he said. "Make sure the knot doesn't come untied. Give me a couple of minutes here to find out what we have, and then take the cord to Northwest and put it on a Property Receipt."

Dohner nodded. He held up a clear plastic bag, and dropped the cord in it.

"I got this from one of the nurses," he said.

A Property Receipt—Philadelphia Police Department Form 75-3—is used to maintain the "*chain of evidence*." As with the biologic samples to be taken from Mary Elizabeth Flannery's body, it would be necessary, presuming the case got to court, for the assistant district attorney to prove that the cord allegedly used to tie the victim's hands had never left police custody from the time Dohner had cut it from her wrists; that the chain of evidence had not been broken.

Property Receipts are numbered sequentially. They are usually kept in the desk of the Operations Room Supervisor in each district. They must be signed for by the officer asking for one, and strict department policy insists that the information on the form must either be typewritten or *printed* in ink. Consequently, evidence is almost always held until the officer using a Property Receipt can find a typewriter.

"Anything happen at the scene?" Dohner asked.

"The Mobile Crime Lab got there when I was there," Hemmings said. "Nobody that looks like the doer has shown up. How long did he have her there?"

"I didn't get hardly anything out of her," Dohner said. "Just her name, and what this guy did to her. She's pretty shook up."

Hemmings finished filling out the form, acknowledging receipt of one length of knotted cord used to tie up Mary Elizabeth Flannery, signed it, and handed the original to Dohner, who handed him the cord.

"You might as well go, Bill," Hemmings said. "I'll take it from here."

"I hope you catch him," Dohner said, standing up and giving his hand to Hemmings.

Then he went outside and got in his car and started the engine and called Police Radio and reported that Fourteen Twenty-Three was back in service.

Mary Elizabeth Flannery looked with frightened eyes at the stranger who had entered the curtained cubicle.

"Miss Flannery, my name is Dick Hemmings, and I'm a detective. How are you doing?"

She did not reply.

"Is there anyone you would like me to call? Your parents, maybe? A friend?"

"No!" Mary Elizabeth Flannery said, as if the idea horrified her.

"I know what you've been going through," Hemmings said.

*"No, you don't!"*

"But the sooner we can learn something about the man who did this to you, the better," Hemmings went on, gently. "Would it be all right if I asked you a couple of questions?"

She eyed him suspiciously, but didn't reply.

"I need your address, first of all," he said.

"210 Henry Avenue," she said. "Apartment C. They call it the Fernwood."

"That's one of those garden apartments, isn't it?" Hemmings asked, as a mental image of that area of Roxborough came to his mind.

"Yes," she said.

"How do you think this man got into your apartment?" Hemmings asked.

"How do I know?" she snapped.

"Is there a fire escape? Were there open windows?"

"There's a back," she said. "Little patios."

"You live on the ground floor?"

"Yes."

"Did you hear any noises, a window breaking, a door being forced, by any chance?"

"The windows were open," she said. "It's been hot."

*She thinks I'm stupid, but at least she's talking.*

"When were you first aware that this man was in your apartment?"

"When I saw him," Mary Elizabeth Flannery snapped.

"Where were you, what were you doing, when you first saw him?"

"I was in my living room, watching television."

"And where was he, when you first saw him?"

"Just standing there, in the door to my bedroom." She grimaced.

"Can you describe him?"

"No."

"Not at all?"

"He was wearing black overalls, coveralls, whatever they call them, and a mask. That's all I could see."

"What kind of a mask?"

"A mask, over his eyes."

"I mean, what color was the mask? Did you notice?"

"It was a Lone Ranger mask," she said. "The kind with a flap over the mouth."

"Black?"

"Yes, black," she said.

*The Lone Ranger*, Hemmings thought, *wore a mask that covered his eyes only, not with a flap over his mouth.*

"Did he have anything with him?"

"He had a knife," she said, impatiently, as if she expected Hemmings to know all these details.

"What kind of knife?"

"A butcher knife."

"Was it your knife?"

"No, it wasn't my knife."

"Do you remember if the windows in your bedroom were open?" Hemmings asked.

"I told you they were; it was hot."

"How big was the knife?" Hemmings asked, extending his index fingers as he spoke, and then moving his hands apart.

"That big," Mary Elizabeth Flannery said, when she thought his hands were as far apart as the knife had been large.

"And it was a butcher knife, right?"

"I told you that."

"I mean, it couldn't have been a hunting knife, or a bayonet, or some other kind of a knife?"

"I know a butcher knife when I see one."

"Miss Flannery, I'm on your side."

"Why do you let people like that run the streets, then?" she challenged.

"We try not to," Hemmings said, sincerely. "We try to catch them, and then to see that they're put behind bars. But we need help to catch them."

There was no response to this.

"What happened then, Miss Flannery?" Hemmings asked, gently.

"I told the cop what that filthy bastard did to me."

"But I have to know, and in some detail, I'm afraid," Hemmings said.

"He threatened me with his knife, and made me . . . oh, Jesus!"

"Can you tell me exactly what he said?"

She snorted. "You want to know exactly what he said? I'll tell you exactly what he said, he said '*Very nice*,' that's what he said."

"What kind of a voice did he have?"

"What do you mean, what kind of a voice?"

"Was it deep, or high pitched? Did he have any kind of an accent?"

"He had a regular voice," she said. "No accent."

"And then what happened?"

"Then . . . he came over to me, and cut my clothes."

"You were sitting where? In an armchair? On a couch?"

"I was laying down on my couch."

"What part of your clothes did he cut? What were you wearing?"

She flushed and turned her face away from him.

"Jesus!" she said.

"Miss Flannery," Hemmings said. "Sometimes, when it's hot like this, and my air conditioner's not working, and there's nobody around to see me, when I watch television, I do it in my underwear. Was that what happened with you?''

She nodded her head, but still kept her head turned away from him.

''Bra and pants, is that what you were wearing, because it was so damned hot?''

''Just my panties,'' she said, faintly, after a moment, and then she flared. ''You're trying to make it sound like it was my fault.''

''No, I'm not, Miss Flannery,'' Hemmings said, with all the sincerity he could muster.

*He probably would have broken in if you had been wearing an ankle-length fur coat, but looking through the window and seeing you wearing nothing but your underpants didn't discourage him any, either,* Hemmings thought. And was immediately ashamed of himself.

''You say he cut your clothing? You mean your underclothes?''

''He came over to me and put the knife down the front of my panties and jerked it,'' she said.

''Did he say anything? Or did you?''

''I tried to scream when I first saw him, and couldn't,'' she said. ''And then when he was using the knife, I was too scared to scream.''

''Did he say anything?''

''He said, 'Let's see the rest,' '' she said, very faintly.

''What was he doing with the knife at this time?'' Hemmings asked, gently.

''Oh, my God! Is this *necessary*?''

''Yes, ma'am, I'm afraid it is.''

''He was pushing me in the breast with it, with the point.''

She turned her face to look at him, then as quickly averted it.

''Then he said, 'Take your panties off,' and I did,'' she said, quickly, softly. ''And then he took me into my bedroom and made me get on the bed, and then he tied me to the bed—''

"What did he use to tie you to the bed?"

"My panty hose," she said. "He went in my dresser and got panty hose and tied me up."

"Up?" Hemmings interrupted. "Or to the bed?"

"To the bed," she said. "I've got a brass bed, and he tied me to the headboard and footboard."

"On your back? Or on your stomach?"

"On my back," she said.

"And then what?"

"Then he started talking dirty," she said.

"Do you remember what he said?"

"What do you think?" she flared.

"Can you tell me exactly what he said?" Hemmings asked.

"Jesus!" she said. "He used words like 'teats' and . . . and 'pussy' and words like that."

"Anything else?"

"Isn't that enough? Or do you mean what he did to me?"

"Anything and everything you can tell me, Miss Flannery . . ."

"Then he started taking off his overalls—"

"Let's get that fact straight," Hemmings said. "*Overalls* are what farmers wear, if you follow me. They have straps over the shoulders, and a sort of flap in front. *Coveralls* are what mechanics sometimes wear. They cover everything; they have sleeves. Which was he wearing?"

"Coveralls," she said. "Black coveralls."

"Black, or maybe dark blue?"

"*Black*," she said firmly.

"Sometimes people who wear coveralls get them at work," Hemmings said. "And they have embroidery on them, or little patches. 'Joe's Garage,' or something like that. Or a name embroidered. Did you notice anything like that?"

"No," she said, surely.

"When he took off his coveralls, did you notice what kind of underclothes he was wearing?"

"When I saw what he was doing, I closed my eyes."

"And?"

"And said Hail Marys," she said.

"And then what happened?"

"He wasn't wearing a T-shirt," she said, "an undershirt. I saw that much. He was barechested. He was hairy. He had a lot of hair."

"And then what happened."

"I felt him getting on the bed, and when I opened my eyes, he was on top of me."

"Lying on top of you?"

"No! Kneeling, squatting, over me. Over my head. And he had all his clothes off."

"And then what did he do?"

"He told me to suck it," she said, bitterly.

"He meant his penis?"

"What do you think?"

"Was he erect? Did he have an erection?"

"No," she said. "No. He said, 'Suck it and make it hard.' "

"And he put his penis in your mouth?"

"He had his goddamned knife on my throat!"

"And forced his penis into your mouth?"

"Yes, God damn you, yes!"

"And did he ejaculate?"

"What? Oh. No. No, thank God, he didn't."

"What did he do?"

"After a while he took it out, and sat back on his heels and . . . played with himself."

"Did he ejaculate then?"

"All over me," she said, almost moaning, "my face, my mouth, my chest . . ."

"You said he was hairy," Hemmings asked. "Did you notice anything else? Were there any scars on his body? Any marks? Any tattoos? Anything like that?"

"I was trying not to look at him."

"You had your eyes closed all this time?"

"He pushed me with the knife and made me open them," she said. "He said he wanted me to watch."

"And after he had masturbated, what did he do?"

"He sat there, on my legs, for a while, and then he got off and put his overalls, coveralls, back on."

"Did he go to the bathroom, anything like that?"

"He went to the bathroom on me," she said, in mingled horror and fury. "He got off me, off the bed, and then stood by the side of it and . . . pissed all over me."

"He stood by the side of the bed and urinated on you. Before or after he put his coveralls back on?"

"Before," she said.

"And you didn't see any markings of any kind on his body?"

"I told you already; no."

"And then what happened?"

"He cut me loose and made me roll over, and then he tied me up again," she said.

"When Officer Dohner found you, Miss Flannery, your hands were tied with lamp cord. Do you remember where he got that?"

"No," she said.

"He cut the panty hose with which you were tied, is that right? He didn't untie you?"

"He tried," she said. "And then when he couldn't, he got mad. And then he got even madder when he couldn't find any more panty hose. He pulled the dresser drawer all the way out and threw it on the floor."

"And after he had tied your hands behind you, what did he do?"

"He said we were going for a little ride, he wanted everybody to—"

"To what?"

"To have a look at me."

"Are those, more or less, his exact words?"

"He said he wanted everybody to see . . . my private parts, and to see his come all over me."

"Then what?"

"He found my raincoat. . . ."

"Where was that?"

"In the hall closet," she said. "And he told me to get up, and he put my raincoat over my shoulders. And he said that if I tried to run away, he'd . . . he'd stick the knife up . . . in me . . . he'd stick the knife between my legs."

"And then?"

"He took me out the back and put me in the back of his van."

"Tell me about the van," Hemmings said. "Where was it?"

"In the parking lot behind my apartment."

Hemmings tried and failed to recall a mental image of the garden apartment complex parking lot.

"What kind of a van was it?"

"A *van*," she said, impatiently.

"Where did he put you in the van?"

"In the back."

"Was there a door on the side, a sliding door, maybe? Or did you get in the front?"

"There was a sliding door. He opened it, and told me to get in and lay down on my face."

"Did you see anything in the back of the van? I mean, was it plain in there, or did he have it fixed up with chairs and upholstery? Was there a carpet, maybe?"

"No. The floor was metal. And there was nothing in there. Just a *van*."

"Did it look to you like a new van, or one that has been around awhile? Was it scratched up, maybe? Was there a peculiar smell? Anything like that?"

"It was dark, and I had my face on the floor, and I couldn't see anything," she said.

"And then what happened?"

"He got in front and started it up, and I guess he just drove me to where he pushed me out and the cop found me."

"Did anything happen while you were in the van? Did you hear something, maybe, that stuck in your mind. Can you think of anything at all?"

"I thought he was going to kill me," she said. "I was praying."

"Tell me about what happened when you got to Forbidden Drive," Hemmings said.

"I knew we'd left the street," she said. "A regular street, I mean. It sounded different under the wheels."

That response disappointed Dick Hemmings a little; if she had picked up on that, she more than likely would have picked up on anything else odd that had happened. Therefore, nothing interesting had happened.

"And?"

"And then he stopped, and I heard him opening the door, and then he told me to get out. He said that I should walk away from him, and if I turned around to look, he would kill me."

"And he was still wearing his mask?"

"Yeah."

"And then?"

"He took my raincoat off, and pushed me, and I started walking," she said. "And then I heard him driving off."

"Did you know where you were?"

"I thought the park," she said. "We hadn't come that far. But where in the park, I didn't have any idea."

"Did anyone come by before Officer Dohner got there?"

"No," she said. "I saw lights, headlights, and started walking toward where they were going past."

"I'll certainly be talking to you again, Miss Flannery," Hemmings said. "But this is enough to get us started. Thank you for being so frank with me."

"I hope he runs away when you catch him, so you can shoot the sonofabitch!" she said.

"Maybe we'll get lucky," Hemmings said.

*I shouldn't have said that.*

"What happens to me now?" Mary Elizabeth Flannery said.

"Well, I guess that's up to the doctor," Hemmings said. "He'll probably want you to spend the night here."

"I don't want to spend the night here," she said, angrily. "I want to go home."

"Well, that's probably your decision. . . ."

"How am I going to get home? I don't have any clothing, my purse . . ."

"If you'd like me to, Miss Flannery," Hemmings said, "I'll be going to your apartment. I could bring you some clothing, and if you can work it out with the doctor, I'd be happy to drive you home. But if you want my advice, I'd stay here, or at least spend the night with your family, or a friend—"

" 'Hello, Daddy, guess what happened to me?' "

"I'm sure your father would understand," Hemmings said. She snorted.

"What my father would say would be, 'I told you if you insisted on getting an apartment by yourself, something like this would happen.' "

"Well, what about a friend?"

"I don't want to have to answer any more questions from anybody," she said.

"Well, I'll go get you some clothing," Hemmings said. "And bring it here. You think about it."

# THREE

As Mickey O'Hara had walked across the fine carpets laid over the marble floor of the lobby of the Bellevue-Stratford Hotel, and then onto South Broad Street, 6.3 miles to the north, where Old York Road cuts into Broad Street at an angle, about a mile south of the city line, the line of traffic headed toward downtown Philadelphia from the north suddenly slowed, taking the driver of a 1971 Buick Super sedan by surprise.

He braked sharply and the nose of the Buick dipped, and there was a squeal from the brakes. The driver of the Mercury in front of him looked back first with alarm, and then with annoyance.

*I'm probably a little gassed,* the driver of the Buick thought. *I'll have to watch myself.*

His name was David James Pekach, and he was thirty-two years old. He was five feet nine inches tall, and weighed 143 pounds. He was smooth shaven, but he wore his hair long, parted in the middle, and gathered together in the back in a pigtail held in place by a rubber band. He was wearing a white shirt and a necktie. The shirt was mussed and sweat stained. The jacket of his seersucker suit was on the seat beside him.

The Buick Super was not quite three years old, but the odometer had already turned over at 100,000 miles. The shocks were shot, and so were the brakes. The foam rubber cushion under David James Pekach's rear end had long ago lost its resilience, and the front-end suspension was shot, and the right-rear passenger door had to be kicked to get it open. But the air conditioner still worked, and Pekach had been running it full blast against the ninety-eight percent humidity and ninety-three degree temperature of the late June night.

David James Pekach was on his way home from upper Bucks County. His cousin Stanley had been married at eleven o'clock that morning at Saint Stanislaus's Roman Catholic Church in Bethlehem, and there had been a reception following at the bride's home near Riegelsville, on the Delaware River, at the absolute upper end of Bucks County.

The booze had really flowed, and he had had more than he could handle. He was a little guy, at least compared to his brothers and cousins, and he couldn't handle very much, anyway.

There had been the usual cracks about his size, and of course the pigtail, at the reception (*"You know what Davie is? With that pigtail? One Hung Low. The world's only Polack Chink."*) and every time he'd looked at the priest, he'd found the priest looking at him, then suddenly turning on an uneasy smile. He wasn't their priest, he was the bride's family's priest, and what he was obviously thinking was, *"What's a bum like that doing in the Pekach family?"*

He saw the reason for the sudden slowdown, flashing blue lights on two Philadelphia police cars at the corner. A wreck. *Probably a bad one*, he thought, with two cars at the scene.

He hadn't been paying much attention to where he was. He looked around to see where he was.

When he got to the cop directing traffic, the cop signaled him to stop. Dave Pekach rolled down the window.

"You almost rear-ended the Mercury," the cop accused. From the way the cop looked at him, Dave Pekach knew that he didn't like men who wore long blond hair in a pigtail any more than the priest had.

"I know," Dave Pekach said, politely. "I wasn't paying attention."

"You been drinking?" It was an accusation, not a question.

"I just came from a wedding," Pekach admitted. "But I'm all right."

The cop flashed his light around the inside of the Buick, to see what he could see, let Pekach sweat twenty seconds, then waved him on.

Pekach drove fifty feet, swore, and then braked hard again. The brakes squealed again, and there was a loud, dull groan from the front end as he bounced over a curb and stopped.

He opened the door and got out and started walking toward two men standing by the hood of a five-year-old Ford sedan.

"Hey, buddy!" the cop who had stopped him called. "What do you think you're doing?"

Pekach ignored him.

The cop, trotting over, reached the old Ford just as Pekach did, just in time to hear one of the men greet Pekach: "Hey, Captain," one of the men said. He was a heavy, redheaded Irishman in a T-shirt and blue jeans. "Don't you look spiffy!"

The cop was embarrassed. He had sensed there was something not quite right with the car, or the man driving it. There were some subtle things. The relatively new automobile had obviously not been washed, much less polished, in some time. It looked as if it had been used hard. The driver's side vent window had a thumb-sized piece of glass missing, and was badly cracked. The tires had black walls, and on closer examination were larger than the tires that had come with the car.

But until right now, the cop had been looking for something-

*wrong*, something that would have given him reasonable cause to see what the clown in the pigtail might have under the seat or in the glove compartment or in the trunk. Now he looked at the car again, and saw that he had missed the real give-away: On the shelf between the top of the backseat and the window was a thin eight-inch-tall shortwave radio antenna.

The battered Buick was a police car, and the funny-looking little guy with the hippy pigtail was a police officer. More than a cop. One of the Narcotics guys had called him "Captain."

And then the cop put it all together. The little guy with the pigtail was Captain David Pekach, of the Narcotics Division of the Philadelphia Police Department. He remembered now, too, that Pektach had just made captain. Now that he was a captain, the cop thought, Pekach was probably going to have to get rid of the pigtail. Captains don't work undercover; neither do lieutenants, and only rarely a sergeant. The cop remembered a story that had gone around the bar of the Fraternal Order of Police. A Narcotics Lieutenant (obviously, now Pekach) had been jumped on by the Commissioner himself for the pigtail. Pekach had stood up to him. If he was supposed to supervise his undercover men working the streets, the only way he could do that was, from time to time, to go on the streets with them. And a very good way to blow the cover of plainclothes cops working Narcotics dressed like addicts was to have them seen talking to some guy in a business suit and a neat, show-your-ears haircut. No questions were likely to be asked about a guy in a dirty sweatshirt and a pigtail. The story going around the FOP bar was that Commissioner Czernick had backed off.

"What's going on?" Captain Pekach asked the red-haired Narc, whose name was Coogan.

"We were cutting the grass in Wissahickon Park," the other Narcotics officer said. He was a Latin American, wearing a sleeveless denim jacket, his naked chest and stomach sweaty under it. He was a small man, smaller than Captain Pekach.

At five feet seven even, he had just made the height requirement for police officers.

"Cutting the grass" was a witticism. Parks have grass. *Cannibas sativa*, commonly known as marijuana, is known on the street as "grass." But arresting vendors of small quantities of grass is not a high-priority function of plainclothes officers of the Narcotics Division. The Narcotics officers knew that, and they knew that Captain David Pekach knew it.

"And?" Pekach asked.

"It was a slow night, Captain," Alexandro Gres-Narino said, uncomfortably.

"Except for the naked lady," Tom Coogan said.

"What naked lady?" Pekach asked.

"Some dame was running around without any clothes in the park by the Wissahickon Bridge," Tom Coogan said. "Every car north of Market Street went in on it."

"Tell me about this," Pekach said, impatiently, gesturing vaguely around him.

"So there was a buy, and they run," Coogan said. "And we chased them. And they run off the road here."

"High-speed pursuit, no doubt?" Pekach asked, dryly.

"Not by us, Captain," Coogan said, firmly and righteously. "We got on the radio and gave a description of the car, and a Thirty-fifth district car spotted it, and they chased them. We only come over here after they wrecked the car."

"So what have you got?" Pekach asked, a tired, disgusted tone in his voice.

Without waiting for a reply, he walked over to one of the Thirty-fifth District patrol cars, and looked through the partially opened rear seat window. There were four white kids crowded in the back, two boys and two girls, all four of them looking scared.

"Anybody hurt?" Pekach asked.

Four heads shook no, but nobody said anything.

"Whose car?" Pekach asked.

There was no reply immediately, but finally one of the boys, mustering what bravado he could, said, "Mine."

"Yours? Or your father's?" Pekach asked.

"My father's," the boy said.

"He's going to love you for this," Pekach said, and walked back to the Narcotics Division officers.

"Well, what have you got on them?" he asked Officer Coogan.

"About an ounce and a half," Coogan replied, uncomfortably.

"An *ounce* and a *half!*" Petach said in sarcastic wonderment.

"Failure to heed a flashing light, speeding, reckless driving," Coogan went on, visibly a little uncomfortable.

"You like traffic work, do you, Coogan? Keeping the streets free of reckless drivers? Maybe rolling on a naked lady?"

Officer Coogan did not reply.

There was the growl of a siren, and Pekach looked over his shoulder and saw a Thirty-fifth District wagon pulling up. The two policemen in it got out, spoke to one of the patrol car cops, and then one of them went to the van and opened the rear door while the other went to the patrol car with the patrol car cop. The patrol car cop opened the door and motioned the kids out.

"Wait a minute," Pekach called. He walked over to them.

One of the girls, an attractive little thing with long brown hair parted in the middle and large dark eyes, looked as if she was about to cry.

"You got any money?" Pekach asked.

"Who are you?" the van cop asked.

"I'm Captain Pekach," he said. "Narcotics."

The girl shook her head.

Pekach pointed at one of the boys, the one who had told him it was his father's car. "You got any money, Casanova?"

There was a just perceptible pause before the boy replied, "I got some money."

"You got twenty bucks?" Pekach asked.

The boy dug his wallet out of his hip pocket.

"Give it to her," Pekach ordered. Then he turned to the patrol car cop. "You have the names and addresses?"

"Yes, sir."

"Put the girls in a cab," Pekach said.

He turned to the girl with the large dark eyes.

"Your boyfriends are going to jail," he said. "First, they're going to the District, and then they'll be taken downtown to Central lockup. When they get out, ask them what it was like."

Pekach found Officers Alexandro Gres-Narino and Thomas L. Coogan.

"If you can fit me into your busy schedule, I would like a moment of your time at half-past three tomorrow in my office," he said.

"Yes, sir," they said, almost in unison.

Pekach took one more look at the girl with the large dark eyes. There were tears running down her cheeks.

"Thank you," she said, barely audibly.

Captain Dave Pekach then walked to the worn-out Buick, coaxed the engine to life, and drove home.

At five minutes after nine the next morning, Mickey O'Hara again pulled his battered Chevrolet Impala to the curb in front of the Bellevue-Stratford Hotel by the NO PARKING AT ANY TIME TOW AWAY ZONE sign. He was not worried about a ticket. There was about as much chance a police officer would cite him for illegal parking, much less summon a police tow truck to haul Mickey O'Hara's car away, as there was for a white hat to slap a ticket on his Honor, Mayor Jerry Carlucci's mayoral Cadillac limousine.

There were perhaps a couple of dozen police officers among the eight thousand or so cops on the force who would not recognize the battered, antennae-festooned Chevrolet as belonging to Mr. Mickey O'Hara, of the editorial staff of the *Philadelphia Bulletin*. The others, from Commissioner Taddeus Czernick to the most recent graduates of the Police Academy, if they saw Mickey O'Hara climb out of his illegally parked vehicle, would wave cheerfully at him, or, if they were close enough, offer their hands, and more than likely say, "Hey, Mickey, how's it going? What's going on?"

It was generally conceded that Mickey O'Hara knew more of what was going on at any given moment, in the area of interesting crime, than the entire staff of the Police Radio Room on the second floor of the Roundhouse. Equally important, Mickey O'Hara was nearly universally regarded as a good guy, a friend of the cops, someone who understood their problems, someone who would put it in the paper the way it had really gone down. Mickey O'Hara, in other words, was accustomed to ignoring NO PARKING signs.

But today, when he got out of his car, Mickey looked at the sign, and read it, and for a moment actually considered getting back in, and taking the car someplace to park it legally. The cold truth was that right now he was not a police reporter. The Bull could call it "*withholding professional services*" all day and all night, but the truth of the matter was that Mickey O'Hara was out of work. If you didn't have a job, and nobody was going to hand you a paycheck, you were, *ergo sum*, out of work.

Mickey decided against moving the car someplace legal. That would have been tantamount to an admission of defeat. He didn't *know* that the *Bulletin* was going to tell him, more accurately tell his agent, to "go fuck yourselves, we don't need him." That struck Mickey as the most likely probability in the circumstances, but he didn't *know* that for *sure*.

He had hoped to have the issue resolved, one way or the other, last night. But the Bull's plane had been late, so that hadn't happened. It had been pretty goddamned depressing, and he had woken up, with a minor hangover, rather proud of himself for not, after he'd drained the last bottle of Ortleib's, having gone out and really tied one on.

Mickey straightened his shoulders and marched resolutely toward the revolving door giving access to the lobby of the Bellevue-Stratford. There was nothing to really worry about, he told himself. For one thing, he was the undisputed king of his trade in Philadelphia. There were four daily newspapers in the City of Brotherly Love, and at least a dozen people, including, lately, a couple of females, who covered crime. The best crime coverage was in the *Bulletin*, and the best reporter on the *Bulletin* was Michael J. O'Hara, even if most of the other reporters, including both women, had master's degrees in journalism from places like Columbia and Missouri.

Mickey himself had no college degree. For that matter, he didn't even have a high school diploma. He had begun his career, as a copy boy, in the days when reporters typed their stories on battered typewriters, and then held it over their head, bellowing "copy" until a copy boy came to carry it to the city desk.

Mickey had been expelled from West Catholic High School in midterm of his junior year. The offenses alleged involved intoxicants, tobacco, and so far as Monsignor John F. Dooley, the principal, was concerned, incontrovertible proof that Michael J. O'Hara had been running numbers to the janitorial staff and student body on behalf of one Francisco Guttermo, who, it was correctly alleged, operated one of the most successful numbers routes in Southwest Philly.

It had been Monsignor Dooley's intention to teach Mickey something about the wages of sin by banishing him in shame from the company of his classmates for, say, three weeks, and then permitting him to return, chastened, to the halls of academe.

The day after he was expelled, Mickey spotted a sign, crudely lettered, thumbtacked to the door of the *Philadelphia Daily News*, which in those days occupied a run-down building on Arch Street, way up by the Schuylkill River. The sign read, simply, COPY BOY WANTED.

Mickey had no idea what a copy boy was expected to do, but in the belief that it couldn't be any worse than his other options, becoming a stock boy in an Acme Supermarket, or an office boy somewhere, he went inside and upstairs to the second floor and applied for the position.

James T. "Spike" Dolan, the City Editor of the *Daily News*, saw in young Mickey O'Hara a kindred soul and hired him. Within hours Mickey realized that he had found his niche in life. He never went back to West Catholic High School, although many years later, in a reversal of roles in which he found himself the interviewee for a reporter for *Phildalephia Magazine*, he gave West Catholic High, specifically the nearly three years of Latin he had been force-fed there, credit for his skill with words. The interview came after Mickey had been awarded the Pulitzer Prize for investigative reporting. The series of stories had dealt with chicanery involving the bail bond system then in effect.

He told himself too that not only was he the best police reporter in town, but that his agent was one of the best agents there was, period. He didn't do too well with this, because there were a couple of things wrong with it, and he knew it. For one thing, newspaper reporters don't have agents. Movie stars have agents, and television personalities have agents, and sports figures have agents, but not newspaper police beat reporters.

Police reporters don't have contracts for their professional services. Police reporters are employed at the pleasure of the city editor, and subject to getting canned whenever it pleases the city editor, or whenever they displease the city editor. Mickey, who had been fired at least once from every newspaper in Philadelphia, plus the *Baltimore Sun* and the *Washington Post* during his journalistic career, knew that from experience. And police reporters don't make the kind of money his agent had assured him he would get him, or kiss his ass at Broad and Market at high noon.

What had happened was that Casimir "the Bull" Bolinski had come to town a month before, and Mickey had gone to see him at the Warwick. Mickey and the Bull went way back, all the way to the third grade at Saint Stephen's Parochial School, at Tenth and Butler Streets where Roosevelt Boulevard turns into the Northeast Extension. So far back that he still called the Bull "Casimir" and the Bull called him "Michael."

Sister Mary Magdalene, principal of Saint Stephen's, had had this thing about nicknames. Your name was what they had given you when you were baptized, and since baptism was a sacrament, sacred before God, you used that name, not one you had made up yourself. Sister Mary Magdalene had enforced her theologic views among her charges with her eighteen-inch, steel-reinforced ruler, which she had carried around with her, and used either like a cattle prod, jabbing it in young sinners' ribs, or like a riding crop, cracked smartly across young bottoms.

Casimir Bolinski had gone on to graduate from West Catholic High School, largely because when Monsignor Dooley had caught Michael J. O'Hara with a pocketful of Frankie the Gut Guttermo's numbers slips, Mickey had refused to name his accomplice in that illegal and immoral enterprise.

Casimir Bolinski had gone on to Notre Dame, where he was an all-American tackle, and then on to a sixteen-year career with the Green Bay Packers. His professional football career ended only when the chief of orthopedic surgical services at the University of Illinois Medical College informed Mrs. Bolinski that unless she could dissuade her husband from returning to the gridiron she should start looking for a wheelchair in which she could roll him around for the rest of his life.

It was then, shortly after Bull Bolinski's tearful farewell-to-professional-football news conference, that his secret, carefully kept from his teammates, coaches and the management of the Green Bay Packers came out. Bull Bolinski was also Casimir J. Bolinski, D. Juris (*Cum Laude*), the University of Southern California, admitted to the California, Pennsylvania, Wisconsin, Illinois, and New York bars, and admitted to practice before the Supreme Court of the United States of America.

He had not, as was popularly believed, spent his off seasons on the West Coast drinking beer on the beach and mak-

ing babies with Mrs. Bolinski. And neither was Mrs.
Antoinette Bolinski quite what most people on the Packers
thought her to be, that is just a pretty, good li'l old broad
with a spectacular set of knockers who kept the Bull on a
pretty short leash.

Mrs. Bolinski had been a schoolteacher when she met her
husband. She had been somewhat reluctantly escorting a
group of sixth-graders on a field trip to watch the Packers in
spring training. She held the view at the time that professional football was sort of a reincarnation of the Roman
games, a blood sport with few if any redeeming societal
benefits.

The first time she saw Casimir, he had tackled a fellow
player with such skill and enthusiasm that there were three
people kneeling over the ball carrier, trying to restore him to
consciousness and feeling for broken bones. Casimir, who
had taken off his helmet, was standing there, chewing what
she later learned was Old Mule rough cut mentholated chewing tobacco, watching.

Antoinette had never before in her entire (twenty-three-
year) life seen such tender compassion in a man's eyes, or
experienced an emotional reaction such as that she felt when
Casimir glanced over at her, spat, smiled shyly, winked, and
said, "Hiya, honey!"

By the time, two months later, Mr. and Mrs. Casimir Bolinski returned from their three-day honeymoon in the Conrad
Hilton Hotel in Chicago, she had him off Old Mule rough cut
mentholated chewing tobacco and onto mint Life Savers, and
already thinking about his—now their—future, which, pre-
Antoinette, had been a vague notion that when he couldn't
play anymore, he would get a job as a coach or maybe get a
bar and grill or something.

Two days after the management of the Green Bay Packers
had stood before the lights of the television cameras of all
three networks and given Bull Bolinski a solid gold Rolex
diver's watch, a set of golf clubs, a Buick convertible and
announced that the number he had worn so proudly on his

jersey for sixteen years would be retired, they received a letter on the engraved crisp bond stationery of Heidenheimer & Bolinski, Counselors At Law, advising them that the firm now represented Messrs. J. Stanley Wozniski; Franklin D. R. Marshall; and Ezra J. Houghton, and would do so in the upcoming renegotiation of the contracts for their professional services, and to please communicate in the future directly with Mr. Bolinski in any and all matters thereto pertaining.

This was shortly followed by that legendary television interview with linebacker F. D. R. Marshall and quarterback E. J. Houghton, during which Mr. Marshall had said, "If the *bleep*ing Packers don't want to deal with the Bull, so far's I'm concerned, they can shove that *bleep*ing football up their *bleep*," only to be chastised by Mr. Houghton, who said, "Shut up, FDR, you can't talk dirty like that on the *bleep*ing TV."

So Mickey O'Hara was aware from the very beginning that the Bull had not only succeeded in getting a fair deal for his former teammates from the Packers, but had also, within a matter of a couple of years, become the most successful sports agent in the business, and grown rich in the process.

But it wasn't until the Bull had come to town and Mickey had picked him up at the Warwick and they had driven into South Philadelphia for some real homemade Italian sausage and some really good lasagna that he even dreamed that it could have anything to do, however remotely, with him.

"Turn the fucking air conditioner on, Michael, why don't you?" the Bull said to Mickey when they were no more than fifty yards from the Warwick.

"It's broke," Mickey had replied.

"What are you riding around in this piece of shit for anyway?" The Bull then looked around the car and warmed to the subject. "Jesus, this is really a goddamned junker, Michael."

"Fuck you, Casimir. It's reliable. And it's paid for."

"You always were a cheapskate," the Bull said. "Life ain't

no rehearsal, Michael. Go buy yourself some decent wheels. You can afford it, for Christ's sake. You ain't even married.''

"Huh!" Mickey snorted. "That's what you think."

"What *do* they pay you, Michael?"

Mickey told him and the Bull laughed and said, "Bullshit," and Mickey said, "That's it. No crap, Casimir."

"I'll be goddamned, you mean it," the Bull had said, genuinely surprised. Then he grew angry: "Why those cheap sonsofbitches!"

Three days later, the publisher of the *Bulletin* had received a letter on Heidenheimer & Bolinski stationery stating that since preliminary negotiations had failed to reach agreement on a satisfactory interim compensation schedule for Mr. Michael J. O'Hara's professional services, to be in effect while a final contract could be agreed upon between the parties, Mr. O'Hara was forced, effective immediately, to withhold his professional services.

When Mickey heard that what the Bull meant by "interim compensation schedule" was $750 a week, plus all reasonable and necessary expenses, he began to suspect that, despite the Bull's reputation in dealing with professional sports management, he didn't know his ass from second base *vis-à-vis* the newspaper business. Mickey had been getting $312.50 a week, plus a dime a mile for the use of his car.

"Trust me, Michael," the Bull had said. "I know what I'm doing."

That was damned near a month ago, and there hadn't been a peep from the *Bulletin* in all that time.

The good-looking dame, from last night, her hair now done up in sort of a bun, was behind the marble reception desk in the lobby of the Bellevue-Stratford.

*What the hell is that all about? How many hours do these bastards make her work, for Christ's sake?*

This time there was no line, and she saw Mickey walking across the lobby, and Mickey smiled at her, and she smiled back.

"Good morning, Mr. O'Hara," she said.

"Mickey, please."

"Mr. and Mrs. Bolinski are in the house, Mr. O'Hara. If you'll just pick up a house phone, the operator will connect you."

"If I wanted to talk to him on the telephone," Mickey replied, "I could have done that from home. I want to see him."

"You'll have to be announced," the good-looking dame said, her delicate lips curling in a reluctant smile.

"You got your hair in a bun," Mickey said.

"I've been here all night," she said.

"How come?"

"My relief just never showed up," she said.

"Jesus! She didn't phone or anything?"

"Not a word," she said.

"You didn't get any sleep at all?"

She shook her head.

"You sure don't look like it," Mickey blurted.

Her face flushed, and she smiled shyly.

Then she picked up a telephone. She spoke the Bull's room number so softly he couldn't hear it.

The phone rang a long time before the Bull's wife answered it.

"Good morning, Mrs. Bolinski," she said. "This is Miss Travis at the front desk. I hope I haven't disturbed you. Mr. O'Hara is here."

*Travis, huh? It figures she would have a nice name like that.*

"May I send him up?" Miss Travis said, glancing at Mickey. Then she said, "Thank you, madam," and hung up. "Mr. Bolinski is in the Theodore Roosevelt Suite, Mr. O'Hara. That's on ten. Turn to your right when you exit the elevator."

"Thanks."

"My pleasure."

Mickey turned and started to walk to the bank of elevators. Then he turned again.

"You get yourself some sleep," he commanded.

The remark startled her for long enough to give Mickey the opportunity to conclude that whenever it came to saying exactly the right thing to a woman he really liked, he ranked right along with Jackie Gleason playing the bus driver on TV. Or maybe the Marquis de Sade.

But she smiled. "Thank you. I'll try," she said. "I should be relieved any minute now."

Mickey nodded at her, and walked to the elevator. When he got inside and turned around and looked at her, she was looking at him. She waved as the elevator door closed.

*It doesn't mean a fucking thing. She was smiling at the old blue-haired broad last night, too.*

Mickey had no trouble finding the Theodore Roosevelt Suite, and when he did the door was open, and he could hear Antoinette's voice. He rapped on the door, and pushed it open.

Antoinette was sitting on one of the two couches in front of a fireplace, in a fancy bathrobe, her legs tucked under her, talking on the telephone. She waved him inside, covered the mouthpiece with her hand, and said, "Come in, Michael. Casimir's in the shower."

Then she resumed her conversation. Mickey picked up that she was talking to her mother and at least one of the kids.

Casimir Bolinski entered the room. He was wearing a towel around his waist. It was an average-sized towel around an enormous waist, which did little to preserve Mr. Bolinski's modesty.

"I can't find my teeth, sweetie," he mumbled.

Mrs. Bolinski covered the mouthpiece again.

"They're in that blue jar I bought you in Vegas," Mrs. Bolinski said.

"Be with you in a jiff, Michael," the Bull mumbled, adding, "You're early."

He walked out of the sitting room. Mickey saw that his back, and the backs of his legs, especially behind the knees, were laced with surgical scars.

"Kiss, kiss," Antoinette said to the telephone and hung up. "We left the kids with my mother," she said. "Casimir and I have to really work at getting a little time alone together. So I came with him."

"Good for you," Mickey said.

"I didn't know we were coming here," Antoinette said, "until we got to the airport."

Mickey wondered if he was getting some kind of complaint, so he just smiled, instead of saying anything.

"How's your mother, Michael?" Antoinette asked.

"I had dinner with her yesterday."

"That's nice," Antoinette said. Then she picked up the telephone again, dialed a number, identified herself as Mrs. Casimir Bolinski, and said they could serve breakfast now.

The Bull returned to the room, now wearing a shirt and trousers, in the act of hooking his suspender strap over his shoulder.

"I told them to come at ten," he announced, now, with his teeth in, speaking clearly. "We'll have time to eat breakfast. How's your mother?"

"I had dinner with her yesterday. Who's coming at ten?"

"She still think the other people are robbing her blind?"

"Yeah, when they're not . . . making whoopee," Mickey said. "Who's coming at ten?"

"Who do you think?" the Bull said. "I told them we were sick of fucking around with them."

"Clean up your language," Antoinette said, "there's a lady present."

"Sorry, sweetie," the Bull said, sounding genuinely contrite. "Ain't there any coffee?"

"On that roll-around cart in the bedroom," Antoinette said.

The Bull went back into the bedroom and came out pushing a cart holding a coffee service. He poured a cupful and handed it to Mickey, then poured one for himself.

"What am I, the family orphan?" Antoinette asked.

"I thought you had yours," the Bull said.

"I did, but you should have asked."

"You want a cup of coffee, or not?"

"No, thank you, I've got to get dressed," Antoinette said, snippily, and left the sitting room.

"She's a little pissed," the Bull said. "She didn't know I was coming here. She thought I was going to Palm Beach."

"Palm Beach?"

"Lenny Moskowitz is marrying Martha Bethune," the Bull explained. "We got to get the premarital agreement finalized."

Mickey knew Lenny Moskowitz. Or knew *of* him. He had damned near been the Most Valuable Player in the American League.

"Who's Martha Whateveryousaid?"

"Long-legged blonde with a gorgeous set of knockers," the Bull explained. "She's damned near as tall as Lenny. Her family makes hub caps."

"Makes what?"

"Hub caps. For cars? They have a pisspot full of dough, and they're afraid Lenny's marrying her for her dough. Jesus, I got him five big ones for three years. He don't need any of her goddamned dough."

Mickey smiled uneasily, as he thought again of the enormous difference between negotiating a contract for the professional services of someone who was damned near the Most Valuable Player in the American League and a police reporter for the *Philadelphia Bulletin*.

A few minutes later, two waiters rolled into the suite with a cart and a folding table and set up breakfast.

"I told you, I think," the Bull said, as he shoveled food onto his plate, "that you can't get either Taylor ham or scrapple on the West Coast?" Scrapple, a mush made with pork by-products, which was probably introduced into Eastern Pennsylvania by the Pennsylvania Dutch (actually Hessians) was sometimes referred to as "poor people's bacon."

"Yeah, you told me," Mickey said. "How do you think we stand, Casimir?"

"What do you mean, stand? Oh, you mean with those bastards from the *Bulletin*?"

"Yeah," Mickey said, as Antoinette came back into the room, and Casimir stood up and politely held her chair for her.

"Thank you, darling," Antoinette said. "Has Casimir told you, Michael, that they don't have either Taylor ham or scrapple on the West Coast?"

"I could mail you some, if you like," Mickey said.

"It would probably go bad before the goddamned post office got it there," the Bull said, "but it's a thought, Michael."

"I never heard of either before I met Casimir," Antoinette said, "but now I'm just about as crazy about it as he is."

"Casimir was just about to tell me how he thinks we stand with the *Bulletin*," Mickey said.

"Maybe you could send it Special Delivery or something," the Bull said. "If we wasn't going from here to Florida, I'd put a couple of rolls of Taylor ham and a couple of pounds of scrapple in the suitcase. But it would probably go bad before we got home."

"Of course it would," Antoinette said. "And it would get warm and greasy and get all over our clothes."

"So how do you think we stand with the *Bulletin*?" Mickey asked, somewhat plaintively.

"You sound as if you don't have an awful lot of faith in Casimir, Michael," Antoinette said.

"Don't be silly," Mickey said.

"It would probably take two days to get to the Coast Air-Mail Special Delivery," the Bull said. "What the hell, it's worth a shot."

He reached into his trousers pocket, took out a stack of bills held together with a gold clip in the shape of a dollar sign, peeled off a fifty-dollar bill, and handed it to Mickey.

"Two of the big rolls of Taylor ham," The Bull ordered thoughtfully, "and what—five pounds?—of scrapple. I wonder if you can freeze it."

"Probably not," Antoinette said. "If they could freeze it, they would probably have it in the freezer department in the supermarket."

"What the hell, we'll give it a shot anyway. You never get anywhere unless you take a chance, ain't that right, Michael?"

"Right."

# FOUR

The Philadelphia firm of Mawson, Payne, Stockton, McAdoo & Lester maintained their law offices in the Philadelphia Savings Fund Society Building at Twelfth and Market Streets, east of Broad Street, which was convenient to both the federal courthouse and the financial district. The firm occupied all of the eleventh floor, and part of the tenth.

The offices of the two founding partners, Brewster Cortland Payne II and Colonel J. Dunlop Mawson, together with the Executive Conference Room and the office of Mrs. Irene Craig, whose title was Executive Secretary, and whose services they had shared since founding their partnership, occupied the entire eastern wall of the eleventh floor, Colonel Mawson in the corner office to the right and Mr. Payne to the left, with Mrs. Craig between them.

Although this was known only to Colonel Mawson and Mr. Payne, and of course to Mrs. Craig herself, her annual remuneration was greater than that received by any of the twenty-one junior partners of the firm. She received, in addition to a generous salary, the dividends on stock she held in the concern.

Although her desk was replete with the very latest office equipment appropriate to an experienced legal secretary, it had been a very long time since she had actually taken a letter, or a brief, or typed one. She had three assistants, two women and a man, who handled dictation and typing and similar chores.

Irene Craig's function, as both she and Colonel Mawson and Mr. Payne saw it, was to control the expenditure of their time. It was, after all, the only thing they really had to sell, and it was a finite resource. One of the very few things on which Colonel Mawson and Mr. Payne were in complete agreement was that Mrs. Craig performed her function superbly.

Brewster C. Payne, therefore, was not annoyed when he saw Mrs. Craig enter his office. She knew what he was doing, reviewing a lengthy brief about to be submitted in a rather complicated maritime disaster, and that he did not want to be disturbed unless it was a matter of some import that just wouldn't wait. She was here, *ergo sum*, something of bona fide importance demanded his attention.

Brewster Cortland Payne II was a tall, dignified, slim man in his early fifties. He had sharp features and closely cropped gray hair. He was sitting in a high-backed chair, upholstered in blue leather, tilted far back in it, his crossed feet resting on the windowsill of the plate-glass window that offered a view of the Benjamin Franklin Bridge and Camden, New Jersey. The jacket of his crisp cord suit was hung over one of the two blue leather upholstered Charles Eames chairs facing his desk. The button-down collar of his shirt was open, and his regimentally striped necktie pulled down. His shirt cuffs were rolled up. He had not been expecting anyone, client or staff, to come into his office.

"The building is gloriously aflame, I gather," he said, smiling at Irene Craig, "and you are holding the door of the very last elevator?"

"You're not supposed to do that," she said. "When there's a fire, you're supposed to walk down the stairs."

"I stand chastised," he said.

"I hate to do this to you," she said.

"But?"

"Martha Peebles is outside."

Brewster C. Payne II's raised eyebrows made it plain that he had no idea who Martha Peebles was.

"Tamaqua Mining," Irene Craig said.

"Oh," Brewster C. Payne said. "She came to us with Mr. Foster?"

"Right."

One of the factors that had caused the Executive Committee of Mawson, Payne, Stockton, McAdoo & Lester to offer James Whitelaw Foster, Esq., a junior partnership with an implied offer somewhere not too far down the pike of a full partnership was that he would bring with him to the firm the legal business of Tamaqua Mining Company, Inc. It was a closely held corporation with extensive land and mineral holdings in northeast Pennsylvania near, as the name implied, Tamaqua, in the heart of the anthracite region.

"And I gather Mr. Foster is not available?" Payne asked.

"He's in Washington," Irene said. "She's pretty upset. She's been robbed."

"Robbed?"

"Robbed. I think you better see her."

"Where's the colonel?" Payne asked.

"If he was here, I wouldn't be in here," she said. Payne couldn't tell if she was annoyed with him, or tolerating him. "He's with Bull Bolinski."

"With whom?"

"World-famous tennis player," Irene Craig said.

"I don't place him, either," Payne said, after a moment.

"Oh, God," she said, in smiling exasperation. "*Bull Bolinski*. He was a tackle for the Green Bay Packers. You really never heard the name, did you?"

"No, I'm afraid I haven't," Payne said. "And now you have me wholly confused, Irene."

"The colonel's at the Bellevue-Stratford, with the Bull, who is now a lawyer and representing a reporter, who's negotiating a contract with the *Bulletin*."

"Why is he doing that?" Payne asked, surprised, and thinking aloud. The legal affairs of the *Philadelphia Bulletin* were handled by Kenneth L. McAdoo.

"Because he wanted to meet the Bull," Irene Craig said.

"I think I may be beginning to understand," Payne said. "You think I should talk to Mrs. . . . Whatsername?"

"Peebles," Irene Craig replied. "*Miss* Martha Peebles."

"All right," Payne said. "Give me a minute, and then show her in."

"I think you should," Irene Craig said, and walked out of the office.

"Damn," Brewster C. Payne said. He slipped the thick brief he had in his lap and the notes he had made on the desk into the lower right-hand drawer of his desk. Then he stood up, rolled down and buttoned his cuffs, buttoned his collar, pulled up his tie, and put his suit jacket on.

Then he walked to the double doors to his office and pulled the right one open.

A woman, a young one (he guessed thirty, maybe thirty-two or -three) looked at him. She was simply but well dressed. Her light brown hair was cut fashionably short, and she wore short white gloves. She was almost, but not quite, good-looking.

Without thinking consciously about it, Brewster C. Payne categorized her as a lady. What he thought, consciously, was that she, with her brother, held essentially all of the stock in Tamaqua Mining, and that that stock was worth somewhere between twenty and twenty-five million dollars.

*No wonder Irene made me see her.*

"Miss Peebles, I'm Brewster Payne. I'm terribly sorry to have kept you waiting. Would you please come in?"

Martha Peebles smiled and stood up and walked past him

into his office. Payne smelled her perfume. He didn't know the name of it, but it was, he thought, the same kind his wife used.

"May I offer you a cup of coffee? Or perhaps tea?" Payne asked.

"That would be very nice," Martha Peebles said. "Coffee, please."

Payne looked at Irene Craig and saw that she had heard. He pushed the door closed, and ushered Martha Peebles onto a couch against the wall, and settled himself into a matching armchair. A long teakwood coffee table with drawers separated them.

"I'm very sorry that Mr. Foster is not here," Payne said. "He was called to Washington."

"It was very good of you to see me," Martha Peebles said. "I'm grateful to you."

"It's my pleasure, Miss Peebles. Now, how may I be of assistance?"

"Well," she said, "I have been robbed . . . and there's more."

"Miss Peebles, before we go any further, how would you feel about my turning on a recording machine? It's sometimes very helpful. . . ."

"A recording machine?" she asked.

"A recording is often very helpful," Payne said.

She looked at him strangely, then said, "If you think it would be helpful, of course."

Payne tapped the switch of the tape recorder, under the coffee table, with the toe of his shoe.

"You say you were robbed?"

"I thought you said you were going to record this," Martha Peebles said, almost a challenge.

"I am," he said. "I just turned it on. The switch is under the table. The microphone is in that little box on the table."

"Oh, really?" she said, looking first at the box and then under the coffee table. "How clever!"

"You were saying you were robbed?"

"You could have turned it on without asking, couldn't you?" Martha Peebles said. "I would never have known."

"That would have been unethical," he said. "I would never do something like that."

"But you could have, couldn't you?"

"Yes, I suppose I could have," he said, realizing she had made him uncomfortable. "But you were telling me you were robbed. What happened?"

There was a brief tap at the door, and Edward F. Joiner, a slight, soft-spoken man in his middle twenties who was Irene Craig's secretary, came in, carrying a silver coffee set. He smiled at Martha Peebles, and she returned it shyly, as he set the service on the table.

"I'll pour, Ed," Payne said. "Thank you."

Martha Peebles took her coffee black, and did not care for a doughnut or other pastry.

"You were saying you were robbed?" Payne said.

"At home," she said. "In Chestnut Hill."

"How exactly did it happen? A burglar?"

"No, I'm quite sure it's not a burglar," she said. "I even think I know who did it."

"Why don't you start at the very beginning?" Payne said.

Martha Peebles told Brewster Payne that two weeks before, two weeks plus a day, her brother Stephen had brought home a young man he had met.

"A tall, rather good-looking young man," she said. "His name was Walton Williams. Stephen said that he was studying theater at the University of Pennsylvania."

"And is your brother interested in the theater?" Payne asked, carefully.

"I think rather more in young actors than in the theater, per se," Martha Peebles said, matter-of-factly, with neither disapproval nor embarrassment in her voice.

"I see," Payne said.

"Well, they stayed downstairs, in the recreation room, and I went to my room. And then, a little after midnight, I heard them saying good night on the portico, which is directly under my windows.''

''And you think there's a chance this Williams chap is involved in the robbery?''

''There's no question about it,'' she said.

''How can you be sure?''

''I saw him,'' she said.

''I'm afraid I've become lost somewhere along the way,'' Payne said.

''Well, the next night, about half-past eight, I was having a bath when the doorbell rang. I ignored it—''

''Was there anyone else in the house? Your brother? Help?''

''We keep a couple,'' she said. ''But they leave about seven. And Stephen wasn't there. He had gone to Paris that morning.''

''So you were alone in the house?''

''Yes, and since I wasn't expecting anyone, I just ignored the bell.''

''I see. And then what happened?''

''I heard noises in my bedroom. The door opening, then the sound of drawers opening. So I got out of the tub, put a robe on, and opened the door a crack. And there was Walton Williams, at my dresser, going through my things.''

''What did you do then?'' Payne asked. *This is a very stupid young woman*, he thought. *She could have gotten herself in serious difficulty, killed, even, just walking in on a situation like that.*

And then he changed ''*stupid*'' in his mind to ''*naive*'' and ''*inexperienced and overprotected.*''

''I asked him just what he thought he was doing,'' Martha Peebles said, ''and he just looked at me for a moment, obviously surprised to find someone home, and then he ran out of the room and down the stairs and out of the house.''

''And you believe he stole something?'' Payne asked.

''I *know* he stole things,'' she said. ''I know *exactly* what he stole from me. All my valuable pins and pendants, and all of Mother's jewelry that was in the house.''

"And where was your mother when this was going on?" Payne asked.

This earned him a cold and dirty, almost outraged, look.

"Mother passed on in February," she said. "I would have thought you would know that."

"I beg your pardon," Payne said. "I did not."

"Most of her good things were in the bank, of course, but there were some very nice pieces at home. There was a jade necklace, jade set in gold, that she bought in Dakarta, and this Williams person got that. I know she paid ten thousand dollars for that; I had to cable her the money."

"You called the police, of course?" Payne asked.

"Yes, and they came right away, and I gave them a description of Stephen's friend, and an incomplete list, later completed, of everything that was missing. Mr. Foster took care of that for me."

"Well, I'm glad the firm was able to be of some help," Payne said. "Would you take offense if I offered a bit of advice?"

"I came here seeking advice," Martha Peebles said.

"I don't think anything like this will ever happen to you again in your lifetime," Payne said. "But if it should, I really think you would be much better off not to challenge an intruder. Just hide yourself as well as you can, let him take what he wants, and leave. And then you call the police."

"It's already happened again," she said, impatiently.

"I beg your pardon?"

"Last Sunday, Sunday a week ago, not yesterday. I had gone out to the Rose Tree Hunt for the buffet—"

"I was there," Payne interrupted, "my wife and I. And my oldest son."

"—and when I returned home," Martha Peebles went on, oblivious to the interruption, "and stepped inside the door from the driveway, I heard sounds, footsteps, in the library. And then he must have heard me. . . . I'm convinced it was Stephen's young man, but I didn't actually see him, for he ran out the front door."

"You didn't confront him again?"

"No, I called the police from the telephone in the butler's pantry."

"And they came?"

"Right away," she said. "And they searched the house, and they found where he had broken a pane of glass in the greenhouse to gain entrance, and I found out what was stolen this time. A Leica camera, Stephen's—I don't know why he didn't take it to France, but he didn't, I had seen it that very morning—and some accessory lenses for it, and Daddy's binoculars . . . and some other things."

"Miss Peebles," Payne said. "The unpleasant fact is that you will probably never be able to recover the things that were stolen. But if Mr. Foster has been looking after your interests, I'm confident that your insurance will cover your loss."

"I'm not concerned about a *camera*, Mr. Payne," she said. "I'm concerned for my safety."

"I really don't think whoever has done this will return a third time, Miss Peebles," Payne said. "But a few precautions—"

"He was back again last night," she interrupted him. "That's why I'm here now."

"I didn't know," Payne said.

"This time he broke in the side door," she said. "And cut himself when he was reaching through the pane he broke out; there was blood on the floor. This time he stole a bronze, a rather good Egyptian bronze Daddy had bought in Cairo as a young man. Small piece, about eight inches tall. And some other, personal items."

"Such as?"

Her face flushed.

"He went through my dresser," she said, softly, embarrassed, "and stole a half dozen items of underclothing."

"I see," Payne said.

"Specifically," she said, apparently having overcome her

discomfiture, "he made off with all my black undies, brassieres, and panties."

"Just the black?" Payne asked, furious with himself for wanting to smile. What this young woman was telling him was not only of great importance to her, but very likely was symptomatic of a very dangerous situation. While a perverse corner of his brain was amused by the notion of an "actor," almost certainly a young gentleman of exquisite grace, making off with this proper young woman's black underwear, it wasn't funny at all.

"Just the black," she said.

"Well, the first thing I think you might consider is the installation of a security system—"

"We've had Acme Security since Daddy built the house," she said. "Until now, I thought it provided a measure of security. Their damned alarm system doesn't seem to work at all."

"May I suggest that you ask them to come and check it out?" Payne said.

"I've already done that," she said. "They say there's absolutely nothing wrong with it. What *I* think is that people like Stephen's young man know about things like that, and know how to turn them off, render them useless, and Acme just doesn't want to admit that's possible."

*She's probably right.*

"Another possibility, for the immediate future," Payne said, "until the police can run this Williams chap to ground, is to move, temporarily, into a hotel."

"I have no intention of having someone like that drive me from my home," Martha Peebles said, firmly. "What I had hoped to hear from Mr. Foster, Mr. Payne, is that he has some influence with the police, and could prevail upon them to provide me with more protection than they so far have."

"I frankly don't know what influence Mr. Foster has with the police, Miss Peebles—"

"Well, that's certainly a disappointment," she interrupted him.

"But as I was about to say, Colonel Mawson, a senior partner of the firm, is a close personal friend of Police Commissioner Czernick."

"Well, then, may I see him please?"

"That won't be necessary, Miss Peebles. As soon as he walks through the door, I'll bring this to his attention."

"Where is he now?"

"Actually," Payne said, "he's at the Bellevue-Stratford. With a chap called Bull Bolinski."

"The Packers' Bull Bolinski?" Miss Peebles asked, brightening visibly.

"Yes, the Packers' Bull Bolinski."

"Oh, I almost cried when he announced his retirement," Martha Peebles said.

"He's now an attorney, you know."

"I hadn't heard that," she said. "And I'd forgotten this has all been recorded, hasn't it?"

"Yes, it has. And I'll have it transcribed immediately."

Martha Peebles stood up and offered Brewster C. Payne II her hand.

"I can't tell you how much better I feel, Mr. Payne, after having spoken to you. And thank you for seeing me without an appointment."

"That was my pleasure," Payne said. "Anytime you want to see me, Miss Peebles, my door is always open. But I wish you would consider checking into a hotel for a few days. . . ."

"I told you, I will not be run off by people like that," she said, firmly. "Good morning, Mr. Payne."

He walked with her to the door, then to the elevator, and saw her on it.

When he walked back into his office, Irene Craig followed him.

"What the devil is wrong with the cops?" she asked. "She gave them a description of this creep, even if that was a phony name."

"Why do I suspect that you were, as a figure of speech, out there all the time with your ear to my keyhole?" he asked.

"You knew I would be monitoring that," she said. "I also had Ed take it down on the stenotype machine. I should have a transcript before the colonel gets back."

"Good girl!" he said.

"There are some women in my position who would take high umbrage at a sexist remark like that," she said. "But I'll swap compliments. You handled her beautifully."

"Now may I go back to work, boss?" Payne said.

"Oh, I think the colonel can handle this from here," she said, and walked out of his office.

Brewster Cortland Payne II returned to his brief.

# FIVE

The eight men gathered in the conference room of the suite of third-floor offices in the Roundhouse assigned to the Police Commissioner of the City of Philadelphia chatted softly among themselves, talking about anything but business, waiting for the Commissioner to more or less formally open the meeting.

He did not do so until Deputy Commissioner for Administration Harold J. Wilson, a tall, thin, dignified man, entered the room, mumbled something about having been hung up in traffic, and sat down.

Police Commissioner Taddeus Czernick then matter-of-factly thumped the table with his knuckles, and waited for the murmur of conversation to peter out.

"The mayor," Commissioner Czernick said, evenly, even dryly, "does not want Mike Sabara to get Highway Patrol."

Taddeus Czernick was fifty-seven years old, a tall, heavyset man with a thick head of silver hair. His smoothly shaven cheeks had a ruddy glow. He was just starting to jowl. He was wearing a stiffly starched shirt and a regimentally striped necktie with a dark blue, pin-striped, vested suit. He was a handsome, healthy, imposing man.

"He say why?" Chief Inspector of Detectives Matt Lowenstein asked.

"He said, 'In uniform, Mike Sabara looks like a guard in a concentration camp,' " Czernick quoted.

Chief Inspector Lowenstein, a stocky, barrel-chested man of fifty-five, examined the half inch ash on his six-inch-long light green *Villa de Cuba* "*Monarch*" for a moment, then chuckled.

"He does," Lowenstein said, "if you think about it, he does."

"That's hardly justification for not giving Sabara the Highway Patrol," Deputy Commissioner Wilson said, somewhat prissily.

"*You* tell the dago that, Harry," Lowenstein replied.

Deputy Commissioner Wilson glowered at Lowenstein, but didn't reply. He had long ago learned that the best thing for him to say when he was angry was nothing.

And he realized that he was annoyed, on the edge of anger, now. He was annoyed that he had gotten hung up in traffic and had arrived at the meeting late. He prided himself on being punctual, and when, as he expected to do, he became Police Commissioner himself, he intended to instill in the entire department a more acute awareness of the importance of time, which he believed was essential to efficiency and discipline, than it had now.

He was annoyed that when he had walked into the meeting, the only seat remaining at the long conference table in the Commissioner's Conference Room was beside Chief Inspector Lowenstein, which meant that he would have to inhale the noxious fumes from Lowenstein's cigar for however long the meeting lasted.

He was annoyed at Chief Inspector Lowenstein's reference to the mayor of the City of Philadelphia, the Honorable Jerry Carlucci, as "the dago," and even more annoyed with Commissioner Czernick for not correcting him for doing so, and sharply, on the spot.

So far as Deputy Commissioner Wilson was concerned, it was totally irrelevant that Mayor Carlucci and Chief Lowenstein were lifelong friends, going back to their service as young patrolmen in the Highway Patrol; or that the mayor very often greeted Chief Lowenstein in similarly distasteful terms. ("How's it going, Jew boy?") The mayor was the mayor, and senior officials subordinate to him were obliged to pay him the respect appropriate to his position.

Deputy Commissioner Wilson was also annoyed with the mayor. There was a chain-of-command structure in place, a standing operating procedure. When it became necessary to appoint a senior police officer to fill a specific position, the Deputy Commissioner for Administration, after considering the recommendations made to him by appropriate personnel, and after personally reviewing the records of the individuals involved, was charged with furnishing the Commissioner the names, numerically ranked, of the three best qualified officers for the position in question. Then, in consultation with the Deputy Commissioner for Administration, the Commissioner would make his choice.

Deputy Commissioner for Administration Wilson had not yet completed his review of the records of those eligible, and recommended for, appointment as Commanding Officer, Highway Patrol. Even granting that the mayor, as chief executive officer of the City of Philadelphia, might have the right to enter the process, voicing his opinion, doing so interfered with both the smooth administration of Police Department personnel policy, and was certain to affect morale adversely.

It had to do with Mayor Carlucci's mind-set, Deputy Commissioner Wilson believed. It was not that the mayor thought of himself as a retired policeman. Mayor Carlucci thought of himself as a cop who happened to be mayor. And even worse than that, Mayor Carlucci, who had once been Captain Carlucci, Commanding Officer, Highway Patrol, thought of himself as a Highway Patrolman who also happened to be mayor.

The mayoral Cadillac limousine, in previous administrations chauffeured by a plainclothes police officer, was now driven by a uniformed Highway Patrol sergeant. It was equipped with shortwave radios tuned to the Highway Patrol and Detective bands, and the mayoral limousine was famous, or perhaps infamous, for rolling on calls the mayor found interesting.

Police Radio would, in Deputy Commissioner Wilson's judgment, far too often announce that there was a *robbery in progress*, or *officer needs assistance*, or *man with a gun, shots fired,* only to have the second or third reply—sometimes the first—be "M-Mary One in on the shots fired," from the mayoral Cadillac limousine, by then already racing down Lancaster Avenue or South Broad Street or the Schuylkill Expressway with the siren whooping and red lights flashing.

Deputy Commissioner Wilson was not really sure in his own mind why the mayor behaved this way, whether it was because, as the mayor himself had said, he was unable to dilute his policeman's blood to the point where he could *not* respond to an *officer needs assistance* call, or whether it was calculated, on purpose. The mayor very often got his picture in the newspapers, and his image on the television, at one crime scene or another, often standing with his hands on his hips, pushing back his suit jacket so that the butt of his Smith & Wesson *Chief's Special* .38-caliber snub-nosed revolver could be seen.

Commissioner Wilson was very much aware that one did not become mayor of the nation's fourth largest city if one was either stupid, childish, or unaware of the importance of public relations and publicity. There were a lot of voters who liked the idea of having their mayor rush to the scene of a crime wearing a gun.

"I think it probably has to do with the *Ledger* editorial last Sunday," Commissioner Czernick said now.

This produced a chorus of grunts, and several mildly profane expressions. Following a Highway Patrol shooting, in which two North Philadelphia youths, interrupted while they were holding up a convenience store, were killed, one of them having six wounds in his body, the *Ledger* published an indignant editorial, under the headline, "POLICE FORCE? OR A JACKBOOTED GESTAPO?"

It was not the first time the *Ledger* had referred to the highly polished motorcyclist's black leather boots worn by police officers assigned to Highway Patrol as Gestapo Jackboots.

"Has he got someone in mind?" Chief Inspector Dennis V. Coughlin asked.

Coughlin looked not unlike Commissioner Czernick. He was tall, and large boned, and had all his teeth and all his curly hair, now silver. He was one of eleven Chief Inspectors of the Police Department of the City of Philadelphia. But it could be argued that he was first among equals. Under his command, among others, were the Narcotics Unit, the Vice Unit, the Internal Affairs Division, the Staff Investigation Unit, and the Organized Crime Intelligence Unit.

The other ten Chief Inspectors reported to either the Deputy Commissioner (Operations) or the Deputy Commissioner (Administration), who reported to the Commissioner. Denny Coughlin reported directly to the Commissioner, and not unreasonably, believed that what happened anywhere in the Police Department was his business.

"The mayor has several things in mind," Commissioner Czernick said, carefully, "thoughts which he has been kind enough to share with me."

"Uh oh," Lowenstein said.

"He thinks that David Pekach would make a fine commander of Highway," Commissioner Czernick said.

Chief Lowenstein considered that for a moment, then said, chuckling, "But he'd have to cut off his pigtail. Do you think David would be willing to do that?"

There were chuckles from everyone around the conference table except for Deputy Commissioner for Administration

Wilson. Newly promoted Captain Pekach wasn't even on the preliminary list of fourteen captains Commissioner Wilson had drawn up to fill the vacancy of Commanding Officer, Highway Patrol, created when Captain Richard C. Moffitt had been shot to death trying to stop an armed robbery.

"Mike Sabara was next in line for Highway," Chief Inspector Coughlin said. "And he's qualified. I guess the mayor's thought about that?"

· "The mayor thinks Mike would fit in neatly as Deputy Commander of Special Operations Division," Commissioner Czernick said, "especially if I went along with his suggestion to take Highway away from Traffic and put it under Special Operations. Then it would be sort of a promotion for Sabara, the mayor says."

"I thought that Special Operations Division idea was dead," Deputy Commissioner for Operations Francis J. Cohan said. It was the first time he'd spoken. "I didn't like it, said so, and now I'm going to get it anyway?"

"Denny's going to get it," Commissioner Czernick said, nodding his head toward Chief Inspector Coughlin.

"My God!" Cohan said. "If Highway isn't Operations, what is?"

"Everything you have now, except Highway," Commissioner Czernick said. "Highway is now under *Special* Operations."

"Highway and what else?" Cohan asked.

"Highway and ACT," Czernick said.

"The ACT grant came through?" Deputy Commissioner Wilson asked, both surprised and annoyed.

ACT was the acronym for Anti-Crime Teams, a federally funded program administered by the Justice Department. It was a test, more or less, to see what effect saturating a high-crime area with extra police, the latest technology, and special assistance from the district attorney in the form of having assistant district attorneys with nothing to do but push ACT-arrested criminals through the criminal justice system would have, short and long term, on crime statistics.

"When did all this happen?" Cohan asked.

"The mayor told me he had a call from the senator Friday afternoon about the ACT grant," Czernick said. "I suppose it'll be in the papers today, or maybe on the TV tonight. The mayor says we'll start getting money, some of it right away."

"I meant about this Special Operations," Cohan said.

"Wait a minute," Czernick said. "I'm glad this came up." He shifted in his chair to look at Deputy Commissioner for Administration Wilson. "Harry, I don't want to be told that, in setting up Special Operations, something can't be done because there's no money. You authorize whatever is necessary, using contingency funds, until the federal money comes in. Then reimburse the contingency fund. Understand?"

"Yes, sir." Deputy Commissioner Wilson said.

Czernick turned back to Deputy Commissioner Cohan.

"To answer your question, it happened yesterday. I don't know how long he's been thinking about it, but it happened about half-past ten yesterday morning. When he came home from mass, he called me up and said if I didn't have anything important going on, I should come by and he'd give me a cup of coffee."

"Was that before or after he read the *Ledger*?" Lowenstein asked.

"He asked me if I'd seen it the moment I walked in the door," Czernick said.

"And when is all this *going* to happen?" Cohan asked.

"It's happening right now, Frank," Czernick said. "It's effective today."

"Am I going to get to pick a commander for this Special Operations Division?" Coughlin asked.

"Anybody you want, Denny," Commissioner Czernick said, "just so long as his name is Peter Wohl."

"Jesus," Coughlin exploded, "why doesn't he just move in here if he's going to make every goddamned decision?" He paused, then added, "Not that I have anything against Peter Wohl. But . . . Jesus!"

"He doesn't have to move in here, Denny," Commissioner Czernick said. "Not as long as he has my phone number."

"Did Mayor Carlucci give you his reasons for all this?" Deputy Commissioner Wilson asked. "Or for any of it?"

"No, but what he did do when he explained everything— there's a little more I haven't gotten to yet—was to ask me if I had any objections, if there was something wrong with it that he'd missed."

"And you couldn't think of anything?" Cohan asked, softly.

"He wants a Special Operations Division," Czernick said. "He knows you don't want it. So he gave it to Denny Coughlin. He wants Peter Wohl to run it. What was I supposed to say, 'Peter isn't qualified'? He thinks Mike Sabara is bad for Highway's image. What was I supposed to say, for Christ's sake, that 'beauty is only skin deep'?"

Cohan shrugged. "You said there's more," he said.

"Just as soon as Peter Wohl has a little time to get his feet wet," Czernick said, "Denny will ask him to recommend, from among Highway Patrol sergeants, someone to take over as the mayor's driver. Sergeant Lucci, who is driving the mayor now, made it onto the lieutenants' list. As soon as Peter can find a replacement for him, *Lieutenant* Lucci will return to ordinary supervisory duties commensurate with his rank, in Highway."

"You don't happen to think," Chief Lowenstein said, dryly sarcastic, "that Lieutenant Lucci might have in mind getting some of this ACT money for Highway, do you? Or that he might just happen to bump into the dago every once in a while, say once a week, and just happen to mention in idle conversation that Highway didn't get as much of it as he thinks they should? Nothing like that could be happening, could it, Tad?"

"I don't know," Czernick said, coldly. "But if he did, that would be Peter Wohl's problem, wouldn't you say? Wohl's and Denny's?"

"What's he really got in mind, long term, for this Special Operations?" Chief Coughlin asked.

"Long term, I haven't any idea," said Czernick. "Short term, yeah, I know what he's got in mind."

There was a pause, and when it didn't end, Denny Coughlin said, "You going to tell us?"

"What he said, Denny, was that he thought it would be nice if he could hold a press conference in a couple of weeks, where he could announce that an Anti-Crime Team of the new Special Operations Division, which was a little suggestion of his to the Police Department, had just announced the arrest of the sexual pervert who had been raping and terrorizing the decent women of Northwest Philadelphia."

"That scumbag is none of the Anti-Crime Team, or Special Operations, or Highway's business," Chief Inspector Lowenstein said, coldly angry. "Rape is the Detective Bureau's business. It always has been."

"It still is, Matt," Czernick said, evenly, "except for what's going on in Northwest Philadelphia. That's now in Peter Wohl's lap because Jerry Carlucci says it is."

"He was at it again last night," Deputy Commissioner Cohan said. "He broke into the apartment of a woman named Mary Elizabeth Flannery, on Henry Avenue in Roxborough, tied her to her bed, cut her clothes off with a hunting knife, took of his clothes, committed an incomplete act of oral sodomy on her, and when that didn't get his rocks off, he pissed all over her. Then he tied her hands behind her back, loaded her in a van, and dumped her naked on Forbidden Drive in Fairmount Park."

"What do you mean, dumped her naked in the park?" Lowenstein asked.

"Just that, Matt. He carried her over there in a van, then pushed her out. Hands tied behind her back. Not a stitch on her."

"You catch somebody like that," Lowenstein said, "what you should do is cut the bastard's balls off and leave him to bleed to death."

"Let's just hope that Peter Wohl can catch him," Czernick said.

At five minutes after ten, Colonel J. Dunlop Mawson, of Mawson, Payne, Stockton, McAdoo & Lester, legal counsel to the *Philadelphia Bulletin*, presented himself at the door of the Theodore Roosevelt Suite.

"Mr. Bolinski," Colonel Mawson said, as he enthusiastically pumped the Bull's hand, "I'm one of your greatest fans."

"And I of yours, Colonel," the Bull said. Before the sentence was completely out of the Bull's mouth, Mickey O'Hara realized that the Bull no longer sounded like your typical Polack Catholic product of West Philly. "I can only hope that the presence of the dean of the Philadelphia Criminal Bar does not carry with it any suggestion that larceny is at hand."

Colonel J. Dunlop Mawson beamed.

"Bull," he said, "—may I call you Bull?"

"Certainly," the Bull said. "I do hope we're going to be friends."

"Bull, the truth of the matter is that I pulled a little rank. I'm a senior partner in the firm, and I took advantage of that so that I would have a chance to meet you."

"I'm flattered," the Bull said, "and honored to meet you, Colonel."

"The honor is mine," Mawson said, "to meet the man who is arguably the best tackle football has ever known."

"This is my wife, Colonel," the Bull said, "and I believe you know Mr. O'Hara?"

"A privilege to meet you, ma'am," Mawson said.

"May we offer you some coffee, Colonel? Or perhaps something else?" Antoinette said.

"Coffee seems like a splendid idea," Colonel Mawson said. He nodded at Mickey, but said nothing and did not offer his hand.

This was followed by a ten-minute tour, conducted by Colonel J. Dunlop Mawson, down Football Memory Lane. Then came a detour, via Bull's mentioning that he represented Lenny Moskowitz, lasting another ten minutes, in which the intricacies of premarital agreements were discussed in terms Mickey couldn't understand at all.

Finally, the Bull said, "Colonel, I really hate to break this off, but Antoinette and I are on a tight schedule."

"Of course," Colonel J. Dunlop Mawson said, "forgive me."

He reached into his alligator attaché case and came up with a manila folder, which he passed to the Bull.

"I think you'll find that brings us to a state of agreement," he said.

The Bull read the document very carefully, while Colonel J. Dunlop Mawson hung on every word of Mrs. Bolinski's tour guide of the better restaurants in the Miami/Palm Beach area.

"With one or two minor caveats," the Bull said, "this appears to be what I discussed with—what was his name?"

"Lemuelson," Colonel Mawson said, "Steve Lemuelson. What seems to trouble you, Bull?"

"I'd like to add a phrase here," the Bull said.

Colonel Mawson scurried to Bull's armchair and looked over his shoulder, then read aloud what the Bull had written in: ". . . it being understood between the parties that the annual increase will ordinarily be approximately ten percentum of both compensation and reimbursement of expenses, unless the annual rate of inflation has exceeded four percentum, in which case the annual increase in compensation will ordinarily be ten percentum plus seventy percentum of the rate of inflation, according to the latest then published figures by the U.S. Department of Commerce."

Colonel Mawson grunted.

"You see the problem, of course, Counselor," the Bull said.

"I think we can live with that, Bull," Colonel Mawson said.

Mickey didn't know what the fuck they were talking about.

"And then here in fourteen (c) six," the Bull said, "I think a little specificity would be in order. You can see what I've penciled in."

And again Colonel Mawson read the modified clause aloud: "A Buick Super, Mercury Monterey, or equivalent automobile, including special radio apparatus, satisfactory to Mr O'Hara, including installation, maintenance, and all related expenses thereto pertaining."

Colonel Mawson paused thoughtfully for a moment, then said, "Oh, I see. Well, that certainly seems reasonable enough."

"Good," the Bull said, "and last, I have added a final paragraph, thirty-six." He flipped through the document and then pointed it out to Mawson. This time he read it aloud: "The terms of this agreement shall be effective as of from June 1973."

"But, Bull," the colonel protested, "he hasn't been working all that time."

"He would have been working, if you had then agreed to the terms agreed to here," the Bull said.

The colonel hesitated, then said, "Oh, hell, what the hell, Bull, why not?"

"I don't think Mr. O'Hara is being unreasonable," the Bull said.

"I'm sorry it got as far as withholding services," Colonel Mawson said.

"What I suggest we do now is have Mr. O'Hara sign, and initial all the modified sections," the Bull said. "And then when I get back to the office I'll have my girl run off a half dozen copies on the Xerox and pop them in the mail to you."

When Mickey O'Hara scrawled his initials in the margin beside *Section* 11-*Compensation*, he saw that a line had been drawn through what had originally been typed, SEVEN HUNDRED AND FIFTY DOLLARS AND NO CENTS ($750.00), and that his corrected weekly compensation was to be ONE THOUSAND DOLLARS AND NO CENTS ($1,000.00), *said sum to be paid weekly by check payable to*

*Heidenheimer & Bolinski, P.C., who herewith assume responsibility for the payment of all applicable federal, state, and local income taxes and Social Security contributions.*

When he came down from the Theodore Roosevelt Suite, there were two people behind the front desk of the Bellevue-Stratford, neither of them Miss Travis. He was torn between disappointment and relief that somebody had finally shown up to take her place.

He wondered how she would react if he just happened to come by the Bellevue-Stratford and say hello, and maybe ask her if she wanted to go get something to eat, or go to a movie, or something.

Then he realized that was foolish. She had given him the same smile she had given the blue-haired broad who had bitched about her room. Maybe the smile was a little more genuine, but even so that would be because he was at the Bellevue-Stratford to see the Bull, who was staying in one of the more expensive suites.

But maybe not. She had said she was a—what did she say?—*an avid reader.*

And then Mickey O'Hara pushed through the revolving door and onto South Broad Street, and there she was, coming up the street headed toward City Hall, carrying a paper sack in each arm. He saw paper towels in one of them.

"Hi!" she said.

"I thought you were going to bed."

"I'm on my way," she said.

"Can I take you?"

*There you go, O'Hara, both fucking feet in your mouth!*

"I didn't mean that the way it sounded," Mickey said. "I mean, I got my car . . ."

"I'm probably going nowhere near where you are," she said, after a just perceptible pause.

"Where?"

"Roxborough."

"Practically on my way," he said.

"Really?"

"Really."

*It would be on my way if you were going to Mexico City.*

"Where's your car?" she asked.

He pointed to it.

"You're sure you're really going that way?" she asked.

"Positive."

Miss Travers didn't seem to think anything was wrong with his car, but Mickey managed to drop into their conversation that he was about to get a new one, that he was thinking of either a Mercury or Buick.

More importantly, she told him her first name was Mary, and that she would love to have dinner with him, but it would probably be hard to arrange it, because she was stuck on the seven-to-three-in-the-morning shift—it was determined by seniority—and that made any kind of a normal social life nearly impossible.

"I know," Mickey said. "The *Bulletin* goes to bed at half-past two."

"You mean that's when you quit for the day?"

He nodded and she smiled at him, and he thought, *We already have something in common.*

Forty minutes later, when he steered the battered Chevrolet Impala off North Broad Street and into the parking lot behind the Thirty-fifth District Station, where he stopped in a space marked INSPECTOR PARKING ONLY, Mickey still wasn't sure he really believed what had happened.

*I've got a date with Mary Travis. Tonight. Tomorrow morning. At five minutes after three, at the front door of the Bellevue-Stratford.*

And that wasn't all that had happened.

*I'm making as much dough as the fucking Police Commissioner, for Christ's sake!*

He sat there for a moment, then lit a cigarette. Then he got out of the car, entered the building through a door marked POLICE USE ONLY and went inside. He waved at the uniformed cops in the ground-floor squad room, then climbed the stairs to the second floor, which housed the Northwest Detectives Division.

On the landing at the top of the stairs were several vending machines, a garbage can, and two battered chairs. A concrete block wall with a wide open window counter and a door separated the landing from the squad room of Northwest Detectives. A sign beneath the window counter read POLICE PERSONNEL ONLY BEYOND THIS POINT, and just inside the door the desk man, a detective, sat at a battered desk.

Mickey walked through the door, waved at the desk man, and exchanged casual greetings, a nod of the head, or a smile, with the half dozen detectives working at their own battered desks, then took a quick, practiced glance at the large, yellow legal pad on the desk man's desk. On it, the desk man would have written the names of any citizens brought into the squad room for "interviews" on the shift. It was an informal record, intended primarily to remind the desk man who had hauled in who, and was responsible for the critter. If a citizen got as far as the detective squad room, the odds were the "interview" would be followed by an arrest.

Mickey found nothing that looked particularly interesting, so he walked across the squad room to a small alcove at the rear, which held a coffee machine. He helped himself to a cup, black, then tucked a dollar bill in the coffee kitty can.

When he came out of the alcove, he looked into the window of the small office used by the Lieutenants of Northwest Detectives. Lieutenant Teddy Spanner, who had the watch, and Lieutenant Louis Natali of Homicide were inside. That was unusual; you rarely saw a Homicide Lieutenant in one of the Detective District Squad Rooms, unless something important was going down.

Lou Natali, a slight, olive-skinned man who was losing his hair, was leaning on the glass wall. Behind the desk, Spanner, a very large fair-skinned man in his shirtsleeves, waved at Mickey, calling him inside.

"How goes it, Mickey?" Spanner said, as Mickey leaned over the desk to shake his hand.

"Can't complain," Mickey said, and turned to Lou Natali. "What do you say, Lou?"

"Haven't seen you around lately, Mick," Natali said. "You been sick or something?"

"I took a couple of weeks off," Mickey said.

"You go down to the shore?" Spanner asked.

"The shore?" Mickey asked.

"You told me, Mick, the last time I saw you, that what you needed was to go lay on the beach."

"I just hung around the house and watched the wallpaper peel," Mickey said.

"So what's new, Mick?" Natali asked, chuckling.

*What's new? I'm now making a thousand bucks a week, less a hundred for the Bull, plus a Buick Super, Mercury Monterey, or equivalent automobile. And I just met a really interesting girl. That's what's new.*

"Nothing much," Mickey said. "You tell me."

Both police officers shrugged their shoulders.

Mickey was disappointed. He had had a gut feeling when he saw Lou Natali that something was up. Mickey knew both of them well enough not to press the question. Probably nothing was. If there was, either Spanner or Natali would have told him, maybe prefacing it with "*Off the record, Mick*" but they would have told him.

"Tell me about the naked lady in Fairmount Park," Mickey said. "I heard the call last night."

"Every car in the District, plus half the Highway Patrol, went in on that, Mick," Spanner said. "But aside from that, it's not very funny. Lou and I were just talking about it."

"Tell me," Mickey said.

"Off the record?"

*Goddamn, I knew there was something!*

"Sure."

"You heard, I suppose, about the guy who's been raping women in Manayunk and Roxborough?"

Mickey nodded.

"From what I understand, he's the same guy who dumped the woman in Fairmount Park."

"Raped her first, you mean?"

"Not quite," Spanner said. "This is a real sick guy. Getting sicker, too."

"I don't know what you mean," Mickey said.

"He's not even screwing them anymore," Spanner said. "What he's doing now is getting his rocks off humiliating them. Pissing on them, and worse."

"Jesus!" Mickey said. "Worse?"

"What he did last night was put a knife to her throat and make her take it in the mouth. Then when he couldn't get his rocks off, he pissed all over her. Then he tied her hands behind her back and dumped her out on Forbidden Drive."

"Nice fella," Mickey said.

"Sure as Christ made little apples," Natali said, "unless they bag this scumbag, he's going to kill somebody. Cut 'em up, probably. I'm afraid he's going to start going after young girls."

"Jesus," Mickey said. He felt a little sick to his stomach when he thought of some slimeball doing something like that to a nice girl like Mary Travis. "You got anything going?"

"Not much. No good description. All we know is that he's a white guy with a van. And likes to wear a mask," Spanner said.

"You didn't get that here, Mickey," Natali said. "What I'm worried about is that I don't want to give the sonofabitch any ideas."

Mickey made a gesture signifying that he wouldn't violate the confidence.

"Who's got this job?" Mickey asked.

"Dick Hemmings," Spanner said. Mickey knew Dick Hemmings to be a brighter than usual Northwest Detective, which was saying something because, with a couple of exceptions, Northwest Division had some really good detectives.

"Who was the cop who answered the call?" Mickey asked.

"Bill Dohner," Spanner said. "I don't know where you can find him until he comes in tonight, but Dick Hemmings is in court. I got the feeling he'll be in there all day."

"Well, then I guess I'd better get down there," Mickey said. "And start earning my living."

He returned to the coffee machine alcove and washed out his cup, then put it in the rack. Then he picked up a telephone on one of the unoccupied desks in the detective squad room and dialed a number from memory.

"City desk," a male voice came on the line.

"This is O'Hara," he said.

"Mr. Michael J. O'Hara?" Gerald F. Kennedy, the city editor of the *Bulletin* replied, in mock awe. "Might one dare to hope, Mr. O'Hara, that there is a small germ of truth in the rumor going around that you are no longer withholding your professional services?"

"Fuck you, Kennedy."

"Then to what do I owe the honor of this telephone call, Mr. O'Hara?"

"Who's been covering the Northwest Philly rapes?"

"Why do you want to know, Mickey?"

"I think I'm onto something."

"Are you?" Gerry Kennedy asked.

"Yeah, I am," Mickey said.

"Odd, but I don't seem to recall assigning this story to you."

"Are we going to play games? In which case, Kennedy, go fuck yourself. I get paid whether or not I work."

"I assigned the story to Cheryl Davies," Kennedy said. "She's not going to like it if I take it away from her and give it to you."

"Fuck her."

"I would love to," Gerry Kennedy said. "But I don't think it's likely. What do you want with her, Mickey?"

"Not a goddamned thing," Mickey said. "What I'm going to do, Kennedy, is cover this myself. And you decide whose stuff you want to run."

"How about working together with her, Mick?" Gerry Kennedy asked. "I mean, she's been on it for three weeks—"

He broke off in midsentence when he realized that Mickey O'Hara had hung up.

# SIX

"Good afternoon, sir," Jesus Martinez, who was of Puerto Rican ancestry, and who was five feet eight inches tall and weighed just over 140 pounds, said to the man who had reached into the rear seat of a 1972 Buick sedan in the parking lot of the Penrose Plaza Mall at Lindbergh Avenue and Island Road in West Philadelphia, and taken out two shopping bags, one of them emblazoned *John Wanamaker & Sons*.

"What the fuck?" the man replied. His name was Clarence Sims, and he was six feet three and weighed 180 pounds.

"Been doing a little shopping, have you, sir?"

"Get out of my face, motherfucker," Clarence Sims replied.

"I'm a police officer," Jesus Martinez said, pulling up his T-shirt, which he wore outside his blue jeans, so that his badge, through which his belt was laced, came into sight. "May I see your driver's license and vehicle registration, please?"

Clarence Sims considered, briefly, the difference in size

87

between them, and his options, and then threw the *John Wan-amaker & Sons* shopping bag at Jesus Martinez and started running.

He got as far as the Buick's bumper when he stumbled over something. The next thing Clarence Sims knew he was flat on the ground, with an enormous honky sitting on him, and painfully twisting his arms behind him. He felt a steel hand-cuff snap shut around one wrist, and then around the other.

And the little spick was in his face, the spick and a gun, shoved hard against his nostrils.

"Don't you *ever* call me motherfucker, you motherfucker!" Officer Jesus Martinez said, furiously. "I ought to blow your fucking brains out, cocksucker!"

"Hay-zus," the enormous honky said, "cool it!"

"I don't like that shit!" Officer Martinez replied, still angry. But the revolver barrel withdrew from Clarence Sims's nostril.

Clarence Sims felt hands running over his body. From one hip pocket a switchblade was removed, from the other his wallet. His side pockets were emptied, spilling a collection of coins and chewing gum wrappers onto the macadam of the parking lot. His groin was probed dispassionately, and then he felt the hands moving down his legs. From his right sock, fingers removed a joint of marijuana, a small plasticine bag of marijuana—known on the street as a "nickel bag," because they sold for five dollars—and a book of matches.

"Oh, my God!" a female voice said, in shock.

"It's all right, ma'am," Clarence heard the spick say, "we're police officers. Is this your car, ma'am?"

"Yes, it is," the female voice said, and then she spotted the shopping bags, and a tone of indignation came into her voice. "Those are my things!"

"Somehow, I didn't think they were his," Martinez said.

Clarence felt the weight of the man kneeling on his back go away.

"Your name Clarence Sims?" Martinez asked.

"Go fuck yourself!"

Clarence Sims's face, which he had raised off the macadam of the parking lot, suddenly encountered it again, as if something—a foot, say—had pushed the back of his head.

"You're under arrest, Clarence," the honky said.

"What happened here?" the female voice asked.

"I saw him taking those bags out of the backseat," Martinez said. "Ma'am, can you tell me how much the stuff in them is worth?"

The victim thought about that a moment. "Two hundred dollars," she said, finally. "Maybe a little more."

"It would help if you could tell us if it's *for sure* worth more than two hundred dollars," Martinez pursued.

The victim considered that for a moment, then said, "Now that I've had a chance to think, it's all worth closer to three hundred dollars than two."

"Bingo," Charley McFadden said. "M-1."

The victim looked at him strangely.

The crime of which Clarence Sims now stood accused, *theft from auto*, was a misdemeanor. There were three subcategories: M-3, where the stolen property is worth less than fifty dollars; M-2, where the property is worth between fifty and two hundred dollars; and M-1, where the property is worth more than two hundred dollars.

Like most police officers, Charley McFadden was pleased that the critter he had arrested was not as unimportant as he might have been. An M-1 thief was a better arrest than an M-3.

A faint but growing glimmer of hope that he might be able to extricate himself from his current predicament came into Clarence Sims's mind: The fucking pigs had not read him his goddamned rights. Like most people in his line of work, Clarence Sims was well aware of what had come to be known as the *Miranda* Decision. If the fucking pigs didn't read you the whole goddamned thing, starting with "*You have the right to remain silent*" and going through the business about them getting you a lawyer if you couldn't afford one, and could prove it, then you told the judge and the judge let you walk.

Clarence Sims erred. Under the law it is necessary to advise a suspect of his rights under *Miranda* only when the suspect is to be questioned concerning a crime. Since it was not the intention of the arresting officers to ask him any questions at all about the crime, it was not necessary for them to inform Mr. Sims of his rights under *Miranda*.

The man Clarence Sims thought of as the big honky, who was a twenty-two-year-old police officer named Charles McFadden, opened the door of a battered old Volkswagen, and picked up a small portable radio.

The battered old Volkswagen was his personal automobile. He had been authorized to use it on duty. Authorized, but not required. Since he had chosen to use it, he had been issued sort of a Police Department credit card, which authorized him to gas up at any Police Department gas pump—there is one at every District Headquarters—up to a limit of one hundred gallons per month, no questions asked. If he had not elected to use his personal vehicle on duty, he could have performed that duty on foot.

"Twelfth District BD," Charley McFadden said into the radio. (Burglary Detail.)

"Twelfth District BD," Police Radio promptly responded.

"Twelfth District BD," Charley McFadden said. "I need a wagon for a prisoner. We're in the parking lot of the Penrose Plaza at Island Road and Lindbergh."

Police Radio did not respond to Officer McFadden directly, but instead, after checking the board to see what was available, called the Emergency Patrol Wagon directly:

"Twelve Oh One."

"Twelve Oh One," the wagon replied.

"Meet the burglary detail at the parking lot of Penrose Plaza, Island at Lindbergh, with a prisoner."

"Twelve Oh One, okay," EPW 1201 replied.

Charley McFadden put the portable radio back on the seat of his Volkswagen.

When the two police officers assigned to 1201, the Twelfth District wagon responding to the call to transport a prisoner, arrived at the scene, they found that the arresting officers were having more trouble with the victim than with the prisoner.

The prisoner was on his feet, his hands cuffed behind him, leaning on the victim's car and apparently resigned to his fate. Even, to judge by the look on his face, a little smug about it.

The victim, having been informed that her two packages had become evidence, and could not be returned to her until released by proper authority, was engaged in a heated conversation with Officer McFadden, telling him that she had to have the shopping bags, at least the one from *John Wanamaker & Sons* which contained a formal dress shirt for her husband, a shirt he absolutely had to have for a dinner party that night.

"Ma'am, if you'll just go the West Detectives, at Fifty-fifth and Pine, and sign the Property Receipt, they'll give you your stuff right back."

"What I don't understand is why I can't sign whatever it is I have to sign right here," she said.

"I don't have the form, lady; you have to do it at West Detectives," Charley McFadden said. "That's the rules."

That was not the truth, the whole truth, and nothing but the truth. But it had been Officer McFadden's experience that if he gave the victim back her property here and now, that would be the last he, or more importantly, the criminal justice system, would ever see of her. It had been his experience that the ordinary citizen's interest in law enforcement ended when they had to make their own contribution, like showing up in court and swearing under oath that the stuff the critter had stolen belonged to her.

The chances of her showing up in court, and thus perhaps aiding in sending Mr. Sims off to jail, would be aided if she got the idea, by signing a Property Receipt, that she was already involved and *had* to show up in court.

"And what if I refuse to press charges?" the victim said, finally, in desperate exasperation.

"Lady, I'm pressing charges," Charley McFadden said, equally exasperated. "Or Hay-zus is. The *city* is. We *caught* him stealing that stuff from your car."

"Well, we'll see about that, young man," the victim said. "We'll just see about that. My brother-in-law just happens to be a very prominent attorney."

"Yes, ma'am," Charley McFadden said. He turned to the two wagon cops. "You can take him," he said.

"And I'm going to get on the telephone right now and tell him about this," the victim said. "This is simply outrageous."

"Yes, ma'am," Charley McFadden said.

Clarence Sims was led to the wagon, helped inside, and driven to the West Detectives District at Fifty-fifth and Pine Streets, where his glowing ember of hope that he was going to walk was extinguished by a detective who began their discussion by explaining his rights under *Miranda*.

Lieutenant Ed Michleson, the Day Watch commander at the Twelfth District, was not at all surprised to get the telephone call from Sergeant Willoughby of Chief Inspector Coughlin's office informing him that he was about to lose the services of Officers Jesus Martinez and Charles McFadden.

When they had been assigned to the Twelfth District, it had been with the understanding that it was only temporary, that they would be reassigned. The District Commander had told him that he had gotten it from Chief Coughlin himself that their assignment was only until he could find a good job for them.

They had been previously working plainclothes in Narcotics, a good, but not unusual assignment for young cops who showed promise and whose faces were not yet known on the street, and who, if they let their hair grow and dressed like bums could sort of melt into the drug culture.

When their faces became known, which was inevitable, the next step was usually back into uniform. But McFadden and Martinez had, on their own, staked out the Bridge & Pratt

Street terminal of the subway, and there found the junkie who had shot Captain Dutch Moffitt, of Highway Patrol, to death. McFadden had chased Gerald Vincent Gallagher down the tracks where Gallagher had fallen against the third rail and then gotten himself run over by a subway train.

In the movies, or in a cop-and-robbers program on TV, with the mayor and assorted big shots beaming in the background, the Commissioner would have handed them detectives' badges, and congratulations for a job well done. But this was real life, and promotions to detective in the Philadelphia Police Department came only after you had taken, and passed, the civil service examination. Martinez had taken the exam and flunked it, and McFadden hadn't been a cop long enough to be eligible to even take it.

But it was good police work, and Chief Inspector Coughlin, who was a good guy, didn't want to put them back into uniform—which young cops working plainclothes considered a demotion—even though with their pictures on the front page of every newspaper in Philadelphia, and on TV, their effectiveness as undercover Narcs was destroyed.

So he'd loaned them to Twelfth District, which was understrength, and had a problem with thieves working shopping mall parking lots, until he could find someplace to assign them permanently. And now he had.

Lieutenant Michleson got up and walked into the Operations Room and asked the corporal where Mutt and Jeff were. They looked like Mutt and Jeff. McFadden was a great big kid, large boned, tall and heavy. Martinez was a little Latin type, wiry and just over Department minimums for height and weight.

"They're on their way in," the corporal said. "They just arrested a guy robbing a car in the parking lot at Penrose Plaza. That makes five they caught since they been here."

"When they finish up the paperwork, send them in to me," Michleson said. "We're going to lose them."

"Where they going?"

"Highway."

"Highway?" the corporal replied, surprised, then laughed. "Those two?"

"That's not kind, Charley," Michleson said, smiling at the mental image of Mutt and Jeff all decked out in Highway Patrol regalia.

"I don't think Hay-zus is big enough to straddle a Harley," the corporal said.

"Maybe somebody figures they paid their dues," Lieutenant Michleson said. "Highway didn't catch the critter who shot Captain Moffitt. They did."

"When are they going?"

"They're to report in the morning."

Staff Inspector Peter Wohl, at thirty-five the youngest of the eighteen Staff Inspectors of the Police Department of the City of Philadelphia, who was lying on his back, looked up from what he was doing and found himself staring up a woman's shorts at her underpants. The underpants were red, and more or less transparent, and worn under a pair of white shorts.

He pushed himself, on his mechanic's crawler, the rest of the way out from under the Jaguar XK-120, and sat up. There was grease on his face, and on his bare, smoothly muscled chest, but there was still something about him that suggested more the accountant, or the lawyer, than a mechanic. Or a police officer.

"Hi," the wearer of the red underpants and white shorts said.

"Hi," Peter Wohl said, noticing now that she was also wearing a man's white shirt, the bottom rolled up and tied in a knot under her bosom, which served to bare her belly and put her not at all unattractive navel on display.

"I saw you working out the window," the woman said, "and I figured you could use this." She extended a bottle of Budweiser to him.

Peter Wohl noticed now that the hand holding the bottle

had both an engagement and a wedding ring on the appropriate finger.

He took the beer.

"Thank you," he said, and took a pull at the neck.

"Naomi," the woman said. "Naomi Schneider."

"Peter Wohl," he said.

Naomi Schneider, it registered on Peter Wohl's policeman's mind, was a white female, approximately five feet six inches tall, approximately 130 pounds, approximately twenty-five years of age, with no significant distinguishing marks or scars.

"We're in Two-B," Naomi Schneider volunteered. "My husband and I, I mean. We moved in last week."

"I saw the moving van," Peter said.

Two-B was the apartment occupying the rear half of the second floor of what Peter thought of as the House. There were six apartments in the House, a World War I-era mansion on the 8800 block of Norwood Road in Chestnut Hill, which had been converted into what the owner, a corporation, called "luxury apartments." The apartments in the rear of the building looked out on the four-car garage, and what had been the chauffeur's quarters above it. Peter Wohl lived in the ex-chauffeur's quarters, and to the often undisguised annoyance of the tenants of the House occupied two of the four garages.

It was possible, he thought, that Mr. Schneider had suggested to his wife that maybe if they made friends with the guy in the garage apartment with the Jaguar and *two* garages they could talk him out of one of them. There had been, he had noticed lately, a Porsche convertible coupe parked either on the street, or behind the house. They could probably make the argument that as fellow fine sports car *aficionados* he would appreciate that it was nearly criminal to have to leave a Porsche outside exposed to the elements.

But he dismissed that possible scenario as being less likely than the possibility that Mr. Schneider knew nothing of his wife's gesture of friendliness, and that Naomi had something in mind that had nothing to do with their Porsche.

"My husband travels," Naomi offered. "He's in floor coverings. He goes as far west as Pittsburgh."

*Bingo!*

"Oh, really?"

He now noticed that Naomi Schneider's eyes were very dark. Dark-eyed women do not have blond hair. Naomi's hair was, therefore, dyed blond. It was well done, no dark roots or anything, but obviously her hair was naturally black, or nearly so. Peter had a theory about that. Women with dark hair who peroxided it should not go out in the bright sunlight. Dyed blond hair might work inside, especially at night, but in the sunlight, it looked . . . dyed.

"He's generally gone two or three nights a week," Naomi offered. "What do you do?"

Peter elected to misunderstand her. "I just had the seats out," he said. "I took them to a place downtown and had the foam rubber replaced, and now I'm putting them back in."

Naomi stepped to the car and ran her fingers over the softly glowing red leather.

"Nice," she said. "But I meant, what do you do?"

"I work for the city," Peter said. "I see a Porsche around. That yours?"

"Yeah," Naomi said. "Mel, my husband, sometimes drives it on business, but there's not much room in it for samples, so usually he takes the station wagon, and leaves me the Porsche."

"I don't suppose," Peter agreed amiably, "that there *is* much room in a Porsche for floor-covering samples."

"This is *nice*," Naomi said, now stroking the Jaguar's glistening fender with the balls of her fingers. "New, huh?"

Peter Wohl laughed. "It's older than you are."

She looked at him in confusion. "It looks new," she said.

"Thank you, ma'am," Peter said. "But that left Coventry in February 1950."

"Left where?"

"Coventry. England. Where they make them."

"But it looks new."

"Thank you again."

"I'll be damned," Naomi said. She looked down at Peter and smiled. "You hear what happened last night?"

"No."

"About the woman who was raped? Practically right around the corner?"

"No," Peter Wohl replied truthfully. He had spent the previous day, and the day before that, the whole damned weekend, in Harrisburg, the state capital, in a hot and dusty records depository.

"He forced her into his van, did—you know—to her, and then threw her out of the van in Fairmount Park. It was on the radio, KYW."

"I hadn't heard."

"With Mel gone so much, it scares me."

"Did they say, on the radio, if it was the same man they think has done it before?" Peter asked.

"They said they *think* it is," Naomi said.

*Interesting,* Peter Wohl thought, *if it is the same guy, it's the first time he's done that.*

"Naked," Naomi said.

"Excuse me?"

"He threw her out of the van naked. Without any clothes."

*Well, that would tie in with the humiliation that seems to be part of this weirdo's modus operandi.*

There was the sound of tires moving across the cobblestones in front of the garages, and Peter's ears picked up the slightly different pitch of an engine with its idle speed set high; the sound of an engine in a police car.

He hoisted himself off the mechanic's crawler. A Highway Patrol car pulled to a stop. The door opened, and a sergeant in the special Highway Patrol uniform (crushed crown cap, Sam Browne belt, and motorcyclist's breeches and puttees) got out. Wohl recognized him. His name was Sergeant Alexander W. Dannelly. Wohl remembered the name because the last time he had seen him was the day Captain Dutch

Moffitt had been shot to death at the Waikiki Diner, over on Roosevelt Boulevard. Sergeant Dannelly had been the first to respond to the call, "Officer needs assistance; shots fired; officer wounded."

And Dannelly recognized him, too. He smiled, and started to wave, and then caught the look in Wohl's eyes and the barely perceptible shake of his head, and stopped.

"Can I help you, Officer?" Wohl asked.

"I'm looking for a man named Wohl," Sergeant Dannelly said.

"I'm Wohl."

"May I speak to you a moment, sir?"

"Sure," Wohl said. "Excuse me a minute, Naomi."

She smiled uneasily.

Wohl walked to the far side of the Highway Patrol car.

"What's up, Dannelly?" he asked.

"You're not answering your phone, Inspector."

"I've got the day off," Wohl said. "Who's looking for me?"

"Lieutenant Sabara," Dannelley said. "He said to send a car by here to see if you were home; that maybe your phone wasn't working."

"The phone's upstairs," Wohl said. "If it's been ringing, I didn't hear it."

"Okay with you, sir, if I get on the radio and tell him you're home?"

"Sure." Wohl wondered what Sabara wanted with him that was so important he had sent a car to see if his phone was working. "Tell him to give me fifteen minutes to take a bath, and then I'll wait for his call."

"You want to wait while I do it?"

"No," Wohl said, smiling. "You get out of here and then you call him."

"I understand, sir," Dannelly said, nodding just perceptibly toward Naomi.

"No, you don't," Wohl said, laughing. "The only thing I'm trying to hide, Sergeant, is that I'm a cop."

"Whatever you say, Inspector," Dannelly said, un-abashed, winking at Wohl.

Wohl waited until Sergeant Dannelly had gotten back in the car and driven off, then walked back to Naomi Schneider. Her curiosity, he saw, was about to bubble over.

"I saw an accident," Peter lied easily. "I have to go to the police station and make a report."

Sometimes, now for example, Peter Wohl often wondered if going to such lengths to conceal from his neighbors that he was a cop was worth all the trouble it took. It had nothing to do with anything official, and he certainly wasn't ashamed of being a damned good cop, the youngest Staff Inspector in the department; but sometimes, with civilians, especially civilians like his neighbors—bright, young, well-educated, well-paid civilians—it could be awkward.

Before he had, just after his promotion to Staff Inspector, moved into the garage apartment, he had lived in a garden apartment on Montgomery Avenue in the area of West Philadelphia known as Wynnfield. His neighbors there had been much the same kind of people, and he had learned that their usual response to having a cop for a neighbor was one of two things, and sometimes both. What was a lowlife, like a cop, doing in among his social betters? And what good is it having a cop for a neighbor, if he can't be counted on to fix a lousy speeding ticket?

He had decided, when he moved into the garage apartment, not to let his neighbors know what he did for a living. He almost never wore a uniform, and with his promotion to Staff Inspector had come the perk of an official car that didn't look like a police car. Not only was it unmarked, but it was new (the current car was a two-tone Ford LTD) and had white-wall tires and no telltale marks; the police shortwave radio was concealed in the glove compartment and used what looked like an ordinary radio antenna.

When his neighbors in the garage apartment asked him what he did, he told them he worked for the city. He didn't actually come out and deny that he was a cop, but he managed to convey the impression that he was a middle-level civil servant, who worked in City Hall.

He didn't get chummy with his neighbors, for several reasons, among them that, like most policemen, he was most comfortable with other policemen, and also because there was no question in his mind that when he was invited to come by for a couple of beers, at least marijuana, and probably something even more illegal, would be on the menu as well.

If he didn't see it, he would not have to bust his neighbors.

"Oh," Naomi Schneider said, when he told her about the accident he had seen and would have to go to the station to make a report about.

"Actually," Peter said, "I'm a suspect in a bank robbery."

Naomi laughed delightedly, which made her bosom jiggle.

"Well, it was nice to meet you, Naomi," Peter said. "And I thank you for the beer—"

"My pleasure," Naomi interrupted. "You looked so *hot*!"

"And I look forward to meeting Mr. Schneider."

"Mel," she clarified. "But he won't be home until Thursday. He went to Pittsburgh, this time."

"But now I have to take a shower and go down to the police station."

"Sure, I understand," Naomi said. "How come you're home all the time in the daytime, if you don't mind my asking?"

"I have to work a lot at night," he explained. "So instead of paying me overtime, they give me what they call compensatory time."

"Oh," Naomi said.

He handed her the empty Budweiser bottle, smiled, and went up the stairs at the end of the building to his apartment.

The red light on his telephone answering machine in the bedroom was flashing. That was probably Sabara, he decided. But even if it wasn't, if it was either business, or more likely his mother, who was not yet convinced that he was really eating properly living by himself that way, it would have to wait until he had his shower.

He showered and shaved in the shower, a trick he had learned in the army, and started to dress. After he pulled on a pair of DAK slacks, he stopped. He knew Mike Sabara— now the Acting Commander of Highway Patrol, until they made it official—but they were not close friends. That made it likely that what Sabara wanted was official; that he would have to meet him somewhere, and he could not do that in lemon-colored DAKs and a polo shirt.

Barefoot, wearing only the DAKs, he pushed the PLAY button on the answering machine. The tape rewound, and then began to play. He had had a number of calls while he was outside putting the seats back in the XK-120. But most of the callers had either hung up when they heard the re-corded message, or cussed and then hung up. Finally, he heard Mike Sabara's voice:

"Inspector, this is Mike Sabara. I'd like to talk to you. Would you call Radio and have them give me a number where you can be reached? Thank you."

This was followed by his mother's voice ("I don't know why I call, you're never home") and three more beeps and clicks indicating his callers' unwillingness to speak to a damned machine.

He looked at his watch and decided he didn't want to hang around until Sabara called him. He dialed the number of Police Radio from memory.

"This is Isaac Seventeen," he said. "Would you get word to Highway One that I'm at 928-5923 waiting for his call? No. Five nine *two* three. Thank you."

He decided another beer was in order, and went to the refrigerator in the kitchen and got one. Then he went back into the living room and sat down on his long, low, white leather couch and put his feet on the plate-glass coffee table before it to wait for Sabara's call.

Peter Wohl had once had a girlfriend, now married to a lawyer and living in Swarthmore, who had been an interior decorator, and who had donated her professional services to the furnishing of the apartment when it had seemed likely they would be married. From time to time he recalled what the couch, two matching chairs, and the plate-glass coffee table had cost him, even with Dorothea's professional discount. Everytime he did, he winced.

His door chimes went off. They were another vestige of Dorothea. She said they were darling. They played the first few bars of *"Be It Ever So Humble, There's No Place Like Home."* They were "custom," and not only had cost accordingly, but were larger than common, ordinary door chimes, so that when, post-Dorothea, he had tried to replace them, he couldn't, without repainting the whole damned wall by the door.

It was Naomi Schneider. He was annoyed but not surprised.

"Hi," she said. "All cleaned up?"

"I hope so," he said. "What can I do for you?"

"Mel, my husband, asked me to ask you something," she said.

The phone began to ring.

"Excuse me," he said, and went toward it. When he realized that she had invited herself in, he walked past the phone on the end table and went into his bedroom and picked up the bedside phone.

"Hello?"

"Tom Lenihan, Inspector," his caller said.

Sergeant Tom Lenihan worked for Peter's boss, Chief Inspector Dennis V. Coughlin. He was sort of a combination driver and executive assistant. Peter Wohl thought of him as a nice guy, and a good cop.

"What's up, Tom?"

"The Chief says he knows you worked all weekend, and it's your day off, and he's sorry, but something has come up, and he wants to see you this afternoon. I've got you scheduled for three-thirty. Is that okay?"

"What would you say if I said no?"

"I think I'd let you talk to the Chief." Lenihan chuckled.

"I'll be there."

"I thought maybe you could fit the Chief into your busy schedule," Lenihan said. "You being such a nice guy, and all."

"Go to hell, Tom," Wohl said, laughing, and hung up. He wondered for a moment if the Chief wanting to see him was somehow connected with Lieutenant Mike Sabara wanting to talk to him.

Then he became aware that Naomi Schneider was standing in the bedroom door, leaning on the jamb, and looking at the bed. On the bed were his handkerchief, his wallet, his keys, the leather folder that held his badge and photo-identification card, and his shoulder holster, which held a Smith & Wesson "Chief's Special" five-shot .38 Special revolver, all waiting to be put into, or between layers of, whatever clothing he decided to wear.

"What are you, a cop or something?" Naomi asked.

"A cop."

"A detective, maybe?" Naomi asked, visibly thrilled.

"Something like that."

*Christ, now it will be all over the House by tomorrow morning!*

"What does that mean?" Naomi asked. "Something like that?"

"I'm a Staff Inspector," he said. "And, Naomi, I sort of like for people not to know that I am."

"What's a Staff Inspector?"

"Sort of like a detective."

"And that's sort of a secret."

The phone rang again, and he picked it up.

"Peter Wohl," he said.

"Inspector, this is Mike Sabara."

Wohl covered the mouthpiece with his hand.

"Excuse me, please, Naomi?"

"Oh, sure," she said, and put her index finger in front of her lips in a gesture signifying she understood the necessity for secrecy.

When she turned around, he saw that her red underpants

had apparently gathered in the decolletage of her buttocks; her cheeks peeked out naked from beneath the white shorts.

"What's up, Mike?" Wohl asked.

"I'd like to talk to you, if you can spare me fifteen minutes."

"Anytime. Where are you?"

"Harbison and Levick," Sabara said. "Could I come over there?"

The headquarters of the Second and Fifteenth districts, and the Northeast Detectives, at Harbison and Levick Streets, was in a squat, ugly, two-story building whose brown-and-tan brick had become covered with a dark film from the exhausts of the heavy traffic passing by over the years.

"Mike, I've got to go downtown," Wohl said, after deciding he really would rather not go to Harbison and Levick. "What about meeting me in DaVinci's Restaurant? At Twenty-first and Walnut? In about fifteen minutes?"

"I'll be there," Lieutenant Sabara said. "Thank you."

"Be with you in a minute, Naomi," Wohl called, and closed the door. He dressed in a white button-down shirt, a regimentally striped necktie, and the trousers to a blue cord suit. He slipped his arms through the shoulder holster straps, shrugged into the suit jacket, and then put the wallet and the rest of the impedimenta in various pockets. He checked his appearance in a mirror on the back on the door, then went into the living room, where he caught Naomi having a pull at the neck of his beer bottle.

"Very nice!" Naomi said.

"Naomi, I don't want to sound rude, but I have to go."

"I understand."

"What was it Mr. Schneider wanted you to ask me?" he asked.

"He said I should see if I could find out if you would consider subletting one of your garages."

"I'm sorry, I can't do that. I need one for the Jaguar, and my other car belongs to the city, and that has to be kept in a garage."

"Why?" It was not a challenge, but simple curiosity.

"Well, there's a couple of very expensive radios in it that the city doesn't want to have boosted."

"Boosted? You mean stolen?"

"Right."

"That makes sense," she said. "I'll tell Mel."

She got off the couch, displaying a large and not at all unattractive area of inner thigh in the process.

"Well," she said. "I'll let you go."

He followed her to the door, aware that as a gentleman he should not be paying as much attention as he was to her naked *gluteus maximus*, which was peeking out the hem of her shorts.

"Naomi," he said, as he pulled the door open for her, "when you talk to your husband about me, would you tell him that I would consider it a favor if he didn't spread it around that I'm a cop?"

"I won't even tell him."

"Well, you don't have to go that far."

"There's a lot of things I don't tell Mel," Naomi said, softly.

And then her fingers brushed his crotch. Peter pulled away, in a reflex action, and had just decided it was an accidental contact, when that theory was disproved. Naomi's fingers followed his retreating groin, found what she was looking for, and gave it a gentle squeeze.

"See you around, Peter," she said, looking into his eyes. Then she let go of him, laughed, and went quickly down the stairs.

# SEVEN

Peter Wohl glanced at the fuel gauge of the Ford LTD as he turned the ignition key off in the parking lot on Walnut Street near the DaVinci Restaurant. The needle was below E; he was running on the fumes. Since he had driven only from his apartment here, that meant that it had been below E when he had arrived home; and *that* meant he had come damned close to running out of gas on the Pennsylvania Turnpike, or on the Schuylkill Expressway, which would have been a disaster. It would have given him the option of radioing for a police wrecker to bring him gas, which would have been embarrassing, or getting drowned in the torrential rain trying to walk to a gas station. Drowned and/or run over.

Periodically in his life, Wohl believed, he seemed to find himself walking along the edge of a steep cliff, a *crumbling* cliff, with disaster a half-step away. He was obviously in that condition now. The gas gauge seemed to prove that; and so did Naomi of the traveling husband and groping fingers. And, he decided, he probably wasn't going to like at all what Mike Sabara had on his mind.

He got out of the car, and locked it, aware that when he got back in it, the inside temperature would be sizzling; that he would sweat, and his now natty and freshly pressed suit would be mussed when he went to see Chief Coughlin. And he had a gut feeling that was going to be some sort of a disaster, too. It wasn't very likely that Coughlin was going to call him in on a day off to tell him what a splendid job he had been doing and why didn't he take some time off as a reward.

A quick glance around the parking lot told him that Sabara wasn't here yet. He would have spotted a marked Highway Patrol car immediately, and even if Sabara was in an unmarked car, he would have spotted the radio antenna and black-walled tires.

And, he thought, as he walked into the DaVinci, if what Coughlin was after was to hear how his current investigation was going, the reason he had been in Harrisburg, he wasn't going to come across as Sherlock Holmes, either. The only thing two days of rooting around in the Pennsylvania Department of Records had produced was a couple of leads that were weak at best and very probably would turn out to be worthless.

The DaVinci restaurant, named after the artist/inventor, not the proprietor, served very good food despite what Peter thought of as restaurant theatrics. As a general rule of thumb, he had found that restaurants that went out of their way to convert their space into something exotic generally served mediocre to terrible food. The DaVinci had gone a little overboard, he thought, trying to turn their space into rustic Italian. There were red checkered tableclothes; a lot of phony trellises; plastic grapes; and empty Chianti bottles with candles stuck in their necks. But the food was good, and the people who ran the place were very nice.

He asked for and got a table on the lower level, which gave him a view of both the upper level and the bar just inside the door. The waitress was a tall, pretty young brunette who looked as though she should be on a college campus. Then he remembered hearing that the waitresses in DaVinci's were aspiring actresses, hoping to meet theatrical people who came to Philly, and were supposed to patronize DaVinci's.

Her smile vanished when he ordered just coffee.

*Or can she tell I'm not a movie producer?*

When she delivered his coffee, he handed her a dollar and told her to keep the change. That didn't seem to change her attitude at all.

Mike Sabara came into the room a few minutes later, immediately after Peter had scalded his mouth on the lip of the coffee cup, which had apparently been delivered to his table fresh from the fires of hell.

Mike was in uniform, the crushed-crown cap and motorcyclist's breeches and puttees peculiar to Highway Patrol, worn with a Sam Browne belt festooned with a long line of cartridges and black leather accoutrements for the tools of a policeman's trade, flashlight, handcuffs, and so on. Mike was wearing an open-collared white shirt, with a captain's insignia, two parallel silver bars, on each collar point.

The Highway Patrol and its special uniform went back a long time, way before the Second World War. It had been organized as a traffic law enforcement force, as the name implied, and in the old days, it had been mounted almost entirely on motorcycles, hence the breeches and puttees and soft-crowned cap.

There were still a few motorcycles in Highway—from somewhere Wohl picked out the number twenty-four—but they were rarely used for anything but ceremonial purposes, or maybe crowd control at Mummers Parades. The Highway Patrol still patrolled the highways—the Schuylkill Expressway and Interstate 95—but the Patrol had evolved over the years, especially during the reign of Captain Jerry Carlucci, and even more during the reign of Mayor Carlucci, into sort of a special force that was dispatched to clean up high-crime areas.

Highway Patrol cars carried two officers, while all other Philadelphia police cars carried only one. Unless they had specific orders sending them somewhere else, Highway Patrol cars could patrol wherever, within reason, they liked, without regard to District boundaries. They regarded themselves, and were regarded by other policemen, as an elite force, and there was always a long waiting list of officers who had applied for transfer to Highway Patrol.

Anyone with serious ambitions to rise in the police hierarchy knew the path led through Highway Patrol. Wohl himself had been a Highway Patrol Corporal, and had liked the duty, although he had been wise enough to keep to himself his profound relief that his service in Highway had been after the motorcycles had been all but retired and he had rarely been required to get on one. Going through the "wheel training course," which he had considered necessary to avoid being thought of as less then wholly masculine, had convinced him that anybody who rode a motorcycle willingly, much less joyfully, had some screws in urgent need of tightening.

Wohl had several thoughts as he saw Mike Sabara walking across the room to him, wearing what for Sabara was a warm smile. He thought that Mike was not only an ugly sonofabitch but that he was menacing. Sabara's swarthy face was marked with the scars of what could have been small pox, but more probably were the remnants of adolescent acne. He wore an immaculately trimmed pencil-line mustache. If it was designed to take attention from his disfigured skin, Wohl thought, it had exactly the opposite effect.

He was a short, stocky, barrel-chested man, with an aggressive walk. He was also hairy. Thick black hair showed at the open collar of his shirt and covered his exposed arms.

All of these outward things, Wohl knew, were misleading. Mike Sabara was an extraordinarily gentle man, father of a large brood of well-cared-for kids. He was a Lebanese, and active—he actually taught Sunday School—in some kind of Orthodox Church. Wohl had seen him crying at Dutch Moffitt's funeral, the tears running unashamedly down his cheeks as he carried Dutch to his grave.

Sabara put out his large hand as he slipped into the seat across from Wohl. His grip was firm, but not a demonstration of all the strength his hand possessed.

"I appreciate you meeting me like this, Inspector," Sabara said.

"I know why you're calling me 'Inspector,' Mike," Wohl said, smiling, "so I'll have to reply, 'My pleasure, *Captain* Sabara.' Congratulations, Mike, it's well deserved, and how come I wasn't invited to your promotion party?"

Wohl immediately sensed that what he had intended as humor had fallen flat. Sabara gave him a confused, even wary, look.

"The Commissioner called me at home last night," Sabara said. "He said to come to work today wearing captain's bars."

*Which you just happened to have lying around,* Wohl thought, and was immediately ashamed of the unkind thought. He himself had bought a set of lieutenant's bars the day the examination scores had come out, even though he had known it would be long months before the promotion actually came through.

"So it's official then?" Wohl said. "Well, congratulations. I can't think of anybody better qualified."

Wohl saw that, too, produced a reaction in Sabara different from what he expected. More confusion, more wariness.

The waitress reappeared.

"Get you something?"

"Iced tea, please," Captain Sabara said. The waitress looked at him strangely. Sabara, Wohl thought, was not the iced tea type.

"Can I get right to it, Inspector?" Sabara asked, when the waitress had left.

"Sure."

"If it's at all possible," Sabara said, "I'd like Highway Patrol."

Sabara had, Wohl sensed, rehearsed that simple statement.

"I'm not sure what you mean, Mike."

"I mean, I'd really like to take over Highway," Sabara said, and there was more uncertainty in his eyes. "I mean, Christ, no one knows it better than I do. And I know I could do a good job."

*What the hell is he driving at?*

"You want me to put in a good word for you? Is that it, Mike? Sure. You tell me to who, and I'll do it."

There was a pause before Sabara replied.

"You don't know, do you?" he said, finally.

"Know what?"

"About Highway and Special Operations."

"No," Wohl said, and searched his memory. "The last I heard about Special Operations was that it was an idea whose time had not yet come."

"It's time has come," Sabara said, "and Highway's going under it."

"And who's getting Special Operations?"

"You are," Sabara said.

*Jesus H. Christ!*

"Where did you get that?" Wohl asked.

Sabara looked uncomfortable.

"I heard," he said.

"I'd check out that source pretty carefully, Mike," Wohl said. "This is the first I've heard anything like that."

"You're getting Special Operations and David Pekach is getting Highway," Sabara said. "I thought Pekach was your idea, and maybe I could talk you out of it."

"Did your source say what's in mind for you?" Wohl asked.

"Your deputy."

"Where the hell did you get this?"

"I can't tell you," Sabara said. "But I believe it."

*And now I'm beginning to. Sabara has heard something he believes. Jesus, is this why Chief Coughlin sent for me?*

*Why me?*

"I'm beginning to," Wohl said. "Chief Coughlin wants to see me at half-past three. Maybe this is why."

"Now I'm on the spot," Sabara said. "I'd appreciate it if you didn't—"

"Tell him we talked? No, of course not, Mike. And I really hope you're wrong."

From the look in Sabara's eyes, Wohl could tell he didn't think there was much chance he was wrong. That meant his source was as good as he said it was. And that meant it had come from way up high in the police department hierarchy, a Chief Inspector, or more likely one of the Deputy Commissioners.

Someone important, who didn't like the idea of Special Operations, of Peter Wohl being given command of Special Operations, of David Pekach being given command of Highway over Mike Sabara. Or all of the above.

"Peter," Mike Sabara said. It was the first time he had used Wohl's Christian name. "You understand . . . there's nothing personal in this? You're a hell of a good cop. I'd be happy to work for you anywhere. But—"

"You think you're the man to run Highway?" Wohl interrupted him. "Hell, Mike, so do I. And I don't think I'm the man to run Special Operations. I don't even know what the hell it's supposed to do."

There was something about Police Recruit Matthew M. Payne that Sergeant Richard B. Stennis, Firearms Instructor and Assistant Range Officer of the Police Academy of the City of Philadelphia, did not like, although he could not precisely pin it down.

He knew when it had begun, virtually the first time he had ever laid eyes on Payne. Dick Stennis, whose philosophy vis-à-vis firearms, police or anyone else's, was *"You never need a gun until you need one badly,"* took his responsibility to teach rookies about firearms very seriously.

Sergeant Stennis—a stocky, but not fat, balding man of forty—was aware that statistically the odds were about twenty to one that his current class of rookies would go through their entire careers without once having drawn and fired their service weapon in the line of duty. He suspected that, the way things were going, the odds might change a little, maybe down to ten to one that these kids would never have to use their service revolvers; but the flip side of even those percentages was that one in ten of them *would* have to use a gun in a situation where his life, or the life of another police officer, or a civilian, would depend on how well he could use it.

Some of Dick Stennis's attitude toward firearms came, and he was aware of this, from the United States Marine Corps. Like many police officers, Stennis had come to the department after a tour in the military. He had enlisted in the Corps at eighteen, a week after graduating from Frankford High School in June of 1950. He had arrived in Korea just in time to miss the Inchon Invasion, but in plenty of time to make the Bug Out from the Yalu and the withdrawal from Hamhung on Christmas Eve of the same year.

He was back from Korea in less than a year, wearing corporal's chevrons and a Silver Star and two Purple Hearts, the reason for the second of which had kept him in the Philadelphia Navy Hospital for four months. When he was restored to duty, the Corps sent him back to Parris Island, and made him a firearms instructor, which was something, but not entirely, like being a drill instructor.

When his three-year enlistment was over and he went back to Philadelphia, he joined the Police Department. Two years after that, about the time he was assigned to the Police Academy, he had gotten married and joined the Marine Corps Reserve because he needed the money.

One weekend a month and two weeks each summer Sergeant Stennis of the Police Department became Master Gunnery Sergeant Stennis of the United States Marine Corps Reserve. He had been called up for the Vietnam War, fully expecting to be sent to Southeast Asia, but the Corps, reasoning that a Philadelphia cop called up from the Reserve was just the guy to fill the billet of Noncommissioned Officer in Charge of the Armed Forces Military Police Detachment in Philadelphia, had sent him back to Philly two weeks after he reported in at Camp LeJeune.

Practically, it had been a good deal. He had done his two years of active duty living at home. The Marine Corps had paid him an allowance in lieu of rations, and an allowance, in lieu of housing, that was greater than the mortgage payment on his house on Leonard Street in Mayfair. And he had been building double-time. His seniority with the Police Department had continued to build while he was "off" in the Corps, and he had added two years of active duty time to his Marine Corps longevity. When he turned sixty, there would be a pension check from the Corps to go with his police pension and, when he turned sixty-five, his Social Security.

When he went on inactive duty again, the Corps gave him a Reserve billet with the Navy Yard, as an investigator on the staff of the Provost Marshal. He generally managed to pick up two or three days of "active duty" a month, sometimes more, in addition to the one weekend, which meant that much more in his Reserve paycheck every three months. It also meant that his Corps pension, when he got to it, would be that much larger.

It was a pretty good deal, he had reminded himself, when he had failed the Police Department's Lieutenant's examination for the second time. If he had passed it, there was no telling where the Department would have assigned him, but it would have meant leaving the Academy, which he liked, and almost certainly would have kept him from picking up an extra two or three days Master Gunnery Sergeant's pay and allowances every month. The Academy had an eight-to-five, Monday-through-Friday work schedule. As a new Lieutenant, he could have expected to work nights and weekends.

And he liked what he was doing, and thought it was important. Sometimes, Dick Stennis thought, very privately, that if his supervision of the firearms instruction at the Police Academy kept *just one* cop, or *just one* civilian, alive, it was worth being thought of by one class of rookies after another as "that bald-headed prick."

The first time Police Recruit Matthew M. Payne had come to the attention of Sergeant Richard Stennis was during the lecture Sergeant Stennis customarily delivered to the class as the first step in the firearms phase of their training. Sergeant Stennis believed, not unreasonably, that over the years he had been able to hone and polish his introductory lecture to the point where it was both meaningful and interesting.

Police Recruit Matthew M. Payne apparently was not so affected. The first time Stennis saw Payne, who was sitting toward the rear of the classroom, he was yawning. He was *really* yawning, holding a balled fist to his widely gaping mouth.

Sergeant Stennis had stopped in midsentence, and pointed a finger at him.

"You!" he said sharply, to get his attention. "What's your name?"

Payne had looked uncomfortable. "Payne, sir."

"Perhaps it would be easier for you to stay awake if you stood up."

Payne had jumped to his feet and assumed what is known in the military as the position of "parade rest," that is, he stood stiffly, with his feet slightly apart, and his hands folded neatly in the small of his back, staring straight ahead.

*That little fucker is making fun of me*, Stennis decided, and then modified that slightly. Payne was not a *little* fucker. He was probably six feet one, Stennis judged, maybe a little over that. And he was well set up, a muscular, good-looking young man.

*Well, fuck you, sonny. I've been dealing with wiseasses like you all my life. You want to stand there at parade rest, fine. You'll stand there until this class is over.*

And Police Recruit Matthew M. Payne had done just that, for the remaining forty, forty-five minutes of the class, which served to give Sergeant Stennis some food for thought. That was the sort of thing a serviceman would do. Perhaps he had jumped the kid a little too hard.

When he checked Payne's records, however, he found no indication that Payne had ever worn any uniform but the one he was wearing now; he was not an ex-serviceman. His records indicated further that Matthew M. Payne had just graduated from the University of Pennsylvania, Bachelor of Arts, *cum laude*.

That was unusual. Very few college graduates took the Civil Service exam for the Police Department. The starting pay for a rookie policeman was low (in Dick Stennis's opinion, a disgrace) and a college degree was worth more money almost anyplace else.

Making an effort not to make a big deal of it, he asked other instructors what they thought of Payne. The responses had been either a shrug, meaning that they hadn't formed an opinion of him one way or another, or that he was just one more recruit, except for a few instructors who replied that he seemed smart. Not smartass, but smart. Bright. Payne had apparently given no one else any trouble; if he had, Stennis would have heard.

The first day of actual firing on the Police Academy Pistol Range was, Stennis had learned, most often one of shock, even humiliation for rookies. Very few recruits, excepting, of course, ex-servicemen, had much experience with any kind of firearm, and even less with handguns.

What they knew of pistols most often came from what they had seen in the movies and on TV, where Hollywood cops, firing snub-nosed revolvers, routinely shot bad guys between the eyes at fifty yards.

The targets on the Academy Pistol Range were life-sized silhouettes, with concentric "kill rings" numbered (K5, K4, and so on) for scoring. Ideally, all bullets would land in a K5 kill ring. The targets were set up for the recruit's first firing at fifteen yards. The weapon used was the standard service revolver, the Smith & Wesson Model 10 "Military & Police." It was a six-shot, .38 Special caliber, fixed-sight weapon, which could be fired in either single action (the hammer was cocked, using the thumb, before the trigger was pulled) or double action (simply pulling the trigger would cock the hammer and then release it).

For their first live firing exercise, the recruits were instructed in the double-hand hold, and told to fire the weapon single action, that is by cocking the hammer before lining up the sights and pulling the trigger.

It seemed so easy when the recruits first took their positions. *Anyone* should be able to hit a man-sized target at that short range. You could practically reach out and touch the damned target. The result of this was that many, even most recruits, decided it would be safe to show off a little, and perhaps even earn a smile from Sergeant Stennis, by shooting the target in the head, a K5 kill ring.

The result of this, many times, was that there were no holes at all in the target, much less in the head, after the recruit had fired his first six rounds. Shooting a pistol is infinitely more difficult than it is made to appear in the movies.

Sergeant Stennis didn't mind that the first six rounds were normally a disaster for their firers. It humbled them; and humbled, they were that much easier to teach.

When Recruit Matthew M. Payne stepped to the firing line, Sergeant Stennis waited until he was in position, and then moved so that he was standing behind him. Payne did not look particularly uncomfortable when, on command, he looked at the revolver. He fed six cartridges into the cylinder without dropping any of them, which sometimes happened, and he closed the cylinder slowly and carefully.

Some recruits, even though cautioned not to do so, followed the practice of Hollywood cops by snapping the pistol sharply to the right, so that the cylinder slammed home by inertia. This practice, Stennis knew, soon threw the cylinder out of line with the barrel, and the pistol then required the services of a gunsmith.

Sergeant Stennis would not have been surprised if Recruit Payne had flipped the cylinder shut. Even when he didn't, he sensed that Payne was going to do something wiseass, like fire his six rounds at the silhouette's head, rather than at the torso of the target.

And when the command to fire was given, Payne did just that.

And hit the silhouette in the head, just above where the right eye would be.

*Beginner's luck,* Stennis decided.

Payne's second shot hit the silhouette in the upper center of the head, where the forehead would be.

*I'll be damned!*

Payne's third shot hit the target head where the nose would be; and so did the fourth. The fifth went a little wide, hitting the tip of the silhouette head, but still inside the K5 ring, which Payne made up for by hitting the silhouette head where the left eye would be with his sixth shot.

*I really will be damned. That wasn't at all bad.*

When the recruits went forward to examine their targets, and to put gummed pasters on the bullet holes, Sergeant Stennis followed Payne.

"Not bad at all," he said to Payne, startling him. "Where did you learn to shoot a pistol?"

"At Quantico," Payne replied. "The Marine base."

"I know what it is," Stennis said. "How come your records don't say anything about you being in the Corps?"

"I was never in the Corps," Payne replied. "I was in the Platoon Leader Program. I went there two summers."

"What happened?" Stennis asked. Payne understood, he saw, what he was really asking: *If you were in the Platoon Leader Program, how come you're here, and not a second lieutenant in the Corps?*

"I busted the commissioning physical," Payne said.

"You tell them that when you joined the Department?" Stennis demanded, sharply.

"Yes, sir."

They locked eyes for a moment, long enough for Stennis to decide that Payne was telling the truth.

*Is that why he came in?* Stennis wondered. *Because he*

*flunked the Marine Corps physical, and wants to prove he's a man, anyway? Well, what the hell is wrong with that?*

"Well, that was pretty good shooting," Stennis said.

"I could do better if the pistol had better sights," Payne said, adding, "and this could use a trigger job, too."

Stennis's anger returned.

"Well, Payne," he replied sarcastically, "I'm afraid you'll just have to learn to cope with what the Department thinks they should give you."

He turned and walked back to the firing line.

Almost immediately, he felt like a hypocrite. Wiseass or not, the kid was right. You couldn't get a very good sight picture with the standard service revolver. The front sight was simply a piece of rounded metal, part of the barrel. The rear sight was simply an indentation in the frame. Stennis's own revolver was equipped with adjustable sights—a sharply defined front sight, and a rear sight that was adjustable for both height and windage, with a sharply defined aperture. That, coupled with a carefully honed action, a "trigger job," which permitted a smooth "let off," resulted in a pistol capable of significantly greater accuracy than an off-the-shelf revolver.

And Stennis was suddenly very much aware that his personal pistol was not regulation, and that he got away with carrying it solely because no one in the Department was liable to carefully scrutinize the pistol carried by the Police Academy's Firearms Instructor.

When he reached the firing line, he was not especially surprised to see Chief Inspector Heinrich "Heine" Matdorf, Chief of the Training Bureaus, and thus sort of the headmaster of the Police Academy, standing at the end of the line, to the right, where a concrete pathway led to the main Police Academy Building.

Heine Matdorf, a large, portly, red-faced man who was nearly bald, believed in keeping an eye on what was going on. Stennis liked him, even if they could not be called friends. When Matdorf had come to the Training Bureau two years before, he had made everyone nervous by his unannounced visits to classrooms and training sites. He was taciturn, and his blue eyes seemed cold.

But they had quickly learned that he was not hypercritical, as prone to offer a word of approval as a word of criticism. The new broom had swept only those areas in need of it.

As was his custom, Stennis acknowledged the presence of Chief Matdorf with a nod, expecting a nod in return. But Matdorf surprised him by walking over to him.

"Chief," Stennis greeted him.

"That kid you were talking to, Payne?"

"Yes, sir."

"I want a word with him," Matdorf said. "Stick around."

"He put six shots into the head, first time up," Stennis offered.

Matdorf grunted again, but didn't otherwise respond.

Matthew Payne finished pasting his target and walked back to the firing line. Stennis saw in his eyes that he was curious, but not uneasy, to see Chief Matdorf standing there beside him.

"You know who I am?" Matdorf asked as Payne walked up.

"Yes, sir."

"We met at Captain Moffitt's wake," Chief Matdorf said. "Chief Coughlin introduced us."

"Yes, sir, I remember."

*What the hell was this kid doing at Dutch Moffitt's wake? And Chief Coughlin introduced him to Matdorf?*

"I just had a call from Chief Coughlin about you," Matdorf said.

"Yes, sir?"

"Turn in your gear," Matdorf said. "Clean out your locker. If anybody asks what you're doing, tell them 'just what I'm told.' At eight-thirty tomorrow morning, report to Captain

Sabara at Highway Patrol. You know where that is? Bustleton and Bowler?''

"I don't understand.''

"I'm sure Captain Sabara will explain everything to you tomorrow morning,'' Matdorf said. "If I didn't make this clear, you won't be coming back here.''

"And I'm to . . . clean out my locker right now?''

"That's right,'' Matdorf said. "And don't tell anybody where you're going.''

"Yes, sir,'' Payne said. Stennis saw that he didn't like what he had been told, but was smart enough to sense that asking Chief Matdorf would be futile.

"So get on with it,'' Matdorf said.

"Yes, sir,'' Payne said. Then he picked up his earmuffs and other shooting equipment from the firing position and walked off the line.

"You don't say anything to anybody about him going to Highway, either, Dick,'' Matdorf said.

"No, sir,'' Stennis said.

"Curiosity about to eat you up?'' Matdorf asked, flashing a rare, shy smile.

"Yes, sir.''

"The reason he was at Dutch Moffitt's funeral was that Dutch was his uncle.''

"I didn't know that.''

"His father was a cop, too. Sergeant John X. Moffitt,'' Matdorf went on. "He got himself killed answering a silent burglar alarm in a gas station in West Philadelphia.''

"I didn't know that, either. What are they going to do with him in Highway?'' Stennis asked, and then, without giving Matdorf a chance to reply, went on, "How come his name is Payne?''

"His mother remarried; the new husband adopted him,'' Matdorf said. "And I don't know what they're going to do with him in Highway. This was one of those times when I didn't think I should ask too many questions.''

''Coughlin set it up?'' Stennis asked.

Matdorf nodded. ''Chief Coughlin and the boy's father went through the Academy together. They were pretty tight. I know, because I was in the same class.''

His face expressionless, Matdorf met Stennis's eyes for a long moment. Then he turned and walked off the firing line.

# EIGHT

When Peter Wohl drove into the parking lot behind the Police Administration Building at Eighth and Arch, he pulled up to the gasoline pump and filled the Ford's gas tank.

It took 19.7 gallons. He had heard somewhere that the Ford held 22 gallons. That meant that despite the gas gauge needle pointing below E, he really had been in no danger of running out of gas.

There was a moral to be drawn from that, he thought, as he drove around the parking lot, looking for a place to park. *For yea, though I walk along the edge of the crumbling cliff, I seem to have an unnatural good luck that keeps me from falling off.*

He pulled the Ford into one of the parking slots reserved for official visitors and got out, leaving the windows open a crack to let the heat out. There was, he rationalized, not much of a chance that even the most dedicated radio thief would attempt to practice his profession in the Roundhouse parking lot.

The Police Administration Building was universally known as the Roundhouse. It was not really round, but curved. The building and its interior walls, including even those of the elevators, were curved. It was, he thought, called the Roundhouse because that came easier to the tongue than "Curved House."

He entered the building by the rear door. Inside, to the right, was a door leading to the Arraignment Room. The Roundhouse, in addition to housing the administrative offices of the Police Department on the upper floors, was also a jail. Prisoners were transported from the districts around the city to a basement facility where they were fingerprinted, photographed, and put in holding cells until it was their turn to face the magistrate, who would hear the complaint against them, and either turn them loose or decide what their bail, if any, should be.

There was sort of a small grandstand in which the family and friends of the accused could watch through a plate-glass wall as the accused was brought before the magistrate.

To the left was the door leading to the lobby of the Roundhouse. It was kept closed and locked. A solenoid operated by a Police Officer, usually a Corporal, sitting behind a thick, shatterproof window directly opposite the door, controlled the lock.

Most senior officers of the Police Department of the City of Philadelphia, that is to say from Deputy Commissioners on down through the Captains, were known by sight to the cop controlling the door. Peter Wohl, as a Staff Inspector, was rather high in the police hierarchy. He was one of seventeen Staff Inspectors, a rank immediately superior to Captains, and immediately subordinate to Inspectors. On the rare occasions when Staff Inspector Wohl wore his uniform, it carried a gold oak leaf, identical to that of majors in the armed forces. Inspectors wore silver oak leaves, and Chief Inspectors a colonel's eagle.

Senior officers were accustomed, when entering the Roundhouse, to having the solenoid to the locked door to the lobby buzzing when they reached it. When Peter Wohl reached it, it remained firmly locked. He looked over his shoulder at the cop, a middle-aged Corporal behind the shatterproof glass. The Corporal was looking at him, wearing an official, as opposed to genuine, smile, and gesturing Wohl over to him with his index finger.

Peter Wohl had been keeping count. This made it thirteen-six. Of the nineteen times he had tried to get through the door without showing his identification to the cop behind the shatterproof glass window, he had failed thirteen times; only six times had he been recognized and passed.

He walked to the window.

"Help you, sir?" the Corporal asked.

"I'm Inspector Wohl," Peter said. The corporal looked surprised and then uncomfortable as Wohl extended the leather folder holding his badge (a round silver affair embossed with a representation of City Hall and the letters STAFF INSPECTOR) and identification for him to see.

"Sorry, Inspector," the Corporal said.

"You're doing your job," Peter said, and smiled at him.

He went back to the door, and through it, and walked across the lobby to the elevators. Then he stopped and walked to a glass case mounted on the wall. It held the photographs and badges of Police Officers killed in the line of duty. There was a new one, of an officer in the uniform of a captain of Highway Patrol. Richard C. Moffitt.

Captain Dutch Moffitt and Peter Wohl had been friends as long as Wohl could remember. Not close friends—Dutch had been too flamboyant for that—but friends. They had known they could count on each other if there was a need; they exchanged favors. Wohl thought that the last favor he had done Dutch was to convince Jeannie, the Widow Moffitt, that Dutch had business with the blonde Dutch had been with in the Waikiki Diner on Roosevelt Boulevard when he had been fatally wounded by a junkie holding the place up.

Wohl turned and entered the elevator and pushed the button for the third floor, the right wing of which was more or less the Executive Suite of the Roundhouse. It housed the offices of the Commissioner, the Deputy Commissioners, and some of the more important Chief Inspectors, including that of Chief Inspector Dennis V. Coughlin.

The corridor to that portion of the building was guarded by a natty man in his early thirties, either a plainclothesman or a detective, sitting at a desk. He knew Wohl.

"Hello, Inspector, how are you?"

"About to melt," Wohl said, smiling at him. "I heard some of the cops in Florida can wear shorts. You think I could talk Chief Coughlin into permitting that?"

"I don't have the legs for that," the cop said, as Wohl went down the corridor.

Chief Inspector Dennis V. Coughlin shared an outer office with Police Commissioner Taddeus Czernick, separated from it by the Commissioner's Conference Room.

Sergeant Tom Lenihan sat at a desk to the left. A pleasant-faced, very large man, his hair was just starting to thin. He was in his shirtsleeves; a snub-nosed revolver could be seen on his hip.

"Well, I'm glad you could fit the Chief into your busy schedule," Lenihan said, with a smile. "I know he'll be pleased."

"How do you think you're going to like the last-out shift in the Seventeenth District, Sergeant?" Wohl said.

Lenihan chuckled. "Go on in. He's expecting you."

Wohl pushed open the door to Chief Inspector Coughlin's office. Coughlin's desk, set catty-cornered, faced the ante-room. Coughlin was also in his shirtsleeves, and he was talking on the telephone. He smiled and motioned Wohl into one of the two chairs facing his desk.

"Hold it a minute," he said into the telephone. He tucked it under his chin and searched through the HOLD basket on his desk. He came out with four sheets of teletype paper and handed them to Wohl. He smiled—rather smugly, Peter thought—at him, and then he resumed his telephone conversation.

The teletype messages had been passed over the Police Communications Network. There was a teletype machine in each of the twenty-two districts (in New York City, and many other cities, the term used for district police stations was "precinct"); in each Detective Division; and elsewhere.

Wohl read the first message.

GENERAL: 0650 06/30/73 FROM COMMISSIONER
PAGE 1 OF 1

\*\*\*\*\*\*\*\*\*\*\*   CITY OF PHILADELPHIA   \*\*\*\*\*\*\*\*\*\*\*
\*\*\*\*\*\*\*\*\*\*\*   POLICE DEPARTMENT   \*\*\*\*\*\*\*\*\*\*\*

...........................

ANNOUNCEMENT WILL BE MADE AT ALL ROLL CALLS OF
THE FOLLOWING COMMAND ASSIGNMENT: EFFECTIVE
IMMEDIATELY CAPTAIN DAVID S. PETACH IS REASSIGNED
FROM NARCOTICS BUREAU TO HIGHWAY PATROL AS
COMMANDING OFFICER.

...........................

*Well, there goes whatever small chance I had to plead Mike Sabara's case. Now that it's official, it's too late to do anything about it.*

He read the second message.

GENERAL: 0651 06/30/73 FROM COMMISSIONER
PAGE 1 OF 1

\*\*\*\*\*\*\*\*\*\*\*   CITY OF PHILADELPHIA   \*\*\*\*\*\*\*\*\*\*\*
\*\*\*\*\*\*\*\*\*\*\*   POLICE DEPARTMENT   \*\*\*\*\*\*\*\*\*\*\*

...........................

THE FOLLOWING COMMAND REORGANIZATION WILL BE
ANNOUNCED AT ALL ROLL CALLS: EFFECTIVE
IMMEDIATELY A SPECIAL OPERATIONS DIVISION IS
FORMED WITH HEADQUARTERS IN THE 7TH POLICE
DISTRICT/HIGHWAY PATROL BUILDING. COMMANDING
OFFICER SPECIAL OPERATIONS DIVISION WILL BE
IMMEDIATELY SUBORDINATE TO THE COMMISSIONER,

REPORTING THROUGH CHIEF INSPECTOR COUGHLIN. THE
SPECIAL OPERATIONS DIVISION WILL CONSIST OF THE
HIGHWAY PATROL, THE ANTI-CRIME TEAM (ACT) UNIT,
AND SUCH OTHER UNITS AS MAY BE LATER ASSIGNED.
THE SPECIAL OPERATIONS DIVISION HAS CITYWIDE
JURISDICTION. SPECIAL OPERATIONS DIVISION MOTOR
VEHICLES (EXCEPT HIGHWAY PATROL) ARE ASSIGNED
RADIO CALL SIGNS S-100 THROUGH S-200, AND WILL
USE THE PHONETIC PRONUNCIATION "SAM."

..............................

The radio designator "Sam" was already in use, Wohl
knew. Stakeout and the Bomb Squad used it. It was "Sam"
rather than the military "Sugar" because the first time a
Bomb Squad cop had gone on the air and identified himself
as "S-Sugar Thirteen" the hoots of derision from his brother
officers had been heard as far away as Atlantic City.

Special Operations had been given, he reasoned, the
"Sam" designator because Special Operations, also "S" was
going to be larger than "S" for Stakeout. So what were they
going to use for Stakeout and the Bomb Squad? It would not
work to have both using the same designator.

But that was a problem that could wait.

He read the third and fourth teletype messages.

GENERAL: 0652 06/30/73 FROM COMMISSIONER
PAGE 1 OF 1
*********** CITY OF PHILADELPHIA ************
************ POLICE DEPARTMENT *************

..............................

ANNOUNCEMENT WILL BE MADE AT ALL ROLL CALLS OF
THE FOLLOWING COMMAND ASSIGNMENT: EFFECTIVE
IMMEDIATELY STAFF INSPECTOR PETER F. WOHL IS
REASSIGNED FROM INTERNAL AFFAIRS DIVISION TO
SPECIAL OPERATIONS DIVISION AS COMMANDING
OFFICER.

..............................

GENERAL: 0653 06/30/73 FROM COMMISSIONER
PAGE 1 OF 1

\*\*\*\*\*\*\*\*\*\*\*\* CITY OF PHILADELPHIA \*\*\*\*\*\*\*\*\*\*\*\*
\*\*\*\*\*\*\*\*\*\*\*\* POLICE DEPARTMENT \*\*\*\*\*\*\*\*\*\*\*\*

..............................

ANNOUNCEMENT WILL BE MADE AT ALL ROLL CALLS OF
THE FOLLOWING COMMAND ASSIGNMENT: EFFECTIVE
IMMEDIATELY CAPTAIN MICHAEL J. SABARA IS
REASSIGNED FROM (ACTING) COMMANDING OFFICER
HIGHWAY PATROL TO SPECIAL OPERATIONS DIVISION AS
DEPUTY COMMANDER.

..............................

"I'll be in touch," Chief Coughlin said to the telephone,
and hung up. He turned to Wohl, smiling.

"You don't seem very surprised, Peter," Coughlin said.

"I heard."

"You did?" Coughlin said, surprised. "From who?"

"I forget."

"Yeah, you forget," Coughlin said, sarcastically. "I don't
know why I'm surprised."

"I don't suppose I can get out of this?" Wohl asked.

"You're going to be somebody in the Department, Peter,"
Coughlin said. "It wouldn't be much of a surprise if you got
to be Commissioner."

"That's very flattering, Chief," Wohl said. "But that's not
what I asked."

"Don't thank me," Coughlin said. "I didn't say that. The
mayor did, to the Commissioner. When the mayor told him
he thought you should command Special Operations."

Wohl shook his head.

"That answer your question, Inspector?" Chief Coughlin
asked.

"Chief, I don't even know what the hell Special Operations
is," Wohl said, "much less what it's supposed to do."

"You saw the teletype. Highway and ACT. You were Highway, and you've got Mike Sabara to help you with Highway."

"I don't suppose anybody asked Mike if he'd like to have Highway?" Wohl asked.

"The mayor says Mike looks like a concentration camp guard," Coughlin said. "Dave Pekach, I guess, looks more like what the mayor thinks the commanding officer of Highway Patrol should look like."

"This is a reaction to that *'Gestapo in Jackboots'* editorial? Is that what this is all about?"

"That, too, sure."

"The *Ledger* is going after Carlucci no matter what he does," Wohl said.

"His Honor the Mayor," Coughlin corrected him.

"And after me, too," Wohl said. "Arthur J. Nelson blames me for letting it out that his son was . . . involved with other men."

Arthur J. Nelson was Chairman of the Board and Chief Executive Officer of Daye-Nelson Publishing, Inc., which owned the *Ledger* and twelve other newspapers across the country.

" 'Negro homosexuals,' " Coughlin said.

It had been a sordid job. Jerome Nelson, the only son of Arthur J. Nelson, had been murdered, literally butchered, in his luxurious apartment in a renovated Revolutionary War-era building on Society Hill. The prime suspect in the case was his live-in boyfriend, a known homosexual, a man who called himself "Pierre St. Maury." A fingerprint search had identified Maury as a twenty-five-year-old black man, born Errol F. Watson, with a long record of arrests for minor vice offenses and petty thievery. Watson had himself been murdered, shot in the back of the head with a .32 automatic, by two other black men known to be homosexuals.

Wohl believed he knew what had happened: It had started as a robbery. The almost certain doers, and thus the almost certain murderers, were Watson's two friends. They were currently in the Ocean County, New Jersey jail, held without bail on a first-degree murder charge. Watson's body had been found buried in a shallow grave not far from Atlantic City, near where Jerome Nelson's stolen Jaguar had been abandoned. When the two had been arrested, they had been found in possession of Jerome Nelson's credit card, wristwatch, and ring. Other property stolen from Jerome Nelson's apartment had been located and tied to them, and their fingerprints had been all over the Jaguar.

The way Wohl put it together in his mind, the two critters being held in New Jersey had gotten the keys to the Nelson apartment from Watson, probably in exchange for a promise to split the burglary proceeds with him. Surprised to find Jerome Nelson at home, they had killed him. And then they had killed Watson to make sure that when the police found him, he couldn't implicate them.

But the two critters had availed themselves of their right under the *Miranda* Decision to have legal counsel. And their lawyer had pointed out to them that while they were probably going to be convicted of the murder of Watson, if they professed innocence of the Nelson robbery and murder, the Pennsylvania authorities didn't have either witnesses or much circumstantial evidence to try them with.

It was a statement of fact that sentences handed down to critters of whatever color for having murdered another critter tended to be less severe than those handed down to black men for having murdered a rich and socially prominent white man. And if the two critters in the Ocean County jail hadn't known this before the State of New Jersey provided them with free legal counsel, they knew it now.

Their story now was that they had met Watson riding around in a Jaguar, and bought certain merchandise he had for sale from him. They had last seen him safe and sound near the boardwalk in Atlantic City. They had no idea who had killed him, and they had absolutely no knowledge whatever of a man named Jerome Nelson, except that his had been the name on the credit card they bought from Errol Watson/Pierre St. Maury.

Ordinarily, it wouldn't have mattered. It would have been just one more sordid job in a long, long list of sordid jobs.

The critters would have gone away, even if the New Jersey prosecutor had plea-bargained Watson's murder down to second-degree murder or even first-degree manslaughter. They would have gotten twenty-to-life, and the whole job would have been forgotten in a month.

But Jerome Nelson was not just one more victim. His father was Arthur J. Nelson, who owned the *Ledger,* and who had naturally assumed that when Mayor Jerry Carlucci and Police Commissioner Taddeus Czernick had called on him immediately after the tragedy to assure him that the full resources of the Philadelphia Police Department would be brought to bear to bring whoever was responsible for this heinous crime against his son to justice, that the Police Department would naturally do what it could to spare the feelings of the victim's family. That, in other words, the sexual proclivities of the prime suspect, or his racial categorization, or that he had been sharing Jerome's apartment, would not come out.

Mayor Carlucci had seemed to be offering what Arthur J. Nelson had, as the publisher of a major newspaper, come to expect as his due: a little special treatment. Commissioner Czernick had even told Nelson that he had assigned one of the brightest police officers in the Department, Staff Inspector Peter Wohl, to oversee the detectives in the Homicide Division as they conducted their investigation, and to make sure that everything that could possibly be done was being done.

That hadn't happened.

Mr. Michael J. O'Hara, of the *Bulletin*, had fed several drinks to, and stroked the already outsized ego of, a Homicide Division Lieutenant named DelRaye, which had caused Lieutenant DelRaye to say something he probably would not have said had he been entirely sober. That resulted in a front page, bylined story in the *Bulletin* announcing that "according to a senior police official involved in the investigation" the police were seeking Jerome Nelson's live-in lover, who happened to be a black homosexual, or words to that effect.

Once Mickey O'Hara's story had broken the dam, the other

two major newspapers in Philadelphia, plus all the radio and television stations, had considered it their sacred journalistic duty to bring all the facts before the public.

Mrs. Arthur J. Nelson, who had always manifested some symptoms of nervous disorder, had had to be sent back to the Institute of Living, in Hartford, Connecticut, said to be the most expensive psychiatric hospital in the country, after it had come out, in all the media except the *Ledger*, that her only child had been cohabiting with a Negro homosexual.

Mr. Arthur J. Nelson had felt betrayed, not only by his fellow practitioners of journalism, but by the mayor and especially by the police. If that goddamned cop hadn't had diarrhea of the mouth, Jerome could have gone to his grave with some dignity, and his wife wouldn't be up in Hartford again.

Peter Wohl had been originally suspected by both Arthur J. Nelson and the mayor as the cop with the big mouth, but Commissioner Czernick had believed Wohl's denial, and found out himself, from Mickey O'Hara, that the loudmouth had been Lieutenant DelRaye.

When Mayor Carlucci had called Mr. Nelson to tell him that, and also that Lieutenant DelRaye had been relieved of his Homicide Division assignment and banished in disgrace— and in uniform—to a remote district; and also to tell him that Peter Wohl had been in on the arrest of the two suspects in Atlantic City, what had been intended as an offering of the olive branch had turned nasty. Both men had tempers, and things were said that could not be withdrawn.

And it had quickly become evident how Arthur J. Nelson intended to wage the war. Two days later, a young plainclothes Narcotics Division cop had caught up with Gerald Vincent Gallagher, the drug addict who had been involved in the shooting death of Captain Dutch Moffitt. It had been a front-page story in all the newspapers in Philadelphia, the stories generally reflecting support for the police, and relief that a drug-addict cop-killer had been run to ground. The *Ledger* had buried the story, although factually reported, far inside the paper. The *Ledger* editorial, headlined "*Vigilante Justice?*" implied that Gerald Vincent Gallagher, who had fallen to his death under the wheels of a subway train as he tried to escape the Narcotics cop, had instead been pushed in front of the train.

The most recent barrage had been the "*Jackbooted Gestapo*" editorial. Arthur J. Nelson wanted revenge, and apparently reasoned that since Mayor Carlucci had risen to political prominence through the ranks of the Police Department, a shot that wounded the cops also wounded Carlucci.

"What is he doing," Wohl asked, "putting me between him and the *Ledger*?"

"Peter, I think what you see is what you get," Coughlin said.

"What I see is me," Wohl said, "who hasn't worn a uniform or worked anywhere but headquarters in ten years being put in charge of Highway, and of something called ACT that I don't know a damned thing about. I don't even know what it's supposed to do."

"The mayor told the Commissioner he has every confidence that, within a short period of time—I think that means a couple of weeks—he will be able to call a press conference and announce that his Special Operations Division has arrested the sexual deviate who has been raping the decent women of Northwest Philadelphia."

"Rape is under the Detectives' Bureau," Wohl protested.

"So it is," Coughlin said. "Except that the Northwest Philly rapist is yours."

"So it *is* public relations."

"What it is, Peter, is what the mayor wants," Coughlin said.

"Matt Lowenstein will blow a blood vessel when he hears I'm working his territory."

"The Commissioner already told him," Coughlin said. "Give up, Peter. You can't fight this."

"Who's in ACT? What kind of resources am I going to find there?"

"I've sent you three people," Coughlin said, "to get you started. Officers Martinez and McFadden. They've been ordered to report to you at eight tomorrow morning."

Officer Charley McFadden was the plainclothes Narc the *Ledger* had as much as accused of pushing Gerald Vincent Gallagher in front of the subway train; Officer Jesus Martinez had been his partner.

Wohl considered that for a moment, then said, "You said three?"

"And Officer Matthew Payne," Coughlin said. "Dutch's nephew. You met him."

After a moment, Wohl said, "Why Payne? Is he through the Academy?"

"I had a hunch, Peter," Coughlin said, "that Matt Payne will be of more value to you, and thus to the Department, than he would be if we had sent him to one of the districts."

"I'm surprised he stuck it out at the Academy," Wohl said.

"I wasn't," Coughlin said, flatly.

"What are you talking about? Using him undercover?" Wohl asked.

"Maybe," Coughlin said. "We don't get many rookies like him. Something will come up."

"The only orders I really have are to do something about this rapist?" Wohl asked.

"Your orders are to get the Special Operations Division up and running. That means trying to keep Highway from giving the *Ledger* an excuse to call them the Gestapo. And it means getting ACT up and running. There's a Sergeant, a smart young guy named Eddy Frizell, in Staff Services, who's been handling all the paperwork for ACT. The Federal Grant applications, what kind of money, where it's supposed to be used, that sort of thing. I called down there just before you came in and told him to move himself and his files out to Highway. He'll probably be there before you get there. Czernick told Whelan to give you whatever you think you need in terms of equipment and money, from the contingency fund, to be reimbursed when the Federal Grant comes in. Frizell should be able to tell you what you need.''

"The mayor expects me to catch the rapist," Wohl said, and paused.

"That's your first priority."

"Who am I supposed to use to do that? Those kids from Narcotics?" He saw a flash of annoyance, even anger, on Coughlin's face. "Sorry, Chief," he added quickly. "I didn't mean for that to sound the way it came out."

"The initial manning for ACT is forty cops, plus four each Corporals, Sergeants, and Lieutenants; a Captain, four Detectives, and of course, you," Coughlin said. "I already sent a teletype asking for volunteers to transfer in. You can pick whoever you want."

"And if nobody volunteers? Or if all the volunteers are guys one step ahead of being assigned to rubber gun squad or being sent to the farm in their districts?"

Coughlin chuckled. "Being sent to the farm" was the euphemism for alcoholic officers being sent off to dry out; the rubber gun squad was for officers whose peers did not think they could be safely entrusted with a real one.

"Then you can pick, within reason, anybody you want," Coughlin said. "Making this thing work is important to the mayor; therefore to Czernick and me. You're not going to give me trouble about this, Peter, are you?"

"No, of course not, Chief," Wohl said. "It just came out of the blue, and it's taking some getting used to."

Chief Coughlin stood up and put out his hand.

"You can handle this, Peter," Coughlin said. "Congratulations and good luck."

He had, Peter Wohl realized as he put out his hand to take Coughlin's, not only been dismissed but given all the direction he was going to get.

"Thank you, Chief," he said.

Wohl went to the parking lot, opened the door of his car, and rolled down the windows, standing outside a moment until some of the heat could escape. Then he got in and started the engine, and turned on the air conditioner. He cranked up the window and shifted into reverse.

Then he changed his mind. He reached over to the glove compartment and took out the microphone.

"Radio, S-Sam One Oh One," he said.

"S-Sam One Oh One, Radio," Police Radio replied. They didn't seem at all surprised to hear the new call sign, Wohl thought.

"Have you got a location on Highway One?" Wohl asked.

The reply was almost immediate: "Out of service at Highway."

"What about N-Two?" Wohl asked, guessing that Dave Pekach, who was, now that he had been promoted, the second-ranking man in Narcotics, would be using that call sign.

"Also out of service at Highway, S-Sam One Oh One," Police Radio replied.

"If either of them come back on the air, ask them to meet me at Highway. Thank you, Radio," Wohl said, and put the microphone back in the glove compartment. Then he backed out of the parking space and headed for Highway Patrol headquarters.

# NINE

Elizabeth Joan Woodham did not like to be called "Woody" as most of her friends did. She thought of herself as too tall, and skinny, and somewhat awkward, and thus "wooden."

She was, in fact, five feet ten and one-half inches tall. She weighed 135 pounds, which her doctor had told her was just about right for her. She thought she had the choice between weighing 135, which she was convinced made her look skinny, and putting on weight, which would, she thought, make her a large woman.

She thought she had a better chance of attracting the right kind of man as a skinny woman. Large women, she believed, sort of intimidated men. Elizabeth J. Woodham, who was thirty-three, had not completely given up the hope that she would finally meet some decent man with whom she could develop a relationship. But she had read a story in *Time* that gave statistics suggesting that the odds were against her. Apparently someone had taken the time to develop statistics showing that, starting at age thirty, a woman's chances of ever marrying began to sharply decline. By age thirty-five, a woman's chances were remote indeed, and by forty practically negligible.

She had come to accept lately that what she wanted, really, was a child, rather than a man. She wondered if she really wanted to share her life with a man. Sometimes, in her apartment, she conjured up a man living there with her, making demands on her time, on her body, confiscating her space.

The man was a composite of the three lovers she had had in her life, and she sometimes conjured him up in two ways. One was a man who had all the attractive attributes of her three lovers, including the physical aspects, rolled into one. The other man had all the unpleasant attributes of her lovers, which had ultimately caused her to break off the relationships.

The conjured-up good man was most often the lover she had had for two and a half years, a kind, gentle man with whom the physical aspects of the relationship had been really very nice, but who had had one major flaw: he was married, and she had gradually come to understand that he was never going to leave his wife and children; and that in fact his wife was not the unfeeling and greedy bitch he had painted, but rather someone like herself, who must have known he was playing around when he came home regularly so late, and suffered through it in the belief that it was her wifely duty; or because of the children; or because she believed practically any man was better than no man at all.

Elizabeth had decided, at the time she broke off the relationship, that it was better to have no man at all than one who was sleeping around.

Elizabeth Woodham, during the winters, taught the sixth grade at the Olney Elementary School at Taber Road and Water Street. This summer, more for something to do than for the money, she had taken a job as a storyteller with the Philadelphia Public Library system, the idea being that the way to get the kids to read was to convince them that something interesting was between the covers of a book; and the way to do that was by gathering them together and telling them stories.

If it also served to keep them off the streets at night, so much the better. Mayor Carlucci had gotten a Federal Grant for the program, and Elizabeth Woodham, the Project Administrator had told her when she applied for the job, was just the sort of person she had hoped to attract.

The hours were from three to nine, with an hour off for dinner. Elizabeth usually got to the playground at two, to set things up and attract a crowd for the three-thirty story hour for the smaller children. The story "hour" almost always ran more than an hour, usually two. She kept it up until she sensed her charges were growing restless. And she took a sort of professional pride in keeping their attention up as long as she could, scrupulously stopping when they showed the first signs of boredom, but taking pride in keeping it longer than you were supposed to be able to keep it.

The playground was on East Godfrey Avenue in Olney. West Godfrey Avenue becomes East Godfrey when it crosses Front Street. It is close to the city line, Cheltenham Avenue. East Godfrey is a dead-end street. A playground runs for two blocks off it to the south, down to where Champlost Avenue turns north and becomes Crescentville Avenue, which forms the western boundary of Tacony Creek Park.

The evening story hour was at seven-thirty, and was thus supposed to be over at eight-thirty, to give Elizabeth time to close things up before the park was locked for the night at nine.

But she'd managed to prolong the expected attention span and it was close to nine before she had told the kids the story of *The Hound of the Baskervilles*, and sown, she hoped, the idea that there were more stories by A. Conan Doyle about Sherlock Holmes and Dr. Watson available in the public library.

It was thus a few minutes after nine when she left the park and walked down East Godfrey Avenue toward where she had parked her car, a two-year-old Plymouth coupe.

"If you scream, I'll cut off your boobies right here," the man with the black mask covering his face said as he pulled Elizabeth J. Woodham through the side door of a van.

Barbara Crowley, a tall, lithe woman of twenty-six, entered Bookbinder's Restaurant at Second and Walbut Streets and looked around the main dining room until she spotted Peter Wohl, who was sitting at a table with an older couple. Then she walked quickly across the room to the table.

Peter Wohl saw her coming and got up.

"Sorry I'm late," Barbara Crowley said.

"We understand, dear," the older woman said, extending her cheek to be kissed. She was a thin, tall woman with silver gray hair simply cut, wearing a flower-print dress. She was Mrs. Olga Wohl, Peter Wohl's mother. It was her birthday. The older man, larger and heavier than Peter, with a florid face, was his father, Chief Inspector (Retired) August Wohl.

"How are you, Barbara?" Chief Wohl said, getting half out of his chair to smile at her and offer his hand.

"Bushed," Barbara Crowley said. As she sat down, she put her purse in her lap, opened it, and removed a small tissue-wrapped package. She handed it to Olga Wohl. "Happy birthday!"

"Oh, you shouldn't have!" Olga Wohl said, beaming, as she tore off the tissue. Underneath was a small box bearing the *Bailey, Banks & Biddle, Jewelers, Philadelphia* logotype. Olga Wohl opened it and took out a silver compact.

"Oh, this is too much," Olga Wohl said, repeating, "You shouldn't have, dear."

"If you mean that, Mother," Peter said, "she can probably get her money back."

His father chuckled; his mother gave him a withering look.

"It's just beautiful," she said, and leaned across to Barbara Crowley and kissed her cheek. "Thank you very much."

"She doesn't look seventy, does she?" Peter asked, innocently.

"I'm fifty-seven," Olga Wohl said, "still young enough to slap a fresh mouth if I have to."

August Wohl laughed.

"Watch it, Peter," he said.

"So how was your day?" Barbara asked, looking at Peter.

"You mean aside from getting my picture in the papers?" Peter asked.

"What?" Barbara asked, confused.

A waiter appeared, carrying a wine cooler on a three-legged stand.

"Peter was promoted," Olga Wohl said. "You didn't see the paper?"

"I don't think 'promoted,' " Peter said. " 'Reassigned.' "

The waiter, with what Peter thought was an excessive amount of theatrics, unwrapped the towel around the bottle, showed Peter the label, uncorked the bottle, and poured a little in a glass for his approval.

"I didn't see the paper," Barbara said.

"Mother just happens to have one with her," Peter said, and then, after sipping the wine, said to the waiter, "That's fine, thank you."

The waiter poured wine in everyone's glass and then rewrapped the bottle in its towel as Olga Wohl took a folded newspaper from her purse, a large leather affair beside her chair, and handed it to Barbara Crowley. The story was on the front page, on the lower right-hand side, beside an old photograph of Peter Wohl. The caption line below the photograph said, simply, "P. Wohl."

## POLICE ORGANIZATION RESHUFFLED

By Cheryl Davies
Bulletin Staff Writer

Police Commissioner Taddeus Czernick today announced the formation of a new division, to be called Special Operations, within the Philadelphia Police Department. Although Czernick denied the reshuffling has anything to do with recent press criticism of some police operations, knowledgeable observers believe this to be the case.

Highway Patrol, the elite police unit sometimes known as "Carlucci's Commandos," which has been the subject of much recent criticism, has been placed under the new Special Operations Division, which will be commanded by Inspector Peter Wohl. Captain Michael J. Sabara, who had been in temporary command of the Highway Patrol since Captain Richard C. Moffitt was shot and killed, was named as Wohl's deputy. Captain David J. Pekach, who had been assigned to the Narcotics Bureau, was named to command the Highway Patrol.

Inspector Wohl, who was previously assigned to the Special Investigations Division, and Pekach are little known outside the police department, but are regarded by insiders as "straight arrows," officers who go by the book, lending further credence to the theory that the reorganization is intended to tame the Highway Patrol, and lessen press criticism of its alleged excesses. One Philadelphia newspaper recently editorialized that the Highway Patrol was acting like the Gestapo.

The new Special Operations Division will also have under its wing a special, federally funded, yet-to-be-formed unit called Anti-Crime Teams (ACT). According to Commissioner Czernick, specially trained and equipped ACT teams will be sent to high-crime areas in Philadelphia as needed to augment existing Police resources.

"That's very nice," Barbara said. Peter Wohl snorted derisively. "Congratulations, Peter." Peter snorted again. "Am I missing something?" Barbara asked, confused. "What's wrong with it?"

"I'm a Staff Inspector, for one thing," Peter said. "Not an Inspector."

"Well, so what? That's a simple mistake. She didn't know any better."

"For another, there's a pretty clear implication in there that Highway has been doing something wrong, and they haven't, and that Mike Sabara, who is a really good cop, didn't get Highway because he's involved with what's wrong with it."

"Why didn't he get it?"

"Because the mayor thinks he looks like a concentration camp guard," Peter said.

"Really?" Barbara said.

"Really," Peter said. "And I wasn't sent over there to 'tame' Highway, either."

"But Carlucci will be very pleased if you can keep the newspapers from calling it the Gestapo," Chief Inspector August Wohl said.

"Only one newspaper's doing that, Dad," Peter replied, "and you know why."

"*I* don't," Barbara said.

"Arthur J. Nelson, who owns the *Ledger*, has got it in for the police," Peter said, "because it got out that his son, the one who was murdered—Jerome?—was a homosexual."

"Oh," Barbara said. "How did it get out?"

"A cop who should have known better told Mickey

O'Hara,'' Peter said. "Not that it wouldn't have come out inevitably, but he blames the Police."

Barbara considered that a moment, and then decided to change the subject: "Well, what are you going to do over there, anyway?" she asked.

"He's the commanding officer," Olga Wohl said, a touch of pride in her voice.

"You asked me how my day was," Peter said, dryly.

"Yes, I did."

"Well, I went over to my new *command*," he said, wryly, "about four-thirty. Special Operations will operate out of what until this morning was Highway Patrol headquarters, at Bustleton and Bowler. Three people were waiting for me. Captain Mike Sabara, his chin on his knees, because until this morning, he thought he was going to get Highway; Captain Dave Pekach, who had his chin on his knees because he's got the idea that somebody doesn't like him; *because* they gave *him* Highway—in other words he thinks he's being thrown to the wolves; and a sergeant named Ed Frizell, from Staff Planning, whose chin is on his knees because when he dreamed up this ACT thing it never entered his mind that he would be involved in it—banished, so to speak, in disgrace from his office in the Roundhouse to the boondocks, forced to wear a uniform and consort with ordinary cops, and possibly even have to go out and arrest people."

Chief Wohl chuckled.

"And then I went to the Highway roll call," Peter went on. "*That* was fun."

"I don't understand, dear," his mother said.

"Well, I was practicing good leadership techniques," Peter said. "I thought I was being clever as hell. I got there, and made my little speech. I was proud to be back in Highway, as I was sure Captain Pekach was. I said that I had always thought of Highway as the most efficient unit in the Department, and felt sure it would stay that way. I even included the standard lines that my door was always open, and that I looked forward to working with them."

"What's wrong with that?" Barbara asked.

"Well, I didn't know that they thought I was the SOB who took Highway away from Mike Sabara, who everybody likes, and gave it to Pekach, who nobody in Highway likes."

"Why don't they like Pekach?" Chief Wohl asked. "I thought he was a pretty good cop. And from what I hear, he did a good job in Narcotics. And he came out of Highway."

"He did a great job in Narcotics," Peter said. "But what I didn't know—and it was my fault I didn't—was that the *one* time a Highway cop got arrested for drugs, Dave Pekach was the one who arrested him."

"The Sergeant? About a year ago?" Chief Wohl asked, and Peter nodded.

"I knew about that," Chief Wohl said, "but I didn't know Pekach was involved."

"And I hadn't seen Miss Cheryl Davies's clever little newspaper article, and they had," Peter went on, "so my attempt at practicing the best principles of command left the indelible impression on my new command that I am a fool or a liar, or both."

"Oh, Peter," his mother said. "You don't know that!"

"I know cops, Mother," Peter said. "I know what those guys were thinking."

"If they think that now, they'll come to know better," Barbara said, loyally.

"Would you care to order now?" the waiter asked.

"Yes, please," Peter said. "I'm going to have something hearty. That's traditional for condemned men."

Chief Wohl chuckled again. Barbara leaned across the table and put her hand on Peter's. Mrs. Wohl smiled at them.

They were on dessert when the manager called Peter to the telephone.

"Inspector Wohl," Peter said.

"Lieutenant Jackson, sir," the caller said. "You said you wanted to be notified when anything came up."

Wohl now placed the name and face. His caller was the Highway Tour Commander on duty.

"What's up, Jackson?"

"We got a pretty bad wreck, I'm afraid. Highway Sixteen was going in on a call and hit a civilian broadside. At Second and Olney."

"Anybody hurt?"

"Both of our guys were injured," Jackson said, reluctance in his voice. "One of the passengers in the civilian car is dead; two others are pretty badly injured."

"My God!"

"It was a little boy that got killed, Inspector," Jackson said.

"Jesus H. Christ!" Wohl said. "Has Captain Pekach been notified?"

"Yes, sir."

"You say they were answering a call?"

"Yes, sir," Jackson said. "They went in on a call to the Thirty-fifth District. Somebody saw a woman being forced into a van by a guy with a knife at Front and Godfrey, one of the apartment buildings. In the parking lot."

"Where are you?"

"At the scene, sir."

"What scene, the wreck or the kidnapping?"

"The wreck, sir. I sent Sergeant Paster to the kidnapping."

"Get on the radio, and tell Captain Pekach I said for him to handle the wreck, and then tell Sergeant—"

"Paster, sir," Lieutenant Jackson furnished.

"Tell Sergeant Paster to meet me at the scene of the kidnapping," Wohl said.

"Yes, sir."

Wohl hung up without saying anything else.

He found the manager and arranged to settle the bill before returning to the table.

"A Highway car hit a civilian," he said, looking at his father. "A little boy is dead."

"Oh, God!" his father said.

"They were going in on a Thirty-fifth District call," Peter

said. "Someone reported a woman being forced into a van at knife point. I've got to go."

His father nodded his understanding.

Peter looked at Barbara. "Sorry," he said. "And I don't know how long this will take."

"I understand," she said. "No problem, I've got my car."

"And I'm sorry to have to walk out on your party, Mother."

"Don't be silly, dear," she said. "At least you got to eat your dinner."

"I'll call you," he said, and walked quickly out of the restaurant.

*You are a prick, Peter Wohl,* he thought, as he walked through the parking lot. *A little boy has been killed and a woman has been kidnapped, and your reaction to all this is that you are at least spared the problem of how to handle Barbara.*

Until Dutch Moffitt had gotten himself killed, everybody concerned had been under the impression that he and Barbara had an *understanding*, which was a half-step away from a formal engagement to be married. But the witness to the shooting of Captain Moffitt had been a female, specifically a stunning, long-legged, long-haired, twenty-five-year-old blonde named Louise Dutton, who was co-anchor of WCBL-TV's *Nine's News*.

Less than twenty-four hours after he had met Louise Dutton in the line of duty, they had been making the beast with two backs in his apartment, and Peter had been convinced that he had finally embarked on the Great Romance of his life. And for a little while, the Grand Passion had seemed reciprocal, but then there had been, on Louise's part, a little sober consideration of the situation.

She had asked herself a simple question: "Can a talented, ambitious young television anchor whose father just happens to own a half dozen television stations around the country find lasting happiness in the arms of an underpaid cop in Philadelphia?"

The answer was no. Louise Dutton was now working for a television station in Chicago, one that not coincidentally happened to be owned by her father—who, Peter understood, while he liked Peter *personally*, did not see him as the father of his grandchildren.

There was no question in Peter's mind that Barbara knew about Louise, and not only because he had covered Dutch's ass one last time by telling the Widow Moffitt that Dutch could not have been fooling around with Louise Dutton because she was his, Peter's, squeeze. That he was "involved" with Louise Dutton had been pretty common knowledge around the Department; even Chief Coughlin knew about it. Barbara had two uncles and two brothers in the Department. Peter had known them all his life, and there is no human being more self-righteous than a brother who hears that some sonofabitch is running around on his baby sister. Barbara knew, all right.

But Barbara had decided to forgive him. Her presence at his mother's birthday dinner proved that. He had called her twice, post-Louise, and both times she hadn't "been able" to have dinner or go to a movie with him. He would not have been surprised if she hadn't "been able" to have dinner with him and his parents, but she'd accepted that invitation. And there wasn't much of a mystery about how she planned to handle the problem: she was going to pretend it didn't exist, and never had.

And when her knee found his under the table, he had understood that after they had said good night to his parents, they would go either to his apartment or hers, and get in bed, and things would be back to normal.

The problem was that Peter wasn't sure he wanted to pick things up where they had been, pre-Louise. He told himself that he had either been a fool, or been made a fool of, or both; that Barbara Crowley was not only a fine woman, but just what he needed; that he should be grateful for her tolerance and understanding; that if he had any brains, he would be grateful for the opportunity she was offering; and that he should manifest his gratitude by taking a solemn, if private, vow never to stray again from the boundaries of premarital fidelity.

But when he had looked at Barbara, he had thought of Louise, and that had destroyed ninety percent of his urge to take Barbara to bed.

He got in his car, started the engine, and then thought of Mike Sabara.

"Jesus!" he said.

He reached into the glove compartment and took out the microphone.

"Radio, S-Sam One Oh One," he said. "Have you got a location on S-Sam One Oh Two?"

After a longer than usual pause, Police Radio replied that S-Sam One Oh Two was not in service.

Peter thought that over a moment. If he and Pekach had been informed of the crash, Sabara certainly had. And Sabara was probably still using his old radio call, Highway Two, for the number two man in Highway.

"Radio, how about Highway Two?"

"Highway Two is at Second and Olney Avenue."

"Radio, please contact Highway Two and have him meet S-Sam One Oh One at Front and Godfrey Avenue. Let me know if you get through to him."

"Yes, sir. Stand by, please."

*I'm going to have to get another band in here,* Peter thought, as he backed out of the parking space. *Bands. I'm going to have to get Highway and Detective, too.*

Every Police vehicle was equipped with a shortwave radio that permitted communication on two bands: the J-Band and one other, depending on what kind of car it was. Cars assigned to the Detective Bureau, for example, could communicate on the J-Band and on H-Band, the Detective Band. Cars assigned to a District could communicate on the J-Band and on a frequency assigned to that District. Peter's car had the J-Band and the Command Band, limited to the Commissioner, the Chief Inspector, the Inspectors, and the Staff Inspectors.

He was six blocks away from Bookbinder's Restaurant when Radio called him.

"S-Sam One Oh One, Radio."

"Go ahead."

"Highway Two wants to know if you are aware of the traffic accident at Second and Olney Avenue."

"Tell Highway Two I know about it, and ask him to meet me at Front and Godfrey."

"Yes, sir," Radio replied.

Peter put the microphone back in the glove compartment and slammed it shut.

Now Sabara, who had very naturally rushed to a scene of trouble involving "his" Highway Patrol, was going to be pissed.

*It can't be helped,* Peter thought. *Mike's going to have to get it through his head that Highway is now Pekach's.*

When Matthew Payne walked into the kitchen of the house on Providence Road in Wallingford, he was surprised to find his father standing at the stove, watching a slim stream of coffee gradually filling a glass pot under a Krups coffee machine.

"Good morning," his father said. He was wearing a light cotton bathrobe, too short for him, and a pair of leather bedroom slippers. "I heard you in the shower and thought you could probably use some coffee."

"Can I!" Matt replied. He was dressed in a button-down-collar shirt and gray slacks. His necktie was tied, but the collar button was open, and the knot an inch below it. He had a seersucker jacket in his hand. When he laid it on the kitchen table—of substantial, broad-planked pine, recently refinished after nearly a century of service—there was a heavy thump.

"What have you got in there?" Brewster C. Payne asked, surprised.

"My gun," Matt said, raising the jacket to show a Smith

& Wesson Military & Police Model .38 Special revolver in a shoulder holster. "What every well-dressed young man is wearing these days."

Brewster Payne chuckled.

"You're not wearing your new blue suit, I notice," he said.

"He said, curiosity oozing from every pore," Matt said, gently mockingly.

"Well, we haven't had the pleasure of your company recently," his father said, unabashed.

"I communed with John Barleycorn last night," Matt said, "at Rose Tree. I decided it was wiser by far to spend the night here than try to make it to the apartment. Particularly since the bug is one-eyed."

"Anything special, or just kicking up your heels?" Brewster Payne asked.

"I don't know, Dad," Matt said, as he took two ceramic mugs from a cabinet and set them on the counter beside the coffee machine. "All I know is that I had more to drink than I should have had."

"You want something to eat?" Brewster Payne asked, and when he saw the look on Matt's face, added, "If you've been at the grape, you should put something in your stomach. Did you have dinner?"

"I don't think so," Matt replied. "The last thing I remember clearly is peanuts at the bar."

His father went to the refrigerator, a multidoored stainless steel device filling one end of the room. He opened one door after another until he found what he was looking for.

"How about a Taylor ham sandwich? Maybe with an egg?"

"I'll make it," Matt said. "No *egg*."

Brewster Payne chuckled again, and said, "You were telling me what you were celebrating. . . ."

"No, I wasn't," Matt said. "You're a pretty good interrogator. You ever consider practicing law? Or maybe becoming a cop?"

"Touché," Brewster Payne said.

"I was on the pistol range yesterday," Matt said, "when Chief Matdorf, who runs the Police Academy, came out and told me to clean out my locker and report tomorrow morning, this morning, that is, at eight o'clock, to the commanding officer of Highway Patrol." He paused and then added, "In plainclothes."

"What's that all about?" Brewster Payne said.

"John Barleycorn didn't say," Matt said. "Although I had a long, long chat with him."

"You think Dennis Coughlin is involved?"

"Uncle Denny's involved in everything," Matt said as he put butter in a frying pan. "You want one of these?"

"Please," Brewster Payne said. "Were you having any trouble in the Academy?"

"No, not so far as I know."

"Highway Patrol is supposed to be the elite unit within the Department," Brewster Payne said. "You think you're getting special treatment, is that it?"

"Special, yeah, but I don't know what kind of special," Matt said. "To get into Highway, you usually need three years in the Department, and then there's a long waiting list. It's all volunteer, and I didn't volunteer. And then, why in plainclothes?"

"Possibly it has something to do with ACT," Brewster Payne said.

"With what?"

"ACT," Brewster Payne said. "It means Anti-Crime Team, or something like that. It was in the paper yesterday. A new unit. You didn't see it?"

"No, I didn't," Matt said. "Is the paper still around here?"

"It's probably in the garbage," Brewster Payne said.

Matt left the stove and went outside. His father shook his head and took over frying the Taylor ham.

"It's a little soggy," Matt called a moment later, "but I can read it."

He reappeared in the kitchen with a grease-stained sheet of

newspaper. When he laid it on the table, his father picked it up and read the story again.

"May I redispose of this?" he asked, when he had finished, holding the newspaper distastefully between his fingers.

"Sorry," Matt said. "That offers a lot of food for thought," he added. "This ACT, whatever it is, makes more sense than putting me in Highway. But it still smacks of special treatment."

"I think you're going to have to get used to that."

"What do you mean?"

"How many of your peers in the Academy had gone to college?" Brewster Payne asked.

"Not very many," Matt said.

"And even fewer had gone on to graduate?"

"So?"

"Would it be reasonable to assume that you were the only member of your class with a degree? A *cum laude* degree?"

"You think that's it, that I have a degree?"

"That's part of it, I would guess," Brewster Payne said. "And then there's Dennis Coughlin."

"I think that has more to do with this than my degree," Matt said.

"Dennis Coughlin was your father's best friend," Brewster C. Payne said. "And he never had a son; I'm sure he looks at you in that connection, the son he never had."

"I never thought about that," Matt said. "I wonder why he never got married?"

"I thought you knew," Brewster Payne said, after a moment. "He was in love with your mother."

"And she picked you over him?" Matt said, genuinely surprised. "I never heard that before."

"He never told her; I don't think she ever suspected. Not then, anyway. But I knew. I knew the first time I ever met him."

"Jesus!" Matt said.

"Would you like to hear my theory—theories—about this mysterious assignment of yours?"

"Sure."

"I think Dennis Coughlin is about as happy about you being a policeman as I am; that is to say he doesn't like it one little bit. He's concerned for your welfare. He doesn't want to have to get on the telephone and tell your mother that you've been hurt, or worse. Theory One is that you are really going to go to Highway. Dennis hopes that you will hate it; realize the error of your decision, and resign. Theory Two; which will stand by itself, or may be a continuation of Theory One, is that if you persist in being a policeman, the best place for you to learn the profession is from its most skilled practitioners, the Highway Patrol generally, and under Inspector Wohl. I found it interesting that Wohl was given command of this new Special Operations Division. Even I know that he's one of the brightest people in the Police Department, a real comer."

"I met him the night of Uncle Dutch's wake," Matt said. "In a bar. When I told him that I was thinking of joining the Department, he told me I would think better of it in the morning; that it was the booze talking."

"Theory Three," Brewster Payne said, "or perhaps Two (a), is that Dennis has sent you to Wohl, with at least an indication on his part that he would be pleased if Wohl could ease you out of the Police Department with your ego intact."

Matt considered that a moment, then exhaled audibly. "Well, I won't know will I, until I get there?"

"No, I suppose not."

Matt wolfed down his Taylor ham on toast, then started to put on his shoulder holster.

"They issue you that holster?" Brewster Payne asked.

"No, I bought it a week or so ago," Matt said. "When I wear a belt holster under a jacket, it stands out like a sore thumb."

"What about getting a smaller gun?"

"You can't do that until you pass some sort of examination,

qualify with it," Matt said. "I wasn't that far along in the Academy when I was—I suppose the word is 'graduated.' "

"There's something menacing about it," Brewster Payne said.

"It's also heavy," Matt said. "I'm told that eventually you get used to it, and feel naked if you don't have it." He shrugged into the seersucker jacket. "Now," he said, smiling. "No longer menacing."

"Unseen, but still menacing," his father responded, then changed the subject. "You said you were having headlight trouble with the bug?"

The bug, a Volkswagen, then a year old, had been Matt Payne's sixteenth-birthday present, an award for making the Headmaster's List at Episcopal Academy.

"I don't know what the hell is the matter with it; there's a short somewhere. More likely a break. Whenever I start out to fix it, it works fine. It only gives me trouble at night."

"There is, I seem to recall, another car in the garage," Brewster Payne said. "On which, presumably, both headlights function as they should."

The other car was a silver, leather-upholstered Porsche 911T, brand new, presented to Matthew Payne on the occasion of his graduation, *cum laude*, from the University of Pennsylvania.

"Very tactfully phrased," Matt said. "Said the ungrateful giftee."

He had not driven the Porsche to Philadelphia, or hardly at all, since he had joined the Police Department.

His father read his mind: "You're afraid, Matt, that it will . . . set you apart?"

"Oddly enough, I was thinking about the Porsche just now," Matt said. "Hung for a sheep as a lion, so to speak."

"I think you have that wrong; it's sheep and lamb, not lion," Brewster Payne replied, "but I take your point."

"I am being—what was it you said?—being 'set apart' as it is," Matt said. "Why not?"

"I really do understand, Matt."

"If I am sexually assaulted by one or more sex-crazed females driven into a frenzy when they see me in that car . . .''

"What?'' his father asked, chuckling.

"I'll tell you how it was,'' Matt said, and smiled, and went out of the kitchen, pausing for a moment to throw an affectionate arm around Brewster C. Payne.

Payne, sipping his coffee, went to the kitchen window and watched as Matt opened one of the four garage doors, then emerged a moment later behind the wheel of the Porsche.

*He should not be a policeman*, he thought. *He should be in law school. Or doing almost anything else.*

Matt Payne tooted "Shave and a Haircut, Two Bits'' on the Porsche's horn, and then headed down the driveway.

# TEN

Officers Jesus Martinez and Charles McFadden arrived together, in Officer McFadden's Volkswagen, at Highway Patrol
headquarters at quarter to eight, determined to be on time
and otherwise to make a good first impression. They were
both wearing business suits and ties, McFadden a faintly
plaided single-breasted brown suit, and Martinez a sharply
tailored double-breasted blue pinstripe.

He looked, McFadden accused him, not far off the mark,
like a successful numbers operator on his way to a wedding.

The available parking spaces around the relatively new
building were all full. There were a row of Highway motorcycles parked, neatly, as if in a military organization, at an
angle with their rear wheels close to the building; and a row
of Highway radio cars, some blue-and-whites identifiable by
the lettering on their fenders, and some, unmarked, by their
extra radio antennae and black-walled high-speed tires.

There were also the blue-and-whites assigned to the Seventh District, the Seventh District's unmarked cars, and sev-

eral new-model cars, which could have belonged to any of the department's senior officers.

And there was a battered Chevrolet, festooned with radio antennae, parked in a spot identified by a sign as being reserved for Inspectors.

"That's Mickey O'Hara's car," Charley McFadden said. "I wonder what he's doing here?"

"There was a woman kidnapped last night," Hay-zus said. "It was on the radio."

"Kidnapped?" McFadden asked.

"Couple of people saw some nut forcing her into a van, with a knife," Hay-zus said.

They had driven through the parking area without having found a spot to park. McFadden drove halfway down the block, made a U-turn, and found a parking spot at the curb.

"That's *abducting*," McFadden said.

"What?"

"What you said was kidnapping was abducting," McFadden said. "Kidnapping is when there's ransom."

"Screw you," Hay-zus said, in a friendly manner, and then, "Hey, look at them wheels!"

A silver Porsche was coming out of the parking lot, apparently after having made the same fruitless search for a place to park they had.

"I'd hate to have to pay insurance on a car like that," McFadden said.

"You got enough money to buy a car like that, you don't have to worry about how much insurance costs," Hay-zus said.

Both of them followed the car as it drove down Bowler Street past them.

"I know that guy," Charley McFadden said. "I seen him someplace."

"Really? Where?"

"I don't know, but I know that face."

Jesus Martinez looked at his watch, a gold-cased Hamilton with a gold bracelet and diamond chips on the face instead of numbers, and on which he owed eighteen (of twenty-four) payments at Zale's Credit Jewelers.

"Let's go in," he said. "It's ten of."

McFadden, not without effort, worked himself out from under the Volkswagen's steering wheel, then broke into a slow shuffle to catch up with Martinez.

They went into the building through a door off the parking lot, through which they could see Highway Patrolmen entering.

They looked for and found the to-be-expected window counter opening on the squad room. A Corporal was leaning on the counter, filling out a form. They waited until he was through, and looked at them curiously.

"We were told to report to the Commanding Officer of Highway at eight," Hay-zus said.

"You're a police officer?" the Corporal asked, doubtfully.

"Yeah, we're cops," Charley McFadden said.

"I know you," the Corporal said. "You're the guy who ran down the shit who was the doer in Captain Moffitt's shooting."

McFadden almost blushed.

"*We* were," he said, nodding at Martinez. "This is my partner, Hay-zus Martinez."

"What do you want to see the Captain about? The reason I ask is that he's busy as hell right now; I don't know when he'll be free."

"Beats me," McFadden said. "We was told to report to him at eight."

"Well, have a seat. When he's free, I'll tell him you're here. There's a coffee machine and a garbage machine around the corner." He pointed.

"Thanks," Charley said, and walked around the corner to the machines, not asking Hay-zus if he wanted anything. Hay-zus was a food freak; he didn't eat anything that had preservatives in it, or drink anything with chemical stimulants in it, like coffee, which had caffeine, or Coke, which had sugar and God only knows what other poison for the body.

When Charley returned, a minute or two later, holding a Mounds bar in one hand and a can of Coke in the other, Hay-zus nodded his head toward the counter. The guy they had seen in the Porsche, the one Charley said he knew from someplace, was talking to the Corporal. As Charley watched, he turned and headed for where Hay-zus was sitting on one of the row of battered folding metal chairs.

Charley walked over and sat down, and then leaned over Hay-zus.

"Don't I know you from somewheres?"

"Is your name McFadden?" Matt Payne asked.

"Yeah."

"I was at your house the night you got Gerald Vincent Gallagher."

"You were?" Charley asked. "I don't remember that."

"I was there with Chief Coughlin," Matt said. "And Sergeant Lenihan."

"Oh, yeah, I remember now," Charley said, although he did not. "How are you?"

"Fine," Matt said. "Yourself?"

There was a sort of stir as someone else came through the door from the parking lot. Matt recognized Peter Wohl; he wondered if Wohl would recognize him.

Wohl recognized all three of the young men on the folding metal chairs. He gave them a nod, and kept walking toward his office.

*God damn it, you're a commanding officer now. Act like one.*

He turned and walked to the three of them, his hand extended first to Martinez.

"How are you, Martinez?" he said, and turned before Martinez, who wasn't quite sure of Wohl's identity, could reply. "And McFadden. How's it going? And you're Payne, right?"

"Yes, sir."

"I'll be with you as soon as I'm free," Wohl said. "The way things are going, that may be a while."

"Yes, sir," McFadden and Martinez said, having found their voices.

Wohl then walked across the room and through the door to his outer office. Three people were in it: a Highway Sergeant, who had been Dutch Moffitt's Sergeant, then Mike Sabara's, and was *not* Dave Pekach's; Sergeant Eddy Frizell, in uniform, and looking a little sloppy compared to the Highway Sergeant; and Michael J. O'Hara, of the *Bulletin*.

The Highway Sergeant got to his feet when he saw Wohl, and after a moment, Frizell followed suit.

"Good morning, Inspector," the Highway Sergeant said.

"Good morning," Wohl said. "What do you say, Mickey? You waiting to see somebody?"

"You," O'Hara said.

"Well, then, come on in," Wohl said. "You can watch me drink a cup of coffee." He turned to look at the Highway Sergeant. "There *is* coffee?"

"Yes, sir," the Sergeant said. "Sir, Chief Coughlin wants you to phone as soon as you get in."

"Get me and Mickey a cup of coffee, and then get the Chief on the line," Wohl ordered.

Captains Sabara and Pekach were in what until yesterday had been the office of the Commanding Officer of Highway Patrol, and what was now, until maybe other accommodations could be found, the office of the Commanding Officer of Special Operations Division. Sabara, who was wearing black trousers and plain shoes, and not the motorcyclist's boots of Highway, was sitting in an armchair. Petach, who was wearing Highway boots, and a Sam Browne belt, was sitting across from him on a matching couch.

They both started to get up when they saw Wohl. He waved them back into their seats.

"Good morning," Wohl said.

"Good morning, Inspector," they both said. Wohl wondered if that was, at least on Mike Sabara's part, intended to show him that he was pissed, or whether it was in deference to the presence of Mickey O'Hara.

"Chief Coughlin wants you to call him as soon as you get in," Sabara said.

"The sergeant told me," Wohl said. "Well, anything new?"

"No van and no woman," Sabara said.

"Damn!" Peter said.

"I called the hospital just a moment ago," Pekach said. "We have two still on the critical list, one of ours and the wife. The other two, the husband and our guy, are 'stabilized' and apparently out of the woods."

The Highway Sergeant came in and handed first Wohl and then Mickey O'Hara a china mug of coffee.

"Nothing on the woman? Or the van? *Nothing?*" Wohl asked.

"All we have for a description is a dark van, either a Ford or a Chevy," Sabara said. "That's not much."

One of the two telephones on Wohl's desk buzzed. He looked at it to see which button was illuminated, punched it, and picked up the handset.

"Inspector Wohl," he said.

"Dennis Coughlin, Peter," Chief Coughlin said.

"Good morning, sir."

"You got anything?"

"Nothing on the van or the woman," Peter said. "Pekach just talked to the hospital. We have one civilian, the wife, and one police officer on the critical list. The husband and the other cop are apparently out of danger."

"Have you seen the paper? The *Ledger*, especially?"

"No, sir."

"You should have a look at it. You'll probably find it interesting," Coughlin said. "Keep me up to date, up to the moment, Peter."

"Yes, sir," Peter said.

He heard Coughlin hang the phone up.

"Has anybody seen the *Ledger*?" Peter asked.

Pekach picked up a folded newspaper from beside him on

the couch, walked across the room to Wohl's desk and laid it out for him.

There was a three-column headline, halfway down the front page, above a photograph of the wrecked cars.

**SPEEDING HIGHWAY PATROL CAR KILLS FOUR-YEAR-OLD**

Below the photograph was a lengthy caption:

> This Philadelphia Highway Patrol car, racing to the scene of a reported abduction, ran a red light on Second Street at Olney Ave. and smashed into the side of a 1970 Chevrolet sedan at 8:45 last night, killing Stephen P. McAvoy, Jr., aged four, of the 700 block of Garland Street, instantly. His father and mother, Stephen P., 29, and Mary Elizabeth McAvoy, 24, were taken to Albert Einstein Northern Division Hospital, where both are reported in critical condition. Both policemen in the police car were seriously injured.
>
> The tragedy occurred the day after Peter Wohl, a Police Department Staff Inspector, was given command of the Highway Patrol, in a move widely believed to be an attempt by Commissioner Taddeus Czernick to tame the Highway Patrol, which has been widely criticized in recent months.
>
> (More photos and the full story on page 10A. The tragedy is also the subject of today's editorial.)

Peter shook his head and looked around the office.

"We didn't run the stop light," David Pekach said. "The guy in the Ford ran it."

Peter met his eyes.

"Hawkins told me the light had just turned green as he approached Olney Avenue," Pekach said. "I believe him. He was too shook up to lie."

"He was driving?" Peter asked.

"Nobody's going to believe that," Mickey O'Hara said. "You guys better find a witness."

"I hope we're working on that," Wohl said.

"I've got guys ringing doorbells," Pekach said.

"How's the *Bulletin* handling this story, Mickey?" Wohl asked.

"It wasn't quite as bad as that," Mickey O'Hara said. "Cheryl Davies wrote the piece. But I'm here for a statement."

"We deeply regret the tragedy," Wohl said. "The incident is under investigation."

O'Hara shrugged. "Why did I suspect you would say something like that?" he said.

"It's the truth," Wohl said. "It's all I have to give you."

"What about the abducted female? The Northwest Philly rapist? On or *off* the record," O'Hara said.

Wohl's phone buzzed again, and he picked it up.

"Inspector Wohl," he said.

"Taddeus Czernick, Peter. How are you?"

"Good morning, Commissioner," Peter said.

Both Pekach and Sabara got up, as if to leave.

*Probably*, Peter thought, *because they figure if they leave, Mickey O'Hara will take the hint and leave with them.*

He waved them back into their seats.

"Fine, sir. How about yourself?"

"It looks as if we sent you over at just the right time," Czernick said. "You've seen the papers?"

"Yes, sir. I just finished reading the *Bulletin*."

"A terrible thing to have happened," Czernick said, "in more ways than one."

"Yes, sir, it is."

"Anything on the missing woman?"

"No, sir."

"Well, I have full confidence in your ability to handle whatever comes up; otherwise we wouldn't have sent you over there. But let me know if there's anything at all that I can do."

"Thank you, sir."

"The reason I'm calling, Peter—"

"Yes, sir?"

"Colonel J. Dunlop Mawson called me yesterday afternoon. You know who I mean?"

"Yes, sir."

"Under the circumstances, if you take my meaning, we can use all the friends we can get."

"Yes, sir."

"He has a client, a woman named Martha Peebles. Chestnut Hill. Very wealthy woman. Has been burglarized. Is *being* burglarized. She is not happy with the level of police service she's getting from the Fourteenth District and/or Northwest Detectives. She complained to Colonel Mawson, and he called me. Got the picture?"

"I'm not sure," Peter said.

"I think it would be a very good idea, Peter," Commissioner Czernick said, "if police officers from the Special Operations Division visited Miss Peebles and managed to convince her that the Police Department—strike that, *Special Operations*—is taking an avid interest in her problems, and is doing all that can be done to resolve them."

"Commissioner, right now, Special Operations is me and Mike Sabara and Sergeant Whatsisname—Frizell."

"I don't care how you do this, Peter," Czernick said, coldly. "Just do me a favor and do it."

"Yes, sir."

"I seem to recall that Denny Coughlin got me to authorize

the immediate transfer to you of forty volunteers. For openers."

"Yes, sir."

"Well then, you ought to have some manpower shortly," Czernick said.

"Yes, sir."

"Keep me informed about the abducted woman, Peter," Czernick said. "I have an unpleasant gut feeling about that."

"Yes, sir, of course."

"Tell your dad I said hello when you see him," Czernick said, and hung up.

Peter put the handset back in its cradle and turned to Mickey O'Hara.

"What can I do for you, Mickey?"

"Don't let the doorknob hit me in the ass?" O'Hara said.

"No. What I said was 'What can I do for you, Mickey?' When I throw you out, I won't be subtle. Is there something special, or do you just want to hang around?"

"I'm interested in the abducted woman," O'Hara said. "I figure when something breaks, this will be the place. So I'll just hang around, if that's okay with you."

"Fine with me," Wohl said. He turned to Mike Sabara. "Mike, get on the phone to the Captain of Northwest Detectives, and the Fourteenth District Commander. Tell them that Commissioner Czernick just ordered me to stroke a woman named Peebles, and that before I send a couple of our people out to see her, I'm going to send them by to look at the paperwork. She's—what the commissioner said was—*being* burglarized, and she's unhappy with the service she's been getting, and she has friends in high places."

"Who are you going to send over?"

"Officers Martinez and McFadden," Wohl said.

"Who are they?" Sabara asked, confused.

"Two of the three kids sitting on the folding chairs in the foyer," Wohl said. "I'm doing what I can with what I've got. Then, the next item on the priority list: We need people. I would like to have time to screen them carefully, but we don't have any time. A teletype went out yesterday, asking for volunteers. I don't know if there have been any responses yet, but find out. If there have not been any, or even, come to think of it, if there have—''

"McFadden and Martinez used to work undercover for me in Narcotics,'' Pekach said to Sabara. "They're the two that found Gerald Vincent Gallagher. They're here?"

"Chief Coughlin sent them over," Wohl said. "To Special Operations, David, not Highway."

"They're good cops. Not much experience in Chestnut Hill . . ." Pekach said.

"Like I said, I'm doing what I can with what I have," Wohl said. "As I was saying, Mike, get us some people. If you, or Dave, can think of anybody you can talk into volunteering, do it. Then call around, see if there have been volunteers. Check them out. Have them sent here today. Go to the Districts if that's necessary. The only thing: tell them that if they don't work out, they go back where they came from.''

"You want to talk to them?" Sabara asked. "Before we have them sent over here?"

"After you've picked them, I want to talk to them, sure," Wohl said. "But you know what we need, Mike."

Peter picked up his telephone and pushed one of the buttons. "Sergeant, would you ask Sergeant Frizell to come in here? And send in the three plainclothes officers waiting in the foyer?" There was a pause, then: "Yeah, all at once."

"Now, I'll be polite," Mickey O'Hara said. "Am I in the way?"

"Not at all," Peter said. "I'll let you know when you are, Mickey."

Sergeant Frizell, trailed by Officers McFadden, Martinez, and Payne, came into the office.

"What do we know about cars?" Wohl asked.

"For the time being," Frizell replied, "we have authority to draw cars, unmarked, from the lot at the Academy on the ratio of one car per three officers assigned."

"And then they'll have to be run by Radio, right, to get the proper radios?"

"Right."

"I want all our cars to have J-Band, Detective, Highway, and ours, whenever we get our own," Peter said.

"I'm not sure that's in the plan, Inspector," Frizell said.

"I don't give a damn about the plan," Peter said. "You call Radio and tell them to be prepared to start installing the radios. And call whoever has the car pool, and tell them we're going to start to draw cars today. Tell them we have fifty-eight officers assigned; in other words that we want twenty cars."

"But we don't have fifty-eight officers assigned. We don't have any."

"We have three at this moment," Wohl said. "And Captain Sabara is working hard on the others."

"Yes, sir," Sergeant Frizell said. "But, Inspector, I really don't think there will be fifteen unmarked cars available at the Academy."

"Then take blue-and-whites," Wohl said. "We can swap them for unmarked Highway cars, if we have to."

"Inspector," Frizell said, nervously, "I don't think you have the authority to do that."

"Do that right now, please, Sergeant," Wohl said, evenly, but aware that he was furious and on the edge of losing his temper.

*The last goddamned thing I need here is this Roundhouse paper pusher telling me I don't have the authority to do something.*

Frizell, sensing Wohl's disapproval, and visibly uncomfortable, left the room.

Wohl looked at the three young policemen.

"You fellows know each other, I guess?"

"Yes, sir," they chorused.

"Okay, this is what I want you to do." He threw car keys at Matt Payne, who was surprised by the gesture, but managed to snag them. "Take my car, and drive McFadden and

Martinez to the motor pool at the Police Academy. There, you two guys pick up two unmarked cars. Take one of them to the radio shop and leave it. You take my car to the radio shop, Payne, and stay with it until they put another radio in it. Then bring it back here. Then you take Captain Sabara's car and have them install the extra radios in it. Then you bring that back. Clear?''

"Yes, sir,'' Matt Payne said.

"You two bring the other car here. I've got a job I want you to do when you get here, and when you finish that, then you'll start shuttling cars between the motor pool and the radio garage and here. You understand what I want?''

"Yes, sir.''

*Getting cars, and radios for them, and handing out assignments to newly arrived replacements, is a Sergeant's job,* Wohl thought, *except when the man in charge doesn't really know what he's doing, in which case he is permitted to run in circles, wave and shout, making believe he does. That is known as a prerogative of command.*


Lieutenant Teddy Spanner of Northwest Detectives stood up when Peter Wohl walked into his office, and put out his hand.

"How are you, Inspector?'' he said. "I guess congratulations are in order.''

"I wonder,'' Wohl said, "but thanks anyway.''

"What can Northwest Detectives do for Special Operations?''

"I want a look at the files on the burglary—is it burglaries?—job on a woman named Peebles, in Chestnut Hill,'' Wohl said.

"Got them right here,'' Spanner said. "Captain Sabara said somebody was coming over. He didn't say it would be you.''

"The lady,'' Wohl said, "the Commissioner told me, has friends in high places.''

Spanner chuckled. "Not much there; it's just one more burglary."

"Did Mike say we were also interested in the Flannery sexual assault and abduction?"

"There it is," Spanner said, pointing to another manila folder.

Wohl sat down in the chair beside Spanner's desk and read the file on the Peebles burglary.

"Can I borrow this for a couple of hours?" Wohl asked. "I'll get it back to you today."

Spanner gave a deprecatory wave, meaning *Sure, no problem,* and Wohl reached for the Flannery file and read that through.

"Same thing," he said. "I'd like to take this for a couple of hours."

"Sure, again."

"What do you think about this?" Wohl said.

"I think we're dealing with a real sicko," Spanner said. "And I'll lay odds the doer is the same guy who put the woman in the van. Anything on that?"

"Not a damned thing," Wohl said. "Push me the phone, will you?"

He dialed a number from memory.

"This is Inspector Wohl," he said. "Would you have the Highway car nearest Northwest Detectives meet me there, please?"

He hung up and pushed the telephone back across the desk.

"I need a ride," he explained.

"Something wrong with your car? Hell, I'd have given you a ride, Inspector. You want to call and cancel that?"

"Thanks but no thanks," Wohl said.

"Well, then"—Spanner smiled—"how about a cup of coffee?"

"Thank you," Wohl said.

A Highway Patrol officer came marching through the Northwest Detectives squad room before Wohl had finished his coffee. Wohl left the unfinished coffee and followed him downstairs to the car.

"I need a ride to the Roundhouse," Wohl said, as he got in the front beside the driver. "You can drop me there."

"Yes, sir," the driver said.

They pulled out of the District parking lot and headed downtown on North Broad Street. Wohl noticed, as he looked around at the growing deterioration of the area, that the driver was scrupulously obeying the speed limit.

"If you were God," Wohl said to the driver, "or me, and you could do anything you wanted to, to catch the guy who's been assaulting the women in Northwest Philly—and I think we're talking about the same doer who forced the woman into the van last night—what would you do?"

The driver looked at him in surprise, and took his time before answering, somewhat uneasily. "Sir, I really don't know."

Wohl turned in his seat and looked at the Highway Patrol officer in the backseat. "What about you?"

The man in the backseat raised both hands in a gesture of helplessness.

"The way I hear, we're doing everything we know how."

"You think he's going to turn the woman loose?" Wohl asked.

"I dunno," the driver replied. "This is the first time he's . . . kept . . . one."

"If you think of something, anything," Wohl said, "don't keep it to yourself. Tell Captain Pekach, or Captain Sabara, or me."

"Yes, sir," the driver said.

"Something wrong with this unit?" Wohl asked.

"Sir?"

"Won't it go faster than thirty-five?"

The driver looked at him in confusion.

"Officer Hawkins says it was the civilian who ran the stop-light last night," Wohl said. "I believe him. We're looking for witnesses to confirm Hawkins's story."

The driver didn't react for a moment. Then he pushed harder on the accelerator and began to move swiftly through the North Broad Street traffic.

*With a little luck,* Wohl thought, *these guys will have a couple of beers with their pals when their tour is over, and with a little more luck, it will have spread through Highway by tomorrow morning that maybe Inspector Wohl ain't the complete prick people say he is; that he asked for advice; said he believed Hawkins; and even told the guy driving him to the Roundhouse to step on it.*

# ELEVEN

As they drove down Delaware Avenue Officer Charley McFadden pushed himself off the backseat of Staff Inspector Peter Wohl's car and rested his elbows on the backrest of the front seat.

"I never been in an Inspector's car before," he said, happily. "Nice."

"It certainly doesn't look like a police car, does it?" Matt Payne, who was driving, said.

McFadden looked at him curiously.

"It's not supposed to," Jesus Martinez said, and then put into words what was in his mind. "Where'd you come from, if you don't mind my asking?"

"The Academy," Matt said.

"You was teaching at the Academy?"

"I was going through the Academy," Matt said. "I was on the range yesterday when Chief Matdorf came out and told me to report to Highway in plainclothes this morning."

"I'll be goddamned," Charley McFadden said, and then

added, "we was in Narcotics. Hay-zus and me. We were partners, working undercover."

"For the last week, we were over in the Twelfth District, catching guys robbing stuff from parked cars," Jesus said. "I wonder what the hell this is all about?"

Both Matt Payne and Charley McFadden shrugged their shoulders.

"We're gonna find out, I guess."

"Where we're going is to that area behind the fence on the way to the Academy, right?" Matt asked.

"Yeah," Martinez said.

"I sure like your wheels," Charley said. "Porsche, huh?"

"Nine Eleven T," Matt said.

"What did something like that set you back?" Charley asked.

"Christ, Charley!" Martinez said. "You don't go around asking people how much things cost."

"I was just curious, Hay-zus, is all," Charley said. "No offense."

"I don't know what it cost," Matt said. "It was a present. When I graduated from college."

"*Nice* present!" Charley said.

"I thought so," Matt said. "What do you call him? Hay-zus?"

"That's his name," Charley said. "It's spick for Jesus."

"*Spanish*, you fucking Mick," Jesus Martinez said.

"I didn't get your name," Charley said, ignoring him.

"Matt Payne," Matt said.

Charley put his hand down over Matt's shoulder.

"Nice to meet you," Charley said as Matt shook it.

"Me, too," Jesus said, offering his hand.

They were able to draw two cars—both new Plymouths, one blue, and the other a dark maroon—from the Police Motor Pool without trouble, but when they got to the Police Radio Shop in the 800 block of South Delaware Avenue, things did not go at all smoothly.

It even began badly. The man in coveralls in the garage

examined all three cars carefully as they drove in, and then returned his attention to what he was doing, which was reading *Popular Electronics*.

He did not look up as, one after the other, Matt, Jesus, and Charley walked up to stand in front of his desk.

"Excuse me." Matt spoke first. "I have Inspector Wohl's car."

"Good for you," the man said without looking up.

"You're supposed to install some communications equipment in it," Matt said.

"I ain't seen nothing on it," the man said. "You got the paperwork?"

"No," Matt said. "I'm afraid I wasn't given any."

"Well, then," the man said, returning to *Popular Electronics*.

"My instructions are to wait while the work is done," Matt said.

"And my instructions are no paperwork, no work," the man said. "And we don't do work while people wait. Who the hell do you guys think you are, anyway?"

"We're from Special Operations," Matt said.

"La dee da," the man said.

"Well, I'm sorry you fell out of bed on the wrong side," Matt said, "but that doesn't help me with my problem. Where can I find your supervisor?"

"I'm in charge here," the man flared.

"Good, then you pick up the telephone and call Inspector Wohl and tell him what you told me."

"What are you, some kind of a wiseass?"

Matt didn't reply.

"You can leave the car here, and when the paperwork catches up with it, we'll see what we can do," the man said.

"May I use your telephone, please?" Matt asked.

"What for?"

"So I can call Inspector Wohl, and tell him that not only are you refusing to do the work, but refusing, as well, to telephone him to say so."

The man gave him a dirty look, then reached for the telephone. He dialed a number.

"Sergeant, I got a hotshot here, says he's from Special Operations, without a sheet of paperwork, and demanding we do something—I don't know what—to three unmarked cars."

There was a reply, unintelligible, and then the man handed Matt the telephone.

"This is Sergeant Francis," the voice said. "What can I do for you?"

"My name is Payne. I'm assigned to Special Operations, and there has apparently been a breakdown in communications somewhere," Matt said. "I'm here with three unmarked cars, one of them Inspector Wohl's. Somebody was to have telephoned down here to arrange all this."

"I don't know anything about it," Sergeant Francis said. "Why don't you go back where you came from and ask somebody?"

"No, Sergeant," Matt said. "What I would like to do is speak to your commanding officer. Can you give me his number, please?"

"I'll do better than that," Sergeant Francis said. And then, faintly, Matt heard, "Lieutenant, you want to take this?"

"Lieutenant Warner."

"Sir, this is Officer Payne, of Special Operations. I'm at the radio shop. I was told to bring Inspector Wohl's car here to have—"

"Christ, you're there already?"

"Yes, sir. With Inspector Wohl's car, and two others."

"I thought when your Sergeant called, he was talking about tomorrow, at the earliest."

"We're here now, sir. Inspector Wohl sent us."

"So you said. Is there a man named Ernie around there, somewhere?"

Matt looked at the man at the desk.

"Is there somebody named Ernie here?" he asked.

"I'm Ernie."

"Yes, sir, there is," Matt said.

"Let me speak to him," Lieutenant Warner said.

Matt handed him the telephone.

Ernie, to judge by the look on his face, did not like what he was being told.

"Yes, sir, I'll get right on it," Ernie said, finally, and hung up. He looked at Matt. "Four bands in every car? What the fuck is this Special Operations, anyway?"

"We're sort of a super Highway Patrol," Matt said, with a straight face.

"Well, what do you think of him?" Charley McFadden asked as Jesus Martinez turned the unmarked Plymouth onto Harbison Avenue and headed north, toward Highway Patrol headquarters.

"I think he's a rich wiseass," Jesus said.

"Meaning you don't like him? I sort of like him."

"Meaning he's a rich wiseass," Jesus said. "Either that or he's a gink."

"Well, he got that shit-for-brains working on the radios, didn't he? I thought he handled that pretty well."

Jesus grunted. "That's what makes me think he may be a gink. He didn't act like a rookie in there. He as much as told that sergeant on the phone to go fuck himself. Rookies don't do that."

"Why would Internal Affairs send a gink in? Christ, they just formed Special Operations today. Internal Affairs sends somebody in undercover when they hear something is dirty. There hasn't been time for anything dirty to happen."

"He could be watching Highway."

"I think you're full of shit," Charley said, after a moment's reflection. "Whatever he is, he's no gink."

"So, you tell me: what is a rich guy who went to college doing in the Police Department?"

"Maybe he wants to be a cop," Charley said.

"Why? Ask yourself that, Charley."

"I dunno," Charley replied. "Why do you want to be a cop?"

"Because, so far as I'm concerned, it's a good job where I can make something of myself. But I didn't go to college, and nobody gave me a Porsche."

"Well, fuck it. I sort of like him. I liked the way he told that shit-for-brains where to head in."

When they got to Highway, the corporal told them that Captain Sabara wanted to see them. There were a lot of people in the outer office, and they both figured they were in for a long wait. Jesus settled himself in as comfortably as he could, and Charley went looking for the Coke and garbage machines.

He had just returned with a ham and cheese on rye and a pint of chocolate drink when the door to the Commanding Officer's office opened, and a middle-aged cop with a white-topped Traffic Bureau cap in his hand came out.

"Is there somebody named McFadden out here?"

Charley couldn't reply, for his mouth was full of ham and cheese, but he waved his hand, with the rest of the sandwich in it, over his head, and caught the traffic cop's attention.

"Captain Sabara wants to see you," the traffic cop said. "You and Gonzales, I think he said."

"*Martinez?*" Jesus asked, bitterly.

"Yeah, I think so."

Charley laid the sandwich on the chair next to Jesus, and, chewing furiously, followed him into the office.

"You wanted to see us, sir?" Jesus asked, politely.

"Yeah," Sabara said. "You got the cars all right?"

"Yes, sir, we left the blue-and-white at Radio," Jesus said.

"This is bullshit," Sabara said. "But from time to time, like when the Commissioner says to, we do bullshit. There have been a couple of minor burglaries in Chestnut Hill. A lady named Peebles. She's rich, and she has friends. And she doesn't think that she's been getting the service she deserves from the Police Department. She talked to one of her friends and he talked to the Commissioner, and the Commissioner called Inspector Wohl. Getting the picture?''

"Yes, sir," Jesus said.

Charley McFadden made one final, valiant swallow of the ham and cheese and chimed in, a moment later, "Yes, sir."

"Here's the file. Inspector Wohl borrowed it from Northwest Detectives. Read it. Then go see the lady. Charm her. Make her believe that we, and by we I mean Special Operations especially, but the whole Department, too, are sympathetic, and are going to do everything we can to catch the burglar, and protect her and her property. Getting all this?''

"Yes, sir," they chorused.

"On the way back, return the file to Northwest Detectives," Sabara said, "and be prepared to tell me, and Inspector Wohl, what you said to her, and how she reacted."

"Yes, sir."

"Okay, go do it," Sabara said, and they said "yes, sir" again and turned to leave. Jesus was halfway through the door when Sabara called out, "Hey!"

They stopped and turned to look at him.

"I know what a good job you guys did getting the doer in the Captain Moffitt shooting," Sabara said. "And Captain Pekach told me you did a good job for him in Narcotics before that. But you got to understand that Chestnut Hill isn't the street, and you have to treat people like this Miss Peebles gentle. It's bullshit, but it's important bullshit. So be real concerned and polite, okay?''

"Yes, sir," they chorused.

Peter Wohl had to show the officer on duty his identification before he was permitted to go through the locked door into the lobby of the Roundhouse. That made the score fourteen-six.

He got on the elevator and went to the Homicide Bureau on the second floor. When he pushed open the door to the main room, he saw that Captain Henry C. Quaire was in his small, glass-walled office.

The door was closed, and Quaire, a stocky muscular man in his early forties, was on the telephone, but when he saw Wohl he gestured for him to come in.

"I'll be in touch," he said after a moment, and then hung up the telephone. Then he half got out of his chair and offered his hand.

"Congratulations on your new command," Quaire said.

"Thank you, Henry," Wohl said.

"I don't know what the hell it is," Quaire said, "but it sounds impressive."

"That sums it up very neatly," Wohl said. "I'm already in trouble, and I just got there."

"I heard about the little boy," Quaire said. "That's a bitch."

"The civilian ran the red light, not our guy," Peter said.

"I hope you can prove that," Quaire said.

"That's what Mickey O'Hara said," Wohl said. "I've got people looking for witnesses. I really hope they can turn some up. But that's not why I'm here, Henry."

"Why do I think I'm not going to like what's coming next?" Quaire asked, dryly.

"Because you won't," Wohl said. "I want two of your people, Henry."

"Which two?"

"Washington and Harris," Wohl said.

"Can I say no, politely or otherwise?"

"I don't think so," Wohl said. "Chief Coughlin said I can have anybody I want. I'm going to hold him to it."

"Can I ask why, then?" Quaire said, after a moment.

Wohl laid the file he had borrowed from Lieutenant Teddy Spanner of Northwest Detectives on Captain Quaire's desk.

"That's what Northwest Detectives has on the Northwest Philly rapist," he said.

"They found the woman he forced into the van?"

"No. Not yet."

"I'll say the obvious, Inspector," Quaire said, tapping the folder with his fingertips but not opening it. "Rape, sexual assault, is none of Homicide's business. What are you showing this to me for?''

"The Northwest Philadelphia rapist is now my business, Henry,'' Wohl said.

"Okay. But still, why are you showing this to me?"

"I don't think we're going to find that woman alive,'' Wohl said.

"Then it will be my business,'' Quaire said. "But not until.''

"No. It will still be my business,'' Wohl said.

Quaire's eyebrows rose.

"Not that it's any of my business, but how did that sit with Chief Lowenstein when he heard that? Or has he?''

Chief Inspector Matt Lowenstein, under whom Homicide operated, was notoriously unsympathetic to what he considered invasions of his territory.

"I devoutly hope he knows it wasn't my idea,'' Wohl said. "But he's been told.''

"What are you asking for, Inspector?'' Quaire asked. "That if this abduction turns into homicide, that I assign Washington and Harris? Frankly, I don't like being told how to run my shop.''

"No, I want them transferred to Special Operations, now,'' Peter said.

Quaire considered that for a moment.

"I was about to say no,'' he said, finally, "but you've already told me I can't, haven't you?''

"Why don't you call Lowenstein?'' Wohl said.

"I believe you, Peter, for Christ's sake,'' Quaire said.

"Thank you,'' Wohl said. "But maybe Lowenstein would like to think he's not the only one pissed off about this.''

Quaire looked at him a moment, and then grunted.

He dialed a number from memory and told Chief Inspector Lowenstein that Staff Inspector Wohl was in his office, saying he wanted Detectives Washington and Harris transferred to Special Operations.

The reply was brief, and then Captain Quaire put the handset back in its cradle without saying good-bye.

"That was quick," Peter said with a smile. "What did he say?"

"You don't want to know," Quaire said.

"Yeah, I do."

"Okay," Quaire said, with a strange smile. " 'Give the little bastard whatever he wants, and tell him I said I hope he hangs himself.' End quote."

"That's all? He must be in a very good mood today," Wohl said, smiling. *But it's not funny. Lowenstein is, understandably, angry, and if he thinks I'm abusing the authority Czernick and Coughlin gave me, I'll pay for it. Maybe tomorrow, maybe next year, but sometime.*

"So when would you like Detectives Washington and Harris?" Quaire asked.

"Now."

"You mean today?" Quaire asked, incredulously.

"Yeah, and if they could keep their cars for a couple of days, until I can get cars for them, I'd appreciate it."

Quaire thought that over for a moment.

"Inspector, I'm short of cars. If you *tell* me to let them keep their cars, I will, but—"

"Okay. I'll work something out with the cars," Wohl said. "But I want them today."

"They're working the streets," Quaire said. "I'll get word to them to come in here. And then I'll send them out to you. Where are you, in Highway?"

"Yeah. Henry, there is a chance we can do something before that woman is . . . before the abduction turns into a homicide. That's why I need them now."

"What you're saying is that you don't like the way Northwest Detectives are handling the job," Quaire said.

Now it was Wohl's turn to consider his reply.

"I hadn't thought about it quite that way, Henry. But yeah, I guess I am. The Northwest Philly rapist is out there somewhere; Northwest Detectives doesn't seem to have been able to catch him. Look at the file—nothing.''

Quaire pushed the file across the desk to Wohl.

''I don't want to look at that file, Inspector,'' he said. ''It's none of my business.''

Wohl bit off the angry reply that popped into his mind before it reached his mouth. He picked up the file and stood up.

''Thank you, Captain,'' he said.

''Yes, sir,'' Captain Quaire said.

In the elevator on the way down to the lobby, Peter's stomach growled, and then there was actually pain.

*I didn't have any breakfast, that's what it is.*

And then he realized that his having skipped breakfast because he didn't want to be late his first morning on his new command had nothing to do with it.

He thought of a sandwich shop not far from the Roundhouse where he could get an egg sandwich or something and a half pint of milk. But when he walked out of the rear door of the Roundhouse, he saw a Highway Patrol car coming out of the Central Lockup ramp.

He trotted over to it, tapped on the closed window, and told the surprised driver to take him to Highway.

As Peter got out of the Highway car, out of the corner of his eye he saw another unmarked car, Sabara's, pull into the parking lot. The driver was Matt Payne. He looked around the parking lot and saw that his car, now wearing another shortwave antenna, was in the parking spot marked INSPEC-TOR.

He waited until Payne found a spot to park Sabara's car and then walked to the building.

''Payne!''

Payne looked around and saw him, and walked over.

''Yes, sir?''

''You got radios in the cars?''

''Yes, sir.''

"That was quick," Wohl thought aloud.

"Well, there really wasn't much to it," Payne said. "Just screw the mounting to the transmission tunnel, install the antenna, and make a couple of connections."

"Come on in the office," Wohl said. "I want to talk to you."

"Yes, sir," Payne said.

Wohl had a quick mental picture of himself having a short chat in his office, to feel the boy out, to get a better picture of him to see what he could do with him.

As soon as he got in the building, he saw that would be impossible. All the folding chairs were occupied. Some of the occupants were in uniform, and he didn't have to be Sherlock Holmes to decide that the ones in plainclothes were policemen, too.

Sabara had gotten right to work, he decided. These people appeared to be looking for a job.

Sergeant Frizell immediately confirmed this: "Captain Sabara is interviewing applicants in there, sir," he said.

"Wait here a minute, Payne," Wohl said.

"Inspector," Payne said, as Wohl put his hand on the office doorknob, and Wohl looked at him. "Captain Sabara's keys, sir," Payne said, handing them to him.

"Thank you," Wohl said. He took the keys and went inside.

Sabara was behind the desk, with a personnel folder spread out before him. A uniformed cop sat nervously on the edge of a straight-backed chair facing the desk. Sabara started to get up, and Wohl waved him back.

There was something about the uniformed cop Wohl instinctively disliked. He had a weak face, Wohl decided. He wondered how he knew. Or if he knew.

"This is Inspector Wohl," Sabara said, and the cop jumped to his feet and put out his hand.

"How do you do, sir?" the cop said.

Confident that the cop couldn't see him, Sabara made a wry face, and then shook his head, confirming Wohl's own snap judgment that this cop was something less than they desired.

*Why am I surprised? When there is a call for volunteers, ninety percent of the applicants are sure to be people unhappy with their present assignment, and, as a general rule of thumb people are unhappy with their jobs because they are either lazy or can't cut the mustard.*

"Here's your keys, Mike," Wohl said.

"So quick?" Sabara asked.

Before Wohl could reply, one of the phones rang and Sabara picked it up.

"Yes?" he said, and listened briefly, and then covered the receiver with his hand. "Detective Washington for you, sir."

Wohl took the telephone.

"Hello, Jason," he said.

"Sir, I'm ordered to report to you," Washington said, his tone of voice making it quite clear what he thought of his orders.

"Where are you, Jason?" Wohl asked.

"At the Roundhouse, sir."

"You need a ride?"

"Sir, I called to ask if you wanted me to drive my car out there."

"Wait around the rear entrance, Jason," Wohl said. "I'll have someone pick you up in the next few minutes."

"Yes, sir," Washington said.

"Is Tony Harris there, too?"

"No, sir," Washington said, and then blurted, "Him, too?"

"I'm trying to get the best people I can, Jason," Wohl said.

"Yes, sir," Washington said, dryly, making it quite clear that he was not in a mood to be charmed.

"I'll have someone pick you up in a couple of minutes, Jason," Wohl said, and hung up.

He looked at Mike Sabara. "Detectives Washington and Harris will be joining us, Captain," he said. "That was

Washington. I'm going to have someone pick him up and bring him here.''

"You want me to take care of that, Inspector?" Sabara asked.

"I can do it," Wohl said, and smiled at the cop. "Nice to have met you," he said. *I hope he doesn't take that guy.*

Matt Payne was leaning on the concrete-block wall of the outside room when Wohl returned to it. When Payne saw him, he pushed himself off the wall.

"Payne, take my car again—" Wohl began and then stopped.

"Yes, sir?"

"How long did it take you to get a car out of the motor pool?"

"Just a couple of minutes," Payne said. "They have a form; you have to inspect the car for damage and then sign for it."

"Okay, let's go get another one," Wohl said, making up his mind.

As they walked to the car, Payne asked, "Would you like me to drive, sir?"

Wohl considered the question.

*I liked my first ride downtown; it gave me a chance to look around. All I usually see is the stoplight of the car ahead of me.*

"Please," he said, and handed Payne the keys.

Three blocks away, Payne looked over at Wohl and said, "I don't know the ground rules, sir. Am I expected to keep the speed limit?"

"Christ," Wohl replied, annoyed, and then looked at Payne. *It was an honest question, he decided, and deserves an honest answer.*

"If you mean, can you drive like the hammers of hell, no. But on the other hand . . . use your judgment, Payne." And then he added, "That's all police work really is, Payne, the exercise of good judgment."

"Yes, sir," Payne said.

*Well, didn't you sound like Socrates, Jr., Peter Wohl?*

But then he plunged on: "It's not like you might think it is. Brilliant detective work and flashing lights. Right now every cop in Philadelphia, and in the area, is looking for a woman that some lunatic with sexual problems forced into the back of his van at the point of a knife. Since we don't have a good description of the van, or the tag number—and, even if we had the manpower, and we don't—we can't stop every van and look inside. That's unlawful search. So we're just waiting for something to happen. I don't like to consider what I think will happen."

"My sister says rapists are more interested in dominating their victims, rather than in sexual gratification," Payne said.

"Your sister, no doubt," Wohl said, sarcastically, "is an expert on rape and rapists?"

"She's a psychiatrist," Payne said. "I don't know how much of an expert she is. As opposed to how much of an expert she thinks she is."

Wohl chuckled. "Well, maybe I should talk to her. I need all the help I can get."

"She'd love that," Payne said. "She would thereafter be insufferably smug, having been consulted by the cops, but if you mean it, I could easily set it up."

"Let's put it on the back burner," Wohl said. "What we're going to do now . . . Chief Coughlin gave me the authority to pick anybody I want for Special Operations. I just stole two of the best detectives from Homicide, which has grievously annoyed the head of Homicide, Chief Lowenstein, and at least one of the two detectives. I haven't talked to the other one yet. Anyway, after we pick up the car, we're going to go to the Roundhouse and pick up a detective named Jason Washington, Jr. I think he's the best detective in Homicide. The car we're going to pick up is for him. I want him to interview all the previous victims. He's damned good at that. Maybe he can get something out of them the other guys missed. Maybe we can find the rapist that way. And maybe Jason Washington would like to talk to your sister."

Payne didn't reply.

Thirty-five minutes later, Matt Payne, at the wheel of a light green Ford LTD, followed Peter Wohl's light tan LTD into the parking area behind the Roundhouse. Wohl pulled to the curb by the rear entrance and got out.

"Stay in the car," he said. "I'll be right out."

He went inside the building, waited in line behind the civilian who was talking to the Corporal behind the shatter-proof glass, and then showed his identification.

"Oh, hell, Inspector," the Corporal said, "I know you."

"Thank you," Peter said.

*That makes it fourteen-seven,* Peter thought.

When the solenoid buzzed, he pushed the door open and entered the lobby.

Two men sitting on chairs stood up. One of them was very large, heavy, and dressed very well, looking more like a successful businessman than a cop.

*Or a colored undertaker,* Peter thought, wondering if that made him racist; and then decided it didn't. Jason Washington was more than colored, he was jet black; and in his expensive, well-tailored suit, he looked like an undertaker.

The other man was white, slight, and looked tired and worn. His clothes were mussed and looked as if they had come, a long time ago, from the bargain basement at Sears. His name was Anthony C. "Tony" Harris, and he was, in Wohl's judgment, the second sharpest detective in Homicide.

Neither smiled when Wohl walked over to them.

"Sorry to keep you waiting," Wohl said. "I stopped by to get you a car."

"Inspector," Tony Harris said, "before this goes too far can we talk about it?"

"Have either of you had lunch?" Peter asked.

Both shook their heads no.

"Neither have I," Peter said. "So, yes, Tony, we can talk about it, over lunch. I'll even buy."

"I'd appreciate that, Inspector," Tony Harris said.

"Where would you like to eat? The Melrose Diner okay?"

There was no response from either of them.

"Jason, I'm not sure the kid driving your car knows where the Melrose is," Wohl said. "You want to ride with him and show him? I'll take Tony with me."

"Where's the car?" Jason Washington asked. It was the first time he had opened his mouth.

"Behind mine," Wohl said, "at the curb."

Washington marched out of the lobby.

*He's really pissed,* Peter thought, and wondered again if he was doing the right thing. And then he felt a wave of anger. *Fuck him! He's a cop. Cops do what they're told. Nobody asked me if I wanted this goddamned job, either!*

"Tony," Wohl said, "aside from telling you that you can make as much overtime in Special Operations as you've been making in Homicide, what we're going to talk about at lunch is how I want you to do this job, not whether or not you like it."

Tony Harris met his eyes, looked as if he was going to reply, but didn't; then he walked toward the door from the lobby.

# TWELVE

Officer Matt Payne had more than a little difficulty complying with Staff Inspector Peter Wohl's order to "Call the office, Payne; tell them where we are. And you better ask if anything's new about the abduction."

It was, he thought, as he fished the thick Philadelphia telephone book from under the pay phone in the foyer of the Melrose Diner, the first time he had ever called the Police Department.

And the phone book was not much help.

The major listing under POLICE was the POLICE ATHLETIC LEAGUE. A dozen addresses and numbers were furnished, none of which had anything to do with what he wanted.

Under POLICE DEPARTMENT were listings to

|  |  |
|---|---|
| STOP A CRIME | 911 |
| OR SAVE A LIFE | 911 |

neither of which were what he was looking for.

A little farther down the listing was

| FOR OTHER POLICE HELP | 231-3131 |
| ADMIN OFCS 7&RACE | 686-1776 |
| POLICE ACADEMY | 686-1776 |

Matt tried the OTHER POLICE HELP number first.

"Police Emergency," a male voice responded on the fifth ring. "May I help you?"

"Sorry," Matt said, "wrong number," and hung up. He chuckled and said, "Shit," and put his finger back on the listing. By ADMIN OFCS 7&RACE they obviously meant the Roundhouse. But the number listed was the same as the one listed for the POLICE ACADEMY, which was to hell and gone the other side of town.

He put another dime in the slot and dialed 686-1776.

"City of Philadelphia," a bored female replied on the ninth ring.

"May I speak to the Special Operations Division of the Police Department, please."

"What?"

"Special Operations, please, in the Police Department."

"One moment, please," the woman replied, and Matt exhaled in relief.

But there was no ringing sound, and after a long pause, the woman came back on the line. "I have no such listing, sir," she said, and the line went dead.

He fumbled through his change for another dime and couldn't find one. But he had a quarter and dropped it in the slot and dialed 686-1776 again.

"City of Philadelphia," another bored female answered on the eleventh ring.

"Highway Patrol Headquarters, please," Matt said.

"Is this an emergency, sir?"

"No, it's not."

"One moment, please."

Now the phone returned a busy signal.

"That number is busy," the operator said. "Would you care to hold?"

"Please."

"What?"

"I'll hold."

"Thank you, sir," she said, and the line went dead.

He dropped his last quarter in the slot, dialed 686-1776 again, and asked a third woman with a bored voice for Highway Patrol.

"Special Operations, Sergeant Frizell."

"This is Officer Payne, Sergeant," Matt said. That was, he thought, the first time he had ever referred to himself as "Officer Payne." It had, he thought, a rather nice ring to it.

"You a volunteer, Payne?"

"Excuse me?"

"I said, are you a volunteer?"

"No, I'm not," Matt said.

"Well, what can I do for you?"

"Inspector Wohl told me to check in," Matt said. "We're at the Melrose Diner."

"Oh, you're his driver. Sorry, I didn't catch the name."

"The number here is 670-5656," Matt said.

"Got it. He say when he's coming in?"

"No. But he said to ask if anything has happened with the abducted woman."

"Not a peep."

"Thank you," Matt said. "Good-bye."

"What?"

"I said good-bye."

"Yeah," Sergeant Frizell said, and the line went dead.

When he went into the dining room of the Melrose Diner, he looked around until he spotted them. They were in a corner banquette, and a waitress was delivering drinks.

"Anything?" Inspector Wohl asked him.

"No, sir."

"Damn," Wohl said. "What are you drinking?"

Drinking on duty, Matt saw, was not the absolute no-no he had been led to believe, from watching *Dragnet* and the other cop shows on television. Both Wohl and Washington had small glasses dark with whiskey in front of them, obviously something-on-the-rocks, and Harris had a taller glass of clear liquid with a slice of lime on the rim, probably a vodka tonic.

"Have you any ale?" Matt asked the waitress.

She recited a litany of the available beers and ales and Matt picked one.

"You going to eat, too?" the waitress asked. "I already got their orders."

Matt took a menu, glanced at it quickly, and ordered a shrimp salad.

From the look—mixed curiosity and mild contempt—he got from Detective Washington, Matt surmised that both the ale and the shrimp salad had been the wrong things to order.

When the waitress left, Peter Wohl picked up his glass, and with mock solemnity said, "I would like to take this happy occasion to welcome you aboard, men."

"Shit," Jason Washington said, unsmiling.

"Jason, I need you," Wohl said, seriously.

"Oh, I know why you did it," Washington said. "But that doesn't mean I agree that it was necessary, or that I have to like it."

Wohl looked as if he had started to say something and then changed his mind.

"I told Tony in the Roundhouse lobby, Jason, that if it's overtime you're worried about, you can have as much as you want."

"I should have drowned you when you were a sergeant in Homicide," Washington said, matter-of-factly. "Inspector, you know what Homicide is."

"Yeah, and I know you two guys are the best detectives in Homicide. *Were* the best two."

"When he's through shoveling the horseshit, Tony," Washington said, "hand the shovel to me. It's already up to my waist, and I don't want to suffocate."

Harris grunted.

"What you're doing, Inspector, is covering your ass, and using Tony and me to do it."

"Guilty, okay?" Wohl said. "Now can we get at it?"

"Now that the air, so to speak, is clear between us," Washington said, "why not?"

"Special Operations has the Northwest Philadelphia rapist job," Wohl said. "That came from the Commissioner, and I think he was following orders."

Jason Washington's eyebrows rose.

"This is the file," Wohl said. "I borrowed it from Northwest Detectives."

They were interrupted by the waitress, who set a bottle of ale and a glass in front of Matt, and then a shrimp cocktail in front of each of the others.

"I want it handled like a homicide," Wohl said.

"It's not a homicide," Washington said. "Yet. Or is it?"

"Not yet," Wohl said.

Tony Harris, who had been sitting slumped back in his chair, now leaned forward and pulled the manila folder from under Wohl's hand. He laid it beside his plate, then picked up his seafood fork. He stabbed a shrimp, dipped it in the cocktail sauce, put it in his mouth, and started to read the file.

"Who had the job at Northwest Detectives?" Jason Washington asked.

"As they came up on the wheel," Wohl said. "But, starting with the Flannery job—"

"That's the one that's missing?" Washington interrupted.

"The one before that. The one he turned loose naked with her hands tied behind her in Fairmount Park."

Washington nodded his understanding, put a shrimp in his mouth, and waited for Wohl to continue.

"Dick Hemmings got the Flannery job on the wheel," Wohl said. "Then Teddy Spanner gave him the whole job. When it became pretty certain what it was, one doer."

"Dick Hemmings is a good cop," Washington said. "What do you think we can do he hasn't already done?"

Then he raised his whiskey glass, which Matt saw was now empty, over his head. When he had caught the waitress's eye, he raised his other hand and made a circular motion, ordering another round.

Matt took another sip of his ale. He was doing his best to follow the conversation, which he found fascinating. He wondered what "the wheel" they were talking about was, but decided it would not to be wise to ask. Washington had already made it plain he held him in contempt; a further proof of ignorance would only make things worse.

"The one thing we need is a—two things. We need first a good description of the doer. Since we don't have a description, we need a profile. I've been thinking of talking to a psychiatrist—"

"Save your time," Tony Harris said. "I can tell you what a shrink will tell you. We're dealing with a sicko here. He gets his rocks off humiliating women. He hates his mother. Maybe he was screwing his mother, or she kept bringing guys home and taking them to bed. Something. Anyway, he hates her, and is getting back at her by hitting on these women. No hookers, you notice. Nice little middle-class women. That's what you'd get from a shrink."

He closed the file and handed it across the table to Washington.

"Jason's very good with people," Wohl said. "I thought it would be a good idea if he reinterviewed all the victims."

If Jason Washington heard Wohl, there was no sign. He was very carefully reading the file.

"I'll lay you ten to one that when we finally catch this scumbag," Tony Harris said, "it will come out that he's been going to one of your shrinks, Inspector, and that one of *those* scumbags has been reading the papers and knows fucking well his seventy-five-dollar-an-hour patient is the guy who's been doing this. But he won't call us. Physician-patient confidentiality is fucking sacred. Particularly when the patient is coughing up seventy-five bucks an hour two, three times a week."

"I don't know how far Hemmings, or anybody, has checked out sexual offenders," Wohl said.

"I'll start there," Harris said. "These fuckers don't just start out big. Somewhere there's a record on him. Even if it's for something like soliciting for prostitution."

He said this as the waitress delivered the fresh round of drinks. She gave him a very strange look.

"I'm going to be in court most of this week and next," Washington said, without looking up from the file any longer than it took to locate the fresh drink.

"I figured that would probably be the case," Wohl said. "So why don't you work the four-to-midnight shift? It is my professional judgment that the people you will be interviewing will be more readily available in the evening hours."

Washington snorted, but there was a hint of a smile at his eyes and on his lips. He knew the reason Wohl had assigned him to the four-to-twelve shift had nothing to do with more readily available witnesses. It would make all the time he spent in court during the day overtime.

"I'm going to be in court a lot, too," Tony Harris said. "That apply to me, too?"

"Since it is also my professional judgment that you can do whatever you plan to do during the evening hours better than during the day, sure," Wohl said.

Peter Wohl had been in Homicide and knew that, because of the overtime pay, Homicide detectives were the best paid officers in the Police Department. There was no question in his mind that Washington and Harris were taking home as much money as a Chief Inspector. That was the major, but not the only, reason they were unhappy with their transfer to Special Operations; they thought it was going to cut their pay.

It posed, he realized, what Sergeant Frizell would term a "personnel motivation problem" for him: if they didn't want to work for him, they didn't have to. About the only weapon he had as a supervisor short of official disciplinary action—and both Washington and Harris were too smart to make themselves vulnerable to something like that—was to send his men back where they had come from. Which would not make either Washington or Harris at all unhappy.

He had a somewhat immodest thought: *if they didn't like me, to the point where they are willing to give me and Special Operations a chance, they would already have come up with twenty reasons to get themselves fired.*

"Is the Flannery woman still in the hospital?" Washington asked.

"I don't know," Wohl said.

"She saw more of this guy than any of the others," Washington said, closing the file. "Can I have this?"

"No," Wohl said. "But I'll get you both a copy. Payne, when we get back to the office, Xerox this in four copies."

"Yes, sir."

"Ah," Washington said, looking around the room. "Here comes my lunch!"

The waitress delivered two New York Strip steaks, a filet mignon (to Washington) and a shrimp salad.

*If I had ordered a steak,* Matt thought, *they would have ordered bacon, lettuce, and tomato sandwiches.*

Nobody spoke another word until Washington laid his knife and fork on the plate, and delicately dabbed at his mouth with his napkin.

"We work for you, right?" he asked. "I don't have to check with Sabara every time I sharpen a pencil?"

"Mike is the Deputy Commander," Wohl said.

"We work for you, right?" Washington repeated.

"Mike is the Deputy Commander," Wohl repeated, "but I will tell him that the only job you two have is the Northwest Philly rapist. What have you got against Sabara?"

"He's a worrier," Washington said. "Worriers make me nervous."

Wohl chuckled.

Washington looked at Matt Payne. "You open to a little advice, son?"

"Yes, sir," Payne said.

" 'Yes, sir,' " Harris quoted mockingly.

"That's a very nice jacket," Washington said, giving Harris a dirty look, and then turning his face to Matt. "Tripler?"

"Yes," Matt said, surprised. "As a matter of fact it is."

"If you're going to wear a shoulder holster, you have to have them make allowance for it," Washington said. "Cut it a little fuller under the left arm. What you look like now, with the material stretched that way, is a man carrying a pistol in a shoulder holster."

Matt, smiling uneasily, looked at Inspector Wohl, whom he found grinning at him.

"Listen to him, Payne," Wohl said. "He's the recognized sartorial authority in the Police Department."

"The whole idea of plainclothes is to look like anything but a cop," Washington said. "What you really should do, in the summer, is get a snub-nose and carry it in an ankle holster. Very few people look at your ankles to see if you're carrying a gun, and even if they do, unless you wear peg-leg trousers like Harris here, they're pretty much out of sight on your ankles."

Wohl laughed.

Washington stood up and put out his hand to Wohl.

"Thank you for the lunch," he said. "I'll check in if I come up with anything."

"My pleasure," Wohl said. "Jason, what you have for radios in the car is J-Band and I don't know what else. It's arranged with Radio to give you Detectives and Highway, too. I mean, if you take the car there, they're set up to do the work right away. Tony, you paying attention?"

"When do I get a car?" Harris asked.

"As soon as Jason drives you over to get one."

Harris grunted.

"Sabara's not going to worry if I take the car home with me at night, is he?" Washington asked.

"No, he's not," Wohl said. "You stop worrying. You're going to be the star of our little operation."

"Here comes the horse manure again," Washington said, and walked out of the room.

"Nice to meet you, Payne," Harris said, offering him his hand. "See you around."

When they had left the restaurant, Wohl held up his coffee cup to catch the waitress's attention, and when she had refilled his cup from a stainless steel pot, he turned to Matt.

"Now we get to you, Officer Payne," he said.

"Sir?"

"It is generally accepted as a fact of life in the Police Department that before you do anything else with a rookie, you give him a couple of years in a District. In the case of someone your size, you assign him to a wagon. You know what a wagon is?"

"Yes, sir, a paddy wagon."

"Be careful where you say that," Wohl said. "To some of our brother officers of Irish extraction, paddy wagon is a pejorative term, dating back to the days when Irishmen were known as 'Paddys' and were hauled off to jail in a horse-drawn vehicle known as the 'Paddy Wagon.' "

"Sir, I'm half-Irish."

"Half doesn't count. It's not like being a little pregnant. My mother's Catholic. But neither you nor I are products of the parochial school system, or alumni of Roman or Father Judge or North Catholic High. Neither are we Roman Catholics. Half-Irish or ex–Roman Catholic doesn't count."

"Yes, sir," Matt said, smiling. "I'll say 'wagon.' "

"As I was saying, broad-backed young rookies like yourself generally begin their careers in a District with a couple of years in a wagon. That gives them practical experience, and the only way to really learn this job is on the job. After a couple of years in a wagon, rookies move on, either, usually, to an RPC, or somewhere else. There are exceptions to this, of course. Both Charley McFadden and Jesus Martinez went right from the Academy to Narcotics, as plainclothes, undercover. The reasoning there was that their faces weren't known to people in the drug trade, and that, presuming they dressed the part, they could pass for pushers or addicts. But that sort of thing is the exception, not the rule."

"Yes, sir."

"Speaking of our Irish-American friends, when was the last time you saw Chief Coughlin?"

"I had dinner with him one night last week," Matt said.

"Would you be surprised to learn that Chief Coughlin sent you to Special Operations?"

"Chief Matdorf told me that he had arranged for me to be sent to Highway," Matt said, hesitated, and then went on, "but Chief Coughlin didn't say anything to me about it."

"He told me he was sending you over," Wohl said, "but he didn't tell me what he expected me to do with you. What would you like to do?"

The question surprised Matt; he raised both his hands in a gesture of helplessness.

"I don't think he had in mind putting you on a motorcycle," Wohl said. "And since, for the moment at least, I'm not even thinking of any kind of undercover operations, I really don't know what the hell to do with you. Can you type?"

"Yes, sir."

"Well?"

"Yes, sir. I think so."

"Well, I don't think Chief Coughlin wants me to turn you into a clerk, either," Wohl said, "but we're going to start generating a lot of paperwork to get Special Operations up to speed. More than Sergeant Frizell can handle. More than he can handle while he does things for me, too, anyway. The thought that occurs to me is that you could work for me, as sort of a gofer, until I can sort this out. How does that sound?"

"That sounds fine, sir."

"And, for the time being, anyway, I think in plain-clothes," Wohl said.

He looked around, caught the waitress's eye, and gestured for the check.

He turned back to Matt. "Jason Washington was right," he said. "You should get yourself a snub-nose and an ankle holster. You'll have to buy it yourself, but Colosimo's Gun Store offers an alleged police discount. Know where it is?''

"No, sir."

"The-nine-hundred block on Spring Garden," Wohl said.

"Sir, I thought you had to qualify with a snubnose," Matt said.

"How did you do on the pistol range in the Academy?" Wohl asked.

"All right, I think," Matt said. "Better than all right. I made Expert with the .45 at Quantico."

"That's right," Wohl said. "You told me that the night I first met you, the night of Dutch's wake. You were planning to be a Marine, weren't you? And then you busted the physical."

"Yes, sir."

"Is that why you came on the cops? To prove you're a man, anyway?"

"That's what my sister says," Matt said. "She says I was psychologically castrated when I flunked the physical, and that what I'm doing is proving my manhood."

"Your sister the psychiatrist?"

"Yes, sir."

"Did you get the feeling that Tony Harris is not too impressed with psychiatrists?" Wohl asked.

"Yes, sir, that came through pretty clearly."

"Or did you come on the job because of what happened to Dutch? And/or your father?" Wohl asked, picking that up again.

"That's probably got something to do with it," Matt said. "It probably was impulsive. But from what I've seen so far—"

"What?"

"It's going to be fascinating," Matt said.

"You haven't seen enough of it to be able to make that kind of judgment," Wohl said. "All you've seen is the Academy."

"And Washington and Harris," Matt argued gently.

"You're a long way, Matt, from getting close to guys like those two. The folklore is that being a detective is the best job in the Department; and that being a Homicide detective is the best of detective jobs. Washington and Harris, in my judgment, are the best two Homicide detectives, period. But that does trigger a thought: it would be a good idea for you to hang around with somebody, some people, who know what they're doing. I'm talking about McFadden and Martinez. I'll tell them to show you the ropes. That'll mean a lot of night work, overtime. How do you feel about overtime?"

"I really don't have anything better to do," Matt said, honestly. "Sure, I'd like that."

"The eyes of the average police officer would light up when a supervisor mentioned a lot of overtime," Wohl said.

"Sir?" Matt asked, confused.

The waitress appeared with the check on a small plastic tray. Matt had to wait until Wohl had carefully added up the bill and handed her his American Express card before he got an explanation.

"Overtime means extra pay," Wohl said. "Washington and Harris take home as much money as I do. More, probably. Supervisors get, at least, compensatory time, not pay for overtime. To most cops, overtime pay is very important."

"I wondered why you kept mentioning to them they could have all the overtime they wanted," Matt said.

"My point is that you weren't thinking about the money, were you? Money isn't much of a consideration for you, is it? You remember, you told me about that the night we met."

"I don't think that will keep me from doing my job," Matt said.

"I don't think it will, either," Wohl said. "But I think you should keep it in mind."

"Yes, sir."

"About the snub-nose," Wohl said, as he signed the American Express bill, "I don't think anyone will challenge you, but if that happens, the paperwork will come through me, and I'll handle it. But don't buy a Smith & Wesson *Undercover*, or a Colt with a hammer shroud.''

"Sir?''

"An *Undercover* comes with a built-in shroud over the hammer; it's intended to keep you from snagging the gun on your clothing, if you should ever need to get at it in a hurry. And they sell shrouds for Colts. The problem is you can't carry a gun with a shroud in an ankle holster; there's no place for the strap on the holster to catch.''

"I understand, sir.''

"The odds that you will ever have to use your revolver, which I hope they told you at the Academy, are about a thousand to one. But as the Boy Scouts say, *''Be Prepared!''*

He smiled at Matt and got up and walked out of the restaurant with Matt at his heels.

When Peter Wohl walked into what had been Mike Sabara's office as Acting Commanding Officer of Highway Patrol, and was now his, it was empty; all of Mike's photographs and plaques were gone from the walls, and so were the pistol shooting and bowling trophies Sabara had had on display on top of filing cabinets and other flat surfaces. Wohl walked to the desk, pulled drawers open, and saw that they too had been emptied.

He walked to the door.

"What happened to Captain Sabara?'' he asked Sergeant Frizell.

"He and Captain Pekach moved in there,'' Frizell said, pointing to a door.

Wohl walked to it and pulled it open. He had been unaware of the room's existence until that moment, and now that he saw it, he realized that it was really too small for two captains, and felt a moment's uneasiness at having the relatively large office to himself. He hadn't had an office when he had been just one more Staff Inspector. He had shared a large room with all of his peers, and he had not had a Sergeant to handle his paperwork.

*I guess it goes with the territory,* he decided, *but I don't like it.*

"We're going to have to do better than that," he said, to Sergeant Frizell. "In your planning, did the subject of space come up?"

"Space is tight, Inspector."

"That's not what I asked."

"There's an elementary school building at Frankford and Castor," Frizell said. "Not being used. The Department's been talking to the Board of Education about that."

"And?"

"It's a *school building,*" Frizell said. "There's no detention cells, nothing but a bunch of classrooms. Not even much space for parking."

"And there's no room in this building to move in fifty, maybe a hundred, maybe two hundred cops," Wohl said. "Find out what's being said, and to whom, about us getting it, will you?"

"Yes, sir," Frizell said. "There was some discussion about giving Special Operations, if it grows as large as it might with the ACT Grants, Memorial Hall."

"At Forty-forth and Parkside in Fairmount Park?"

"Yes, sir."

"That would be nice. Keep your ears open and keep me advised," Wohl said.

Frizell nodded. "Inspector, what do you want me to do about these?" He held up the Northwest Philadelphia rape files.

"I told Payne to Xerox them in four copies."

"Our Xerox is down."

"What about the machine in the District?"

"Well, they're not too happy with us using theirs," Frizell said. "They'll do it, but they make us wait."

*I will be damned if I will go find the District Captain and discuss Xerox priorities with him.*

"Sergeant," Wohl said, his annoyance showing in his voice, "high on your list of priorities is getting us a new

Xerox machine. Call Deputy Commissioner Whelan's office and tell them I said we need one desperately.''

''Yes, sir,'' Frizell said. ''And in the meantime, sir, what do I do with this?''

''Payne,'' Wohl ordered. ''Go get that Xeroxed someplace. You're a bright young man, you'll find a machine somewhere.''

''Yes, sir,'' Matt said.

''There's one more thing, Inspector,'' Sergeant Frizell said, and handed him a teletype message.

GENERAL: 0698 06/30/73 FROM COMMISSIONER
PAGE 1 OF 1

*********** CITY OF PHILADELPHIA ***********
*********** POLICE DEPARTMENT ***********

..........................

THE FOLLOWING WILL BE ANNOUNCED AT ALL ROLL
CALLS: EFFECTIVE IMMEDIATELY SPECIAL OPERATIONS
DIVISION MOTOR VEHICLES (EXCEPT HIGHWAY PATROL)
ARE ASSIGNED RADIO CALL SIGNS W-1 THROUGH W-200,
AND WILL USE THE PHONETIC PRONOUNCIATION
''WILLIAM.''

..........................

*Jesus! I just got here, and they're already changing things.*
*''William''? That's awkward. Why not ''Whiskey''?*
*Obviously, ''Whiskey'' wouldn't work.*
*And ''Wine'' and ''Women'' wouldn't work, either. But ''William''?*
*In two or three days, if not already, that will be ''Willy'' and I will get an interdepartmental memorandum crisply ordering me to have my men follow official Department Radio procedures.*

''Did you get the word out?'' Wohl asked Frizell.

''Yes, sir.''

Wohl, without thinking about it, handed the teletype to

Matt Payne. Then he saw Charley McFadden and Jesus Martinez coming into the outer office.

"Wait a minute, Payne," he said, as he walked into the outer office.

"Good afternoon, sir," Martinez said.

"I hope you're here to report that you have seen Miss Peebles, and that she now loves the Police Department and all we're doing for her," Wohl asked.

"I don't know if she loves us or not," McFadden said, smiling. "But she made us a cup of coffee."

"What's going on over there?" Wohl said, gesturing for the two of them to go into his office, and then adding, "You, too, Matt. I want you in on this."

Wohl sat in the upholstered chair and indicated that Martinez, McFadden, and Payne should sit on the couch.

"Okay, what happened? What's going on with Miss Peebles?"

"She's all right," McFadden said. "A little strange. Rich. Scared, too."

"Explain all that to me," Wohl said. "Did Captain Sabara explain that she has friends in high places?"

"Yes, sir," Martinez said. "Well . . . do you want to hear what I think, Inspector?"

"That would be nice," Wohl said, dryly.

"She's a nice lady, with a fag for a brother," Martinez said. "I don't even know if she knows the brother is a fag, she's that dumb. I mean, nice but *dumb*, you follow me?"

"I'm sure that you're going to tell me what her brother's sexual proclivities have to do with the burglary. Burglaries."

"She knows all right," McFadden said.

"Anyway, the brother brought a guy home. An actor."

"Going under the name Walton Williams," McFadden said. "Nothing in criminal records under that name."

"That was in the report I told you to read," Wohl said.

"Anyway, the way we see it," Martinez went on, "the fag took one look around the place, saw all the expensive crap—what do you call it, 'bric-a-brac'?"

"If it's worth more than fifty dollars, we usually say, 'objets d'art,'" Wohl said.

"Expensive *knicknacks*," McFadden offered.

"—and figured he was in a toy store. Especially after the brother went to France. So he's been ripping her off."

"How would you handle this crime wave?"

"Find the fag," McFadden said.

"*Cherchez la pouf,*" Wohl said.

Matt Payne laughed.

"Excuse me?" Martinez said.

"Go on," Wohl said. "How would you do that?"

"Give us a couple of days," McFadden said. "We'll find him."

"You think you know where to look?"

"There's a couple of fairies around who owe me some favors," Martinez said.

"Just off the top of my head, do you think there is any chance this Mr. Williams could be the doer in the rapes?"

"I called Detective Hemmings at Northwest Detectives," McFadden said. "The best description of *that* doer is that he's hairy. Black hairy. The description we got from Miss Peebles is that the brother's boyfriend is blond."

"And 'delicate,'" Martinez said.

*Well, they're thinking,* Wohl thought.

"What about his stealing her underwear?"

"That's a puzzler," Martinez said. "When I catch him, I'll ask him."

"We could stake out the house, Inspector," McFadden said. "Until he comes back. I'm sure he'll be back. But I think the easiest and cheapest way to catch him is for you to let us go look for him."

"What did you say 'cheapest'?" Wohl asked.

"I got the feeling that when we catch this guy, Miss Peebles isn't going to want to go testify against him," McFadden said. "Because of the brother. What he is would get out. And the brother may not want the guy locked up."

"I see."

"But if we can find him, maybe we can talk to him," Martinez said. "Maybe we can even get some of the stuff back. But I think we can discourage him from going back there again."

"You're not suggesting anything that would violate Mr. Williams's civil rights, are you, Martinez?"

"No, sir," Martinez said, straight-faced. "As a minority member myself, I am very sensitive about civil rights."

"I'm glad to hear that," Wohl said. "I would be very annoyed if I learned any of my men were slapping some suspect around. You understand that?"

"Yes, sir."

"You, too, McFadden?"

"Yes, sir."

"Okay, go look for him," Wohl said.

"Yes, sir," they said in unison, pleased.

"Sir, the best time to deal with people like that is at night, say from nine o'clock on, until the wee hours," McFadden said.

"You're talking about overtime?" Wohl asked, looking at Matt Payne as he spoke.

"Yes, sir," McFadden said.

"Put in as much overtime as you think is necessary," Wohl said. "I want you to take Officer Payne along with you, to give him a chance to see how you work."

"Yes, sir," McFadden said, immediately.

"Inspector, that might be a little awkward," Martinez said.

"That wasn't a suggestion," Wohl said.

"Yes, sir," Martinez said.

"Can we keep the car we've been driving, sir?" McFadden asked.

"If you mean, do you have to turn it in when you go off duty, the answer is no, not for the time being. I don't care which one of you keeps it overnight, but I don't want to hear that somebody stole the radios, or the tires, or ran a key down the side to show his affection for the police."

"I'll take good care of it, sir," Martinez said.

"For right now, for the rest of the afternoon, I want you to keep drawing cars and taking them for radios and bringing them here. Take Payne with you. He's doing an errand for me, and he'll need a car to do it."

"Yes, sir," McFadden said.

"That's all," Wohl said. He looked at Payne. "Get that Xeroxed, and then come back here."

"Yes, sir," Payne said.

"I have every confidence that in the morning, Mr. Williams will be in the hands of the law, and that I can call the Commissioner and tell him that not only has justice been done, but that Miss Peebles is more than satisfied with her police support."

Martinez and McFadden flashed smiles that were not entirely confident, and got up. As Payne started to follow them out of the office Wohl said, softly, "Keep your eyes open and your mouth shut tonight, Matt."

# THIRTEEN

Matt Payne turned off Seventh Street into the parking lot behind the Roundhouse at the wheel of an almost new Plymouth Fury. Forty-five minutes before, he had picked it up at the Radio garage, and it was equipped with the full complement of radios prescribed for Special Operations by Staff Inspector Peter Wohl.

He knew the radio worked, because he had tried it.

"W-William Two Oh Nine," he had called on the Highway Band. "Out of service at Colosimo's Gun Store in the nine-hundred block of Spring Garden."

And Radio had called back, "W-William Two Oh Nine, is that the nine-hundred block on Spring Garden?"

The Radio Dispatcher was Mrs. Catherine Wosniski, a plump, gray-haired lady of sixty-two who had been, it was said, a dispatcher since Police Dispatch had been a couple of guys blowing whistles from atop City Hall, long before Marconi had even thought of radio.

Mrs. Wosniski had been around long enough to know, for example, that:

Special units—and Special Operations was certainly a Special Unit—did not have to report themselves out of service as did the RPCs in the Districts. The whole idea of reporting out of (or back in) service was to keep the dispatchers aware of what cars were or were not available to be sent somewhere by the dispatchers. Dispatchers did not dispatch special unit vehicles.

Catherine Wosniski also knew about Colosimo's Gun Store. It was where three out of four cops in Philadelphia, maybe more, bought their guns. And she also knew that many of them stopped by Colosimo's to shop on a personal basis when they had been officially sent to the Roundhouse; that they shopped there, so to speak, on company time, almost invariably "forgetting" to call Police Radio to report themselves out of service.

So what she had here was a car that was not required to report itself out of service doing just that, and at a location where cars rarely reported themselves out of service, because supervisors, who also had radios, frowned on officers shopping on company time.

Although Mrs. Catherine Wosniski was a devout and lifelong member of the Roman Catholic Church, she was also conversant with certain phrases used by those of the Hebraic persuasion: What she thought was, *there's something not kosher here*.

"W-William Two Oh Nine," she radioed back. "Do you want numbers on this assignment?"

What she was asking was whether the officer calling wanted the District Control Number for whatever incident was occurring at Colosimo's Gun Store that he had elected to handle. A District Control Number is required for every incident of police involvement.

Officer Matthew Payne had no idea at all what she was talking about.

"W-William Two Oh Nine. No, thank you, ma'am, I don't need any numbers."

It had been at least two years since anyone had said thank you to Catherine Wosniski over the Police Radio; she could never remember anyone who had ever called her 'ma'am' over the air.

"W-William Two Oh Nine," she radioed, a touch of concern in her voice, "is everything all right at that location?"

"W-William Two Oh Nine," Officer Payne replied, "everything's fine here. I'm just going inside to buy a gun."

There was a pause before Mrs. Wosniski replied. Then, very slowly, she radioed, "Ooooooo-kaaaaaay, W-Two Oh Nine."

Everyone on this band thus knew that Mrs. Wosniski knew that she was dealing with an incredible dummy who hadn't the foggiest idea how to cover his tracks when he was taking care of personal business.

Blissfully unaware of the meaning of his exchange with Police Radio, and actually complimenting himself on the professional way he had handled the situation, Matt Payne got out of the car and went into Colosimo's Gun Store.

Thirty minutes after that, after equipping himself with a Smith & Wesson Model 37 Chief's Special Airweight J-Frame .38 Special caliber revolver and an ankle holster for it, he had called Radio again and reported W-William Two Oh Nine back in service.

Getting the pistol had been far more complicated than he had imagined. He had—naively, he now understood—assumed that since he was now a sworn Police Officer, and equipped with a badge and a photo identification card to prove it, buying a revolver would be no more difficult than buying a pair of shoes.

But that hadn't been the case. First there had been a long federal government form to fill out, on which he had to swear on penalty of perjury, the punishments for which were spelled out to be a $10,000 fine and ten years imprisonment, that he was not a felon, a drunk, or a drug addict; and that neither was he under psychiatric care or under any kind of an indictment. And when that was complete, the salesman took his photo identification to a telephone and called the Police Department to verify that there was indeed a Police Officer named Matthew Payne on their rolls.

But finally the pistol was his. He carried it out to the car and, with more trouble than he thought it would be, managed to fasten the ankle holster to his right ankle. Then, sitting in the car, he had gone through some actually painful contortions to take off his jacket and his shoulder holster.

He took the revolver from the holster, opened the cylinder, and dumped the six shiny, somehow menacing, cartridges into his hand. He loaded five of them, all it held, into the *Undercover* revolver's cylinder and put it back into the ankle holster. He slipped the leftover cartridge into his trousers pocket.

When he tried to put the service revolver and the shoulder holster in the glove compartment, it was full of shortwave radio chassis. He finally managed to shove it all under the passenger-side seat.

The ankle holster, as he drove to the Roundhouse, had felt both strange and precariously mounted, raising the very real possibility that he didn't have it on right.

As he looked for a parking place, other doubts rose in his mind. He had never been inside the Roundhouse; the closest he'd come was waiting outside while Inspector Wohl had gone inside to get Detectives Washington and Harris.

He had no idea where to go inside to gain access to a Xerox machine. And there was, he thought, a very good possibility that as he walked down a corridor somewhere, the ankle holster would come loose and his new pistol would go sliding down the corridor before the eyes of fifty Police Officers, most of them Sergeants or better.

He found a parking place, pulled the Fury into it, and almost immediately backed out and left the Roundhouse parking lot. He knew where there was a Xerox machine, and where to park the car to get to it. He picked up the microphone.

"W-William Two Oh Nine," he reported, "out of service at Twelfth and Market."

"Why hello, Matt," Mrs. Irene Craig, executive secretary to the senior partners of Mawson, Payne, Stockton, McAdoo & Lester, said. "How are you?"

"Just fine, Mrs. Craig," Matt said. "And yourself?"

His confidence in the ankle holster had been restored. He had walked, at first very carefully, and then with growing confidence through the parking building to the elevator, and it had not fallen off.

"What can I do for you?"

"I need to use the Xerox machine," he said.

"Sure," she said. "It's in there. Do you know how to use it?"

"I think so," he said.

"Come on," she said. "I'll show you."

When the fifth sheet was coming out of the Xerox machine, she turned to him.

"What in the world is this?"

"It's the investigation reports of the Northwest Philadelphia rapes," Matt said.

"What are you doing with them?" she asked. "Or can't I ask?"

"I'm working on them," Matt said, and then the lie became uncomfortable. "My boss told me to get them Xeroxed."

"Doesn't the Police Department have a Xerox machine?"

"Ours doesn't work," Matt said. "So they sent me down to the Roundhouse to have it done. And since I'd never been in there, I figured it would be easier to come in here."

"We'll send the city a bill." She laughed. And then, after a moment, she asked, "Is that what they have you doing? Administration?"

"Sort of."

"I didn't think, with your education, that they'd put you in a prowl car to hand out speeding tickets."

"What they would like to have done was put me in a paddy wagon, excuse me, EPW, but Denny Coughlin has put his two cents in on my behalf."

"You don't sound very happy about that," she said. Irene Craig had known Matthew Payne virtually all of his life, liked him very much, and shared his father's opinion that Matt's becoming a cop ranked high on the list of Dumb Ideas of All Time.

"Ambivalent," he said, as he started to stack the Xeroxed pages. "On one hand, I am, at least theoretically, opposed to the idea of special treatment. On the other hand—proving, I suppose, that I am not nearly as noble as I like to think I am—I like what I'm doing."

"Which is?"

"I'm the gofer for a very nice guy, and a very sharp cop, Staff Inspector Peter Wohl."

"He's the one who had his picture in the paper? The one they put in charge of this new—"

"Special Operations," Matt filled in.

"That sounds interesting."

"It's fascinating."

"I'm glad for you," she said.

*Not really,* she thought. *I would be a lot happier if he was miserable as a cop; then maybe he'd come to his senses and quit. But at least Denny Coughlin is watching out for him; that's something.*

"I like it," Matt said. "So much I keep waiting for the other shoe to drop."

"Stick around," she said, laughing. "It will. It always does."

"Thanks a lot," Matt said, chuckling.

"You want to see your father?"

"No," he said, and when he saw the look on her face, quickly added, "I've got to get back. He's probably busy; and I had breakfast with him this morning."

"Well, I'll tell him you were in."

"If you think you have to."

"You're a scamp," she said. "Okay. I won't tell him. How's the apartment?"

"I can't get used to the quiet," he said.

He had, two weeks before, moved into an attic apartment in a refurbished pre–Civil War building on Rittenhouse Square. His previous legal residence had been a fraternity house on Walnut Street near the University of Pennsylvania campus. Irene Craig knew that he knew his father had "found" the apartment for him, in a building owned by Rittenhouse Properties, Inc., the lower three floors of which were on long-term lease to the Delaware Valley Cancer Society. She wondered if he knew that eighty percent of the stock of Rittenhouse Properties, Inc., was owned by Brewster Cortland Payne II. Now that she thought of it, she decided he didn't.

"Maybe what you need is the patter of little feet to break the quiet," Irene Craig said.

"Don't even *think* things like that!" Matt protested.

When the Xerox machine finally finished, Irene Craig gave him thick rubber bands to bind the four copies together, and then, impulsively, kissed him on the cheek.

"Take care of yourself, sport," she said.

When Matt returned to the Highway Patrol building at Bustleton and Bowler, he stopped first at his car, double-parking the Fury to do so, and put his service revolver and shoulder holster under the driver's seat of his Porsche. Then he drove the Fury into the parking lot.

He gave the keys to Sergeant Frizell, who apparently had had a word with Inspector Wohl about Officer Payne's place in the pecking order of Special Operations.

Frizell handed him a cardboard box full of multipart forms.

"The Inspector said do as many of these as you can today," Frizell sad. "There's a typewriter on a desk in there."

"What are they?" Matt asked.

"The requisition and transfer forms for the cars, and for the extra radios," Frizell explained. "On top is one already filled out; just fill out the others the same way."

They were, Matt soon saw, the "paperwork" without which Good Old Ernie in the radio garage had been, at first, unwilling to do any work. Plus the paperwork for the cars themselves, the ones they had already taken from the motor pool, and blank forms, with the specific data for the particular car to be later filled in, for cars yet to be drawn, as they were actually taken from the motor pool.

The only word to describe the typewriter was "wretched." It was an ancient Underwood. The keys stuck. The platen was so worn that the keys made deep indentations in, or actually punched through, the upper layers of paper and carbon, and whatever the mechanism that controlled the paper feeding was called, that was so worn that Matt had to manually align each line as he typed.

He completed two forms and decided the situation was absurd. He looked at his watch. It was quarter to five.

He went into the other room.

"Sergeant," he said. "I think I know where I can get a better typewriter. Would it be all right if I left now and did these forms there?"

"You mean, at home?"

"Yes, sir."

"I don't give a damn where you type them, Payne, just that they get typed."

"Good night, then."

"Yeah."

Matt took the carton of blank forms and carried it to the Porsche. At this time of day, he decided, he would do better going over to I-95 and taking that downtown, rather than going down Roosevelt Boulevard to North Broad Street. He could, he decided, make better time on I-95. There was not much fun driving a car capable of speeds well over one hundred if you couldn't go any faster than thirty-five.

Two miles down I-95, he glanced in the mirror to see if it was clear to pass a U-Haul van, towing a trailer. It was not. There was a car in the lane beside him. It was painted blue-

and-white, and there was a chrome-plated device on its roof containing flashing lights. They were flashing.

He dropped his eyes to the speedometer and saw that he was exceeding the speed limit by fifteen miles per hour. The police car, a *Highway Patrol* car, he realized with horror, pulled abreast of him, and the Highway Patrolman in the passenger seat gestured with his finger for Matt to pull to the side of the superhighway.

"Oh, Jesus!" Matt muttered, as he looked in the mirror and turned on his signal.

He had a flash of insight, of wisdom.

He broke the law. He would take his medicine. He would not mention that he was a fellow Police Officer, in the faint hope that he could beat the ticket. That way, there was a chance that it would not come to Staff Inspector Wohl's attention that on his very first day on the job, he had been arrested for racing down I-95 somewhere between eighty and eighty-five miles per hour.

He stopped and went into the glove compartment for the vehicle registration certificate. The glove compartment was absolutely empty. Matt had a sudden, very clear, mental image of the vehicle registration. It, together with the bill of sale and the title and the other paperwork, was in the upper right-hand drawer of the chest of drawers in his room in the house in Wallingford.

He glanced in the mirror and saw that both Highway Patrolmen had gotten out of the car and were approaching his. He hurriedly dug his wallet from his trousers and got out of the car.

First one, and then three more cars in the outer lane flashed past him, so close and so fast that he was genuinely frightened. He walked to the back of the car and extended his driver's license to one of the Highway Patrolmen.

"I don't seem to have the registration with me," Matt said.

"You were going at least eighty," the patrolman said. "You had it up to eighty-five."

"Guilty," Matt said, wanly.

"You mind if we examine the interior of your car, sir?" the other Highway Patrolman said. Matt turned his head to look at him; he was at the passenger-side window, looking inside.

"No, not at all," Matt said, obligingly. "Help yourself."

He turned to face the Highway Patrolman who had his driver's license.

"My registration is home," Matt said.

"This your address, 3906 Walnut?"

"No, sir," Matt said. "Actually, I just moved. I now live on Rittenhouse Square."

"Look what I got!" the other Highway Patrolman said.

Matt turned to look. The other Highway Patrolman was holding Matt's service revolver and his shoulder holster in his hand.

He didn't get a really good look. He felt himself being suddenly spun around, and felt his feet being kicked out from under him, and then a strong shove against his back. Just in time, he managed to get his hands out in front of him, so that he didn't fall, face first, against the Porsche.

"*Don't* move!" the Highway Patrolman behind him said.

He felt hands moving over his body, around his chest, his waist, between his legs, and then down first one leg and then the other.

"He's got another one!" the Highway Patrolman said, pulling Matt's right trousers leg up, and then jerking the Chief's Special from the ankle holster.

"I can explain this," Matt said.

"Good," the Highway Patrolman said.

Matt felt himself being jerked around again. A hand found his belt and pulled him erect. A handcuff went around his right wrist, and then his right arm was pulled behind him. His left arm was pulled behind him, and he felt the other half of the handcuff snapping in place. Then he was spun around.

"Have you a permit to carried concealed weapons, sir?" the Highway Patrolman said.

"I'm a policeman," Matt said.

"This one's brand new," the second Highway Patrolman said, shaking the cartridges from the *Undercover* revolver into his palm.

"I just bought it today," Matt said.

"You were saying you're a policeman?" the Highway Patrolman asked.

"That's right," Matt said.

"Where do you work? Who's your Lieutenant?"

"Special Operations," Matt said. "I work for Inspector Wohl."

"Where's that?" the Highway Patrolman asked, just a faint hint of self-doubt creeping into his voice.

"Bustleton and Bowler," Matt said.

"Where's your ID?"

"In my jacket pocket," Matt said.

The Highway Patrolman dipped into the pocket and found the ID.

"Jesus!" he said, then, "Turn around."

Matt felt his wrists being freed.

"What's this?" the second Highway Patrolman said.

"He's a cop," the first one said. "He says he works for Inspector Wohl."

"Why didn't you show us this when we pulled up beside you?" the second asked, more confused than angry.

Matt shrugged helplessly.

"You find anything wrong with the way we handled this?" the first Highway Patrolman asked.

"Excuse me?" Matt asked, confused.

"We stopped an eighty-five-mile-an-hour speeder, and found a weapon concealed under his seat. We asked permission to examine the car. We took necessary and reasonable precautions by restraining a man we found in possession of two concealable firearms. Anything wrong with that?"

Matt shrugged helplessly.

"Isn't that what this is all about? You were checking on us?"

Matt suddenly understood.

"What this is all about is that this is my first day on the job," he said. "And I decided I'd rather pay the ticket than have Inspector Wohl find out about it."

They both looked at him. And both of their faces, by raised eyebrows, registered disbelief.

And then the taller of them, the one who had found the revolver under the seat, laughed, and the other joined in.

"Jesus H. Christ!" he said.

The taller Highway Patrolman, shaking his head and smiling with what Matt perceived to be utter contempt, handed him the Chief's Special and then the cartridges for it. The shorter one looped the shoulder holster harness around Matt's neck. Then, chuckling, they walked back to their car and got in.

By the time Matt got back in his car, they had driven off.

Officer Matthew Payne drove the rest of the way to his apartment more or less scrupulously obeying the speed limit.

It was after the change of watches when Peter Wohl returned to his office. The day-watch Sergeants had gone home; an unfamiliar face of a Highway Patrol Sergeant was behind the desk.

"I'm Peter Wohl," Peter said, walking to the desk with his hand extended.

"Yes, sir, Inspector," the Sergeant said, smiling. "I know who you are. We went through Wheel School together."

Wohl still didn't remember him, and it showed on his face.

"I had hair then," the Sergeant said, "and I was a lot trimmer. Jack Kelvin."

"Oh, hell, sure," Wohl said. "I'm sorry, Jack. I should have remembered you."

"You made a big impression on me back then."

"Good or bad?" Wohl asked.

"At the time I thought it was treason," Kelvin said, smiling. "You spilled your wheel, and I went to help you pick it up, and you said, 'Anybody who rides one of these and likes it is out of his fucking mind.' "

"I said that?"

"Yes, you did," Kelvin said, chuckling, "and you meant it."

"Well, under the circumstances, I'd appreciate it if you didn't go around telling that story."

"Like I said, that was a long time ago, and you'll notice that I am now riding a desk myself. You don't spill many desks."

"I've found that you can get in more trouble riding a desk than you can a wheel," Wohl said. "Did anything turn up on the abduction?"

"No, sir," Kelvin said. "Chief Coughlin called a couple of minutes ago and asked the same thing."

"Did he want me to call him back?"

"No, sir, he didn't. He asked that you call him in the morning."

"Anything else?"

"Sergeant Frizell said to tell you that your driver took the vehicle and radio requisition forms home to fill out," Kelvin said. When Wohl looked at him curiously, Kelvin explained. "Frizell said he didn't like the typewriter here."

Wohl nodded. He understood about the typewriters. It was generally agreed that the only decent typewriters in the Police Department were in the offices of Inspectors, *full* Inspectors, and up.

"He's a nice kid," Wohl said. "Just out of the Academy. He is—was?—how do you say this? Dutch Moffitt was his uncle."

"Oh," Kelvin said. "I heard that Chief Coughlin sent him over, but I didn't get the connections."

"Chief Coughlin also sent over the two Narcotics plainclothesmen who found Gerald Vincent Gallagher," Wohl said. "Until I decide what to do with Payne, I'm going to have him follow them around, and make himself useful in here. He's not really my driver."

"You're entitled to a driver," Kelvin said. "Hell, Captain

Moffitt had a driver. It may not have been authorized, but no one said anything to him about it.''

''Did Captain Sabara? Have a driver, I mean?''

''No, sir,'' Kelvin said. ''After Captain Moffitt was killed, and Sabara took over, he drove himself.''

''Every cop driving a supervisor around is a cop that could be on the streets,'' Wohl said. ''Matt Payne is nowhere near ready to go on the streets.''

Kelvin nodded his understanding.

''Jason Washington called. Homicide detective? You know him?''

''Special Operations,'' Wohl corrected him. ''He transferred in today.''

''He didn't mention that,'' Kelvin said. ''He called in and asked that you get in touch when you have time to talk to him.''

''Where is he?''

''He said he was having dinner in the Old Ale House.''

''Call him, please, Jack, and tell him that when he finishes his dinner, I'll be here for the next hour or so.''

''Yes, sir,'' Kelvin said. ''Captain Sabara left word that he's going to work the First and Second District roll calls for volunteers, and then go home. Captain Pekach left word that he's going to have dinner and then ride around, and that he'll more than likely be in here sometime tonight.''

Wohl nodded. ''Payne was supposed to have Xeroxed some stuff for me. You know anything about it?''

''Yes, sir. I left it on your desk. I'd love to know where he found that Xerox machine. The copies are beautiful.''

''Knowing Payne, he probably waltzed into the Commissioner's office and used his,'' Wohl said. He put out his hand again. ''It's good to see you, Jack,'' he said. ''And especially behind that desk.''

''I'm glad to see you behind your desk, too, Inspector.''

*He meant that*, Wohl decided, flattered. *It wasn't just polishing the apple.*

Wohl went into his office and examined the Xeroxed materials. Kelvin was right, he thought, the copies were beautiful, like those in the Xerox ads on television, not like those to be expected from machines in the Police Department.

He took the original file back out to Sergeant Kelvin and told him to have a Highway Patrol car run it back to Northwest Detectives, and to make sure that it wound up in Lieutenant Spanner's hands, not just dumped on the desk man's desk in the squad room.

Then he sat down and took one of the Xerox copies and started, very carefully, to read through it again.

Fifteen minutes later, he sensed movement and looked up. Jason Washington was at the office door, asking with a gesture of his hand and a raised eyebrow if it was all right for him to come in.

Wohl gestured that it was. Washington did so and then closed the door behind him.

"How was dinner?" Wohl asked.

"All I had was a salad," Washington said. "I have to watch my weight."

"What's on your mind, Jason?"

"Is that the Xerox you said you would get me?"

Wohl nodded, and made a gesture toward it.

Washington took one of the files, then settled himself in an armchair.

"I saw the Flannery girl," he said.

"How did that go?"

"Not very well, as a matter of fact," Washington said. "She wasn't what you could call anxious to talk about it again. Not to anyone, but especially not to a man, and maybe particularly to a black man."

"But?"

"*And,*" Washington said, "I told you Hemmings was a good cop. It was a waste of time. I didn't get anything out of her that he didn't. And then I talked to him. He's pissed, Peter, and I can't say I blame him. Putting me on this job was the same as telling him either that you didn't think he had done a good job, or that he was capable of doing one."

"That's not true, and I'm sorry he feels that way."

"How would it look to you, if you were in his shoes?" Washington asked reasonably.

"When I was a new sergeant in Homicide, Jason," Wohl replied, "Matt Lowenstein took me off a job because I wasn't getting anywhere with it. The wife in Roxborough who ran herself over with her own car. He put the best man he had on the job, a guy named Washington."

"I told Hemmings that story," Washington said. "I don't think it helped much."

After a moment, Wohl said, "Thank you, Jason."

Washington ignored that.

"You read that file?"

"I was just about finished reading it for the third time."

"The one time I read it," Washington said, "I thought I saw a pattern. Our doer is getting bolder and bolder. You see that, something like that, too?"

"Yes, I did."

"If we get the abducted woman back, alive, I'll be surprised."

"Why?"

"That didn't occur to you?" Washington asked.

"Yes, it did, but I want to see if we reached the same conclusion for the same reasons."

"The reason we don't have a lead, not a damned lead, on this guy is because we don't have a good description on him, or his van. And the reason we don't is that, until the Flannery thing, he wasn't with the victims more than fifteen, twenty minutes, and he did what he did where he found them. In the Flannery job, he put her in his van, but in such a way that it didn't give us any better picture of him than we had before. He never took that mask off—by the way, it's not a Lone Ranger–type mask; the Lone Ranger wore one that just covered his eyes."

"I picked up on that," Wohl said.

"That was the one little mistake that Dick Hemmings made, and when I mentioned it to him, he admitted it right away; said that he'd picked up on that, too, and doesn't know why he put it in the report the way he did."

"Go on, Jason."

"In the Flannery job, he put her in his van and drove away with her. I think that convinced him he can take his victims away, and keep them longer. That's what he's really after, I think, having them in his power. That's more important to him, I think, than the sexual gratification he's getting; there's been no incident of him reaching orgasm except by masturbation."

"I agree," Wohl said, "that he's after the domination; the humiliation is part of that."

"So he now knows he can get away with taking the women away from their homes; he proved that by taking the Flannery woman to Forbidden Drive. And since that was so much fun, he took the next victim away, too. Maybe to his house, maybe someplace else, the country, maybe."

"And the longer he keeps them, the greater the possibility . . . that his mask will fall off, or something. . . ."

"Or that the victim will look around and see things that would help us to find where she's been taken," Washington continued. "And this guy is smart, Peter. It is going to occur to him sooner or later, if it hasn't already, that what he's got on his hands is someone who can lead the cops to him; and that will mean the end of his fun."

Not dramatically, but matter-of-factly, Jason Washington drew his index finger across his throat in a cutting motion.

"And he might find that's even more fun than running around in his birthday suit, wearing a mask, and waving his dong at them," Washington added.

"That's the way I see it," Wohl said. "That's why I wanted you over here, working on it. I want to catch this guy before that happens."

"Dick Hemmings, if you'd have asked him, could have told you the same thing."

"It's done, Jason, you're here. So tell me what we should be doing next."

"Tony Harris has come up with a long list of minor sexual offenders," Washington said. "If I were you, Peter, I'd get him all the help he needs to ring doorbells."

"I don't know where I can get anybody," Wohl said, thinking aloud.

"You better figure out where," Washington said. "That's all we've got right now. Tony's been trying to get a match, in Harrisburg, between the names he's got and people who own any kind of a van. So far, zilch."

"Sabara's got some people coming in," Peter said. "Probably some of them will be here in the morning. I'll put them on it. And maybe I could get some help from Northwest Detectives, maybe even tonight."

"I wouldn't count on that," Washington said. "I think they're glad you've taken this job away from them."

"I didn't take it away from them," Wohl flared. "It was given to me."

"Whatever you say."

"Jason, it's been suggested to me that we might find a psychiatric profile of the doer useful."

"Don't you think we have one?" Washington said, getting to his feet. "Whose suggestion was that? Denny Coughlin's? Or Czernick himself?"

Wohl didn't reply.

"I'm going home," Washington said. "It's been a long day."

"Good night, Jason," Wohl said. "Thanks."

"For what, Peter?" Washington said, and walked out of his office.

Wohl felt a pang of resentment that Washington was going home. So long as Elizabeth J. Woodham, white female, aged thirty-three, of 300 East Mermaid Lane in Roxborough, was missing and presumed to have been abducted by a known sexual offender, it seemed logical that they should be doing something to find her, to get her back alive.

And then he realized that was unfair. If Jason Washington

could think of anything else that could be done, he would be doing it.

There was nothing to be done, except wait to see what happened.

And then Wohl thought of something, and reached for the telephone book.

# FOURTEEN

The apartment under the eaves of what was now the Delaware Valley Cancer Society Building was an afterthought, conceived after most of the building had been renovated.

C. Kenneth Warble, A.I.A, the architect, had met with Brewster C. Payne II of Rittenhouse Properties over luncheon at the Union League on South Broad Street to bring him up to date on the project's progress, and also to explain why a few little things—in particular the installation of an elevator—were going a little over budget.

Almost incidentally, C. Kenneth Warble had mentioned that he felt a little bad, *vis-à-vis* space utilization, about the "garret space," which on his plans, he had appropriated to "storage."

"I was there just before I came here, Brewster," he said. "It's a shame."

"Why a shame?"

"You've heard the story about the man with thinning hair who said he had too much hair to shave, and too little to comb? It's something like that. The garret space is really unsuitable for an apartment, a decent apartment—by which I mean expensive—and too nice for storage.''

''Why unsuitable?''

''Well, the ceilings are very low, with no way to raise them, for one thing; by the time I put a kitchen in there, and a bath, which it would obviously have to have, there wouldn't be much room left. A small bedroom, and, I've been thinking, a rather nice, if long and narrow living room, with those nice dormer windows overlooking Rittenhouse Square, *would* be possible.''

''But you think it could be rented?''

''If you could find a short bachelor,'' Warble said.

''That bad?'' Brewster Payne chuckled.

''Not really. The ceilings are seven foot nine; three inches shorter than the Code now calls for. But we could get around that because it's a historical renovation.''

''How much are we talking about?''

''Then, there's the question of access,'' Warble said, having just decided that if he was going to turn the garret into an apartment, it would be Brewster C. Payne's wish, rather than his own recommendation. ''I'd have to provide some means for the short bachelor to get from the third-floor landing, which is as high as the elevator goes, to the apartment, and I'd have to put in some more soundproofing around the elevator motors—which are in the garret, you see, taking up space.''

''How much are we talking about?'' Payne repeated.

''The flooring up there is original,'' Warble went on. ''Heart pine, fifteen-eighteen-inch random planks. That would refinish nicely, and could be done with this new urethane varnish, which is really incredibly tough.''

''How much, Kenneth?'' Payne had asked, mildly annoyed.

''For twelve, fifteen thousand, I could turn it into something really rather nice,'' Warble said. ''You think that would be the way to go?''

"How much could we rent it for?"

"You could probably get three-fifty, four hundred a month for it," Warble said. "There are a lot of people who would be willing to pay for the privilege of being able to drop casually into conversation that they live on Rittenhouse Square."

"I see a number of well-dressed short men walking around town," Brewster C. Payne II said, after a moment. "Statistically, a number of them are bound to be bachelors. Go ahead, Kenneth."

Rental of the apartment had been turned over to a realtor, with final approval of the tenant assumed by Mrs. Irene Craig. There had been a number of applicants, male and female, whom Irene Craig had rejected. The sensitivities of the Delaware Valley Cancer Society had to be considered, and while Irene Craig felt sure they were as broad-minded as anybody, she didn't feel they would take kindly to sharing the building with gentlemen of exquisite grace, or with ladies who were rather vague about their place of employment and who she suspected were practitioners of the oldest profession.

It was, she decided, in Brewster C. Payne II's best interests to wait until the ideal tenant—in Irene's mind's eye, a sixtyish widow who worked in the Franklin Institute—came along. And she waited.

And then Matt Payne had come along, needing a residence inside the city limits to meet a civil service regulation, and about to be evicted from his fraternity house. She called the Director of Administration at the Cancer Society and told him that the apartment had been rented, and that, as he had been previously informed, the two parking spaces in the garage behind the building, which they had until now been permitted to use temporarily, would no longer be available to them.

She assured him that the new tenant was a gentleman whose presence in the building would hardly be noticed, and devoutly hoped that would be the case.

Air conditioning had also been an afterthought, or more accurately an after-afterthought. Not only was their insufficient capacity in the main unit already installed, but there was no room to install the duct work that would have been necessary. Two 2.5-ton window units had been installed, one through the side wall, the second in the bedroom in the rear.

The wave of hot muggy air that greeted Matt Payne when he trotted up the narrow stairway from the third floor and unlocked his door told him that he had forgotten to leave either unit on when he had last been home.

He put the carton of requisition forms on the desk in the living room and quickly turned both units on high. The desk, like the IBM typewriter sitting on it, had been "surplus" to the needs of Mawson, Payne, Stockton, McAdoo & Lester. With a great deal of difficulty, four burly movers had been able to maneuver the heavy mahogany desk up the narrow stairs from the third floor, but, short of tearing down a wall, there had been no chance of getting it into the bedroom, as originally planned.

He then stripped off his clothes and took a shower. Despite the valiant efforts of the air conditioners, the apartment was still hot when he had toweled himself dry. If he got dressed now, he would be sweaty again. Officer Charley McFadden had told him, in response to Matt's question as to how he should dress while they sought to locate Mr. Walton Williams, "Nice. Like you are now. He's an arty fag, not the leather and chains kind."

Matt then did what seemed at the moment to be entirely logical. He went into the living room in his birthday suit, sat down behind the IBM typewriter in that condition, and started typing up the forms.

He had been at it for just over an hour when his concentration was distracted by a soft two-toned bonging noise that he recognized only after a moment as his doorbell.

He decided it was his father, who not only had a key to the downstairs, but was a gentleman, who would sound the doorbell rather than just let himself in.

He trotted naked to the door and pulled it open.

It was not his father. It was Amelia Alice Payne, M.D.,

Fellow of the American College of Psychiatrists, his big sister.

"Jesus Christ, Amy! Wait till I get my goddamned pants on."

"I really hope I'm interrupting something," Amy said as she entered the apartment. She smirked at the sight of her naked brother trotting into his bedroom and then looked around.

Amy Payne was twenty-seven, petite and intense, a wholesome but not quite pretty woman who looked a good deal like her father. She was in fact not related to Matt except in the law. Her mother had been killed in an automobile accident. Six months later, her father had married Matt's widowed mother, and Brewster Payne had subsequently adopted Matthew Mark Moffitt, her infant son. Patricia Moffitt Payne and Matt had been around as far back as Amy could remember.

In Amy's mind, Patricia Moffitt Payne was her mother, and Matt her little brother.

Matt returned to the living room bare-chested and zipping up a pair of khaki pants.

"How'd you get inside?" he asked.

"Dad gave me a key so that I could use the garage," she said. "It also opens the door downstairs, as I just found out."

"Not to the apartment?" he challenged.

"No, not to the apartment," Amy said.

"To what do I owe the honor of your presence?" Matt asked. "You want a beer or a Coke or something?"

"I want to talk to you, Matt."

"Why does that cause me to think I'm not going to like this? The tone of your voice, maybe?"

"I don't care if you like what I have to say or not," she said. "But you're going to listen to me."

"What the hell is the matter with you?"

He looked at the desk, and then at the clock, and then decided he had typed the last form he was going to have to type tonight, and he could thus have a beer.

He walked to the refrigerator and took out a bottle of Heineken. He held it up.

"You want one of these?"

"I don't suppose you would have any white wine in there?"

"Yeah, I do," he said, and took a bottle from the refrigerator door.

"How long has that been in there, I wonder?" she asked.

"You want it or not?" he asked.

She nodded. "Please."

He took a stemmed glass from a cupboard over the sink, filled it nearly full with wine, and handed it to her.

"Make this quick, whatever it is," he said. "I have to work tonight, and between now and nine, I've got to grab a sandwich or something."

She didn't respond to that. Instead she raised her glass toward the mantelpiece of the fireplace, which showed evidence of having recently been bricked in.

"What's this?" she asked. "Your temple of the phallic symbol?"

"What?"

"Firearms are a substitute phallus," she said.

He saw that she was referring to his pistols, both of which he had placed on the wooden mantelpiece.

"Only for people with performance problems," Matt snorted. "I don't have that kind of problem. Not only did I take Psychology 101, too, Amy, but I stayed awake through the parts you missed."

"That's why you have two of them, right?" she replied. "I hope they're not loaded."

"One of them is," he said. "Leave them alone."

"Why two?"

"I bought the little one today; it's easier to conceal," he said. "Is that the purpose of your uninvited visit, to lay some of your psychiatric bullshit on me?"

She turned to face him.

"I had lunch with Mother today," she said. "She worries me."

"What's the matter with Mother?" he asked, concern coming quickly into his voice.

"Why you are, of course," she said. "Don't tell me that hasn't run through your mind."

"Oh, not that again!"

"Yes, that again," she said. "And she has every reason to feel that way. She's had a husband killed, *and* a brother-in-law, and she'd be a fool if she closed her mind to the possibility that could happen to a son, too."

"Did she say anything?"

"Of course not," Amy said. "Mother's not the type to whine."

"We have, I seem to recall," Matt said, "been over this before. My position, I seem to recall, was that I had—there was a much greater chance of my getting myself blown away if I had made it into the Marines. I didn't hear any complaints, I seem to recall, from you about my going in the Marines."

"You had no choice about that," she said. "You do about being a policeman."

"Oh, shit!" he said, disgustedly. "When you get a real complaint about me from Mother, then come to see me, Amy. In the meantime, butt out."

"You refuse to see, don't you, that this entire insane notion of yours to be a policeman is nothing more than an attempt to overcome the psychological castration you underwent when you failed the Marine physical."

"I seem to recall your saying something like that, before, Dr. Strangelove."

"Well, I don't have to be a psychiatrist to know that your being a policeman is tearing Mother up!"

"But your being a shrink makes it easier, right?"

The telephone rang. Matt picked it up.

"Dr. Payne's Looney-Bin, Matt the Castrated speaking."

"Peter Wohl, Matt," his caller identified himself.

*Oh, shit! Those two bastards in the highway RPC sure didn't lose any time squealing on me!*

*And, oh, Jesus, what I just said!*

"Yes, sir?"

Amy looked at him curiously. The phrase "yes, sir" was not ordinarily in his vocabulary.

"That was an interesting way to answer your phone," Peter Wohl said.

"Sir," Matt said, lamely. "My sister is here. We were having a little argument."

"Actually, that's what I called you about. You did mean your sister the psychiatrist?"

"Yes, sir."

"Jason Washington was just in to see me. He didn't turn up anything useful interviewing Miss Flannery. I'm sort of clutching at straws. In other words, I was hoping that your offer to talk to your sister was valid."

"Yes, sir, of course. I'm sure she'd be happy to speak with you."

"Who is that?" Amy asked in a loud whisper. Matt held up his hand to silence her, which had the exact opposite reaction. *"Who is that?"* Amy repeated, louder this time.

"I'm talking about now, Matt," Wohl said.

"Yes, sir," Matt said. "Now would be fine."

"I suppose you've eaten?"

"Sir?"

"I asked, have you had dinner?"

"No, sir."

"Well, then, why don't I pick you up, and we'll get a little something to eat, and I can speak with her. Would that be too much of an imposition on such short notice?"

"Not at all, sir."

"You live in the 3800 block of Walnut, right?"

"No, sir. I've moved. I'm now on Rittenhouse Square, South, in the Delaware Valley Cancer Society Building—"

"I know where it is."

"In the attic, sir. Ring the button that says *'Superintendent'* in the lobby."

"I'll be there in fifteen minutes," Wohl said. "Thank you."

The phone went dead.

"What was all that about? Who were you talking to?"

"That was my boss," Matt said. "He wants to talk to you. I told him about you."

"Tell him to call the office and make an appointment," Amy snapped. "My God, you've got your nerve, Matt!"

"It's important," Matt said.

"Maybe it is to you, Dick Tracy, to polish the boss's apple, but it's not to me. The nerve! I don't believe that you really thought I would go along with this!"

"A lunatic who has already raped, so to speak, a half dozen women, grabbed another one last night, forced her into his van at knifepoint, and hasn't been seen since," Matt said, evenly. "Inspector Wohl thinks you might be able to provide a profile of this splendid fellow, and that might possibly help us to find him."

"Doesn't the Police Department have its own psychologists, psychiatrists?" Amy asked.

"I'm sure they do," Matt said. "But he wants to talk to you. Please, Amy."

She looked at him for a long moment, then shrugged.

"Why did you say, 'raped, so to speak'?"

"Because, so far," Matt said, as evenly, "there has been no vaginal or anal penetration, and the forced fellatio has not resulted in ejaculation."

"You should hear yourself," she said, softly. "How cold-blooded and clinical you sound. Oh, Matt!"

It was, she realized, a wail of anguish at the loss of her little brother's innocence.

"Under these circumstances," she added, as cold-bloodedly as she could manage, "I don't have much choice, do I?"

"Not really," Matt said. "He's going to take us to dinner."

"I can't go anywhere looking like this," she said. "I came here right from the hospital."

"Well, then, we'll go someplace where you won't look out of place," Matt said.

"The bathroom, presumably, is in there?" Amy asked, pointing toward his bedroom.

"Vanity, thy name is woman," Matt quoted sonorously.

"Screw you, Matt," Dr. Amelia Alice Payne replied.

Staff Inspector Peter Wohl was not what Amy Payne expected. She wasn't sure exactly what she had expected—maybe a slightly younger version of Matt's "Uncle Denny" Coughlin—but she had not expected the pleasant, well-dressed young man (she guessed that he was in his early thirties) who came through Matt's apartment door.

"Amy," Matt said, "this is Inspector Wohl. Amy Payne, M.D."

Wohl smiled at her.

"Doctor, I very much appreciate your agreeing to talk to me like this," he said. "I realize what an imposition it is."

"Not at all," Amy said, and hearing her voice was furious with herself; she had practically gushed.

"I've been trying to figure out the best way to do this," Wohl said. "What I would like you to do, if you would be so kind, would be to read the file we have on this man, and then tell me what kind of man he is."

"I understand," Amy said.

He gave her a look she understood in a moment was surprise, even annoyance, that she had interrupted him.

He smiled.

"But that isn't really the sort of thing you want to talk about over dinner. And dinner is certainly necessary. Then there's Matt."

"Sir?" Matt said.

*There he goes again with that "Sir" business,* Amy thought. *Who does he think this cop is, anyway?*

"What time are you meeting McFadden and Martinez?"

"Nine o'clock, at the FOP," Matt said.

*What in the world is the Eff Oh Pee?*

"I thought that was it," Wohl said. "So what I propose is that we go to an Italian restaurant I know on Tenth Street, and have dinner. Then I could drop you at the FOP, Matt, and take Dr. Payne to the Roundhouse, and borrow an office there where we could have our talk."

*I really loathe spaghetti and meatballs; but what did I expect?*

"Sir," Matt said, "why don't you come back here? I mean, she has her car in the garage here."

"Well, I don't know. . . ."

"How would you get in if you gave us your key?" Amy asked.

"I wouldn't give you my key," Matt explained tolerantly. "I would leave the door to the apartment unlocked, and you use your key to get in the building."

"Doctor?" Peter asked, politely.

"Whatever would be best," Amy heard herself saying.

*It is absolutely absurd of me to think about being alone in an apartment with a man I hardly know. This is a purely professional situation; he's a policeman and I am a physician. I will do my professional duty, even if that entails pretending I like spaghetti and meatballs. And besides it's important to Matt.*

The tailcoated waiter in *Ristorante Alfredo* bowed over the table, holding out a bottle of wine on a napkin for Peter Wohl's inspection.

"Compliments of the house, sir," he said, speaking in a soft Italian accent. "Will this be satisfactory?"

Wohl glanced at it, then turned to Amy. "That's fine with me. How about you, Doctor? It's sort of an Italian *Pinot Noir*."

"Fine with me," Amy said. She watched as the waiter uncorked the bottle, showed Wohl the cork, then poured a little in his glass for him to taste.

"That's fine, thank you," Wohl said to the waiter, who proceeded to fill all their glasses.

"I think it will go well with the *tournedos Alfredo*," the waiter said. "Thank you, sir."

Peter Wohl had explained to both of them that the *tournedos Alfredo*, which he highly recommended, were sort of an Italian version of steak with a *marchand de vin* sauce, except there was just a touch more garlic to it.

"You must be a pretty good customer in here, Inspector," Amy said, aware that there was more than a slight tone of bitchiness in her voice.

"I come here fairly often," Wohl replied. "I try not to abuse it, to save it for a suitable occasion."

"Excuse me?"

'Well, my money is no good in here," Wohl said.

"I don't think I understand that," Amy said.

"The Mob owns this place," Wohl said, matter-of-factly. "Specifically a man named Vincenzo Savarese—the license is in someone else's name, but Savarese is behind it—and he has left word that I'm not to get a bill."

"Excuse me," Amy flared, "but isn't that what they call 'being on the take'?"

"My God, Amy!" Matt said, furiously.

"No," Wohl said. " 'Being on the take' means accepting goods or services, or money, in exchange for ignoring criminal activity. Vincenzo Savarese knows that I would like nothing better than to put him behind bars; and that, as a matter of fact, before they dumped this new job in my lap, I was trying very hard to do just that."

"Then why does he pick up your restaurant bills?" Amy asked.

"Who knows? The Mob is weird. They operate as if they were still in Sicily or Naples, with a perverted honor code. He thinks he's a 'man of honor,' and thinks I am, too. He thought Dutch Moffitt was, too. Mrs. Savarese and her sister went to his funeral. The wake, too, I think, and when Dutch, before he went to Highway, was in Organized Crime, he tried very hard to lock Savarese up."

Amy decided she was talking too much, and needed time to consider what she had just heard.

The waiter and two busboys, with great élan, served the *tournedos Alfredo* and the side dishes. Amy took four bites of the steak, then curiosity got the best of her.

"And it doesn't offend your sense of right and wrong to take free meals from a gangster?" she asked.

"Come on, Amy!" Matt protested again.

"No," Wohl said, making a gesture with his hand toward Matt to show that since he didn't mind the question, Matt should not be upset. "What I will do in the morning is send a memo to Internal Affairs, reporting that I got a free meal here. As far as taking it—why not? Savarese knows he'll get nothing in return, and this is first-class food."

"But you know he's a gangster," Amy argued.

"And he knows I'm a cop, an honest cop," Wohl countered. "Under those circumstances, if it gives both of us pleasure, what's wrong with it?"

Amy Payne could think of no withering counterargument, and was furious. Then doubly furious when she saw Matt smiling smugly at her.

Matt glanced at his watch as the pastry cart was wheeled to the table, then jumped to his feet.

"I better get over to the FOP," he said. "You finish your dinner. I'll catch a cab. Or run."

When he was gone, Wohl said, "He's a very nice young man, soaking wet behind the ears, but very nice."

"I think I should tell you, Inspector," Amy said, "that I'm not thrilled with his choice of career."

"I would be very surprised if you were," Wohl said. "Your mother must really be upset."

*Damn it, you weren't supposed to agree with me!*

"She is," Amy said. "I had lunch with her today."

"I feel a little sorry for myself, too," Wohl said. "Dennis Coughlin sent him to me, with the unspoken, but very obvious, implication that I am to look after him. I think Coughlin is probably as unhappy as you and your family about his taking the job.''

He looked at her, and when she didn't reply, added, ''He's twenty-one years old, Dr. Payne. I suspect that he has been very humiliated by having failed the Marine Corps physical. He has decided he wants to be a policeman, and I don't think there's anything anyone can do, or could have done to dissuade him.''

*I don't need you to explain that to me, damn you again!*

''You don't agree?'' Wohl asked.

''I suppose that's true,'' Amy said. ''Where's he going tonight? What's the Eff Oh Pee?''

''Fraternal Order of Police,'' Wohl said, ''They have a building on Spring Garden, just off Broad. He's meeting two of my men there. They're going to look for a man we think is connected with a couple of burglaries in Chestnut Hill. I told them to take Matt with them, to give him an idea how things are, on the street.''

''Oh,'' she said.

''That chocolate whateveritis looks good,'' Wohl said. ''Would you like a piece?''

''No, thank you,'' Amy snipped. ''Nothing for me, thank you.''

''You don't mind if I do?''

''No, of course not,'' Amy said.

*Damn this man, he has a skin like an elephant, the smug sonofabitch!*

Matt got out of the taxi in front of the Fraternal Order of Police Building on Spring Garden Street and looked at his watch. He was five minutes late.

*Damn!* he thought, and then *Double Damn, either I've got the wrong place, or this place is closed!*

Then, on the right corner of the building, he saw movement, a couple going into a door. He walked to it, and saw there were stairs and went down them. He had just relaxed with the realization that he had found ''the bar at the FOP,'' even if five minutes late, when a large man stepped in front of him.

"This is a private club, fella," he said.

"I'm meeting someone," Matt replied. "Officer Mc-Fadden."

The man looked at him dubiously, but after a moment stepped out of his way, and waved him into the room.

Matt wondered how one joined the FOP; he would have to ask.

The room was dark and noisy. There was a dance floor crowded with people and what he thought at first was a band, but quickly realized was a phonograph playing records, very loudly, through enormous speakers. At the far end of the room, he saw a bar, and made his way toward it.

He found Officers McFadden and Martinez standing at the bar, at the right of it.

"Sorry to be late," Matt said.

"We was just starting to wonder where you were," Charley McFadden said. "Talking about you, as a matter of fact."

"You got to learn to be on time," Jesus Martinez said.

"He said he was sorry, Hay-zus," McFadden defended him.

McFadden, Matt saw, was drinking Ortlieb's beer, from the bottle. Martinez had what looked like a glass of water.

"You want a beer, Matt?"

"Please," Matt said. "Ortlieb's."

"Hey, Charley," McFadden called to the bartender. "Give us another round here!"

"Two beers and a glass of water?" the bartender said. "Or is Jesus still working on the one he has, taking it easy?"

"Call him, Hay-zus," McFadden said. "He likes that better. Charley, say hello to Matt Payne."

Matt was at the moment distracted by something to his right. A woman leaned up off her bar stool, supported herself with one hand on the bar, and threw an empty cigarette package into a plastic garbage can behind the bar. In doing so, her dress top fell open, and her brassiere came into view. Her brassiere was one that Matt had yet to see in the flesh, but had seen in *Playboy, Penthouse*, and other magazines of the type young men buy for the high literary content of their articles and fiction.

It was black, lacy, and instead of the cloth hemispheres of an ordinary brassiere, this one had sort of half hemispheres, on the bottom only, which presented the upper portion of the breast to Matt's view, including the nipple.

Matt found this very interesting, and was grossly embarrassed when the woman glanced his way, saw him looking, said "Hi!" and then returned to her bar stool.

She was old, he thought, at least thirty-five, and she had caught him looking down her dress.

*Oh, shit! If she says something . . .*

"Matt, say hello to Charley Castel," Charley McFadden repeated.

Matt offered his hand to Charley Castel. "How are you?"

"Matt's out with us in Special Operations," Charley said.

"Is that so?" Charley Castel said.

"He just got out of the Academy," Jesus Martinez offered.

*Thanks a lot, pal,* Matt thought.

"Is that so?" Charley Castel repeated. "Well, welcome to the job, Matt."

"Aren't you going to introduce me to your friend?" a female voice said in Matt's ear. Out of the corner of his eye, he saw it was the woman who had caught him peering down her dress.

"Yeah, why not?" Charley said, chuckling. "Matt, this is Lorraine Witzell, Lorraine, this is Matt Payne."

"How are you, Matt Payne?" Lorraine said, putting her arm between Matt and Charley to shake his hand, which action served to cause her breast to press against Matt's arm. "Is that short for Matthew, or what?"

"Yes, ma'am," Matt said.

"Yes, ma'am," Jesus Martinez parroted sarcastically.

"You're sweet," Lorraine Witzell said to Matt, looking

into his eyes and not letting go of his hand. "Did I hear Charley say you've been assigned to Special Operations?"

"That's right," Matt said.

*For an older woman, she's really not too bad-looking. And she either didn't really catch me looking down her dress, or, Jesus, she doesn't care.*

"That should be an interesting assignment," Lorraine said.

"We're on the job now, Lorraine," Charley McFadden said. "We was just talking about that."

"You're working plainclothes?" she asked. Matt sensed the question was directed to him, but Charley answered it.

"We're looking for a fag burglar," Charley replied. "Been hitting some rich woman in Chestnut Hill."

"Well, if you're going to work the fag joints," Lorraine said, again directly to Matt, "you better keep your hand you-know-where, and I don't mean on your gun. They're going to love you!"

"What we was talking about," Charley McFadden said, "is maybe splitting up. Hay-zus taking the unmarked car—he don't drink, and it's better that way—and you and me go together."

"Whatever you say, Charley," Matt said.

"You got your car? Mine's a dog."

"I came in a cab," Matt said.

"Oh," Charley said.

Matt saw the look of disappointment on McFadden's face.

"But I don't live far; getting it wouldn't be any trouble." McFadden's disappointment diminished.

"What I was thinking was that in a car like yours, we could cruise better," McFadden said.

"I understand," Matt said. "You mean it's the sort of car a fag would drive?"

"I didn't say that," McFadden said, embarrassed. "But, no offense, yeah."

"What kind of car do you have?" Lorraine asked.

"A Porsche 911T," Charley answered for him.

"Oh, they're darling!" Lorraine said, clutching Charley's

arm high up under the armpit, which also caused her breast to press against his arm again.

Which caused a physical reaction in Matt Payne that he would rather not have had under the circumstances, at this particular point in space and time.

"Where do you live, Payne?" Jesus Martinez asked.

"On Rittenhouse Square," Matt said.

"Figures," Martinez said. "Let's get the hell out of here, somebody's liable to spot that car in the parking lot and start asking questions."

"To which we answer, we were picking up Payne, and you were drinking water," McFadden replied, but Matt saw that he picked up his fresh Ortlieb's and drank half of it.

"Hay-zus is a worrier," Charley said to Matt.

"You better be glad I am," Martinez replied.

Lorraine Witzell pushed between Charley and Matt to sit her glass on the bar, which served to place her rear end against Matt's groin and the physiological phenomenon he would have rather not had manifesting itself at that moment. It didn't seem to bother Lorraine Witzell at all; quite the contrary. She seemed to be backing harder against it.

Matt took a pull at his bottle of Ortlieb's.

"I'm ready," he said, signifying his willingness to leave. "Anytime."

Lorraine Witzell chuckled deep in her throat.

"Well," she said, "if it turns out to be a dull night, come on back. I'll probably be here."

# FIFTEEN

At quarter to one, Officer Charley McFadden pulled Matt Payne's Porsche 911T to the curb before a row house on Fitzgerald Street, not far from Methodist Hospital, in South Philadelphia.

"It happens that way sometimes," Charley said to Matt. "Sometimes you can go out and find who you're looking for easy as hell. And other times, it's like this. We'll catch the bastard. Hay-zus will turn up something."

"Yeah," Matt said.

"And you got the fag tour, right?" Charley said. "So it wasn't a complete waste of time, right?"

"It was . . . educational," Matt said, just a little thickly.

"And we wasn't in all of them," McFadden laughed. "Maybe half."

"There seem to be more of those places than I would have thought possible," Matt said, pronouncing each syllable carefully.

"You all right to drive?"

"Fine," Matt said.

"You're welcome to sleep on the couch here," Charley offered.

"I'm all right," Matt insisted.

"Well, drive careful, huh? You don't want to fuck up a car like this."

"I'll be careful," Matt said, and got out of the car and walked around the back.

"We'll get the bastard," Charley McFadden repeated. "And what the hell, we were on overtime, right?"

"Right," Matt said. "Good night, Charley. See you in the morning."

He started the engine, returned to South Broad Street, and pointed the nose toward Willy Penn, surveying the city from atop City Hall.

Matt had asked Charley McFadden about "that woman you introduced me to in the FOP" five minutes after they had picked up the Porsche, and were headed into West Philadelphia.

"She works for the district attorney," Charley said. "They call her the shark."

"Why?"

"Well, she likes cops," Charley said. "Young cops in particular. What did she do, grab your joint?"

"No. Nothing like that," Matt said. "I was just curious, that's all."

"I'm surprised," Charley said. "She looked pretty interested, to me."

"She seemed to know a good deal about the police, about police work."

"As much as any cop," Charley had said.

Matt reached City Hall, and drove around it, and up North Broad to Spring Garden and into the FOP parking lot.

The place was still crowded. He made his way to the bar and ordered a scotch and soda. He had a good deal to drink, some of the drinks paid for by either the proprietors of the bars they visited, or put in front of him by the bartender, who had then said, "The tall fellow at the end of the bar," or something like that.

He saw Lorraine Witzell at the far end of the bar, with three men standing around her.

*Well, it was dumb coming here in the first place.*

And then fingers grazed his neck.

"I was beginning to think you'd found something more interesting to do," Lorraine Witzell said, as she slid onto the bar stool behind, which action caused first one of her knees and then the other to graze his crotch.

"May I buy you a drink?" Matt said, very carefully.

Lorraine Witzell looked at him and smiled.

"You can, but what I think would make a lot more sense, baby, would be for Lorraine to take you home and get some coffee into you. You can take me for a ride in your Porsche some other time. It'll be safe in the parking lot here."

"I'm all right to drive," Matt insisted, somewhat indignantly, as Lorraine led him across the FOP bar and up the stairs to the street.

Peter Wohl walked to his car, and stood outside the door until he saw Dr. Amelia Payne's Buick station wagon come out of the alley beside the Delaware Valley Cancer Society Building and drive past him.

He raised his hand in a wave, but Dr. Payne either did not see it, or ignored it. He shrugged and got in the car, started it up, and reached for the microphone in the glove compartment, realizing only then that was the wrong radio. He put the microphone back, and fumbled around on the seat for the microphone that would give him access to the Highway Band.

He became aware that a car had pulled parallel to him and stopped. He turned to look, and found a pair of Highway Patrolmen looking at him from the front seat of an unmarked Highway car.

He waved and smiled. There was no response from either cop, but the car moved off.

*They either didn't recognize me, or they did and aren't in a particularly friendly mood toward the sonofabitch who took Highway away from Good Ol' Mike and gave it to Dave Pekach.*

He picked up the microphone, and as he did, smiled.

"Highway One, this is S-Sam One."

"Highway One," Pekach came back immediately. Wohl was not surprised that Pekach was up and riding around. Not only was he new to the job, and conscientious, but Pekach was used to working nights; it would take him a week, maybe longer, to get used to the idea that the Commander of Highway worked the day shift.

"I'm on Rittenhouse Square, David. Where are you? Where could we meet?"

Wohl chuckled. The brake lights on the unmarked Highway car flashed on, and the car slowed momentarily. In what he was sure was an involuntary reflex action, the driver had hit the brakes when he heard the New Boss calling Highway One. He was sure he could read the driver's mind: *I thought that was him. Now what's the bastard up to?*

"I'm on the expressway about a mile from the Manayunk Bridge," Pekach said. "You name it."

"You know where I live?"

"Yes, I do."

"I'll meet you there," Wohl said, and laid the microphone down.

Pekach, in full uniform, complete to motorcyclist's boots and Sam Browne belt festooned with shiny cartridges, was leaning on a Highway blue-and-white on the cobblestones before Wohl's garage apartment when Wohl got there.

*I wouldn't be surprised if he was working the expressway with radar for speeders,* Wohl thought, and was immediately sorry. That was both unkind and not true. What David Pekach was doing was what he would have done himself in the circumstances, making the point that Highway could expect to find the boss riding around at midnight, and the second, equally important point, that he was not sneaking around in an unmarked car, but in uniform and in a blue-and-white.

Wohl pulled the nose of the LTD up to the garage and got out.

"Let me put this away, David," he called. "And then I'll buy you a beer. Long night?"

"I thought it was a good idea to ride around," Pekach said.

"So do I," Wohl said, as he unlocked the doors and swung them open. "But it's after midnight."

He put the car in the garage, and then touched Pekach's arm as he led him up the stairs to the apartment.

"You seen the papers?" Pekach said.

"No, should I have?"

"Yeah, I think so. I brought you the *Bulletin* and the *Ledger*."

"Thank you," Wohl said. "It wouldn't take a minute to make coffee."

"I'm coffeed out; beer would be fine."

"Sit," Wohl said, pointing to the couch beneath the oil painting of the voluptuous nude, and went to the refrigerator and came back with two bottles of Schlitz. "Glass?"

"This is fine," Pekach said, "thank you."

"Nothing on Elizabeth Woodham?" Wohl asked. "I expect I would have heard. . . ."

David Pekach shook his head.

"Not a damn thing," he said. "I was so frustrated I actually wrote a speeding ticket."

"Really?" Wohl chuckled.

"Sonofabitch came by me at about eighty, as if I wasn't there. I thought maybe he was drunk, so I pulled him over. He was sober. Just in a hurry."

"It's been a long time since I wrote a ticket," Wohl said.

"When he saw he was going to get a ticket," Pekach said, "he got nasty. He said he was surprised a captain would be out getting people for something like speeding when we had a serial rapist and a kidnapped woman on our hands."

"Ouch," Wohl said.

"I felt like belting the sonofabitch," Pekach said. "That was just before you called."

"I had a disturbing session just before I called you," Wohl said. "With a psychiatrist. You've seen that kid hanging around Bustleton and Bowler? Payne?"

"He's Dutch's nephew or something?"

"Yeah. Well, his sister. I let her read the files and asked her for a profile."

"And?"

"Not much that'll help us find him, I'm afraid. But she said—the way she put it was 'slippery slope'—that once somebody like this doer goes over the edge, commits the first act, starts to act out his fantasies, it's a slippery slope."

"Huh," Pekach said.

"Meaning that he's unable to stop, and starts to think of himself as invincible, starts to think, in other words, that he can get away with anything. Worse, that to get the same charge, the same satisfaction, he has to get deeper and deeper into his fantasies."

"Meaning, she doesn't think we're going to get the Woodham woman back alive?"

"No, she doesn't," Peter said. "And worse, that because he's starting to think he's invincible, that he's not going to get caught, that he'll go after somebody else, a new conquest, more quickly than he has before."

"I'm not sure I understand that," Pekach said.

"What she said is that the first time, after he'd done it, he was maybe ashamed and afraid he would get caught. And then when he didn't get caught, he stopped being afraid. And he remembered how much fun it was. So he did it again, got into his fantasies a little deeper, and was a little less frightened, and a lot less ashamed."

"Jesus!"

"What she, Dr. Payne, said was that it "*evolves into frenzy.*"

"She meant he loses control?"

"Yeah."

"You think she knows what she's talking about?"

"I'm afraid she does," Wohl said.

"What can be done that isn't being done?" Pekach asked.

"Tony Harris is working minor sexual offenders," Wohl said. "He thinks this guy may have a misdemeanor arrest or two for exposing himself, soliciting a hooker, you know. Mike has been out recruiting people, and as soon as they start coming in, in the morning, I'm going to put them to work ringing doorbells for Harris."

"If there was a van, any kind of van, in Northwest Philly tonight that got away with not coming to a complete stop, or whose taillights weren't working, you know what I mean, I would be very surprised," Pekach said. "But we just can't stop every goddamned van in town, looking for a hairy white male, no further description available."

"I know," Wohl said.

"I went to the roll call tonight," Pekach said, "and reminded Highway that if we catch this scumbag, it might get the goddamned newspapers, especially the goddamned *Ledger*, off our backs. Not that they wouldn't be trying to catch this scumbag anyway."

"I know," Wohl said.

"Czernick on your back, Peter? Coughlin? The mayor?"

"Not yet," Peter said. "But that's going to happen."

"What do they expect?"

"Results," Wohl said. "I'm wide open to suggestion, David."

"I don't have any, sorry," Pekach said.

"What did you decide after tonight?" Wohl asked.

"Excuse me?"

"What shape is Highway in? Isn't that why you were riding around?"

Pekach met Wohl's eyes for a moment before replying.

"I went in on six calls," he said. "One on 95, one on the expressway, both traffic violations, and the other four all over town, a robbery in progress, two burglaries, man with a gun, that sort of thing. I didn't find a damned thing wrong with anything Highway did."

"Did AID come up with any witnesses in the accident?"

Any accident involving a city-owned vehicle is investigated by the Accident Investigation Division of the Police Department.

"Not a damned one."

"Well, I'll check and make sure they keep trying," Wohl said.

"I intended to do that, Inspector," Pekach said, coldly.

"I didn't mean that, David," Wohl said, evenly, "the way you apparently thought it sounded."

"I also let the word get out that maybe AID could use a little help," Pekach said.

"Meaning exactly what, David?" Wohl asked, his voice now chilly.

Pekach didn't reply; it was obvious he didn't want to.

"Come on, David," Wohl insisted.

Pekach shrugged.

"I wouldn't be surprised," Pekach said, "if a bunch of people in sports jackets and ties went around the neighborhood ringing doorbells. And if one of them turned up a witness, and then, anonymously, as a public-spirited citizen, called AID and gave them the witness's name, what's wrong with that?"

"Off-duty people in sports coats and ties, you mean, of course? Who could easily be mistaken for newspaper reporters or insurance investigators because they never even hinted they might be connected with the Police Department?"

"Of course," Pekach said.

"Then in that case, David," Wohl said, smiling at Pekach, "I would say that the new commander of Highway was already learning that some of the things a commander has to do can't be found in the book."

"I'm sorry I snapped at you before," Pekach said. "I don't know what the hell is the matter with me. Sorry."

"Maybe we're both a little nervous in our new jobs."

"You bet your ass," Pekach agreed, chuckling.

"You want another beer, David?"

"No. This'll do it. Now that I had it, I'm getting sleepy."

He got up. "Something will turn up, Peter, it always does," he said.

"I'm afraid of what will," Wohl said. "How long do you think it will take your wife to learn that the Highway Captain doesn't have to work eighteen hours a day?"

"Forever; I don't have a wife," Pekach said. "Or was that to politely tell me not to ride around?"

"It was to politely tell you to knock off the eighteen-hour days," Wohl said.

Pekach looked at him long enough to decide he was getting a straight answer, and gave one in return.

"I think Highway is sort of an honor, Peter. I want to do it right."

"You can do it right on say *twelve* hours a day," Wohl said, smiling.

"Isn't that the pot calling the kettle black?"

"The difference is that you have a kindly, understanding supervisor," Wohl said. "I have Coughlin, Czernick, and Carlucci."

"You may have a point." Pekach chuckled. "Good night, Peter. Thanks for the beer."

"Thanks for the talk," Wohl said. "I wanted to bounce what Dr. Payne said off someone bright."

"I'm very much afraid she's going to be right," Pekach said, and then he added, "Don't read those newspapers tonight. Let them ruin your breakfast, not your sleep."

"That bad?"

"The *Ledger* is really on our ass, yours in particular," Pekach said.

"Now, I'll have to read it," Wohl said, as he walked with Pekach to the door.

Wohl carried the beer bottles to the sink, emptied the inch remaining in his down the drain, and put them both in the garbage can under the sink.

He went to his bedroom, undressed, and then, giving into curiosity, walked naked into the living room and reclaimed the newspapers.

He spread them out on his bed, and sat down to read them.

There was a photograph of Elizabeth J. Woodham on the front page of the *Ledger*, under the headline: KIDNAPPED SCHOOLTEACHER. Below the picture was a lengthy caption.

> Elizabeth J. Woodham, 33, of the 300 block of E. Mermaid Lane in Chestnut Hill, is still missing two days after she was forced at knifepoint into a van and driven away. Her abductor is generally believed to be the serial rapist active in Chestnut Hill.
>
> Inspector Peter Wohl, recently put in charge of a new Special Operations Division, which has assumed responsibility for the kidnapping, was "not available for the press" for comment, and Captain Michael J. Sabara, recently relieved as commander of the Highway Patrol to serve as Wohl's Deputy, refused to answer questions concerning Miss Woodham put to him by a *Ledger* reporter.
>
> Sources believed by the *Ledger* to be reliable, however, have said the police have no clues that might lead them to the abductor, and no description of him beyond that of a "hairy, well-spoken white male." [Further details and photographs on page B-3. The Police Department's handling of this case is also the subject of today's *Ledger* editorial, page A-7.]

Peter turned to the story, which contained nothing he hadn't seen before, and then to the editorial:

## HOUSECLEANING NEEDED, NOT WHITEWASH

It is frankly outrageous, considering the millions of dollars Philadelphia's taxpayers pour unquestioningly into their police department, that a woman can be taken from her home at knifepoint at all. It is even more outrageous that twenty-four hours after the kidnapping, the police, rather than devoting all of their time and effort to apprehending the individual responsible for the kidnapping, and rescuing a kidnapped schoolteacher, have instead elected to assign many members of the so-called elite Highway Patrol to finding witnesses willing to say that the father of the four-year-old boy killed when a stoplight-running Highway Patrol smashed into his car was at fault, not them.

It was unconscionable that Inspector Peter Wohl, a crony of Police Commissioner Czernick, who is the responsible senior police official involved, should make himself "not available" to the press. The people have a right to know how well—or how poorly—their police are protecting them.

Mayor Carlucci should replace Czernick and Wohl with police officers dedicated to protecting the public, and not to whitewashing the Highway Patrol's unjustified, frequent, and well-documented excesses and failures. Anything less is malfeasance in office.

"Oh, *shit*," Peter Wohl said, tiredly, closing the newspaper. Then he picked up the *Bulletin*. There were two stories about the Woodham abduction. One, a tearjerker, was written by a woman, Cheryl Davies, and chronicled the anguish of Elizabeth J. Woodham's family and friends. She had done her homework, Peter admitted grudgingly. There was a photograph of, and the reactions of, two sixth-graders who had been in her classes.

Mickey O'Hara's story was more or less upbeat. He wrote that Czernick had agreed to transfer to

> . . . Staff Inspector Peter Wohl's just-forming new command two of the most highly respected homicide detectives, Jason Washington and Anthony Harris. Wohl, who himself enjoys a wide reputation as an investigator, has turned over the Woodham abduction to Washington and Harris, and is reported to be himself working around the clock on the investigation.

He finished reading Mickey's story, then folded the *Bulletin* closed, too. He exhaled audibly, stood up, and carried the newspapers into the kitchen, intending to put them in the garbage. Then he changed his mind and simply laid them on the counter by the sink.

When he went back into his bedroom, he smashed his right fist into his open palm, grimaced, considered for a moment getting drunk, and wound up with his head pressing against the closed venetian blinds on the window beside his bed.

Without knowing why he did it, he pulled on the cord, and the blinds twisted open, and he could see the Big House thirty yards away.

There were lights in only several of the windows, and he had just decided they were the windows of Two B, Chez Schneider, when there was proof. Naomi Schneider, wearing only her underpants, pranced into view, smiling happily at someone else in the room, and handing him a drink.

Without thinking about it, Peter turned off the lights in his bedroom.

"Peel him a grape, Naomi," Peter said, aloud.

And then he wondered if Mr. Schneider had come home unexpectedly, or whether Naomi had pulled on someone else's dong to lure him into what obviously was her bedroom.

*Nice boobs!*

And then a wave of chagrin hit him.

"Oh, shit," he said. He closed the blinds quickly, turned the light on, and sat on the bed.

*"You're a fucking voyeur, you goddamned pervert! You were really getting turned on watching her boobs flop around like that.*

*You ought to be ashamed of yourself!*

And then he had a second thought, not quite as self-critical: *Or get your ashes hauled, so that you won't get horny, peeking through people's bedroom windows.*

And then he had a third thought, considered it a moment, and then dug the telephone book from where he kept it under his bed.


Amelia Alice Payne, M.D., lived on the tenth floor of the large, luxurious apartment building on the 2600 block of the Parkway, said to be the first of its kind in Philadelphia, and somewhat unimaginatively named the *2601 Parkway.*

She got off the elevator, walked twenty yards down the corridor, and let herself into her apartment.

She pushed the door closed with her rear end, turned and fastened the chain, and started to unbutton her blouse. She was tired, both from a long day, and from her long session with Staff Inspector Peter Wohl.

She walked into her living room and slumped into the armchair beside a table, which held the telephone answering device. She snapped it on.

She grunted as she bent to take off her shoes.

There were a number of messages, but none of them were important, or required any action on her part tonight. She had no intention of returning the call of one female patient who announced that she just had to talk to her as soon as possible. Listening to another litany of the faults of the lady's husband would have to wait until tomorrow.

She reset the machine, turned it off, and, carrying her shoes, walked into her bedroom, turning to the drapes and closing them. Open, they had given her a view of downtown Philadelphia, and, to the right, the headlights moving up and down the Schuylkill Expressway.

Amy decided against taking a shower. No one was going to be around to smell her tonight, and it would be better to use the shower as both cleanser and waker-upper in the morning.

She took off her blouse and pushed her skirt off her hips, and jerked the cover of her bed.

She probably had met more offensive men than Peter Wohl in her life, but she couldn't call one to mind at the moment. He represented everything she found offensive in men, except, she thought, that he didn't have either a pencil-line mustache or a pinky ring. But everything else she detested was there, starting with the most advanced (regressive?) case of Male Supremacist Syndrome she had ever encountered.

It was probably his cultural background, she thought. Wohl was certainly German. What was it the Germans said to define their perception of the proper role of females in society, *Kinder, Kirche, und Kuche*? Children, church, and kitchen. He obviously thought that Moses had carried that down from Mount Sinai with the other Commandments.

And he was a cop, the son of a cop. Had he said the grandson of a cop, too? That, obviously, had had a lot to do with what he was, and how he thought.

It wasn't, she thought, that he had implied she was stupid. He had been perfectly willing to pick her mind about this seriously ill man who was raping the women in Northwest Philadelphia. He was willing, as he had proved by *interro-*

*gating* her for over three hours after they had gone back to Matt's apartment, to recognize her expertise, and take advantage of it. Men who couldn't fry an egg were always perfectly willing to allow themselves to be fed by the Little Woman.

Peter Wohl, Amy knew, had believed, and had been alarmed by, her announcement that the man he was looking for was rapidly losing what control he had left. He had asked her why she had felt that way, and she had explained, and then he had made her explain her explanations. And in the end, she knew he had accepted everything she had told him.

But he had never let her forget for a moment that he was a great big policeman, charged by God and the City of Philadelphia with protecting the weak and not-too-bright, such as she. He admired her skill and knowledge, Amy thought, the way he would have admired a dog who had been trained to walk on its hind legs. *Isn't that amazing!*

He had actually insisted on walking her to her car and then telling her *"to make sure"* to lock the doors from the inside, *"there were all sorts of people running loose at night."*

And if he had said *"Good Girl"* one more time, she would have thrown something at him.

Which, of course, would only have confirmed his devout belief that women were unstable creatures who needed a great big male to protect them from the world, and from themselves.

She pulled her slip over her head, and unfastened her brassiere and took that off, examining the marks it had left on the lower portion of her breasts.

The telephone rang. She reached down to her bedside table and picked it up.

*If it's that hysterical bitch calling again, I'll scream!*

"Yes?"

"Dr. Payne?"

"Yes."

*I'll be damned, it's him!*

"Peter Wohl, Doctor."

"How nice of you to call," Amy said, sarcastically.

"I'm glad I caught you before you got to bed," he said.

"Just barely," she said. "What is it, Inspector?"

*Was that a Freudian slip?* Amy wondered. She had, quite unintentionally, caught her reflection in the triple mirror of her vanity table. She was, except for her underpants, *bare.* She covered her breasts with her free arm.

"I wanted to say how grateful I am for all the help you gave me, for your time," Peter Wohl said.

*That's absurd! What am I modestly concealing? From whom? Mr. High and Mighty is on the telephone; he can't see me.*

"You said that earlier," she said.

She pushed her panties off her hips and stepped out of them, found her reflection again, put her free hand on her hip, and thrust it out.

*I have nothing whatever to be embarrassed about.*

"And I have one more question," he said.

"What?"

"What effect on our doer would seeing a naked woman have? I mean, if he saw one through her window?"

She felt herself flushing.

*Why the hell did he ask that?*

She looked quickly around the room to see that her own blinds were tightly drawn.

"As opposed to a woman . . . a fully clothed woman," Wohl went on.

"What did you do, Inspector, just see something like that?" Amy asked, sarcastically.

"As a matter of fact, yes," he said, unabashed. "Quite inadvertently."

"I'm sure," Amy said. "But it had no effect on you, right, but you're wondering if it would on . . . a mentally ill man?"

"No," he said. "Actually, it had quite an effect on me. It was rather embarrassing."

*Most men would deny that,* Amy thought. *How interesting.*

"The nude female, at least a reasonably attractive one," Amy said seriously, and then saw her reflection and almost giggled as she thought, *like me for example*, "has a certain effect on the male. The normal male. A mentally ill male? Let me think." She did, and then went on. "Probably, given a man with mental problems, it would have a more profound effect. I'm not sure what that would be. If he hates women, it might trigger disgust. He might become highly aroused. The disgust might trigger anger, a sense that he thereafter had the right to punish. Innocent nudity, changing clothes, having a bath, might lead him to thinking about the helplessness of the woman."

He grunted.

"Is this of any help to you?"

"Mary Elizabeth Flannery was wearing only her underpants when this scumbag—sorry—when this guy showed up."

"I saw that in the file," Amy said.

"Maybe he drives around looking through windows," Wohl thought aloud, "and when he finds a naked, or partially naked, woman, that turns him on."

"That might have been the trigger early on," Amy said. "I can't really say. But now that I'm almost certain this man is out of control, I don't really know what effect, if any, that would have."

"Ummm," Peter Wohl said, thoughtfully.

"If that's all, Inspector, it's very late."

"Actually," Peter Wohl blurted, "I had something else in mind."

It had, in fact, occurred to him two seconds before.

"Yes?" Amy said, impatiently.

"I really enjoyed our time together," Wohl plunged on, "and I hoped that you might have dinner with me sometime. On a nonprofessional basis."

"Oh, I see," she heard herself saying. "We could run through a long line of gangster-owned restaurants where fellow men of honor get free meals, is that it?"

There was a long pause, long enough for Amy to wonder *what's wrong with me? Why did I say that?*

"I beg your pardon, Doctor. I won't trouble you again."

*Oh, God, he's going to hang up!*

"Peter—"

There was no reply for a long moment, and then he said, "I'm here."

"I don't know why I said that. I'm sorry."

He didn't reply.

"I would love to have dinner with you," Amy heard herself blurting. "Call me. Tomorrow. I'm glad you called."

"So'm I," Peter Wohl said, happily. "Good night, Amy."

The line went dead.

She looked at herself in the mirror again.

Oh, God, she thought. *It* was *Freudian. Sex is what that was all about!*

# SIXTEEN

At five minutes to eight, the nineteen police officers assigned to the day shift of the Fourteenth Police District gathered in the Roll Call Room of the district building at Germantown and Haines Streets, and went through the roll call ritual, under the eyes of Captain Charles D. Emerson, the Fourteenth District Commander, a heavyset, gray-haired man of fifty.

The officers formed in ranks, and went through the ritual, obviously based on similar rituals in the armed forces, of inspection in ranks. Trailed by the Sergeant, Captain Emerson marched through the three ranks of men, stopping in front of each to examine his appearance, the length of his hair, whether or not he was closely shaved, and the cleanliness of his weapon, which each officer held up in front of him, with the cylinder open. Several times, perhaps six, Captain Emerson had something to say to an officer: a suggestion that he needed a new shirt, or a shoe shine, or that he was getting a little too fat.

When the Inspection in Ranks was completed, the Sergeant

stood before the men and read aloud from several items on a clipboard.

Some of the items he read were purely administrative, and local in nature, dealing with, for example, vacation schedules; and some had come over the police teletype from the Roundhouse with orders that they be read at roll calls. They dealt with such things as the death and funeral arrangements for two retired and one active police officers.

There were some items of a local nature, in particular the report of another burglary of the residence of a Miss Martha Peebles of 606 Glengarry Lane in Chestnut Hill, coupled with instructions that Radio Patrol cars and Emergency Patrol wagons on all shifts were to make a special effort to ride by the Peebles residence as often as possible.

"And we are still looking for Miss Elizabeth Woodham," the Sergeant concluded. "That's at the top of the list. You all have her description, and what description we have of the probable doer and his van. We have to get the lady back. Report anything you come across."

The day shift of the Fourteenth District was then called to attention, and dismissed, and left the Roll Call Room to get in their cars and go on duty.

Captain Charles D. Emerson walked over to Staff Inspector Peter Wohl, who had entered the room just as the roll call started.

"How are you, Peter?" he said, putting out his hand. "Or is this an occasion when I should call you Inspector?"

Staff Inspector Wohl had no authority whatever over the Fourteenth Police District, and both of them knew it. But he *was* a Staff Inspector, and he *was* the new commander of the new Special Operations Division, and no one, including Captain Emerson, had any idea what kind of clout went with the title.

"I hope I didn't get in the way, Charley," Wohl said, shaking Emerson's hand.

"Don't be silly. Distinguished visitors are always welcome at my roll calls."

Wohl chuckled. He knew the roll call ritual had been a bit more formal than usual, because of his presence.

"Bullshit, Charley," Wohl said, smiling at him.

"What can I do for you, Peter?" Emerson smiled back.

"You want the truth?"

"When all else fails, sometimes that helps."

"I'm covering my ass, Charley. This Peebles woman has friends in high places."

"So Commissioner Czernick has led me to believe," Emerson said, dryly. "He's been on the phone to me, too."

"So now both of us can tell him, if he asks, and I think he will, that you and I are coordinating our resources to bring Miss Peebles's burglar to the bar of justice."

Emerson chuckled.

"That's all, Peter?"

"I have the Woodham job. The Northwest rapist. Did you hear?"

"Czernick must like you."

"Czernick, hell. Carlucci."

"Ouch."

"I was hoping . . . maybe something turned up here?"

"I can't think of a thing, Peter. But come on in the office, and we'll call in the watch commander and whoever and kick it around over a cup of coffee."

"Thanks, but no thanks. I've got another roll call to make. Special Operations' first roll call. But call me, or better Jason Washington or Tony Harris—use the Highway Commander's number to get them—if you think of anything, will you?"

"They're working for you?" Emerson asked, surprised.

"Somewhat reluctantly."

"You must have some clout to get them transferred to you."

"I think the word is 'rope,' Charley. As in 'he now has enough rope to hang himself.' "

Captain Emerson's eyebrows rose thoughtfully. He did not offer even a *pro forma* disagreement.

"Say hello to your dad for me when you see him, will you, Peter?" he said.

• • •

Fifteen minutes later, Wohl walked into the Roll Call Room at Bustleton and Bowler. He had arrived just in time for the roll call. Captains Pekach and Sabara, and Detectives Washington and Harris, were already in the room, and ultimately, sixteen other police officers came into the room and formed into two ranks.

The sixteen newcomers were a Sergeant, a Corporal, a Detective, and thirteen Police Officers who had reported for duty to the Special Operations Division that morning, and been directed to the Roll Call Room by Sergeant Frizell when they walked in the door.

"Form in ranks," Captain Sabara called, unnecessarily, as the last of the newcomers was doing just that. Then he turned to Wohl, and asked, rather formally, "You want to take this, Inspector?"

"You go ahead, Mike," Wohl said.

Sabara nodded, and moved in front of the formation of policemen.

"Let me have your attention, please," Sabara said. "You all know me, and you probably know Inspector Wohl and Captain Pekach, too, but in case you don't, that's Captain Pekach, the High Commander, and that's the boss. Special Operations now has Highway, in case that wasn't clear to everybody.

"Welcome to Special Operations. I think you'll find it, presuming you can cut the mustard, a good assignment, an interesting job. And we're going to put you right to work.

"You all have read the papers," Sabara said, "and know that a woman named Elizabeth J. Woodham was abducted at knifepoint by a doer we think is the man who has been raping women all over Northwest Philadelphia. Let me tell you, we have damned little to go on.

"Getting Miss Woodham back alive from this critter is the first priority of business for Special Operations. For those of you who don't know them, the two gentlemen standing beside the Inspector are Detectives Washington and Harris. They came to Special Operations from Homicide and the Inspector has put them in charge of the investigation. They report directly to his office, and if they ask you to do something in connection with this investigation, you can take it as if it came from either me or the Inspector himself.

"We have some cars, and we're getting more. They have the J-Band, of course, and they have—or will have, Sergeant Frizell will talk to you about that—the Highway Band and the Detective Band, and when the Roundhouse gets around to assigning one to us, will have a Special Operations Band. From now until we get this lady back, forget about eight-hour shifts."

He paused, looked thoughtful for a moment, then gestured toward Washington.

"Detective Washington will now tell you what we've got, and what we're looking for."

Wohl saw, except on one or two faces, an expression of interest, perhaps even excitement.

*There is*, he thought, *except in the most jaded, cynical cops, an element of little boy playing cops and robbers, a desire to get involved in something more truly coplike than handing out speeding tickets and settling domestic disputes, in being sent out to catch a bona fide bad guy, to rescue the damsel in distress from the dragon.*

*And Mike Sabara has just told them that's what we want them to do, and the proof stands there in the person of Jason Washington. There is still an element of romance in the title "Detective," and an even greater element of romance in the persona of a homicide detective, and Washington is literally a legend among homicide detectives; sort of real-life Sherlock Holmes. They are in the presence of what they dreamed of being themselves, and maybe still do, and they know it.*

Washington spoke for about five minutes, tracing the activities of the serial rapist from the first job, before anyone even thought of that term. He didn't waste any words, but neither, Wohl thought, did he leave anything even possibly important out.

"And since we have, essentially, nothing to go on," Washington concluded, "we have to do it the hard way, ringing doorbells, digging in garbage cans, asking the same questions over and over again. Tony Harris has the only idea that may turn something up that I can think of, so I'll turn this over to him."

*Tony Harris,* Wohl thought, *does not present anything close to the confident, formidable presence Washington projects. He's a weasel compared to an elephant. No. That's too strong. A mangy lion, the kind you see in the cages of a cheap circus, compared to an elephant. Where the hell does he get his clothes? Steal them from a Salvation Army depository? Did the Judge really give his ex-wife everything? Or is Tony trying to support two women, and taking the cost out of his clothing budget?*

But almost as soon as Tony started to speak, Wohl saw that the interest of the newcomers—who had almost audibly been wondering *Who the hell is this guy?* began to perk up. Within a minute or two, they were listening to him with as rapt attention as they had given Washington. *Who the hell is this guy?* had been replaced with *This sonofabitch really knows what he's talking about!*

Tony delivered a concise lecture on sexual deviation and perversity, went from there to the psychology of the flasher, the molester, the voyeur, the patron of prostitutes, and the rapist, and then presented a profile of the man they were looking for that differed from the one Wohl had got from Dr. Amelia Alice Payne only in that he didn't mention "the slippery slope" or "invincibility."

And then he told them what they were looking for, and how he wanted them to look for it: "What I've come up with is a list of minor sexual offenders, white males who have misdemeanor arrests for any of a long list of weird behavior. I'm still working on coming up with names. . . ."

He stopped and looked at Wohl.

"Inspector, I used to work with Bart Cumings in South

Detectives," he said, indicating the Sergeant among the new-comers. "Could I have him to work with me on the files?"

"You've got him," Wohl said, smiling at Sergeant Cum-ings. He saw Officer Matt Payne enter the Roll Call Room, look around, and then head for him.

*I'll bet I know what Payne wants*, Wohl thought. *And I'll bet Sergeant Cumings will be out of that uniform by tomorrow morning. If he waits that long to get out of it.*

In the Police Department rank structure, the step up from police officer was either to detective or corporal, who re-ceived the same pay. There was no such rank as "detective sergeant," so a detective who took and passed the sergeant's examination took the risk of being assigned anywhere in the department where a sergeant was needed, and that most often meant a uniformed assignment. After a detective had been on the job awhile, the prospect of going back in uniform, even as a sergeant, was not attractive. Very few uniformed sergeants got much overtime. Divisional detectives, counting their overtime, always took home more money than captains. Homicide detectives like Tony Harris and Jason Washington, for example, for whom twenty-four hour days were not at all unusual, took as much money home as a Chief Inspector.

Some detectives, thinking of retirement, which was based on rank, took the Sergeant's exam hoping that when they were promoted they would get lucky and remain assigned to the Detective Division. Wohl felt sure that Sergeant Cumings was one of those who had taken the gamble, and lost, and wound up as a uniformed sergeant someplace that was nowhere as interesting a job as being a detective had been. That ex-plained his volunteering for Special Operations. If he had been a crony of Harris in South Detectives, that meant he had been a pretty good detective.

And if he could work here, in civilian clothes, he would be, Wohl knew, very pleased with the arrangement. He won-dered if Cumings would ask permission to wear plainclothes, and decided he probably would not. He was an experienced cop who had learned that if you ask permission to do something, the answer was often no. But if you did the same thing, like working in an investigative job in plainclothes without asking, probably no one would question you.

Wohl decided that whether Cumings asked for permission to work in civilian clothes, or just did it, it would be all right.

"Anyway, what we need you guys to do," Tony Harris went on, "is check these people out. Very quietly. I don't want anybody going where these people work and asking their boss if they think the guy could be the rapist. You work on the presumption of innocence. What you will look for is whether or not he fits the rough description we have—hairy and well spoken. And we look for the van. We've already run these people through Harrisburg for a match with a van and come up with zilch. But maybe his neighbor's got a van, or his brother-in-law, or maybe he gets to bring one home from work. And that's *all* you do! You hit on something, you report it to Washington or me, and now Sergeant Cumings. Unless there's no way you can avoid it, I don't want you talking to these people. You just thin out the list for us. Anybody got any questions about that?"

"You mean, we find this guy, we don't arrest him?" a voice called out.

"Not unless he's got the schoolteacher in the van with him," Harris said, "with her life clearly in danger. Otherwise, you report it, that's all. We're dealing with a real sicko here, and there's no telling what he'll do if he figures he's about to get grabbed."

"Like what, for example, he hasn't already done?" a sarcastic voice called.

Wohl looked quickly to spot the wiseass, but was not successful.

Harris's face showed contempt, not anger, but Wohl suspected there was both, and Harris immediately proved it.

"Okay," Harris said, "since you apparently can't figure it out yourself. We bag this guy, a hairy guy who speaks as if he went past the eighth grade, and who has a van. We even get one or more of the victims to identify him. But we don't have Miss Woodham, all right? So, if he doesn't figure this out himself, and he's smart, he gets a lawyer and the lawyer says, *'Just keep denying it, Ace. Nobody saw you without your mask, and I'll confuse them when I get them on the stand . . . make them pick you out of a line of naked hairy men wearing masks, or something!'* That's how he would beat the first rapes, unless we can get what we professional detectives call 'evidence.' "

The identity of the wiseass was now clear. At least four of the newcomers had turned around to glower contemptuously at him.

"And we seem to have forgotten Miss Woodham, haven't we?" Harris went on. "Who is the reason we're all out looking for this scumbag in the first place. Now just for the sake of argument, let's say he's got her tied up someplace, like a warehouse or something. Some place we can't connect him to. So our cowboy says, *"Where's the dame?"* and our guy says *"What dame?"* and our cowboy says, *"You know what dame, Miss Woodham,"* and our sicko says, *"Not only did I not piss all over the one lady, I never heard of anybody named Woodham. You got a witness?"* So the latest victim, the one we're trying to find, cowboy, starves or suffocates or goes insane, wherever this scumbag has her tied up. Because once our sicko knows we're on to him, he's not going to go anywhere near the victim. Does that answer your question, smartass?"

*Harris handled that perfectly,* Wohl thought.

"You think she's still alive?" another newcomer asked, softly.

"We won't know that until we find her," Harris said. "That's all I've got, Captain."

Sabara turned to Wohl.

"Have you got anything, Inspector?"

"Going along with what Harris said, Captain," Wohl said. "About not making the man we're looking for any more disturbed than he is, what would you think about putting as many of these officers as it takes in plainclothes? And in unmarked cars?''

''I'll find out how many unmarked cars there are and set it up, sir,'' Sabara said.

''If necessary, Mike, take unmarked cars from Highway.''

''Yes, sir. Anything else, sir?''

Wohl shook his head and turned to face Matt Payne, who was now standing beside him.

''Inspector, Chief Coughlin called,'' Matt said, surprising Peter Wohl not at all. ''He wants you to call him right away.''

''Okay,'' Wohl said, and walked out of the Roll Call Room toward his office.

As he passed Sergeant Frizell's desk, Wohl told him, ''Call Chief Coughlin for me, please.''

''Inspector, the Commissioner just called, too, wanting you to get right back to him.''

''Get me Chief Coughlin first,'' Wohl ordered. He walked into his office, sat down, and watched the telephones until one of the buttons began to flash. He picked it up.

''Inspector Wohl,'' he said.

''Hold one for the Chief,'' Sergeant Tom Lenihan's voice replied.

''Have you seen the papers, Peter?'' Coughlin began, without any preliminaries.

''Yes, sir.''

''What's this about you refusing to talk to the press?''

''I wasn't here,'' Wohl said. ''Somebody must have told him I was unavailable.''

''That's not what it sounded like in the *Ledger*,'' Coughlin said.

''It also said you and I are cronies,'' Wohl said.

''The Commissioner's upset,'' Coughlin said.

''He just called here,'' Wohl said. ''As soon as you're through with me, I'm going to return his call.''

''What about assigning officers to find witnesses to clear the Highway cop?''

''Guilty,'' Peter said. ''Except that I didn't assign them.

They volunteered. Off duty, in civilian clothes. If they turn up a witness, there will be an anonymous telephone call from a public-spirited citizen to AID. It was actually Dave Pekach's idea, I want you to understand that I'm doing the opposite of laying it off on Pekach. If I had thought of it first, I would have done it first. And I'll take full responsibility for doing it."

He heard Coughlin grunt, and there was a pause before Coughlin asked, "Was that smart, under the circumstances?"

"If I could have sent them to find the Woodham woman, I would have," Wohl said.

Matt Payne appeared at his office door. Wohl made a gesture for him to go away, together with a mental note to tell him to learn to knock before he came through a closed door.

"How's that going?" Chief Coughlin asked.

"The first fifteen, maybe sixteen, volunteers just showed up for duty. I turned them all over to Washington and Harris to ring doorbells. That's where I was when you called."

"Maybe, until you get the Woodham woman back, you better put the people who were looking for witnesses to the car wreck to work ringing doorbells, too."

"I will if you tell me to, Chief," Wohl said, "but I'd rather not."

"You want to explain that?"

"Well, for one thing, I think they did all they could, and drew a blank, about finding anyone who saw Mr. McAvoy run the red light."

"Damn," Coughlin said.

"And for another, I don't think having Highway cops going around ringing doorbells is such a good idea. The guy we're looking for is already over the edge. I don't want to spook him."

"You want to go over that again?" Coughlin asked.

Wohl covered the mouthpiece with his hand, and demanded, "What the hell do you want, Payne?"

"Sir, the Commissioner's on Two Six, holding for you," Matt replied.

"Okay," Wohl said, and Matt backed out of the office, closing the door after him.

"Chief, the Commissioner's on the other line. Can I get back to you?"

"Call me when you get something," Coughlin said, impatiently, and then added, "Peter, frankly, I would have a hell of a lot more confidence in the way you're doing things if you had at least been able to keep that Peebles woman from being burgled again."

"I was just talking to Charley Emerson about that—" Wohl said, and then stopped, because Chief Inspector Dennis V. Coughlin had hung up.

He pushed the flashing button on the telephone.

"Good morning, Commissioner," he said. "Sorry to keep you waiting. I was talking to Chief Coughlin."

"Hold on for Commissioner Czernick, please, Inspector Wohl," a female voice Peter did not recognize replied.

"Czernick," the Commissioner snarled a moment later.

"I have Inspector Wohl for you, Commissioner," the woman said.

"It's about time," Czernick said. "Peter?"

"Yes, sir. Sorry to keep you waiting, sir. I was talking to Chief Coughlin."

"You've seen the papers? What's this about you refusing to talk to the press?"

"Sir," Wohl said, "it wasn't quite that way. I wasn't here, and—"

"Lemme have that," a voice said, faintly in the background, and then came over the line full volume. "This is Jerry Carlucci, Peter."

"Good morning, sir," Peter said.

"I know and you know that sonofabitch is after us, Peter," the mayor of the City of Brotherly Love said, "and we both know why, and we both know that no matter what we do, he'll still be trying to cut our throats. But we can't afford to give the sonofabitch any ammunition. You just can't tell the press to go fuck themselves. I thought you were smarter than that.''

"Sir, that's not the way it happened," Peter said.

"So tell me," Mayor Carlucci said.

"Sir, I was not in the office. I *was* 'unavailable.' That's it.''

"Shit," the mayor said. "What about using Highway to look for witnesses to clear our guy? Is that true?"

"Yes, sir, I did that. But in sports coats and ties. Off-duty volunteers.''

"I think I know why you did it," Mayor Carlucci said, "but under the circumstances, was it smart?"

"Sir, I considered it to be the proper thing to do at the time. There was nothing that wasn't already being done to locate Miss Woodham, and I hoped to clear the officers involved of what I considered—consider—to be an unjust accusation.''

"You're saying you'd do the same thing again?" Carlucci asked, coldly.

"Yes, sir."

"They find any witnesses for our side?"

"No, sir."

"They still looking?"

"Sir, I have no intention, without orders to the contrary, to tell my men what they can't do when they're off duty and in civilian clothes.''

"In other words, fuck Arthur Nelson and his goddamned *Ledger*?''

"No, sir. I frankly think that if we were going to find a witness, they'd have found one by now. But I think, for the morale of Highway, that it's important we keep looking. Or maybe I mean that I don't want Highway to think I threw Officer Hawkins to the wolves because of the *Ledger* editorial.''

"Hawkins was the guy driving?"

"Yes, sir. And he says Mr. McAvoy ran the stoplight, and I believe him.''

"Goddamn it, I was right," Mayor Carlucci said.

"Sir?"

"When I sent you out there, gave you Special Operations," Mayor Carlucci said.

Peter Wohl could think of no appropriate response to make to that, and so made none.

"I was about to ask where you are with the Woodham job," Mayor Carlucci said.

"Sir, I have turned over all—"

"I said 'was about to ask,' " the mayor said. "Don't interrupt me, Peter."

"Sorry, sir."

"I've been there," the mayor said. "And I know the one thing a commanding officer on the spot does not need is people looking over his shoulder and telling him what they think he should have done. So I won't do that. I'll tell you what I am going to do, Peter. I'm going to issue a statement saying that I have complete faith in the way you're handling things."

"Yes, sir," Peter said.

"But you better catch this sonofabitch, Peter. You know what I'm saying?"

"Yes, sir."

"This sonofabitch is making the Police Department look like the Keystone Cops. The Department can't afford that. I can't afford that. And you, in particular, can't afford that."

"I understand, sir," Peter said.

"I don't want to find myself in the position of having to tell Tad Czernick to relieve you, and making it look like Arthur Nelson and his goddamned *Ledger* were right all the time," Mayor Carlucci said.

"I hope that won't be necessary, sir."

"You need anything, Peter, anything at all?"

"No, sir, I don't think so."

"If you need something, you speak up. Tad Czernick will get it for you."

"Thank you, sir."

"Tell your dad, when you see him, I said hello," the mayor said. "Hang on, Tad wants to say something."

"Peter," Commissioner Czernick said. "I understand Miss Peebles was burgled again last night."

"Yes, sir," Peter said. "I'm working on it."

"Good," Commissioner Czernick said. "Keep me advised."

Then he hung up.

Wohl took the telephone from his ear, looked at the handset, wondered for perhaps the three hundredth time why he did that, and then put it in its cradle. He got up and walked to his office door and pulled it open.

Matt Payne had been put to work collating some kinds of forms.

"Payne?"

"Yes, sir?"

"You look like death warmed over," Wohl said. "Are you sick?"

Payne looked distinctly uncomfortable.

"Sir, I guess I had a little too much to drink last night."

*That figures,* Wohl thought, *McFadden and Martinez took him to the FOP and initiated him.*

"Where are they?"

"Sir?"

"Where's Sherlock Holmes and the faithful Dr. Watson?"

Matt finally understood that Wohl meant McFadden and Martinez.

"Sir, I don't know," he said.

"Find them," Wohl said. "Tell them as soon as they can fit me into their busy schedule, I want to see them. And find Captain Pekach, too, please, and ask him to come see me."

"Yes, sir."

David Pekach was still in the Seventh District Building. Two minutes later, he was standing in Wohl's doorway waiting for Wohl to raise his eyes from the papers on his desk. Finally, he did.

"Come in, please, David," he said. "You want some coffee?"

Pekach shook his head no, then asked with raised eyebrows if Wohl wanted him to close the door. Wohl nodded that he did.

"I just finished talking to Chief Coughlin and the Commissioner," Wohl said, deciding in that moment not to mention Mayor Jerry Carlucci.

"I thought maybe they would call," David Pekach said, dryly.

"In addition to everything else," Wohl said, "they both seem personally concerned and very upset with me about whatever the hell is going on with this Peebles woman. She was burgled again last night."

"I heard."

"I put your two hotshots, McFadden and Martinez, on the job. They're looking for—"

Pekach's nod of understanding told Wohl that Pekach knew about that, so he stopped. "The way they tackled the job, unless I am very wrong, was to take young Payne out there down to the FOP and get him falling-down drunk."

"I don't know," Pekach said, loyally. "They were always pretty reliable."

"They didn't find the guy—the actor, the boyfriend of the Peebles woman's brother—that I know," Wohl said.

"You want me to talk to them?"

"No. I'll talk to them. I want you to go talk to Miss Peebles."

"What?"

"You go over there right now," Wohl said. "And you ooze sympathy, and do whatever you have to do to convince her that we are very embarrassed that this has happened to her again, and that we are going to take certain steps to make absolutely sure it doesn't happen again."

"What certain steps?"

"We are going to put—call it a stakeout team—on her property from sunset to sunrise."

"You lost me there," Pekach confessed. "Where are you going to get a stakeout team? I mean, my God, if it gets in the paper that you're using manpower to stake out a third-rate burglary site . . ."

"Martinez, McFadden, and Hungover Harry out there," Wohl said. "The wages of sin are death, David. I'm surprised you haven't learned that."

Pekach chuckled. "Okay," he said.

"And you will tell Miss Peebles that a Highway Patrol car will drive past her house not less than once every half hour during the same hours. Then you will tell your shift Lieutenant to set that up, and to tell the guys in the car that they not only are to drive by, but they are to drive into the driveway, making a lot of noise, and slamming the car doors when they get out of the car, so that Miss Peebles, when she looks in curiosity out her window, will see two uniformed officers waving their flashlights around in the bushes."

"That'd spook the guy who's doing this to her," Pekach argued.

"I hope so," Wohl said. "I don't want another burglary at that address on the Overnight Report on the Commissioner's desk tomorrow morning."

"Okay," Pekach said, doubtfully, "you're the boss."

"I'm not going to tell Sherlock Holmes and Dr. Watson this, David," Wohl said. "But I think they're right. I think the doer is the brother's boyfriend. When they're not sitting outside her house, I want them to keep looking for him. Got the picture?"

"Like I said, you're the boss. You're more devious than I would have thought. . . ."

"I'll interpret that as a compliment," Wohl said. "And as devious as I am, I will frankly tell you that the success of this operation will hinge on how well you can charm the lady."

"Then why don't you go charm her?"

"Because I am the commanding officer, and that sort of thing is beneath my dignity," Wohl said, solemnly.

Pekach smiled.

"I'll charm the pants off the lady, boss," he said.

"Figuratively speaking, of course, Captain?"

"I don't know. What does she look like?"

"I don't know," Wohl said.

"Then I don't know about the pants," Pekach said. "I'll let you know how well I do."

"Just the highlights, please, Captain. None of the sordid details."

# SEVENTEEN

Captain David Pekach was tempted to go see both the Captain of Northwest Detectives and the Captain of the Fourteenth District before going to call on the Peebles woman, but finally decided against it. He knew that his success as the new Highway Captain depended in large measure on how well Highway got along with the Detective Bureau and the various Districts. And he was fully aware that there was a certain resentment toward Highway on the part of the rest of the Department, and especially on the part of detectives and uniformed District cops.

He had seen, several times, and as recently as an hour before, what he thought was the wrong reaction to the *Ledger* editorial calling Highway "the Gestapo." This morning, he had heard a Seventh District uniformed cop call "*Ach-tung!*" when two Highway cops walked into the building, and twice he had actually seen uniformed cops throw a straight-armed salute mockingly at Highway Patrolmen.

It was all done in jest, of course, but David Pekach was

enough of an amateur psychologist to know that there is almost always a seed of genuine resentment when a wife zings her husband, or a cop zings another cop. After he had a few words with the cop who had called "*Ach-tung,*" and the two cops who had thrown the Nazi salutes, he didn't think they would do it again. With a little luck, the word would quickly spread that the new Highway Commander had a temper that had best not be turned on.

He understood the resentment toward Highway. Some of it was really unjustified, and could be attributed to simple jealousy. Highway had special uniforms, citywide jurisdiction, and the well-earned reputation of leaving the less pleasant chores of police work, especially domestic disputes, to District cops. Highway RPCs, like all other RPCs, carried fire hydrant wrenches in their trunks. When the water supply ran low, or water pressure dropped, as it did when kids turned on the hydrants to cool off in the summer, the word went out to turn the hydrants off.

David Pekach could never remember having seen a Highway cop with a hydrant wrench in his hand, and he had seen dozens of Highway cars roll blithely past hydrants pouring water into the streets, long after the kids who had turned it on had gone in for supper, or home for the night. That sort of task, and there were others like it—a long list beginning with rescuing cats from trees and going through such things as chasing boisterous kids from storefronts and investigating fender-benders—was considered too menial to merit the attention of the elite Highway Patrol.

The cops who had to perform these chores naturally resented the Highway cops who didn't do their fair share of them, and Highway cops, almost as a rule, managed to let the District cops know that Highway was something special, involved in *real* cop work, while their backward, nonelite brothers had to calm down irate wives and get their uniforms soaked turning off fire hydrants.

So far as the detectives were concerned, it was nearly Holy Writ among them that if Highway reached a crime scene before the detectives did, Highway could be counted on to destroy much of the evidence, usually by stomping on it with their motorcyclists' boots. Lieutenant Pekach of Narcotics had shared that opinion.

One of his goals, now that he had Highway, was to improve relations between Highway and everybody else, and he didn't think a good way to do that would be to visit Northwest Detectives and the Fourteenth District to ask about the Peebles burglaries. They would, quite understandably, resent it. It would be tanamount to coming right out and saying *"since you ordinary cops can't catch the doer in a third-rate burglary, Highway is here to show you how real cops do it!"*

And, David Pekach knew, Peter Wohl had already been to both the Fourteenth District and Northwest Detectives. Wohl could get away with it, if only because he outranked the captains. And Wohl, in Pekach's judgment, was a good cop, and if there had been anything not in the reports, he would have picked up on it and said something.

But Pekach did get out the reports, which he had already read, and he read them again very carefully before getting into his car and driving over to Chestnut Hill.

Number 606 Glengarry Lane turned out to be a very large Victorian house, maybe even a mansion, sitting atop a hill behind a fieldstone-pillar-and-iron-bar fence and a wide expanse of lawn. The fence, whose iron bars were topped with gilded spear tops, ran completely around the property, which Pekach estimated to be at least three, maybe four acres. The house on the adjacent property to the left could be only barely made out, and the one on the right couldn't be seen at all.

Behind the house was a three-car garage that had, Pekach decided, probably started out as a carriage house. The setup, Pekach thought, was much like where Wohl lived, except that the big house behind Wohl's garage apartment had been converted into six luxury apartments. This big house was occupied by only two people, the Peebles woman and her brother, and the brother was reported to be in France.

All three garage doors were open when Pekach drove up the driveway and stopped the car under a covered entrance portal. It was not difficult to imagine a carriage drawn by a matched pair of horses pulling up where the blue-and-white had stopped, and a servant rushing off the porch to assist the Master and his Mistress down the carriage steps.

No servant came out now. Pekach saw a gray-haired black man, wearing a black rubber apron and black rubber boots, washing a Buick station wagon. There was a Mercedes coupe, a new one, and a Cadillac Coupe de Ville in the garage, and a two-year-old Ford sedan parked beside the garage, almost certainly the property of the black guy washing the car.

Pekach went up the stairs and rang the doorbell. He heard a dull bonging inside, and a moment or two later, a gray-haired black female face appeared where a lace curtain over the engraved glass window had been pulled aside. And then the door opened.

"May I help you?" the black woman asked. She was wearing a black uniform dress, and Pekach decided the odds were ten to one she was married to the guy washing the Buick.

"I'm Captain Pekach of the Highway Patrol," David said. "I'd like to see Miss Peebles, please."

"One moment, please," the black woman said. "I'll see if Miss Peebles is at home."

She shut the door.

Pekach glanced around.

*The way this place is built and laid out, it's an open invitation to a burglar to come in and help himself.*

The door opened again a full minute later.

"Miss Peebles will see you," the maid said. "Will you follow me, please?"

Pekach took off his uniform cap, and put his hand to his pigtail, which of course was no longer there.

Inside the door was a large foyer, with an octagonal tile fountain in the center. Closed double doors were on both sides of the foyer, and a wide staircase was directly ahead. There was a stained-glass leaded window portraying, Pekach thought, Saint Whoever-It-Was who slayed the dragon on the stairway landing.

*This place looks like a goddamned museum. Or maybe a funeral home.*

The maid slid open one of the double doors.

"Here's the policeman, Miss Martha," the maid said, and gestured for him to go through the door.

He found himself in a high-ceilinged room, the walls of which were lined with bookshelves.

"How do you do?" Martha Peebles said.

*A fifty-year-old spinster,* Pekach instantly decided, looking at Martha Peebles. She was wearing a white, frilly, high-collared, long-sleeved blouse and a dark skirt.

"Miss Peebles, I'm Captain Pekach, commanding officer of the Highway Patrol," David said. "Inspector Wohl asked me to come see you, to tell you how sorry we are about the trouble you've had, and to tell you we're going to do everything humanly possible to keep it from happening again."

Martha Peebles extended her hand.

The cop, as opposed to the man, in Pekach took over. The cop, the trained observer, saw that Martha Peebles was not fifty. She did not have fifty-year-old hands, or fifty-year-old eyes, or fifty-year-old teeth. These were *her* teeth, not caps, and they sat in healthy gums. There were no liver spots on her hands, and there was a fullness of flesh in the hands that fifty-year-olds have lost with passing time. And her neck had not begun to hang. It was even possible that the firm appearance of her breasts was Miss Peebles herself, rather than a well-fitting brassiere.

"How do you do, Captain . . . *Pekach,* you said?"

"Yes, ma'am."

Her hand was warm and soft, confirming his revised opinion of her age. She was, he now deduced, maybe thirty-five, no more. She just dressed like an old woman; that had thrown him off. He wondered why the hell she did that.

"You'll forgive me for saying I've heard that before, Captain," Martha Peebles said, taking her hand back and lacing it with the other one on her abdomen. "As recently as yesterday."

"Yes, ma'am, I know," David Pekach said, uncomfortably.

"I am really not a neurotic old maid, imagining all this," she said.

"No one suggested anything like that, Miss Peebles," Pekach said. *Oh, shit! McFadden and Martinez!* "Miss Peebles, did the two officers who were here yesterday say anything at all out of line? Did they insinuate anything like that?"

"No," she said. "I don't recall that they did. But, if I may be frank?"

"Please."

"They did seem a little young to be detectives," she said, "and I got the impression—how should I put this—that they were rather overwhelmed by the house."

"I'm rather overwhelmed with it," David said. "It's magnificent."

"My father loved this house," she said. "You haven't answered my question."

"What question was that, Miss Peebles?" Pekach asked, confused.

"Aren't those two a little young to be detectives? Do they have the requisite experience?"

"Well, actually, Miss Peebles, they aren't detectives," Pekach said.

"They were in civilian clothing," she challenged. "I thought, among policemen, only detectives were permitted to wear civilian clothing."

"No, ma'am," Pekach said. "Some officers work in civilian clothing."

"I didn't know that."

"Yes, ma'am," he said. "When it seems appropriate, that's authorized."

"It seems to me that the more police in uniform the better," she said. "That that would tend to deter crime."

"You have a point," Pekach said. "I can't argue with that. But may I explain the officers who were here yesterday?"

"We're talking about the small Mexican or whatever, and the large, simple Irish boy?"

"Yes, ma'am. Miss Peebles, do you happen to recall hearing about the police officer, Captain Moffitt, who was shot to death recently."

"Oh, yes, of course. On the television, it said that he was, unless I'm confused somehow, the commanding officer of the Highway Patrol."

"Yes, ma'am, he was," Pekach said.

"Oh, I see. And you're his replacement, so to speak?"

"Yes, ma'am, but that's not what I was driving at."

"Oh?"

"We knew who had shot Captain Moffitt within minutes," Pekach said. "Which meant that eight thousand police officers—the entire Philadelphia Police Department—were looking for him."

"I can certainly understand that," she said.

"Two undercover Narcotics Division officers found him—"

"They threw him under a subway train," she said. "I read that in the *Ledger*. Good for them!"

"That story wasn't true, Miss Peebles," Pekach said, surprised at her reaction. "Actually, the officer involved went much further than he had to to capture him alive. He didn't even fire his weapon, for fear that a bullet might hit an innocent bystander."

"He should have shot him dead on the spot," Miss Peebles said, firmly.

David looked at her with surprise showing on his face.

"I read in *Time*," Martha Peebles said, "that for what it costs to keep one criminal in prison, we could send four people to Harvard."

"Yes, ma'am," Pekach said. "I'm sure that's about right."

"Now, *that's* criminal," she said. "Throwing good money after bad. Money that could be used to benefit society being thrown away keeping criminals in country clubs with bars."

"Yes, ma'am, I have to agree with you."

"I'm sure that people like yourself must find that sort of thing very frustrating," Martha Peebles said.

"Yes, ma'am, sometimes," Pekach agreed.

"I'm going to draw the blind," Martha Peebles announced. "The sun bleaches the carpets."

She went to the window and did so, and the sun silhouetted her body, for all practical purposes making her blouse transparent. David Pekach averted his eyes.

*Just a bra, huh? I would have thought she'd have worn a slip. Oh, what the hell, it's hot. But really nice boobs!*

She walked back over to him.

"You were saying?" she said.

"Excuse me?"

"There was a point to your talking about the man who shot your predecessor?"

"Oh, yes, ma'am. Miss Peebles, the officer who found Gerald Vincent Gallagher was Officer Charles McFadden."

"Who?"

"Officer McFadden, Miss Peebles. The officer Inspector Wohl sent to see you yesterday. And Officer Martinez is his partner."

"Really?" she replied, genuinely surprised. "Then I certainly have misjudged them, haven't I?"

"I brought that up, Miss Peebles, in the hope you might be convinced that we sent you the best men available."

"Hummm," she snorted. "That may be so, but they don't seem to be any more effective, do they, than anyone else that's been here?"

"They were working until long after midnight last night, Miss Peebles, looking for Walton Williams—"

"They were looking in the wrong place, then," Martha Peebles said. "They should have been looking here. *He* was here."

*Shit, she's right about that!*

"Well, actually, we don't know that," David said. "We don't know if whoever was here last night was Mr. Williams.

For that matter, we don't even know that Mr. Williams is even connected—''

"Don't be silly," Martha Peebles snapped. "Who else could it be?"

"Literally, anyone."

"Captain, I don't like to think of a total figure for all the things that have been stolen from this house by one of Stephen's 'friends.' I don't know whether he actually pays them to do what—whatever they do—but I do know that almost without exception, they tip themselves with whatever they can stick in their pockets before they go back wherever Stephen finds them."

"I didn't see any record of that, prior to this last sequence of events," Pekach said.

"For the good reason that I never reported it. I find it very painful to have to publicly acknowledge that my brother, the last of the line, is, so to speak, going to *be* the last of the line; and that he's not even very good at that, and has to go out and hire prostitutes."

"Yes, ma'am," David said, genuinely sympathetic.

"Is that the correct word? Or is there another term for males?"

"Same word, ma'am."

"I suppose I would have gone on and on, closing my eyes to what was going on, pretending that I didn't really care about the things that turned up missing . . . but this Williams man shows no sign of stopping this harassment—and that's what it is, more than the value of the items he's stolen—and that proves, it seems to me, that it is he and not any other burglar, who would take as much as he could haul off—''

"You may have a point, Miss Peebles," Pekach said.

"But I am also afraid that he will either steal, or perhaps simply vandalize, for his own perverse reasons, Daddy's gun collection. That would break my heart, if any of that was stolen or vandalized."

Pekach's eyes actually brightened at the word *gun*.

*What the hell is going on here? There was not one damned word about guns in any of the reports I read.*

"A gun collection?" Pekach asked. "I wonder if you'd be kind enough to show it to me?"

"If you like," she said. "With the understanding that you may look, but not touch."

"Yes, ma'am."

"Well, then, come along." She led him out of the library and up the stairs, past Saint Whatsisname Slaying the Dragon.

"There were some edged pieces," she said.

"Excuse me?"

Pekach had been distracted by the sight of Miss Martha Peebles's rear end as she went up the stairs ahead of him. The thin material of her skirt was drawn tight over her rump. She was apparently not wearing a half slip, for the outline of her underpants was clearly visible. And the kind of underpants she was wearing were . . .

Pekach searched his limited vocabulary in the area and as much in triumph as surprise came up with "bikinis."

*Or the lower half of bikinis, whatever the hell they were called. Little tiny goddamned things, which, what there was of them, rode damned low.*

*Nice ass, too.*

"Swords, halberds, some Arabian daggers, that sort of thing," Martha Peebles said, "but they were difficult and time consuming to care for, and Colonel Mawson—do you know Colonel Mawson, Captain?"

"I know who he is, Miss Peebles," Pekach said as she stopped at the head of the stairs and waited for him to catch up with her.

"Colonel Mawson worked out some sort of tax arrangement with the government for me, and I gave them to the Smithsonian Institution," she concluded.

"I see."

She led him down a carpeted corridor, and then stopped so suddenly David Pekach bumped into her.

"Sorry," he said.

She gave him a wan smile, and nodded upward, toward the wall behind him.

"That's Daddy," she said.

It was an oil painting of a tall, mean-looking stout man with a large mustache. He was in hunting clothes, one hand resting on the rack of an elk.

It was a lousy picture, Pekach decided. It looked more like a snapshot.

"I had that done after Daddy passed away," Martha Peebles said. "The artist had to work from a photograph."

"I see," Pekach said. "Very nice."

"The photo had Stephen in it, but I told the artist to leave him out. Stephen hated hunting, and Daddy knew it. I think he probably made him go along to . . . you know, expose him to masculine pursuits. Anyway, I didn't think Stephen belonged in Daddy's picture, so I had the artist leave him out."

"I understand."

Martha Peebles then put her arm deep into a vase sitting on the floor and came out with two keys on a ring. She put one and then the other into locks on a door beside the portrait of her father, and then opened the door, and reached inside to snap a switch. Fluorescent lights flickered to life.

The room, about fifteen feet wide and twenty feet long, was lined with glass-fronted gun racks, except for the bar end, which was a bookcase above a felt-covered table. There were two large, wide, glass-enclosed display cases in the center of the room, plus a leather armchair and matching footstool, and a table on which an old Zenith Trans-Oceanic portable radio sat.

"This is pretty much as it was the day Daddy passed away," Martha Peebles said. "Except that I took out his whiskey."

"How long has your father been dead, Miss Peebles?" Pekach asked, as he walked toward the first display case.

"Daddy passed over three years, two months, and nine days ago," she said, without faltering.

Pekach bent over the display case.

*Jesus H. Christ! That's an 1819 J. H. Hall breech action! Mint!*

"Do you know anything about these guns, Miss Peebles?" Pekach asked.

She came to him.

"Which one?" she asked and he pointed and she leaned over to look at it, which action caused her blouse to strain over her bosom, giving David Pekach a quick and unintentional glimpse of her undergarments.

Even though Captain Pekach was genuinely interested in having his identification of the weapon he had pointed out as a U.S. Rifle, Model 1819, with a J. H. Hall pivoted chamber breech action confirmed, a certain portion of his attention was diverted to that which he had inadvertently and in absolute innocence glimpsed.

*Jesus! Black lace! Who would have ever thought! I wonder if her underpants are black, too? Black lace bikinis! Jesus H. Christ!*

"That's an Army rifle," Martha Peebles said. "Model of 1819. That particular piece was made in 1821. It's interesting because—"

"It has a J. H. Hall action," Pekach chimed in.

"Yes," she said.

"I've never seen one in such good shape before," David Pekach said. "That looks unfired."

"It's been test fired," Martha said. "It has Z.E.H. stamped on the receiver just beside the flintlock pivot. That's almost certainly Captain Zachary Ellsworth Hampden's stamp. But I don't think it ever left Harper's Ferry Armory for service."

"It's a beautiful piece," Pekach said.

"Are you interested—I was about to ask 'in breech loaders,' but I suppose the first question should be, are you interested in firearms?"

"My mother says that's the reason I never got married," Pekach blurted. "I spend all my money on weapons."

"What kind?"

"Actually, Remington rolling blocks," Pekach said.

"Daddy loved rolling blocks!" Martha Peebles said. "The whole wall case on the left is rolling blocks."

"Really?"

He walked to the cabinet. She caught up with him.

"I don't have anything as good as these," Pekach said. "I've got a sporting rifle something like that piece, but it's worn and pitted. That's mint. They all look mint."

"Daddy said that he regarded himself as their caretaker," Martha Peebles said. "He said it wasn't in him to be a do-gooder, but preserving these symbols of our heritage for later generations gave him great pleasure."

"What a nice way to put it," Pekach said, absolutely sincerely.

"Oh, I'm so sorry Daddy passed over and can't be here now," Martha said. "He so loved showing his guns to people with the knowledge and sensitivity to appreciate them."

Their eyes met. Martha Peeble's face colored and she looked away.

"That was his favorite piece," she said after a moment, pointing.

"What is it? It looks German."

They were looking at a heavily engraved, double-triggered rifle with an elaborately shaped, carved, and engraved wild cherry stock.

"German-American," she said. "It was made in Milwaukee in 1883 by Ludwig Hamner, who immigrated from Bavaria in 1849. He took a Remington rolling block action, barreled it himself, in 32-20, one turn in eighteen inches, and then did all the engraving and carving himself. That's wild cherry."

"I know," Pekach said. "It's beautiful!"

She turned and walked away from him. He saw her bending down to lift the edge of the carpet by the door. She returned with a key and used it to unlock the case. Almost reverently, she took the rifle from its padded pegs and handed it to Pekach.

"I don't think I should touch it," he said. "There's liable to be acid on my fingertips from perspiration."

"I'll wipe it before I put it back, silly," Martha Peebles said. When he still looked doubtful, she said, "I know Daddy would want you to."

He reached to take the gun, and as he did so, his fingers touched hers and she recoiled as if she was being burned, and he almost dropped the rifle.

But he didn't, and when, after an appropriately detailed and appreciative examination of the piece, he handed it back to her, their fingers touched again, and this time she didn't seem to recoil from his touch; quite the contrary.

"So what does Mr. Walton Williams have to say about the burglaries of the Peebles residence?" Staff Inspector Peter Wohl inquired, at almost the same moment Martha Peebles handed Captain David Pekach the 1893 wild cherry–stocked Ludwig Hamner Remington rolling-block *Schuetzen* rifle.

"We had a little trouble finding him, Inspector," Officer Charley McFadden replied.

"But you did find him?"

"No, sir," McFadden said. "Not really."

"You didn't find him?" Wohl pursued.

"No, sir. Inspector, we was in every other fag bar in Philadelphia, last night."

"Plus the bar in the FOP?" Wohl asked.

"We met Payne there is all, Inspector," McFadden said.

"Oh, I thought maybe you thought you would find Mr. Williams hanging around the FOP."

"No, sir. It was just a place to meet Payne."

"So you had nothing to drink in the FOP?"

"Hay-zus didn't," Charley said.

"Does that mean that you and Payne had a drink? A couple of drinks?"

"We had a couple of beers, yes, sir."

"Payne can't hold his liquor very well, can he?"

"He put it away all right last night, it seemed to me," McFadden said.

"In the FOP, or someplace else?"

"We had to order something besides a soda when we was looking for Williams, sir."

"Hay-zus, too?"

"Hay-zus doesn't drink," McFadden said.

"I thought you just said, or implied, that to look credible in the various bars and clubs in which you sought the elusive Mr. Williams, it was necessary to drink something other than soda."

"I don't know how Hay-zus handles it, sir."

"Weren't you with him?"

"No, sir. We split up. Hay-zus took the plain car, and I took Payne and we looked in different places."

"Using a personal vehicle?"

"Yes, sir."

"Must have been fun," Wohl said. "To judge by the way Payne looks and smells this morning."

"He looked all right to me when we went home," Charley said.

"I'll take your word for that, Officer McFadden," Wohl said. "Far be it from me to suggest that you would consider yourself to be on duty with a bellyful of booze and impaired judgment."

"Yes, sir," McFadden said.

"I have a theory why you were unable to locate Mr. Williams last night," Wohl said. "Would you care to hear it?"

"Yes, sir," McFadden said.

Wohl glared at Jesus Martinez.

"May I infer from your silence that you are not interested in my theory, Officer Martinez?"

"Yes, sir. No, sir. I mean, yes, sir, I'd like to hear your theory."

"Thank you," Wohl said. "My theory is that while you, McFadden, and Payne were running around town boozing it up on what you erroneously believed was going to be the taxpayer's expense, and you, Martinez, were doing—I have no idea what—that Mr. Williams went back to Glengarry Lane and burglarized poor Miss Peebles yet one more time. You did hear about the burglary?"

"Yes, sir," Martinez said. "Just before we came in here."

"Miss Peebles is not going to be burglarized again," Peter Wohl said.

"Yes, sir," they replied in chorus.

"Would either or both of you be interested to know why I am so sure of that?"

"Yes, sir," they chorused again.

"Because, from now until we catch the Peebles burglar, or hell freezes over, which ever comes sooner, between sundown and sunup, one of the three of you is going to be parked somewhere within sight and sound of the Peebles residence."

"Sir," Martinez protested, "he sees somebody in a car, he's not going to hit her house again."

"True," Wohl said. "That's the whole point of the exercise."

"Then how are we going to catch him?" Martinez said.

"I'll leave that up to you," Wohl said. "With the friendly advice that since however you were going about that last night obviously didn't work, that it might be wise to try something else. Are there any questions?"

Both shook their heads no.

Wohl made a gesture with his right hand, which had the fingers balled and the thumb extended. Officers McFadden and Martinez interpreted the gesture to mean that they were dismissed and should leave.

When they were gone, and the door had been closed after them, Captain Michael J. Sabara, who had been sitting quietly on the couch, now quietly applauded.

"Very good, Inspector," he said.

"I used to be a Highway Corporal," Wohl said. "You thought I'd forgotten how to eat a little ass?"

"They're good kids," Sabara said.

"Yes, they are," Wohl said. "And I want to keep them that way. Reining them in a little when they first get here is probably going to prevent me from having to jump on them with both feet a little down the pike."

# EIGHTEEN

"What we're going to do," Officer Jesus Martinez said, turning to Officer Charles McFadden as they stood at the urinals in the Seventh District POLICE PERSONNEL ONLY men's room, "is give your rich-kid rookie buddy the midnight-to-sunup shift."

"What are you pissed at him for?" Charley McFadden asked.

"You dumb shit! Where do you think Wohl heard that you two were boozing it up last night?"

"We wasn't boozing it up last night," McFadden argued.

"Tell that to Wohl," Martinez said, sarcastically.

"If we make him work from midnight, then who's going to be staking out the house from sunset to midnight? Somebody's going to have to be there."

McFadden's logic was beyond argument, which served to anger Martinez even more.

"That sonofabitch is trouble, Charley," he said, furiously. "And he ain't *never* going to make a cop."

"I think he's all right," McFadden said. "He just don't know what he's doing, is all. He just came on the job, is all."

"You think what you want," Martinez said, zipping up his fly. "Be an asshole. Okay. This is what we'll do: We'll park Richboy outside the house from sunset to midnight. We'll go look for this Walton Williams. Then we'll split the midnight to sunrise. You go first, or me, I don't care."

"That would make him work what—what time is sunset, six? Say six hours, and we would only be working three hours apiece."

"Tough shit," Martinez said. "Look, asshole, Wohl meant it: until we catch this Williams guy, we're going to have to stake out the house from sunset to sunrise. So the thing to do is catch Williams, right? Who can do that better, you and me, or your rookie buddy? Shit, he don't even know where to look, much less what he should do if he should get lucky and fall over him."

Sergeant Ed Frizell raised the same question about the fair division of duty hours when making the stakeout of the Peebles residence official, but bowed to the logic that Officer Payne simply was not qualified to go looking for a suspect on his own. And he authorized three cars, one each for what he had now come to think of as Sherlock Holmes, Dr. Watson, and the Kid. He also independently reached the conclusion that unless Walton Williams was really stupid, or maybe stoned, he would spot the car sitting on Glengarry Lane as a police car, and would not attempt to burglarize the Peebles residence with it there. And that solved the problem of how just-about-wholly inexperienced Matt Payne would deal with the suspect if he encountered him; there would be no suspect to encounter.

At two-fifteen, when Staff Inspector Wohl walked into the office after having had luncheon with Detective Jason Washington at *D'Allesandro's Steak Shop*, on Henry Avenue, Sergeant Frizell informed him that Captain Henry C. Quaire, the commanding officer of the Homicide Bureau, had called, said it was important, and would Wohl please return his call at his earliest opportunity.

"Get him on the phone, please," Wohl said. Waving at Washington to come along, he went into his office.

One of the buttons on Wohl's phone began to flash the moment he sat down.

"Peter Wohl, Henry," he said. "What's up?"

"I just had a call from the State Trooper barracks in Quakertown, Inspector," Quaire said. "I think they found Miss Woodham."

"Hold it, Henry," Wohl said, and snapped his fingers. When Jason Washington looked at him, Wohl gestured for him to pick up the extension. "Jason's getting on the line."

"I'm on, Captain," Washington said, as, in a conditioned reflex, he took a notebook from his pocket, then a ballpoint pen.

"They—the Trooper barracks in Quakertown, Jason," Quaire went on, "have a mutilated corpse of a white female who meets Miss Woodham's description. Been dead twenty-four to thirty-six hours. They fed it to NCIC and got a hit."

"Shit," Jason Washington said, bitterly.

"Where did they find it?" Wohl asked, taking a pencil from his desk drawer.

"In a summer cottage near a little town called Durham," Quaire said. "The location is . . ."

He paused, and Wohl had a mental image of him looking for a sheet of paper on which he had written down the information.

". . . 1.2 miles down a dirt road to the left, 4.4 miles west of US 611 on US 212."

Jason Washington parroted the specifics back to Quaire.

"That's right," Quaire said.

"They don't have anything on the doer, I suppose?" Washington said.

"They said all they have so far is what I just gave you," Quaire said.

"If they call back," Wohl said, "get it to me right away, will you?"

"Yes, sir," Quaire said, his tone showing annoyance.

*That was stupid of me,* Wohl thought. *I shouldn't have told Quaire how to do his job.*

"I didn't mean that the way it came out, Henry," Wohl said. "Sorry."

There was a pause, during which, Wohl knew, Henry Quaire was deciding whether to accept the apology.

"The last time we dealt with Quakertown, they were a real pain in the ass, Inspector," Quaire said, finally. "Resented our intrusion into their business. But I know a Trooper Captain in Harrisburg. . . ."

Wohl considered that a moment.

"Let's save him until we need him, Henry," he said. "Maybe we'll be lucky this time."

"Call me if you think I can help," Quaire said.

"Thanks very much, Henry," Wohl said. "I'll keep you advised."

"Good luck," Quaire said, and hung up.

Wohl looked up at Washington.

"I'll get up there just as fast as I can," Washington said. "I'm wondering if I need Tony up there, too."

"Whatever you think," Wohl said.

"Would it be all right if I took the kid with me?" Washington said.

It took Wohl a moment to take his meaning.

"Payne, you mean? Sure. Whatever you need."

"It's in the sticks," Washington explained. "He might be useful to use the phone. . . ."

"You can have whatever you want," Wohl said. "You want a Highway car to go with you?"

"No, the kid ought to be enough," Washington said. "Highway and the Troopers have never been in love. Would you get in touch with Tony and tell him, and let him decide whether he wants to go up there, too?"

"Done."

"Maybe I can get a description of this sonofabitch anyway," Washington said. "Or the van."

"I was afraid we'd get something like this," Wohl said.

"It's not like Christmas finally coming is it?" Washington said, and walked out of Wohl's office.

Matt Payne was sitting at an ancient, lopsided table against the wall beside Sergeant Ed Frizell's desk, typing forms on a battered Underwood typewriter.

"Come on with me, Payne," Washington said.

Matt looked at him in surprise, and so did Sergeant Ed Frizell.

"Where's he going with you?" Frizell said.

"He's going with me, all right?" Washington said, and took Matt's arm and propelled him toward the door.

"I need him here," Frizell protested.

"Tell Wohl your problem," Washington said, and followed Matt outside.

"You know Route 611? To Doylestown, and then up along the river to Easton?" Washington asked.

"Yes, sir," Matt said.

"You drive," Washington said.

Matt got behind the wheel.

"Take a right," Washington ordered, "and then a left onto Red Lion."

"Yes, sir," Matt said, and started off.

There was a line of cars stopped for a red light at Red Lion Road. Matt started to slow.

"Go around them to the left," Washington ordered. "Be careful!"

And then he reached down and threw a switch. A siren started to howl.

"Try not to kill us," Washington ordered. "But the sooner we get out there, the better. Maybe we can find this sonofabitch before he does it again."

"Where are we going?"

"The State Troopers found Miss Woodham," Washington said. "Mutilated. Dead, of course. In the sticks."

Matt edged into the intersection, saw that it was clear, and went through the stop sign.

*My God, I'm actually driving a police car with the siren going, on my way to a murder!*

"Are you sure you'd rather not drive, Mr. Washington?" Matt asked.

"You have to start somewhere, Payne. The first time I was driving and my supervisor turned on the light and siren, I was sort of thrilled. I felt like a regular Dick Tracy."

"Yeah," Matt Payne said, almost to himself, as he pulled the LTD to the left and, swerving into and out of the opposing lane, went around a UPS truck and two civilian cars.

Sergeant Ed Frizell stood in Inspector Wohl's doorway and waited until he got off the telephone.

"Sir, am I going to get Payne back? Detective Washington just took him off somewhere, and I have all those—"

"You'll get him back when Washington's through with him. You better find Sherlock Holmes and Dr. Watson and tell them Payne might not be back by the time he's supposed to be at the Peebles residence."

"Yes, sir," Frizell said, disappointed, and started to leave.

"Wait a minute," Wohl said. "There's something else." He had just that moment thought of it.

"Yes, sir."

"Get somebody on the Highway Band and ask them to get me a location on Mickey O'Hara. I mean me, say 'W-William One wants a location on Mickey O'Hara.' "

"He might be hard to find, sir. Wouldn't it be better to put it out on the J-Band? And have everybody looking for him?"

"I think Mickey monitors Highway," Wohl said.

"Can I ask what that's all about, Inspector?"

"Put it down to simple curiosity," Wohl said. "Thank you, Sergeant."

And then, as Frizell closed the door, Wohl thought of something else, and dug out the telephone book.

"Dr. Payne," Amelia Alice Payne's voice came over the line.

"Peter Wohl," he said.

"Oh," she said, and he sensed that her voice was far less professional, more—what? *girlish*—than it had been a moment before.

"I called to break our date," he said.

"I wasn't aware that we had one," she said, coyly.

"We had one for dinner," he said. "*I* remember."

"So do I," she confessed. "I was waiting for you to call."

"The State Police called," he said.

"They found the Woodham woman," Amy said. "Oh, God!"

"They found the mutilated body of a woman who may be Miss Woodham," he said.

"Where?"

"In the sticks. Bucks County. Near the Delaware River. Way up."

"Mutilated? How?"

*Now she sounds like a doctor again.*

"I don't know that yet," Wohl said. "I just sent a detective up there."

*I did not mention Matt Payne,* he decided, *because her next question would probably be a challenging "why?"*

"This is another of those times I hate having to say, 'I told you so,' " Amy said.

"It'll take him an hour, an hour and a half to get there and have a quick look. I've been reminded that the State Troopers aren't always as cooperative as they could be. I may have to go up there myself and wave a little rank around. So that blows our dinner, I'm afraid."

"I'd like to see the body," Amy said.

*I know she's a doctor, a shrink, so why did that shock the shit out of me?*

"How was she killed?" Amy went on, without waiting for a reply.

"I don't know that, either," Wohl said. "Or even where. All I know is what I told you."

"Where did they find the body?"

"In a summer cottage," he said.

"Maybe if I could look around," Amy said. "Oh, I don't know. I might just be butting in and getting in the way. But you have to find that man, Peter."

"If this body is Miss Woodham," he said.

"Well, what do you think?" she asked, sharply.

"I think it's going to prove to be her," Wohl said. "I have nothing to back up that feeling, of course. It very well could be someone else."

"And thanks but no thanks, huh? Peter, you came to me! I didn't ask to become involved in this."

"Could you get off to go up there with me? Presuming I have to go? In say an hour and a half?"

"I don't want to butt in."

"I'm asking for your help," Wohl said. "Again."

"Yes, I could," she said. "I'll just cancel my appointments, that's all."

"I'll get back to you," he said, "as soon as I hear from Washington."

"From *Washington*?"

"That's the detective's name," Wohl said.

"Oh." She chuckled.

"There's a flock of nice restaurants up there," he said. "We can have dinner in the country, if you'd like."

"Are they run by gangster men of honor, or would you actually have to pay for it?"

"Jesus, you're something," he said. "There goes my other phone. I'll call you."

His caller was an indignant Inspector from the Traffic Division who had wrecked his car, sent someone to get him another from the motor pool, and been informed that Peter Wohl's Special Operations Division had, in the last three days, taken all the available new cars. Peter's explanation that they had drawn what cars the motor pool had elected to give them did not mollify the Inspector from Traffic.

The next call, which came in while the Traffic Inspector was still complaining, was from Mickey O'Hara.

"I understand that you're looking for me," Mickey said. "What's up, Peter?"

"Nothing."

"Bullshit, I heard the call."

"I have no idea what you're talking about," Wohl said. "I thought you had called to demand to know what, if anything, has developed in the Woodham kidnapping."

There was a pause.

"Okay," Mickey said. "What if anything has developed in the Woodham case?"

"Well, since you put that to me as a specific question, which is not the same thing as me volunteering information to one favored representative of the press, I suppose I am obliged to answer it. The State Police have found a body near Durham, Bucks County, 4.4 miles west of US 611 on US 212, which they feel may be that of Miss Woodham."

"When?"

"They reported the incident to the Philadelphia Police less than an hour ago," Wohl said.

"Anybody else have this?"

"Since no one has come to me, as you did, Mr. O'Hara, with a specific question that I am obliged to answer, I have not mentioned this to anyone outside the Police Department."

"Thanks, Peter," Mickey O'Hara said, "I owe you one."

The line went dead.

Wohl broke the connection with his finger and dialed first Chief Coughlin's number and told him what had happened and what (minus Mickey O'Hara) he had done about it. And then he called Commissioner Czernick and told him the same thing.

Then he called Sergeant Frizell in and told him to have a Highway Patrolman take one of the new cars over to Inspector

Paul McGhee in Traffic with the message that he could have the use of it until a car was available to him from the motor pool.

Then he settled down to deal with the mountain of paperwork on his desk until such time as Washington checked in.

A mile the far side of Willow Grove, Jason Washington switched off the siren.

"If this is Miss Woodham," he said. "And we won't know until we get a look at the body—maybe not even then, maybe not until we get her dental records, they didn't say how badly she was mutilated, only that she had been—this may be the first break we've had in this job."

"I don't understand," Matt said. He had been thinking that it was suddenly very quiet in the car, even though the speedometer was nudging eighty.

"Well, maybe somebody saw a van drive in. The site is supposed to be a summer cottage on a dirt road; in other words, not a busy street. People might have noticed. Maybe we can get an identification on the van, at least the color and make. If it's a dirt road, or there's a lawn, or some soft dirt, near the cottage, maybe we can get a cast and match it against the casts on Forbidden Drive—do you know what I'm talking about?"

"Yes, sir," Matt said. "When I Xeroxed the reports, I read them."

"If we get a match on tire casts, that would mean the same vehicle. If we can get a description of the van, that would help. *If* he brought her out here in a van, and *if* the body they have is Miss Woodham. And obviously, he has some connection with the summer cottage. I mean, I don't think he just drove around looking for someplace to take her; he knew where he was taking her. So we start there. Who's the owner? Our guy? If not, who did he rent it to? Does he know a large, hairy, well-spoken white male? Do the neighbors remember seeing anybody, or anything? Hell, we may even get lucky and come up with a name."

Matt wondered if Washington was merely thinking out loud, or whether he was graciously showing him how things were done. The former was more likely; the latter quite flattering.

"I see you got rid of the horse pistol in the shoulder holster," Washington said.

"Yes, sir," Matt said. "I bought a *Chief's Special*."

"After I told you that, I had some second thoughts," Washington said.

"Sir?"

"What kind of a shot are you?" Washington said.

"Actually, I'm not bad."

"I was afraid of that, too," Washington said. "Listen, I may be just making noise, because the chances that you would have to take that pistol out of its holster—ankle holster?"

"Yes, sir," Matt replied.

"The chances that you will have to take that snub-nose out of its holster range from slim indeed to nonexistent, but there's always an exception, so I want to get this across to you. The effective range, if you're lucky, of that pistol is about as long as this car. If you, excited as you would be if you had to draw it, managed to hit a man-sized target any farther away than seven yards, it would be a miracle."

"Yes, sir," Matt said.

"I don't expect you to believe that," Washington said.

"I believe you," Matt said.

"You believe that *'what ol' Washington says is probably true for other people, but doesn't apply to me. I'm a real pistolero. I shot Expert in the service with a .45.'* "

"Well, I didn't make it into the Marines," Matt said. "But I did shoot Expert with a .45 when I was in the training program."

"Do me a favor, kid?"

"Sure."

"The next time you've got a couple of hours free, go to a pistol range. Not the Academy Range, one of the civilian ones. Colosimo's got a good one. Take that *Chief's Special* with you and buy a couple of boxes of shells for it. And then shoot at a silhouette with it. Rapid fire. Aim it, if you want to, or just point it—you know what I'm talking about, you know the difference?''

"Yes, sir.''

"And then count the holes in the target. If you hit it—anywhere, not just in the head or in the chest—half the time, I would be very surprised.''

"You mean I should practice until I'm competent with it?'' Matt asked.

"No. That's *not* what I mean. The point I'm trying to make is that Wyatt Earp and John Wayne couldn't shoot a snub-nose more than seven yards, nobody can, and expect to hit what they're shooting at. I want you to convince yourself of that, and remember it, if—and I reiterate—in the very unlikely chance you ever have to use that gun.''

"Oh, I think I see what you mean,'' Matt said.

"I hope so,'' Washington said. "My own rule of thumb is that if he's too far away to belt in the head with a snub-nose, he's too far away to shoot.''

Matt chuckled.

"Where the hell are we?'' Washington said. "We should be in Canada by now. Pull in the next gas station and ask for directions.''

Route 212, a two-lane, winding road, was fifteen miles from the gas station. They had no trouble finding the dirt road 4.4 miles from the intersection of 611 and 212. There were a dozen cars and vans parked on the shoulder of the road by it, some wearing State Trooper and Bucks County Sheriff's Department regalia, and others the logotypes of radio and television stations.

A sheriff's deputy waved them through on 212, and advanced angrily on the car when Matt turned on the left-turn signal.

"Crime scene,'' the deputy called when Matt rolled the window down.

"Philadelphia Police,'' Washington said, showing his badge. "We're expected.''

"Wait a minute," the deputy said and walked to a State Trooper car. A very large Corporal in a straw Smokey the Bear hat swaggered over.

"Help you?"

"I hope so," Washington said, smiling. "We're from Homicide in Philadelphia. We think we can help you identify the victim."

"The Lieutenant didn't say anything to me," the Corporal said, doubtfully.

"Well, then, maybe you better ask Major Fisher," Washington said. "He's the one that asked us to come up here."

The Corporal looked even more doubtful.

"Look, can't you get him on the radio?" Washington said. "He said if he wasn't here before we got here, he'd be here soon. He ought to be in radio range."

The Corporal waved them on.

When Matt had the window rolled back up, Washington said, "I guess they have a Major named Fisher. Or Smokey thought that he better not ask."

Matt looked at Washington and laughed.

"You're devious, Mr. Washington," he said, approvingly.

"The first thing a good detective has to be is a bluffer," Washington said. "A good bluffer."

The road wound through a stand of evergreens and around a hill, and then they came to the cabin. It was unpretentious, a small frame structure with a screened-in porch sitting on a plot of land not much larger than the house itself cut into the side of a hill.

There was a yellow CRIME SCENE DO NOT CROSS tape strung around an area fifty yards or so from the house. There was an assortment of vehicles on the shoulders of the road, State Trooper and Sheriff's Department cars; a large van painted in State Trooper colors and bearing the legend STATE POLICE MOBILE CRIME LAB; several unmarked law-enforcement cars, and a shining black funeral home hearse.

"Pull it over anywhere," Washington ordered. "We have just found Major Fisher."

Matt was confused but said nothing. He stopped the car and followed Washington to the Crime Scene tape and ducked under it when Washington did. Washington walked up to an enormous man in a State Police Lieutenant's uniform.

The Lieutenant looked at Washington and broke out in a wide smile.

"Well, I'll be damned, look who escaped from Philadelphia!" he said. "How the hell are you, Jason?"

He shook Washington's hand enthusiastically.

"Lieutenant," Washington said, "say hello to Matt Payne."

"Christ, I thought they would send a bigger keeper than that with you," the Lieutenant said. "I hope you know what kind of lousy company you're in, young man."

"How do you do, sir?" Matt said, politely.

"I'm surprised you got in," the Lieutenant said. "When I got here, there was people all over. The goddamned press. Cops from every dinky little dorf in fifty miles. People who watch cop shows on television. Jesus! I finally ran them off, and then told the Corporal to let nobody up here."

"I told him I was a personal friend of the legendary Lieutenant Ward," Washington said.

"Well, I'm glad you did, but I don't know why you're here," Ward said.

"If the victim is who we think it is, a Miss Elizabeth Woodham," Washington said, "she was abducted from Philadelphia."

"I heard they got a hit on the NCIC," Lieutenant Ward said. "But I didn't hear what. I was up in the coal regions on an arson job. Can you identify her?"

"From a picture," Washington said, and handed a photograph to Lieutenant Ward.

"Could be," Ward said. "You want to have a look?"

"I'd appreciate it," Washington said.

Ward marched up the flimsy stairs to the cottage, and led them inside. There was a buzzing of flies, and a sweet, sickly smell Matt had never smelled before. He had never seen so many flies in one place before, either. They practically covered what looked like spilled grease on the floor.

*Oh, shit, that's not grease. That's blood. But that's too much blood, where did it all come from?*

Two men in civilian clothing bent over a large black rubber container, which had handles molded into its sides.

"Hold that a minute," Lieutenant Ward said. "Detective Washington wants a quick look."

One of the men pulled a zipper along the side down for eighteen inches or so, and then folded the rubber material back, in a flap, exposing the head and neck of the corpse.

"Jesus," Jason Washington said, softly, and then he gestured with his hand for the man to uncover the entire body. When the man had the bag unzipped he folded the rubber back.

Officer Matthew Payne took one quick look at the mutilated corpse of Miss Elizabeth Woodham and fainted.

# NINETEEN

Officer Matthew Payne returned to consciousness and became aware that he was being half carried and half dragged down the wooden stairs of the summer cottage, between Detective Washington and Lieutenant Ward of the Pennsylvania State Police, who had draped his arms over their shoulders, and had their arms wrapped around his back and waist.

"I'm all right," Matt said, as he tried to find a place to put his feet, aware that he was dizzy, sweat soaked, and as humiliated as he could possibly be.

"Yeah, sure you are," Lieutenant Ward said.

They half dragged and half carried him to the car and lowered him gently into the passenger seat.

"Maybe you better put your head between your knees," Jason Washington said.

"I'm all right," Matt repeated.

"Do what he says, son," Lieutenant Ward said. "The reason you pass out is because the blood leaves your brain."

Matt felt Jason Washington's gentle hand on his head, pushing it downward.

"I did that," Lieutenant Ward said, conversationally, "on Twenty-Two, near Harrisburg. A sixteen-wheeler jackknifed and a guy in a sports car went under it. When I got there, his head was on the pavement, looking at me. I went down, and cracked my forehead open on the truck fuel tank. If my sergeant hadn't been riding with me, I don't know what the hell would have happened. They carried me off in the ambulance with the body."

"That better, Matt?" Washington asked.

"Yeah," Matt said, shaking his head and sitting up. His shirt was now clammy against his back.

"He's getting some color back," Lieutenant Ward said. "He'll be all right. Lucky he didn't break anything, the way he went down."

Matt saw the two men carrying the black bag with the obscenity in it down the stairs, averted his eyes, then forced himself to watch.

"Did you get any tire casts," Washington asked, "or did the local gendarmerie drive all over the tracks?"

"Got three good ones," Ward said. "The vehicle was a '69 Ford van, dark maroon, with a door on the side. It has all-weather tires on the back."

"How you know that?"

"I told you, I got casts."

"I mean that it was a '69 Ford?"

"Mailman saw it," Ward said. "Rural carrier. There's a couple of houses farther up the road."

"Bingo," Washington said. "I don't suppose he saw who was driving it?"

"Not driving it," Ward said. "But he saw a large white male out in back."

"That's all, 'large, white male'?"

"He had hair," Ward said.

"Had hair, or was hairy?"

"Wasn't bald," Ward said. "Late twenties, early thirties.

The mail carrier lives in that little village down there,'' he added, jerking his thumb in the direction of the highway. ''You want to talk to him?''

''Yes, I do, but what I really want first is a tire cast. Is there a phone in the village?''

''Yeah, sure, there's a store and a post office.''

''Are you back among us, Matt?'' Washington asked. ''Feel up to driving down there and calling the boss?''

''Yes, sir,'' Matt said.

''Well, then, go call him. Tell him what we have—were you with us when Lieutenant Ward gave us the vehicle description?'' He stopped and turned to Ward. ''I don't suppose we have a license number?''

''No,'' Ward said. ''Just that it was a Pennsylvania tag. But he saw that the grill was pushed in on the right. What caught the mail carrier's attention was that the van was parked right up by the steps. He thought maybe somebody was moving in.''

''I heard what Lieutenant Ward said,'' Matt said. ''A '69 dark red Ford with a door on the side.''

''*Maroon*, kid,'' Lieutenant Ward said. ''Not red, *maroon*. This ain't whisper down the lane.''

''Yes, sir,'' Matt said, terribly embarrassed. ''*Maroon*.''

''And a pushed-in, on the right, grill,'' Washington added, quickly.

''Yes, sir.''

''Pennsylvania tag. So tell Inspector Wohl that. Find out if Harris decided to come out here. If he did, tell Wohl that you'll bring the casts in as soon as they're set and dry, and that I'll ride back with Tony. If he's not coming, then I'll do what I can here and go back with you. Or you can take the casts in and come back for me. Ask him how he wants to handle it.''

Forty-five minutes later, five miles north of Doylestown on US 611, a Pennsylvania State Trooper turned on his flashing red light, hit the siren switch just long enough to make it growl, and caught the attention of the driver of a Ford LTD that was exceeding the 50 mph speed limit by thirty miles an hour, and which might, or might not, be an unmarked law enforcement vehicle.

Matt was startled by the growl of the siren, and by the State Trooper car in his rearview mirror. He slowed, and the Trooper pulled abreast and signaled him to pull over. Matt held his badge up to the window, and the Trooper repeated the gesture to pull over.

Matt pulled onto the shoulder and stopped and was out of his car before the Trooper could get out of his. He met him at the fender of the State Police car with his badge and photo ID in his hand.

The Trooper looked at it, and then, doubtfully, at Matt.

"What's the big hurry?" the trooper asked.

"I'm carrying tire casts from the crime scene in Durham to Philadelphia," Matt said. When that didn't seem to impress the trooper very much, he added: "We're trying to get a match. We think the doer is a serial rapist we're looking for."

The trooper walked to the car and looked in the backseat, where the tire casts, padded in newspaper, were strapped to the seat with seat belts.

"I didn't know the Philadelphia cops were interested in that job," the Trooper said, "and I wasn't sure if you were really a cop. I've had two weirdos lately with black-walled tires and antennas that didn't have any radios. And you *were* going like hell."

"Can I go now?"

"I'll take you through Doylestown to the Willow Grove interchange," the Trooper said, and walked back to his car and got in.

There is a stoplight at the intersection of US 611, which at that point is also known as "Old York Road," and Moreland Road in Willow Grove. When Matt stopped for it, the State Trooper by then having left him, his eye fell on the line of cars coming in the opposite direction. The face of the driver of the first car in line was familiar to him. It was that of Inspector Peter Wohl. He raised his hand in sort of a salute. He was sure that Wohl saw him, he was looking right at him, but there was no response. And then Matt saw another familiar face in Wohl's car, that of his sister.

*What the hell is she doing with Inspector Wohl?*

The light changed. The two cars passed each other. The drivers examined each other, Matt looking at Wohl with curiosity on his face, Wohl looking at Matt with no expression that Matt could read. And Amy Payne didn't look at all.

When he had spoken with Wohl from the pay phone in the little general store in Durham, Wohl had ordered him to bring the tire casts into Philadelphia as soon as they could safely be transported. "Harris is on his way out there, and I'm going out there myself. One or the other of us will see that Washington gets home."

*He hadn't mentioned anything about bringing Amy with him. What's that all about? And Harris? I must have passed him on the road. With my luck, when I was being escorted by the Trooper. What would Harris think about that? Or maybe even he drove past when I was stopped for speeding! Oh, Christ, what a fool I'm making of myself!*

He had just begun to wallow in the humiliation of having passed out upon seeing his first murder victim when he became aware of the radio, first that W-William One was calling W-William Two Oh One; next that W-William One was Inspector Wohl, and finally that W-William Two Oh One was Washington's—and at the moment, his—call sign.

He grabbed the microphone.

"W-William Two Oh One," he said.

"The crime lab people are waiting for those casts," Wohl's voice said. "So take them right to the Roundhouse; don't bother stopping at Bustleton and Bowler."

"Yes, sir," Matt said.

As he tried to make up his mind the fastest way to get from where he was to the Roundhouse, he turned up the volume on the J-Band.

There came the three beeps of an emergency message, signifying that the message that followed was directed to all radio-equipped vehicles of the Philadelphia Police Department:

Beep Beep Beep.

*"All cars stand by unless you have an emergency.*

*Wanted for investigation for homicide and rape, the driver of a 1969 Ford van, maroon in color, damage to right portion of the front grill, all-weather tires mounted on the rear. Operator is a white male, twenty-five to thirty years of age, may be armed with a knife. Suspect is wanted for questioning in a rape-homicide and should be considered dangerous."*

There was a brief pause, then the beeps and the message were repeated.

*Jesus*, Matt thought, *I'd like to spot that sonofabitch!*

He did not do so, although he very carefully scrutinized all the traffic on Broad Street, and on the Roosevelt Boulevard Extension, and then down the parkway into downtown Philadelphia, looking for a maroon van.

He had difficulty finding a parking space at the Roundhouse, but finally found one. He unstrapped the casts and carried them into the building. A very stout lady with orange hair came rapidly out of the elevator as he prepared to board it, nearly knocking the casts out of his hands.

That, he decided, would not have surprised him at all. It would be the gilding of the lily. If he had dropped and destroyed the casts, he would have spent the rest of his natural life typing up Sergeant Frizell's goddamned multipart forms.

*No*, he thought, *that's terribly clever, but it's not true. What would have happened if I had carelessly allowed the casts to be broken would be that I would have had to face the question I have been so scrupulously avoiding; whether or not I am, as Amy suggests, simply indulging myself walking around with a gun and a badge, pretending I'm a policeman because I was rejected by the Marines.*

*I'm not a policeman. I proved that today, both by the childish pleasure I took racing through traffic with the siren screaming and then again by passing out like a Girl Scout seeing her first dead rabbit when I saw that poor woman's mutilated body. And just now, again, when I was really looking for a dark red van, so I could catch the bad guy, and earn the cheers and applause of my peers.*

*What bullshit! What the hell would I have done if I'd found him?*

*Maybe it would have been better in the long run if that fat lady had knocked the casts from my hands; the cops, the real cops, are going to catch this psychopath anyway, and if I had dropped the damned things, I would have been out of the Police Department in the morning, which, logic tells me, ergo sum, would be better all around.*

Officer Matthew Payne was not at all surprised to be treated as a messenger boy by the officers in the Forensic Laboratory when he gave them the casts, nor when he returned to Bustleton and Bowler to be curtly ordered by a Corporal he had never seen before to get his ass over to the Peebles residence.

"You're late," the Corporal said. "Where the hell have you been?"

"At the Roundhouse," Matt replied.

"Oh, yeah, I heard," the Corporal said. "You have friends in high places, don't you, Payne?"

Matt did not bother to explain that he had been sent to the Roundhouse by Inspector Wohl, and that it had been in connection with police business. The Corporal had just added the final argument in favor of resignation. He did have friends in high places.

*Even if I wanted to, even if I had the requisite psychological characteristics necessary in a police officer, which I have proven beyond argument today that I do not, it would be impossible to prove myself a man, uncastrate myself, so to speak, with Uncle Denny Coughlin around, watching over me like a nervous maiden aunt, keeping me from doing what every other rookie gets to do, but rather sending me to a sinecure where, I am sure, the word is out to protect me. And where, I am obviously, and with justification, held in contempt by my peers.*

*I'll complete this tour of duty, because it would not be fair to expect McFadden and Martinez to take my duty in addition to their own, but in the morning, I will type out a short, succinct letter of resignation, and have it delivered out here by messenger.*

He took the keys the Corporal had given him in exchange for the keys to Jason Washington's car and drove out to Chestnut Hill.

Charley McFadden had parked his car fifty yards away from the gate to the Peebles residence, on the opposite side of the street. Matt pulled in behind it, got out, and walked up to it.

"I was beginning to wonder if you were going to show up at all," McFadden said, not critically. "Where'd you go with Washington?"

"He went out to Bucks County, where they found the Woodham woman's body," Matt said. "He needed an errand boy."

"Well, all those Homicide guys think they're hotshots," McFadden said, not understanding him. "Don't let it get you down."

"What am I supposed to do here, Charley?"

"This is mostly bullshit," McFadden said. "Most of it is to scare the creep off. Wohl don't want another burglary here on the Overnight Report. And some of it is because he's pissed at me."

"What for?"

"He somehow has the idea I took you out and got you shitfaced last night," Charley said. He looked at Matt's face for a reaction, and then went on: "Hay-zus thinks you told Wohl that."

"No," Matt said. "I told Inspector Wohl that *I* got drunk."

"With me?"

"No," Matt said. "And if he formed that impression, I'll see that I correct it."

"Fuck it, don't worry about it," Charley said. "Now, about

here. I don't think this asshole will show up again. If he does, he's not stupid, he'll spot your car, and disappear. But if he does show up, and he is stupid—in other words, if you see somebody sneaking around the bushes, call for a backup. Don't try to catch him yourself. Highway cars will be riding by here every half hour or so, so what you'll do is sit here and try to stay awake until Hay-zus relieves you at midnight.''

"How do I stay awake?"

"You didn't bring a thermos?"

Matt shook his head.

"I should have said something," Charley said. "I'll go get you a couple of containers of black coffee before I leave. Even cold coffee is better than no coffee. Get out of the car every once in a while, and walk around a little. Wave your arms, get the blood circulating. . . ."

"I get the picture," Matt said.

"Every supervisor around is going to be riding past here tonight," McFadden said. "I wouldn't be surprised if Wohl himself came by. So for Christ's sake, don't fall asleep, or your ass will be in a crack."

"Okay," Matt said. "Thanks, Charley."

"Ah, shit," McFadden said, and started his engine. "You want something with the coffee? An egg sandwich, hamburger, something?"

"Hamburger with onions, two of them," Matt said, digging in his pocket for money. "They give me gas. Maybe that'll keep me awake."

Two hamburgers generously dressed with fried and raw onions (Charley McFadden, not knowing Matt's preference, had brought one of each) and two enormous foam containers of coffee, while they produced gas, did not keep Officer Matthew Payne awake on his post.

Neither did half a dozen walks down the street and up the driveway of the Peebles residence. Neither did getting out of the car and waving his arms around and doing deep knee bends.

At five minutes after eleven, while he was, for the tenth or fifteenth time, mentally composing the letter of resignation he would write in the morning, striving for both brevity and avoiding any suggestion that he would entertain any requests to reconsider, his head dropped forward and he fell asleep.

Five minutes after that, he twisted in his sleep, and slid slowly down on the seat.

Five minutes after that, as Officer McFadden had predicted, a senior supervisor did drive by the Peebles residence. He spotted the car, but paid only cursory attention to it, for he had other things on his mind.

Captain David Pekach thought the odds were about twenty-to-one that he was about to make a complete fool of himself. He was *imagining* that the fingers of Miss Martha Peebles had lingered tenderly and perhaps even suggestively on his when he had damned near dropped the Ludwig Hamner Remington rolling-block *Schuetzen*, and it was *preposterous* to think that he really saw what he thought he saw in her eyes when she had seen him to the door.

What he was going to do, he decided, as he turned into the Peebles driveway, was simply perform his duty, that given to him by Peter Wohl; to assure the lady that everything that could conceivably be done by the Philadelphia Police Department generally and the Highway Patrol, of which he was the commanding officer, specifically, to protect her property from the depredations of Walton Williams; and to apprehend Mr. Williams; was being done. His presence would be that proof.

The odds are, he thought, that she went to bed long ago, anyway.

But there was a light in the library, and the light over the entrance was on, so he went on the air and reported that Highway One was out of service at 606 Glengarry Lane, checking the Peebles residence.

He walked up the stairs and had his finger out to push the doorbell when the door opened.

"I saw you coming up the drive," Martha Peebles said. "I wasn't sure that you would come."

"Good evening," David Pekach said, unable to choose between "Miss Peebles" and "Martha" and deciding quickly on neither one.

"Please come in," she said.

She was wearing a dressing robe.

*Nothing sexy or suggestive or anything like that; it goes from her neck to her ankles. Just what a lady like herself would wear when she was about to go to bed.*

"I said I would stop by and check on you," David Pekach said.

"I know," she said.

She started to walk to the stairway, stopped and looked over her shoulder to see if he was following her.

*Where the hell is she going?*

"And I've ordered cars to check on you regularly," he said.

"I've seen them," she said. "That's why I thought you might not be coming. That you had sent the other cars in your stead."

"If I say I'll do something, I do it," David Pekach said.

"I was almost sure of that, and now that you're here, I'm convinced that you are a man of your word," Martha Peebles said.

They were at the landing before the stained glass window of Saint Whatsisname the Dragon Slayer by then.

"I made a little midnight snack," Martha Peebles said.

"You didn't have to do that."

"I wanted to," she said, and took his arm.

"And there's a plainclothes officer in an unmarked car parked just up the block," David said.

*Or I think there is. I didn't see anybody in the goddamned car, now that I think about it.*

"I saw him, too," she said. "He's been up the drive four times, waving his flashlight around."

"We're doing our very best to take care of you."

"I wasn't sure if you—if you came, that is—if you could drink on duty, so I made coffee. But there's wine. Or whiskey, too, if you'd rather."

They were on the second floor now, moving down the corridor, away from the gun room.

"Oh, I don't think law and order would come crashing down if I had a glass of wine," David said.

"I'm glad. I put out a port, a rather robust port, that Father always enjoyed."

A door was open. Inside, David saw a small round table with a tablecloth that reached to the floor. There was a tray of sandwiches on it, with the crusts cut off, and a silver coffee set, and beside it was a wine cooler with the neck of a bottle of wine sticking out of it.

*Jesus!*

And when he stepped inside, he saw that there was an enormous, heavily carved headboard over a bed on which the sheets had been turned down.

*Jesus!*

"The maiden's bed," Martha Peebles said.

"Excuse me?" David said, not sure that he had heard her correctly.

"The maiden's bed," Martha said. "My bed. I suppose you think that's a bit absurd in this day and age, a maiden my age."

"Not at all." He seemed to have trouble finding his voice.

"I'm thirty-five," Martha said.

"I'm thirty-seven."

"Do you think *I'm* absurd?" Martha Peebles asked.

"No," he said firmly. "Why should I think that?"

"Enticing you, trying to entice you, up here like this?"

"Jesus!"

"Then you do," she said. "I didn't . . . it wasn't my intention to embarrass you, David."

"You're not embarrassing me."

"I'll tell you what is absurd," she said. "I never even thought of doing something like this until you came here this afternoon."

"I don't know what to say," David said. "Christ, I've been thinking about you all day . . . ever since I almost dropped the Hamner *Schuetzen*."

"When our hands touched?"

"Yeah, and when you looked at me that way," he said.

"I thought you were looking into my soul," Martha said. "Jesus!"

"That made you uncomfortable, didn't it?" Martha asked. "For me to say that?"

"I felt the same damned thing!"

"Oh, David!"

He put his arms around her. At first it was awkward, but then they seemed to adjust their bodies to each other, and he kissed the top of her head, then her forehead, and finally her mouth.

"David," Martha said, finally. "Your . . . equipment . . . the belt and whatever, your badge, is hurting me. If we're going—shouldn't we take our things off?"

David backed away from her and looked down at his badge, then started to take off his Sam Browne belt.

When he glanced at Martha, he saw that she had removed her dressing gown. She hadn't been wearing anything under it.

"Are you disappointed?" she asked.

"You're *beautiful*!"

"Oh, I'm so glad you think so!"

At fifteen minutes to midnight, Officer Jesus Martinez drove down Glengarry Lane in Chestnut Hill, saw the unmarked car parked by the side of the Peebles house, recognized it as one he had ferried from the Academy, and wondered who the hell was in it. Obviously, one of the brass hats, stroking the lady. If there had been anything going on, it would have come over the radio.

He saw Matt Payne's unmarked car and drove past it, made a U-turn, and pulled in beside it. Payne wasn't in the car; maybe he was in the house with the supervisor.

He turned the engine off, and slumped back against the seat waiting for Payne to show up.

When ten minutes passed and he had not, Jesus Martinez got out of his car and walked up to Payne's. Payne knew he was coming. Maybe he had left a note for him on the dashboard or something, saying where he was.

When he saw Matt on the seat, the first thing that occurred to him was that violence had occurred, that maybe he'd run into Walton Williams or something. He was just about to jerk the door open when Matt snored.

*The cocksucker's asleep! The cocksucker is really asleep!*

This was followed by a wave of righteous indignation approaching blind fury.

*The sonofabitch is sleeping when I've been out busting my ass all night looking for the asshole burglar! Before I have to baby-sit this fucking place!*

Officer Matthew Payne was a hair's breadth away from being jerked out of the car by his feet when Martinez had one more reaction that infuriated him even more than finding Payne asleep.

*The sonofabitch has been getting away with it! While I have been out busting my ass in every tinkerbell saloon in Philadelphia, he has been sleeping and nobody caught him! Highway cars have been going past here every half hour, and nobody caught him—or gave a damn if they did—and every fucking supervisor around, District, Highway, Northwest Detectives, maybe even Wohl and Sabara and that new Sergeant, have ridden by here and nobody noticed!*

Officer Martinez stood by the side of Matt's car for a moment, his arms folded angrily across his chest, as he considered the various options open to him to fix the rich-boy rookie' ass once and for all for this. When the solution came to him, it was simplicity itself.

Now smiling, he took his penknife from his pocket, tested the sharpness of the blade with his thumb, and then knelt by the left front wheel. He sliced into the rubber tire valve where it passed through the tire. There was a piercing whistle of escaping air, which Martinez quickly muffled with his fist.

On the right front and rear wheels, he used his handkerchief to muffle the whistle of air escaping from sliced air valves.

Then he got back in his car and drove off, wearing a smile of satisfaction. The smile grew broader as he thought of the finishing touch. He reached for his microphone.

"W-William Two Eleven, W-William Two Twelve," he said.

"Go," Charley McFadden's voice came back immediately.

"I'm at Broad and Olney, working on something," Martinez said. "I ain't gonna be able to relieve our friend on time. What should I do?"

"I'll go relieve him," Charley replied immediately. "You want to come when you get loose, or do you want me to take the tour?"

"I'll relieve you at three, if that's all right," Martinez said.

"Yeah, fine," McFadden said.

*That means I've got to hang around until three,* Jesus Martinez thought. *But what the fuck. It's worth it!*

And then he thought that the sonofabitch would probably still be asleep when Charley rode up.

*Good, let Charley see for himself what a useless prick Rich-boy is.*

# TWENTY

Officer Charles McFadden attempted to contact Officer Matthew Payne by radio as he drove to Chestnut Hill. There was no reply, which Charley thought was probably because Payne was walking around, the way he told him to, to keep awake.

But he sensed that something was wrong when he pulled up behind Matt's car and didn't see him. He had had plenty of time to stretch his legs from the time he had called; he should have been back by now. McFadden got cautiously out of his car and walked warily to Matt's.

Then he sensed something was wrong with the car and looked at it and found the four flat tires. McFadden squatted and took his revolver from his ankle holster, then approached the car door, and saw Matt sprawled on the seat.

"Matt!" he called, and then, louder, "Payne!"

Matt sat up, sleepily.

"You dumb fuck!" Charley McFadden exploded. "What in the goddamned hell is wrong with you? If one of the supervisors caught you, you'd be up on charges."

"I guess I fell asleep," Matt said, pushing himself outside the car, and then raising his arms over his head.

"What happened to your tires?" McFadden asked.

"My tires? What about my tires?"

"They're flat," McFadden said. And then he felt rage rise up in him.

*That fucking Hay-zus did this! That's what that bullshit was about him working on something at Broad and Olney! He drove up here, and let the air out of Payne's tires!*

"They're?" Matt asked. "Plural? As in more than one?"

He knelt beside Charley as Charley, pulling on a valve stem, discovered that someone had slit it with a knife.

*Someone, shit! Hay-zus!*

"All four of them, asshole!" Charley said. "Somebody caught you sleeping and slit your valve stems open. And I've got a good fucking idea who."

"It doesn't matter, Charley."

"The fuck it *don't!*" McFadden said. "You call for a police wrecker, how you going to explain this? Vandals? You were supposed to be sitting in the car, or close enough so that you could hear the radio. The guys on the wrecker are going to know what happened, stupid. It'll be all over Highway and Special Operations, the District, *'you hear about the asshole was sleeping on a stakeout? Somebody cut his tire valves.'* "

Matt was touched by Charley's concern. This did not seem to be the appropriate time to tell him that he was going to resign in the morning. It occurred to him that he liked Charley McFadden very much, and wondered if some sort of friendship would be possible after he had resigned.

"Well, now that I've made a jackass of myself, what can be done about it?"

"I'm thinking," Charley said. "There's a Sunoco station at Summit Avenue and Germantown Pike I think is open all night. I think they fix tires."

"Why don't we just call the police wrecker and let me take my lumps?" Matt asked.

"Don't be more of an asshole than you already are," Charley said. "We'll jack your car up, take off two tires at a time, put them in my car, and you get them fixed. Then the other two."

*I have an AAA card,* Matt thought, *but this doesn't seem to be an appropriate time to use it.*

"Come on," Charley said. "Get off the dime! I don't want to have to explain this to a supervisor."

A supervisor did in fact appear thirty minutes later, by which time Matt had returned from the service station with two repaired tires, and departed with the last two.

"What's going on here?" Captain David Pekach asked. "You need some help?"

"No, sir, another officer's helping me," Charley said. "Payne."

"What the hell happened?"

"There was some roofing nails here, Captain. Got two tires."

"You should have called the police wrecker," David Pekach said. "That's what they're for."

"This looked like the easiest way to handle it, sir," Charley said.

"Well, if you say so," David Pekach said. "Good night— or is it good morning?—Charley."

"Good night, sir."

"Charley, I'll have a word with Inspector Wohl tomorrow, and see if he won't reconsider this bullshit stakeout."

"I wish you would, sir."

"Good night, again, Charley," Captain Pekach said. He was in a very good mood. He was going to check in at Bustleton and Bowler, then go home and change his clothes, and then come back. Martha had said she completely understood that a man like himself had to devote a good deal of time to his duty, and that she would make them breakfast when he came back. Maybe something they could eat in bed, like strawberries in real whipped cream. Unless he wanted something more substantial.

*Jesus!*

•  •  •

Matt Payne walked into Bustleton and Bowler thirty minutes later and handed the keys to the car to the same Corporal who had given him hell for being late before he'd gone on the stakeout.

"Where the hell have you been with that car? It's after one."

"Go fuck yourself," Matt said. "Get off my back."

"You can't talk that way to me," the Corporal said.

"Payne!" a voice called. "Is that you?"

"Yeah, who's that?"

"Jason," Washington called. "I'm in here."

"Here" was Wohl's office. Washington was sitting on the couch, typing on a small portable set up on the coffee table.

"Do me a favor?" Washington asked, as he jerked a sheet of paper from the typewriter.

"Sure," Matt said.

"I'm dead on my feet," Washington said, "and you, at least relatively, look bright-eyed and bushy-tailed."

He inserted the piece of paper he had just taken from the typewriter into a large manila envelope and then licked the flap.

"Wohl wants this tonight, at his house," Washington said. "It's a wrap-up of the stuff we did in Bucks County, and what's happening here. You'd think they could find a maroon Ford van, wouldn't you? Well, shit. We'll have addresses on every maroon Ford van in a hundred miles as soon as Motor Vehicles opens in Harrisburg in the morning. Anyway, that's what's in there. He says if there are no lights on, slip it under his door."

"I don't know where he lives," Matt said.

"Chestnut Hill," Washington said. "Norwood Street. In a garage apartment behind a big house in front. You can't miss it. Only garage apartment. I'll show you on the map."

"I can find it," Matt said.

"Thanks, Matt, I appreciate it," Washington said.

"I appreciate . . . today, Mr. Washington," Matt said. "I'll never forget today."

"Hey, it's Jason. I'm a detective, that's all."

"Anyway, thanks," Matt said.

When he was in the Porsche headed for Chestnut Hill, he was glad he had thought to say "*thank you*" to Washington. He would probably never see him again, and thanks were in order. A lesser gentleman would have made merry at the rookie's expense.

He found Norwood Street without trouble. There was a reflective sign out in front with the number on it, and he had no trouble finding the garage apartment behind it, either.

And there was the maroon Ford van that everybody was looking for, parked right under Staff Inspector Peter Wohl's window.

Matt chuckled when he saw it.

*That poor sonofabitch is in for a hell of a surprise when he goes tooling down the street tomorrow, and is suddenly surrounded by eight thousand cops, guns drawn, convinced they've caught the rapist.*

Matt's attention didn't linger long on the Ford van. There was another motor vehicle parked on the cobblestones he really found fascinating. It was a Buick station wagon, and if the decal on the windshield was what he thought it was, a parking permit for the Rose Tree Hunt Club, then it was the property of Amelia Alice Payne, M.D., which suggested that the saintly Amelia and the respectable Peter Wohl were up to something in the Wohl apartment that they would prefer not to have him know about.

He walked to the station wagon and flashed his light on the decal. It was the Rose Tree decal all right.

There were no lights on in the garage apartment. Wohl and Amy were either conducting a séance, or up to something else.

*What the hell, Wohl had no idea I'd bring this envelope. He thought either Jason would, or maybe a Highway car, neither of whom would pay a bit of attention to Amy's car.*

*What I should do is go up there and beat on the door until I wake him up or at least get his attention. "Hi, there, Inspector! Just Officer Payne running one more safe errand. My, but that lady looks familiar!"*

He discarded the notion almost as soon as it formed. Wohl was a good guy, and so, even if he wouldn't want her to hear him say it, was Amy.

He started up the stairs to Wohl's door, intending to slip the envelope under the door. Maybe, later, he would zing Amy with it. That might be fun.

He stopped halfway up the stairs.

*I saw movement inside that van.*

*That makes two things wrong with that van: the grill was damaged. On the right side? Shit, I don't know!*

His heart actually jumped, and he felt a little faint.

*Oh, bullshit. Your fevered imagination is running away with you. The van probably belongs to the superintendent here. Wohl certainly knows about it, and has checked it out even before we knew we were looking for a maroon Ford.*

He stopped for a moment, and then he heard the whine of a starter.

*If he's been in there all this time, why is he just starting the engine now?*

Matt turned and ran down the stairs, fishing in his pocket for his badge.

*What do I say to this character?*

*"Excuse me, sir. I'm a Police Officer. We're looking for a murderer-rapist. Is there any chance that might be you, sir?"*

*No. What I am going to wind up saying is, "I'm sorry to have troubled you, sir. We've been having a little trouble around here, and we're checking, just to make sure. Thank you for your cooperation."*

He didn't get a chance to say anything. As he got between the Porsche and the van, the van headlights suddenly came on and it came toward him.

Bile filled Matt's mouth as he understood that the man was trying to run him down. He backed up, encountered the rear of the Porsche and scurried up it like a crab, terrified that his leg would be in the way when the van hit the Porsche.

The impact knocked him off the Porsche. He fell to the right, between the car and the garage doors, landing painfully on his rear end, the breath mostly knocked out of him.

He thought: *I'm alive.*

He thought: *Why the hell didn't I wake up Wohl? He would know what to do.*

The van made a sweeping turn, didn't make it, backed up ten feet, and started out the drive.

He thought: *Thank God, he's going and is not going to try to kill me again.*

He thought: *I'm a cop.*

He thought: *I'm scared.*

He pulled the Chief's Special from the ankle holster and got to his feet and ran to the end of the garage building. His leg hurt; he had injured it somehow.

The van was almost up the driveway.

He became aware that he was standing with his feet spread apart, holding the Chief's Special in both hands, pulling the trigger and pulling it again, and that the hammer was falling on the primers of cartridges that had already been fired.

The van was at the main house, seeming to be gathering speed.

*Jason told me, "If you can't belt them in the head with a snub-nose, they're out of range."*

*Shit, shit, shit, shit, I fucked this up, too!*

The van reached Norwood Street, crossed the sidewalk, entered the street, kept going, and slammed into a chestnut tree.

A woman began to scream, bloodcurdlingly.

Matt ran up the driveway. His leg was really throbbing now.

*What the fuck am I going to do now? The revolver is empty and I don't have any more shells for it.*

He reached the van, out of breath, his chest hurting almost as much as his leg. The van was moving, trying to push the tree out of the way, burning rubber. There was the smell of antifreeze sizzling on a hot block.

He went to the front door and jerked it open.

The driver was slumped over the wheel.

There was a sickening bloody white mess on the windshield. A 168-grain lead projectile had penetrated the rear window of the van, and then the rear of the driver's skull, with sufficient remaining energy to cause most of his brain to be expelled through an exit wound in his forehead.

Matt reached inside and shut off the ignition. Then he ran around the front, went to the side door, and pulled it open. There was something on the floor of the van, under a tarpaulin. He jerked the tarpaulin away.

Mrs. Naomi Schneider, naked, her hands bound behind her, looked at him out of wide eyes.

"I'm a police officer," Matt said. "You'll be all right, lady. It's all over."

Naomi started screaming again.

Beep Beep Beep.

Tiny Lewis opened his microphone and said, "Officer needs assistance. Shots fired. 8800 block of Norwood Street. Ambulance Required. Police by telephone."

The first response to the call was from a Fourteenth District RPC. The second was, "M-Mary One in on the shots fired."

The Honorable Jerry Carlucci, Mayor of the City of Philadelphia, was returning to his Chestnut Hill home from a late dinner with friends. M-Mary One was the first car on the scene.

Staff Inspector Peter Wohl, followed by Amelia Alice Payne, M.D., entered the Rittenhouse Square residence of Officer Matthew Payne. Chief Inspector Dennis V. Coughlin was already there.

"Here's the newspapers. The *Ledger* and the *Bulletin*," Wohl said. "I bought five of each."

"The *Ledger*? Why did you buy that goddamned rag?" Coughlin asked, surprised and angry.

"I think I'm going to have the *Ledger* story framed," Wohl said.

"What the hell are you talking about?" Coughlin asked as Wohl handed him a copy of the *Ledger*.

There was a photograph of Miss Elizabeth Woodham on the front page, in her college graduation cap and gown, three columns wide, with the caption, "Rapist-Murderer's Latest Victim."

## SCHOOLTEACHER STILL AT LARGE; PUBLIC CRITICISM OF POLICE BUBBLING OVER

By Charles E. Whaley
Ledger Staff Reporter

Police Commissioner Taddeus Czernick confessed tonight that while "everything that can be done is being done" the police have not arrested, or for that matter, even identified, the Northwest Philadelphia rapist-murderer whose latest victim's mutilated body was discovered early today by State Police in Upper Bucks County.

"Our Police Department is a disgrace, and we intend to force the mayor to do something about it," said Dr. C. Charles Fortner, a University of Pennsylvania sociology professor, at a press conference at which he announced the formation of "The Citizens' Committee for Efficient Law Enforcement."

"A recall election would be a

last step," Dr. Fortner said, "but not out of the question if the mayor proves unable or unwilling to shake up the Police Department from top to bottom. The people of Philadelphia are entitled to better police protection than they are getting. We will do everything necessary to see that they get it. The kidnapping and brutal murder of Miss Woodham, and the Police Department's nearly incredible ineptness in dealing with the situation, demands immediate action. We are not going to let them forget Miss Woodham as they have forgotten this psychopath's other victims."

Dr. Fortner said that Arthur J. Nelson, publisher of the *Ledger*, has agreed to serve as Vice-Chairman of the committee, and that Nelson and "a number of other prominent citizens" would be with him when the new organization stages its first public protest today. Fortner said that the committee would form before the Police Administration Building at Seventh and Arch Streets at noon, and then march to City Hall, where they intend to present their demands to Mayor Jerry Carlucci.

(A related editorial can be found on Page 7-A.)

"If they march," Chief Coughlin said, "I'll get a bass drum, and march right along with them."

Matt was leaning on his desk, sipping at a glass dark with whiskey, looking down at the *Bulletin*'s front page. There was a four-column photograph on it, of Officer Matthew Payne and the Honorable Jerry Carlucci, who had an arm around Matt's shoulder, and who was standing with his jacket open wide enough to reveal that His Honor the Mayor still carried his police revolver. The caption below the picture read, "Mayor Carlucci Embraces 'Handsome Hero' Cop."

When he heard Coughlin speak, he looked over at him. "What?"

"You read the *Bulletin* first, Matty," Coughlin said. "Then you'll really enjoy the story in the *Ledger*."

Matt shrugged, and returned to reading the *Bulletin*.

"Mickey O'Hara will do all right by you," Denny Coughlin said. "He told me he thought you'd done a hell of a job. I'll bet that's a very nice story."

"So far it's bullshit," Matt replied.

---

**NORTHWEST SERIAL RAPIST-MURDERER KILLED BY "HANDSOME" SPECIAL OPERATIONS COP AS HE RESCUES KIDNAPPED WOMAN**

By Michael J. O'Hara
Bulletin Staff Writer

Officer Matthew Payne, 22, in what Mayor Jerry Carlucci described as an act of "great personal heroism," rescued Mrs. Naomi Schneider, 34, of the 8800 block of Norwood Street in Chestnut Hill, minutes after she had been abducted at knifepoint from her home by a man the mayor said he is positive is the man dubbed the "Northwest Serial Rapist."

The man, tentatively identified as Warren K. Fletcher, 31, of Germantown, had, according to Mrs. Schneider, broken into her luxury apartment as she was preparing for bed. Mrs. Schneider said he was masked and armed with a large butcher knife. She said he forced her to disrobe, then draped her in a blanket and forced her into the rear of his 1969 Ford van and covered her with a tarpaulin.

"The next thing I knew," Mrs. Schneider said, "there was shots, and then breaking glass, and then the van crashed. Then this handsome young cop was looking down at me and smiling and telling me everything was all right; he was a police officer."

Moments before Officer Payne shot the kidnapper and believed rapist-murderer, according to Mayor Carlucci, the man had attempted to run Payne down with the van, slightly injuring Payne and doing several thousand dollars' worth of damage to Payne's personal automobile.

"Payne then, reluctantly," Mayor Carlucci said, "concluded there was no choice but for him to use deadly force, and proceeded to do so. Mrs. Schneider's life was in grave danger and he knew it. I'm proud of him."

Mayor Carlucci, whose limousine is equipped with police shortwave radios, was en route to his Chestnut Hill home from a Sons of Italy dinner in South Philadelphia when the rescue occurred.

"We were the first car to respond to the 'shots fired' call," the mayor said. "Officer Payne was still helping Mrs. Schneider out of the wrecked van when we got there.''

Payne, who is special assistant to Staff Inspector Peter Wohl, commanding officer of the newly formed Special Operations Division, had spent most of the day in Bucks County, where the mutilated body of Miss Elizabeth Woodham, 33, of 300 East Mermaid Lane, Roxborough, had been discovered by State Police in a summer country cottage.

Miss Woodham was abducted from her apartment three days ago by a masked, knife-wielding man. A Bucks County mail carrier had described a man meeting Mr. Warren K. Fletcher's description, and driving a maroon 1969 Ford van identical to the one in which Mrs. Schneider was abducted, as being at a cottage where her body was discovered. Police all over the Delaware Valley were looking for a similar van.

Payne, who had been assigned to work as liaison between ace Homicide detectives Jason Washington and Anthony Harris and Special Operations Division, had gone with Washington to the torture-murder scene in Bucks County.

He spotted the van in the early hours of this morning as he drove to the Chestnut Hill residence of Inspector Wohl to make his report before going off duty.

''He carefully appraised the situation before acting, and decided Mrs. Schneider's very life depended on his acting right then, and alone,'' Mayor Carlucci said. "She rather clearly owes her life to him. I like to think that Officer Payne is typical of the intelligent, well-educated young officers with which Commissioner Czernick and I intend to staff the Special Operations Division."

Payne, who is a bachelor, recently graduated from the University of Pennsylvania. He declined to answer questions from the press.

"This is going to thrill them in Wallingford," Matt said, when he had finished reading. "When they sit down to read the morning paper."

"Dad already knows," Amy said. "I called him and told him."

"That was smart!" Matt snapped.

"I wanted Dad to know before Mother," Amy said, unrepentant. "Matt, do you want me to give you something . . ."

"I've got it, thanks," he said, picking up his glass. Then he looked around at all of them. "Doesn't anyone but me care that the whole article is bullshit?"

"You've undergone a severe emotional trauma," Amy said.

"Tell me about it," Matt said. "But we were—I was—talking about bullshit."

"I can give you something to help you deal with it," Amy persisted. "Liquor won't help."

"That's what you think," Matt said. "You *are* talking about the bullshit?"

"I'm talking about the shock you've suffered," Amy said.

"I'm talking about bullshit," Matt said. "I damned near killed that peroxide-blond woman," Matt said. "I didn't know she existed until I heard her screaming. I shot that sonofabitch because he tried to run me over. I was not the calm, heroic police officer. I was a terrified and enraged child who had a gun."

"I don't know what you're talking about," she said.

"You're right, Amy," Matt said. "I am not cut out to be a cop."

"You don't want to make a decision like that right now, Matty," Dennis Coughlin said.

"Nobody's listening to me," Matt said. "If there is one thing I learned from this is that I am not my father's—my blood father's— son."

"Matty!" Dennis Coughlin said.

"I was afraid out there," Matt said. "Terrified. *And* insane."

"That's perfectly understandable under the circumstances," Dennis Coughlin said.

"I almost killed that woman!" Matt said, angrily. "Doesn't anybody understand that?"

"You didn't," Wohl said. "You didn't. You kept her alive."

"Did you know I fell asleep on the job tonight?"

"No."

"Did Washington tell you I fainted when I saw the Woodham body?"

"So what?" Wohl asked.

"Matty," Dennis Coughlin said. "Listen to me."

Matt looked at him.

"I admit, Mickey and the mayor laid it on a little thick," Coughlin said. "That it was, excuse me, Amy, bullshit. But so was the story in the *Ledger*. So you're not a hero. But neither is the Police Department as incompetent as Arthur J. Nelson wants the people to think it is. What he's trying to do to us has nothing to do with the truth about the Police. That's pretty rotten. So the bottom line here is you took this critter down. He's not going to rape or murder anyone else. A lot of single young women around town are going to get to sleep tonight. That's all we try to do on the cops, Matty, try to fix things so people can sleep at night. And if they read in the newspapers that we're all stupid, or on the take, or just can't be trusted . . . Am I getting through to you?"

"I don't know," Matt said.

"And as far as your father—your blood father, as you call him— is concerned. He was my best friend. And I know he would be proud of you. I am. You were scared, but you did what had to be done. And there's something else about your father, Matty. They have his picture and his badge hanging in the lobby of the Roundhouse. He's a hero, an officer who got killed in the line of duty. But—I was his best friend, so I can say this—he didn't do his duty. He let that critter kill him. And before we caught him, he killed three civilians. You didn't let this critter kill you. That psychopath isn't going to get to hurt somebody else. In my book that makes you a better cop than your father. That's the bottom line, Matty. Protecting the public. You think about that."

Matt looked at Coughlin for a moment, then at Wohl, who nodded at him, and then at his sister.

"Matt," Amy said. "Maybe you shouldn't be a cop. But now is not the time for you to make that decision."

"Jesus!" Matt said. "From you?"

There was a knock at the door. Wohl went to it and pulled it open.

Charley McFadden was standing there, a brown bag in his hand.

"What do you want, McFadden?" Wohl asked.

"It's all right, Peter," Chief Coughlin said, "I sent for him."

"I came as quick as I could," McFadden said. "I figured he could use a drink. I didn't know if he had any, so I brung some."

"Come on in, McFadden," Dennis Coughlin said. "We were all just leaving." He looked Amy Payne in the eye. "Officer McFadden, Amy, is the man who was about to apprehend Gerald Vincent Gallagher when he fell beneath the train wheels."

"I wondered who he was," Amy said.

"He's a friend of mine, Amy, all right?" Matt snapped.

"No offense meant," Amy said. She looked at Chief Inspector Coughlin.

"I think you're right, Uncle Denny," she said. "You don't mind if I call you that, do you?"

"I'm flattered, darling."

"You take care of him, Mr. McFadden," Amy said.

"Yeah, sure," Charley McFadden said. "Don't worry about it."

# EPILOGUE

Walton Williams was detained three weeks later by officers of the Bureau of Immigration and Naturalization as he attempted to reenter the United States after a vacation in France. He was taken into custody despite the somewhat hysterical protestations of his traveling companion, one Stephen Peebles, that Mr. Williams had not been out of his sight for the past five weeks and could not possibly be the burglar of the home Mr. Peebles shared with his sister.

Following the night Captain David Pekach visited Miss Martha Peebles at her home to assure her that the police were doing everything possible to protect her property from further burglaries, none were ever reported.

When Staff Inspector Peter Wohl reported this happy fact to Chief Inspector Dennis V. Coughlin, he added, with a knowing smile, that this might have something to do with the fact Captain Pekach and Miss Peebles seemed to have developed a friendship. He said he had heard from an impeccable source, specifically, Lieutenant Bob McGrory of the

New Jersey State Police, that Captain Pekach and Miss Peebles had been seen strolling down the Boardwalk in Atlantic City, holding hands, simply enthralled by each other.

Chief Inspector Coughlin smiled back, just as knowingly.

"People who live in glass houses, Peter, my boy, should not toss rocks. I have it from an impeccable source, specifically His Honor the Mayor, that a certain Staff Inspector was seen walking hand in hand down Peacock Alley in the Waldorf-Astoria Hotel in New York, toward the elevators, with a certain female physician, neither of whom were registered there under their own names."

Matthew Payne did not resign from the Police Department.